A PORTABLE

CHAOS

A Novel

Portrait, E.M. Schorb
Sculpture by Natale de la Padura

A PORTABLE

CHAOS

A Novel

E.M. SCHORB

HILL HOUSE   NEW YORK

ISBN: 978-0-578-95498-1

Cover Design: Selah Bunzey

FOR PATRICIA

A fleece of fine doves
is too crude,
Patricia.

A fleece of fine doves,
murdered for love,
is not enough.

Waves of anger and fear
Circulate over the bright
And darkened lands of the earth,
Obsessing our private lives . . .

—*W.H. Auden*

Oh! Blessed rage for order . . .
The maker's rage to order words of the sea . . .

—*Wallace Stevens*

CONTENTS

INTRODUCTION

A tentative word on the title. The bearer of the chaos is the main character of this novel, and the chaos that is borne is he, himself. A chaos that can be described as a tangled web of contrary forces combating without any apparent central or final aim, a chaos which, in Pope's one-and-a-half heroic couplets, is said to be the condition of every one of us:

> Chaos of thought and passion, all confused;
> Still by himself abused or disabused;
> Created half to rise, and half to fall.

Thus viewed, this absorbing novel could have been equally aptly titled, An Essay on Man. Yet from a more particular point of view, the present chaos and its bearer are creatures of our time and place, or more precisely, of the generation of American men who were or could have been drafted and sent to kill or to be killed in Vietnam. Both Schorb and I belong to it. And so does the main character of this novel, who first appears as a boy referred to only by the pronoun "he" and later by the name Jimmy; still later we learn that his last name is Whistler. I recognized him immediately as the hero of some of the short stories in Schorb's 2019 book *Collected Stories*. How could I have failed to recognize him: Jimmy and his friend Marsayas, the Zoroastrian hippie, are unforgettable characters and here, in this new book, you have a feast of their sometimes parallel, some other times orthogonal endeavors.

Parallel and orthogonal? What does that mean? Let's pause here and ask about the contrary forces pulling against each other as part of this chaos that we are. Two of those forces are of old standing, perhaps as old as civilization: on the one hand the wish for innocence and freedom – the freedom of Elysium or of Paradise not yet lost, the leisure or σχολή so dear to the Greek poets and philosophers, whence our "school." The freedom of the anchorite alone with his God in the Thebaid, or of the mystic having lived through her fiery night. On the other hand, the drive for business of the man of affairs, of those who are out to make money or acquire goods, of the professionals. Two different ethics is what it boils down to: in our society it is common to praise a person's "work ethics," but have you ever heard someone being praised for her "free time ethics"? For foregoing three hours of watching a football game on TV, for example, so she can read and mull over four poems by Robert Frost?

Plato in the *Theaetetus* (172c - 173b) has Socrates contrast the two ethics, characterizing the one, the free time ethics, as proper to the free man, and the other as governing the slave bound by the rules of his own ambition and those of his profession (he takes as example the lawyers). If you are objecting, dear reader, that I shouldn't bring up Plato, who was a notorious elitist and the arch-enemy of open and progressive societies, I will counter that Marsayas himself, the Zoroastrian hippie, the free spirit, is an elitist too. Early in the novel, he encourages Jimmy to devote his life to poetry, for, as Marsayas says, Jimmy has what it takes to be a good poet, and those and no others are the choice and natural elite of humankind.

At the beginning, Jimmy follows his friend's advice and resists all temptations. He is told that he is ready to become a great actor and is given a chance to reach the pot of gold at the end of the Hollywood rainbow, but he resists. Jimmy could have chosen from many a brilliant calling, but he prefers to preserve his own freedom and innocence for poetry, and instead joins the Marines. At nineteen he is a marine who reads and rereads the two great poetic Johns: Milton and Donne. Isn't that strange? Not so strange when we consider another basic force always acting in the chaos that we all are:

the need for certainty, for a trustworthy, solid ground under our mental feet. As interpreted by a philosopher whose name I don't wish to remember: feeling the solidity of something seemingly outside you reassures you that you are a solid entity as well.

Jimmy had grown up lacking such ground: the best that could be said about his parents is that they were both untrustworthy, irresponsible liars, besides being a pain in the butt. That Jimmy loved them nevertheless is one of the things that endears him to me, and, I venture to guess, to every reader of this book. I had my own problems with the sticky webs of lies wrapped around me as a boy, so by the time I was eighteen or nineteen I had resolved to devote my life to math, where the ground is as solid as anyone could wish, and where ambiguity is discouraged and contradiction is never allowed. Well, Jimmy chose the Marines, where the situation is much the same. Marines and Math provide solid grounds. We are talking the late 1950s; Jimmy stayed only for a few years with the Marines, and I just a dozen more with Math; Jimmy, though, went as far as naming his child Semper Fi, while it never occurred to me to name one of my boys Dedekind Cut.

You may remember that President Eisenhower warned Americans against the military-industrial complex in his parting speech. The Marines were obviously part of the powerful complex, but relatively few are aware that mathematicians belonged there too. John von Neumann was given the Medal of Freedom by Eisenhower for his many achievements and services – computer architecture, calculations for the atomic and the hydrogen bomb, equilibrium strategy of mutual assured destruction, and the list goes on. He was a towering talent, but thousands of lesser mathematicians and their research papers were "supported" by grants from the U.S. Army, Navy, and Air Force. And then, after the Gulf of Tonkin resolution was passed almost unanimously by

Congress, the Vietnam War turned a good deal nastier: for the first time, the USA was involved in an unwinnable war launched on false pretenses and suspect intelligence reports. The resulting horror soon destroyed the remaining aboriginal faith Americans may have had in the freedom and essential innocence of their society, and therefore all trust in its institutions. And all for what, or to what end? A reporter once asked Lyndon Johnson why the United States was fighting in Vietnam, and the President answered by pulling out his schlong, which he revered and referred to as "jumbo" – pulling it out, showing it off, and saying, "This is why!" People were dying and children were being napalmed for the sake and glory of Johnson's johnson.

Jimmy, like many of his generation, including myself – although I was not an American citizen yet –, fell into despondence. Many opted to drop out of unbearable reality, that reality which Phyllis, a young woman Jimmy had lived with, used to call "the bullshit world." An apt name. It fits my own feelings a little later, in 1970, about my colleagues, who walked on high logical clouds and considered themselves far above such earthly minutiae as the defoliation of Vietnam and the incursion into Cambodia. For young, frail Phyllis, the true, non-bullshit world was rather that of Jimmy's poetry, with its emotional peak in "Obituary," in memory of his slippery father, who had died in a fire. My own first serious poem was about the death of my own slippery father in 1969; a further coincidence that endears me still more to Jimmy and moves me to admire Schorb's psychological penetration, particularly when he writes about the relation between fathers and sons.

Again, when toward the end of the book Jimmy is living with Lani, the beauty from Hawaii, he composes a "Dirge for the Dead Students," after the Kent State killing of unarmed students by the Ohio National Guard on May 4th, 1970. You will be moved by it, as you will be moved by "Obituary" and by the other poems dispersed through the novel. At roughly the same time, I was teaching math at the University of Wisconsin, Madison, and writing and printing anonymous pamphlets against the presence of the Army Math Research Center on campus and against its director, a distinguished logician who stoutly maintained that the activities of the Army Center were no more objectionable than those of the horseshoe craftsmen for the King's Cavalry. A typical example of the bullshit that's the life breath of the bullshit world.

Liquor and beer in prodigious amounts were means Jimmy used to escape the bullshit world. This may sound odd, for he had, in poets such as Donne and Milton, the means to rise above it; but remember, we are created half to rise, and half to fall, and fall he did repeatedly, at one time buried under a ton of garbage, at another sloshing through sewage to earn a few bucks helping a plumber friend.

Schorb is not a writer to hand us happy endings, nor does he kill his Jimmy in the end. He leaves him suspended, on the razor's edge. Epics are supposed to start *in medias res*, in the middle of the action; this novel ends that way. Will Jimmy free himself of his alcohol dependence? What kind of riches will Jimmy heap up? Will he cower and submit to the logos that governs the bullshit world, so as to enjoy its rewards and prestige? Will he drop totally out of it? Or will he undertake the most difficult task, to change that logos from within? When I reached the end, I found myself praying for Jimmy to choose rightly, and I also found that actually I could not presume to know what would be for him the right choice.

Ricardo L. Nirenberg
Editor, Offcourse Literary Journal (offcourse.org)

BEFORE

From the deep recesses of the universe he woke to find himself gumming the blue lead paint from the top rail of his crib, blissfully unaware of the crack in the Liberty Bell, or the Liberty Bell itself, for that matter; Mussolini in Abyssinia, Schicklgruber, in Guernica or the Rhineland, Tojo in China, or any of the crazy problems of the age into which he had been dropped. The lead paint was delicious and maddening, and would, no doubt make a mad poet of him. He looked around and for the first time saw other humanoids (oops, hominids), much bigger, but basically the same. They, also, wobbled on two legs, holding drinks to their lips, as he held his empty baby bottle's nipple to his. One fell back into a faded, flowered easy chair, in what seemed, even to his innocent eyes, a flat, shabby and small, compared with whatever had been before. Years later, photographs would tell him who they were. Someone had taken several Brownie snapshots. Here was his young Aunt, a fourteen-year-old schoolgirl, who hookied to the City of Brotherly Love to help with her new nephew, the young Master, her big sister's first child. An older boy would have noticed the beginnings of her breasts, and that she was a pretty young thing with startling blue eyes and chestnut waves piled up, but he was unaware of these uplifting attractions. The woman was his Mother. Later he would understand that at that point in her life, made-up and Marcelled, people said that she looked like the actress Mary Astor, except for her harlequin-shaped glasses. The central figure, the one who had collapsed in the overstuffed chair, his well-tonsured dark hair staining the antimacassar, a dry-state half-empty bottle of gin on his lap, looked like the famous-at-the-time Arrow Collar Man. Well, that was his old man, tall, dark, and handsome alcoholic, Depression-fallen from Wall Street stocks and bonds salesman, to selling The

Wonder Book of Knowledge, or some such, door-to-door in the territory assigned him in the deep middle of the Depression by the New York based Publisher's Guild. His young Aunt stuck a rubber nipple in his mouth and quickly the picture faded.

*   *   *

When you are about three feet tall, the gray streets of Philadelphia in winter are very long and tiring and slowly climb uphill toward a dark sky. His mother pulled him along. Where were they going? Had War Two begun yet? Their arms were empty. Not shopping? Was the Depression still on? Was there no money? Why were they walking, walking so far? He was beginning to get very cold. Then, on the empty street, a stranger appeared before them. He confronted them. His mother knew the man, yes, and they laughed together too high above him for him to have any idea what was funny, but something obviously was, or had been, for their laughter tinkled down upon him like sprightly snowflakes, like tinsel and sequins, a glittery sprinkling of fairy dust. He tried to get under it, between them, where it fell. His mother pulled him back and away, toward her own back. Then the man seized his mother in his arms and dipped her back toward where he waited and kissed her hard and long. It was wrong, wasn't it? Because this man was not his father. His father was up ahead somewhere, somewhere at the end of the long gray avenue, somewhere up several flights of stairs, in a small apartment that looked down on the avenue. It was wrong, wasn't it? Because his mother did not struggle to be free. Instead, she simply held him behind her, away from them. He could feel the strength of her grip. He thought he might cry, but wasn't sure if crying was the right thing to do. The man seemed to lift his mother off the pavement and to place her back on it, her high heels firm. She pulled him from behind her and around to her side. Her other hand held out to the man as he stepped back, back, and turned and went

17

a little way, and stopped, and turned again, and waved, and blew her a kiss, and turned once again, and went on down the long slowly sinking avenue that his mother and he had just climbed. Who was that? he wanted to know. His mother pulled him forward up the hill. "Who was that?" he asked. His mother climbed on, pulling him along with one hand and wiping tears from her eyes with the other. "Mommy, who was that man?" His mother ignored him until he shouted his question at her. The question and its answer had become imperative, like the bearing down of traffic at the intersection. Finally his mother said, "What man?" He looked back and saw the receding figure of the man who had kissed his mother. He tugged his mother half around and pointed—"That man," he said. "I don't see any man," his mother said. "I haven't seen anyone since we began our walk, and neither have you." He looked back again, desperately, but the man was gone. "You see," said his mother. "There is no one on the street but us." She was lying, wasn't she, or could he not believe the evidence of his own eyes? From then on he struggled to keep his hand free of hers.

*   *   *

The children of Camden roamed the streets in gangs composed not so much of juvenile delinquents as of orphaned children looking for something to do, their parents lost to them at Campbell's Soups or at Lionel Trains, ground up in the Wheels of Industry and War Two. The schools didn't count, were apparently attended out of a need to get indoors for a time, their schedules not fitting the schedules of the factories. Sleepers slept when they could, morning or evening or night. Meals came when they did, now or later, morning or evening or night. A skinny child, he drank containered coffee, ate stale chocolate donuts drizzling in wax paper, and huge greasy cafeteria meat-cakes smothered in sour brown gravy, which often turned his stomach. In winter the snow was black with soot, in summer the air was heavy and stank.

There was a constant grinding out of matter, of war material, of goods, of people, but the funereal unreal light made one feel that no matter how much was made, the making was wages of sin, of death, as he read in the Gideon Bible supplied by the hotel; and the whistles blew and the sirens sounded and the mobs made their moans. The white faces were black and the black faces were white, and everyone seemed to be slow-marching a treadmill to death, once, in Camden, way back when.

*   *   *

His mother and father could not understand the extreme of his grief, for his father's other son was only half his brother, and had not existed in their lives but for letters and occasional photographs taken around the world where the war was, often next to his Wellington, or by a field tent, wearing his wings, a smiling twenty-year-old whom he, the child in a yard, thought must look the way he himself would look at twenty, and be a brave pilot and take up the war against Hitler and Tojo in his turn, not knowing that even wars do not last forever. How could the child be so devastated by the news, who barely knew of his half-brother's existence? How adults box things up the child could not know or believe. Hard rain. Rivers of rain, as when you look up through greenhouse glass on a rainy day, crossed his green eyes blotting out the blue dry sky overhead, and he told the rain of his grief and he told the blurred, ugly yard behind the city row house with its junked, warped furniture and strata of ripped linoleum, roses and geometry, and its wet, stalking cat along the old spiked wooden fence, run with rusted wire meant to throw yourself on, told the whole world, which was all the rain of tears out of his breathless, heaving chest, narrow as a chicken's, out of his pounding seven-year-old heart, and cowlicked hair, that was trapped by the four-sidedness of fence and could not fly with his grief as his brother the pilot had flown, whom he had never known. Let the child race

19

pointlessly in circles, trapped in the square yard, and cry himself out. The letter was already over a year old and smeared with his father's few tears, sad horrible history, but must be set aside so that life could go on. "He'll get over it." "I never thought—" said his mother. "No, of course not," said his father. But the yard was sodden with the child's grief, whose head burned with hope against fact that a mistake had been made, that this fine brother was yet to come to him who had no one, whose loneliness could not be surmised by two wise parents, kept sane by callousing death and full of the hard world's rain.

*　　*　　*

Late evening, once, on the midway of a carnival, amidst the carnival music, the punctuating squeals of the other children, the pop, pop, pop of the rifles at the gallery, and the crazy laughter of the funhouse, he came upon a fortune-telling machine, the illustrations of which showed the requirement of an Indian-head nickel in exchange for what children wish for most: Knowledge of the Future, which gives the feckless and the hapless power over it. He searched through his change and found just such a nickel, plunged it in the slot of his future, and received in return a card the size of a typical business card with the following printed on it: Act the Way you Want to Be and Soon You'll Be the Way you Act. Little people take such advisements seriously, one might even say, with all their hearts; and so he tried to live out that dream, and must assume that what he is, is what he desired to be, when he was an eager if short-sighted child.

*　　*　　*

Like a spider on a thread, the eye dropped down on its optic nerve and drew up out of his range of vision. He was on his knees in a bar in Newark, shining shoes, maybe eight or nine years old. He sat between two men on stools whose heads were high above him. He was close to the level of the

20

brass spittoon and the brass rail. They glittered with the changing lights, but it was hard to see very well down there on the seat of the shoeshine box, hard to see anything but the whiteness of the eye, like an egg suspended on the cord that feeds the yoke. Some extraordinarily quick gesture of violence must have been employed. The shoes he was shining scrambled with the shoes he was about to shine. Crashing sounds, screaming, and he backed off to the wall behind him. A big scuffle of several men ensued. When he returned home late that night, his mother asked him if anything interesting had happened. "Have you ever seen an eye popped out?" he asked her, after stating his preference for the Campbell's Chicken Noodle soup over the Cream of Mushroom. He began counting his money, which he was saving for a bicycle. He was going to become a Western Union boy.

*   *   *

His father, the superior drunk, had left them in this dump in Newark to go off selling his bullshit books in Buffalo, and to shack up with his beautiful vocabulary, a bottle, and a bimbo, and not to have to sit with them under the dripping pipes wrapped in soggy cardboard by the puke-green wall of bricks with a thousand holes in them for the bedbugs, roaches, and rumpled ringdings that came out at night and crawled over them, biting, that swarmed like emigrating bees when the lights came on. The asbestos-insulated furnace belched, farted, and hummed outside the door, a jack-o'-lantern whose serrated teeth did not scare the rats, who warmed to him, in his furry gray suit that glowed in the dark. A giant rodent Golem, one could hear him breathing through the thin walls that divided the superintendent's apartment from the front basement, a pathed indoor junkyard. They had to wend their way out through that La Brea Tar Pit to get to the stairs that climbed and turned out to the street, where they would peep up to see if anybody out there would notice where they were coming from, which was out from among the dented old

21

metal cans full of raw sour garbage, and what peculiar spe-cies of spelunker they were: what Untouchables were surrep-titiously seeking light and air. He lied about his age and became a Western Union boy, having shoeshined his way to the top, saved his money and bought a bicycle, a Western Flyer. He found his mother a pretty little apartment high over a pizza joint, and they moved up into the air and the smell of hot dough. He made his timid mother smile at such daring, daring to fly so high, so near to the sun, and for a while they were content. But his father came home and said, This place is too expensive; we must superintend another sump-pump dump. Another nice basement that drips piss, the boy said, and added, No, I can afford to pay this rent, as I have been doing for some time now. Now stick with me on this one, Mom. But we better do what your father thinks best, she said; and he said to himself, That's it, never again, as he helped to carry their paltry embarrassing possessions, "Impedimenta" his father called them, through the streets, and back to the basement they had escaped from, his father leading the way like a bigshot, soused-up and self-important, his mother fol-lowing him into nothing but worse with a "Wither-thou-goest" and a last wistful look up over the pizza parlor at their window of opportunity, a dutiful wife of the Fifties, and Jimmy planning his next escape.

CHAPTER ONE

CANDY BUTCHER

So much of adolescence is an ill-defined dying,
An intolerable waiting,
A longing for another place and time,
Another condition.
—Theodore Roethke

THE NEW YORK TIMES
SEPTEMBER 24, 1952

NEWARK NJ DENIES MINSKY BURLESQUE PERMIT

THE NEW YORK TIMES
NOVEMBER 5, 1952

EISENHOWER WINS

THE NEW YORK TIMES
APRIL 28, 1953

MINSKY SHOW BAN VETOED IN NEWARK

This was a new kind of burlesque, Harold Minsky's burlesque of 1953, with big production numbers reminiscent of the great follies of an earlier era; and this was the Saturday night crowd, middle-class and wealthy people, husbands who had brought their wives, respectable theater-parties, even an occasional clergyman, come across the Hudson or in from the suburbs to see at the Adams Theatre in Newark what Mayor La Guardia had banned from New York. Now, for the sixth and last time of the day, the oily, tuxedoed singer leaped from the wings singing the theme song, a variation on "The Most Beautiful Girl in the World"—

> *Oh, they're handy—*
> *Oh, they're dandy—*
> *And Minsky girls*

are the most beautiful girls in the W-O-R-L-D! The strippers did a bump-and-grind, twirled the tassels on their pasties, snapped their G-strings, and strutted off in their spike-heels. The chain of chorus girls disappeared into the wings with a sequined kick from its last link. The singer took several bows and stepped off into obscurity. The great purple curtains rushed from the wings, met center-stage, ballooned, and settled.

*   *   *

In his first week at Minsky's Jimmy had his hair cut into a ducktail and bought himself a white-on-white shirt, like the ones the older candy butchers wore. The second week he cut his penny-ante tonk rummy bets—the novelty of the ongoing game was keeping him up till all hours—and managed a pair of blue suede shoes. He had begun to smoke, holding his corktipped cigarettes between his teeth in imitation of Stoney, the hard-faced ex-Marine who was the chief candy butcher for Lou Schenk, the concessionaire. He even attempted to imitate the bitterness Stoney had acquired in an apparently brutal life that had been capped by the Korean War, without quite understanding it to be bitterness, taking it for worldliness, a kind of crude sophistication. But Stoney disliked innocence, and delighted in persecuting it. He practiced his persecution of Jimmy during the all-night card games in the

24

little concession room in the basement of the theater with a form of verbal abuse that had its origins in Marine Corps boot camp and in the black street kids' game of "The Dozens"— piling up ingenious metaphorical insults about one another's mothers. Stoney was the great white hope of "The Dozens." "My balls itch. Whose Mama can get here first with a good ball-scratcher? You're young, Junior. Maybe your Mama's the fastest runner." Jimmy thought it prudent not to offer a rejoinder. Stoney was big and raw boned and quick to anger, as Jimmy had observed. No one said a word. Tex and Big Jim, both of whom had at least five years on Jimmy, just sat patiently on their deep, upended trays and played on.

*　　*　　*

Jimmy leaned on the plateglass of the candy stand, smoking, and saw sad-eyed Marge, the counter girl, staring up at Stoney's hard, handsome face. Jimmy saw her sad eyes and wanted to divert them to himself. He gripped his cigarette in his teeth and swaggered a little in his mind. Marge and Stoney were talking about someone named Sunny.

"Who's Sunny?" he asked.

"A tramp," Stoney said.

"She's not a tramp, Stonewall!"

"Sunny used to be my old lady when she was in the chorus in Bayonne," Stoney said.

"She never was!" cried Marge. "She was a lot too nice for you!"

Stoney ignored her. "She's an usherette," he said, "just hired."

"She's waiting for an opening in the chorus," Marge said, "like me."

Stoney snorted contemptuously. He took Jimmy's elbow and said, "C'mon, Junior. Let's find her."

They pushed through the heavy red padded doors of the lobby and into the auditorium. On stage, Flame O'Hair was

25

strutting her stuff. Stoney led Jimmy toward a blonde in an usherette's uniform. "This is Sunny Day, Jimmy. She asked me to introduce you."

Sunny Day smiled, and said: "Hi! I've seen you around and thought we should get acquainted." She had small, pretty teeth and gray eyes. "I'll be off duty in a half hour. I'm going up to the box on the left side to watch the show. Would you like to join me?"

"I don't know," he said. He realized that his knees were beating unrhythmically against the orchestra's drum gambade and that his heart was beating only between cymbal crashes and then in great, breathless gallops. He could feel his pointed ears burning and guessed they were red, perhaps enlarged.

When Jimmy joined Sunny in the dark, brass-railed box she was in street clothes and had undergone a transformation from the cute usherette into a woman of mystery. In the dim stage light that rose up to them, he could make out the way her knitted dress clung to her voluptuous body. She said, "Hi, again!" as he sat down. Her wide-brimmed hat angled back to the stage. Feathery hopes, fears, and doubts fluttered Jimmy's heart. He was glad that he had stopped to comb his Vaselined, ducktailed hair, and had put on Stoney's suit jacket. His scuffed leather jacket—which he had worn as a Western Union boy, and which had grown much too small for him since he had taken up bodybuilding—would have been out of place, in what he now thought of as this formal setting. It would have completely hidden his white-on-white shirt as well. His knee-bulged dungarees were dark and dirty, but didn't show. He resented the lower darkness, though, for hiding his new, pointed, blue suede shoes.

On stage a long curving sweep of powerful powdered thigh rippled and flexed. From spiked heels two seams ran up mesh-covered flesh, were accented at the round hips and nearly met at the tiny, arching waist. Each gambade shifted the weight of the body from one jutting hip to the other, a pulsing, upside-down heart. Sunny put a hand on his knee and squeezed in rhythm with the music and the stripper's bumps and grinds. Jimmy sat, afraid to move, staring at the stage. Sunny unzipped his jeans, and in a few seconds a crescendo of music and motion coincided. She pressed a piece of paper into his palm. "My address," and got up and left him alone in the dark box. He saw the comics come on but had no idea of what they were saying. He heard, "My address, my address, my address. . ." over and over, like the refrain of a song. He had never before had a woman touch him like that. Never before had such a thing been done, he thought, not in all history.

Jimmy waited for two weeks before going to see Sunny. He wasn't sure whether he had avoided the encounter for two full weeks because he didn't want to seem in too much of a hurry or because he was afraid. He was not afraid, he told himself, he just didn't want to seem too eager. Nuts! He was scared to death.

Sunny took Jimmy's leather jacket and woolen scarf and put them over the back of an armchair. She was just out of the shower and her hair was wrapped in a big yellow towel. She was wearing a quilted pink robe and pink pom-pommed slippers. Her feet seemed incredibly small to Jimmy, and the nail polish on her toes glittered like enamel roses. She made him breathless, yet he tried to breathe evenly. He wanted to be cool and smooth.

"Sit down," she said, indicating the couch. "That thing opens into a bed." She smiled at him. "Are you horny?"

"No, I ate. But I'm thirsty."

She laughed, shaking her head, said, "I'll get some beer," and went into the kitchenette.

Jimmy sat like a collapsed puppet on the couch and clumsily fingered a pack of cigarettes. Finally he tore the pack open and stuck a corked tip between his teeth. This was the tenth brand he had tried in as many weeks. So far, these were the best for biting. He took a drag. The smoke got into his eyes and he wiped them quickly with his sweatered sleeve. He heard Sunny getting the beer, the clinking of bottles. The kitchenette had an oilcloth across its doorway. The walls wore faded flowered wallpaper. There was a metal dining set with a plastic top and maple end-tables and a mahogany dresser with a mirror with cards and letters stuck in it. One of the items stuck in the mirror was a picture of Sunny in G-string, pasties, and spike-heels. His sixteen-year-old lust, which he had carried about in him like an overstuffed piñata, felt a near-bursting blow. Sunny came back with a tray, beer, and two pilsner glasses. She smelled of exotic perfume, passion flowers, his nose told him, not that he quite knew what they were.

"You've got a nice apartment here," he said.

"What, this dump? I rent it by the week."

"Isn't the furniture yours?"

"No, it's furnished. I just took it to tide me over when I came in from Bayonne." She saw his extended cigarette ash. "There's an ashtray."

She sat down beside him and her quilted robe flapped open, exposing a neat, pale knee.

"I never know how to open these things," she said, clinking a bottle-opener on a cap.

"Here," Jimmy said, opening the bottles with shaking hands.

"You're strong," she said. "I can see your biceps through your sweater."

"I lift weights," he said. "I've built myself up from a ninety-eight pound weakling, when I was thirteen, to my present size—almost six feet tall and a hundred and seventy-five pounds—in just over three years. I work out three times a week at the Y, and I've done a lot of bicycle-riding. I was a Western Union boy. That really develops your thighs."

"Well, I understand that," she said, "being a dancer."

"I can see you have strong legs, too," he said.

"I have something else. I have something to celebrate tonight. I got a new gig. I'll be shuffling off to Buffalo in a few days. A chorus job." She removed the towel from her head and shook out her damp, curly hair.

Jimmy could not connect with her words. He looked at her dark-rooted, orange hair, that looked to him like Rapunzel's golden locks, and wondered how old she was. Thirty? He couldn't tell about women. Then he realized that she was leaving town. Leaving town!

"I wish you weren't going away."

He could never understand how women got their clothes to fit them as they did; how, for instance, they got their full hips through the narrow waistbands of their slacks. He had pondered these things.

"Why didn't you come up and see me sooner? I might not have taken the gig in Buffalo."

"Well, I was kind of—"

"Scared? You've never been with a woman, have you? C'mon now, tell Sunny truth." She laughed, touched his cheek, and pushed back some of his fair hair. "I wish you'd change the way you wear your hair. It'd look nice without all that grease in it, loose and curly."

"I will—if you won't go away." He bounced his glass on the table and put his hand decisively on her knee.

She shuddered. "Oh, your hand's still cold!"

Jimmy held his ground for a moment, his eyes widening, then withdrew his hand.

Sunny smiled, and affectionately added to the rumpled state of his hair. "That's all right," she said, putting his hand back. "Go ahead."

"Sure is hot in here."

"Why don't you take off your sweater?"

He stood up and pulled his sweater over his head,

tousling his hair in a wild, electric disarray.

"My," she said. "I think you've got something for me."

*　　*　　*

A few nights later, Jimmy groped through the littered outer cellar of his parents' basement cave, which was the very same superintendent's apartment of the rooming house where they'd lived once before. He was guided only by the demonic red eyes and teeth of the roaring jack-o'-lantern furnace. He reached out before him in the dark, acutely aware of his new gloves. They would protect him should he touch something sharp or hot. Sunny had come to the theater to pick up her final check and had brought them with her. "For my curly-head," she had said. "Your hands looked red and raw when you visited me. But I shouldn't give them to you."

"Why not?"

"Because you told me a lie."

"What lie?"

"You pretended you had never been with a woman. But I know better, don't I?" She had kissed him quickly on the cheek and hurried off.

Now the tight smile of light from under the door of the basement apartment stirred mixed feelings. He wanted to tell somebody about himself and Sunny, but there was nobody to tell, nobody willing to listen. Once inside, he'd be doing the listening. He loitered in the dark, shadow-boxing without shadows to box.

"Take *that!* Stoney—and *that!*" He wondered if Sunny had told Stoney about them. She had sworn to him that she had not told Stoney, but Stoney seemed to know and had been ragging him unmercifully. "Junior finally wet the wick." As Jimmy boxed there in the dark, it occurred to him that Sunny was probably in Buffalo. Would it ever happen again? His gloved hands dropped to his sides. It would never happen again—never, never! And he loved Sunny, *loved* her!

30

Emotion shook through him. He wiped his eyes on his sleeves, the backs of his gloves.

Inside, his father sat at the table, wearing his mother's kimono. He greeted Jimmy with:

"Quoth the Raven, Nevermore!"

Immediately echoed by:

"Quoth the Raven, yourself!" Jimmy's mother rose from a bed in a corner. She was wearing his father's overcoat. "He's been like this for hours, Jimmy. *Quoth the Raven! Quoth the Raven!* I can't stand it anymore. He's been drunk for weeks. He's supposed to sell books. When was the last book you sold? Look at us, here in this hole in the ground! Look!"

Jimmy looked at the dripping, criss-crossing pipes, the painted-over, black-speckled bricks of the walls, where the bedbugs lived, the faded linoleum roses . . . .

"The Wizard of Oz!"

Jimmy looked at his father. "Mom's right, Dad. Look at us! Look at this place! Remember that nice place I got us? Over the pizza parlor? It was *nice!* It was *beautiful* compared with this! We can't live here. Nobody can!"

"That's what I've been telling him. That's what I've been saying. What I've been telling *you*! Nobody'll listen to me. It's mid-winter and we have no back wall, just a rug slung up to keep out the cold. If it weren't for the furnace outside the front door, we'd freeze. In fact, we ought to knock out that beaverboard partition so we can get more heat."

"Mom's right, Dad."

"Just one minute, young man," said his father, raising a finger. "Since when do you decide policy?"

"Since he sees his mother in this terrible condition."

"People can't live like this, Dad."

"People can and do. But let me propose the biblical solution to you both. If your home offends you, pluck yourselves from it!"

"He doesn't know what he's saying, Jimmy. Don't pay any attention to him."

"It is *you* who never knows what you're saying—or doing," said his father. He gave Jimmy a conspiratorial wink. "Did you know that she found a woman's photograph in your suitcase?"

"Sunny's picture?" Jimmy looked at his mother. "Mom, you didn't have any right to go through my things. I have a right to *some* privacy."

"No, you don't! Not when you're only sixteen and might be getting into all kinds of trouble."

"Where is it?"

"I tore it up. What do you think? A picture of a half-naked tramp with 'I'll never forget you' on it! I only hope you didn't have anything to do with her. You might have a social disease."

*   *   *

It was Saturday night again, the big night, and the last show was over. Jimmy sat with his friend, Tex, in a bar that was catty-corner across the intersection from the theater. Through a soft, steady fall of snow he saw the Minsky marquee-lights dowse out. He had plugged the jukebox with a nickel to hear his favorite song, "Rags to Riches." The crooner understood how he felt.

"Look, Junior," said Tex, "the lady's got to live her life. She's got to take a job when she gets the chance. You can't go moping around like this—'taint good for you. Go on, now—drink your beer. The chorus line's full of girls who would be glad to sleep with you."

"Nobody else is like Sunny. She made me feel like somebody cared about me."

Stoney and his ne'er-do-well buddy, Big Jim, emerged from the backroom, where they'd been shooting pool.

"How's the virgin?" said Stoney. He was drunk and disgruntled, having lost a game and a fivespot to Big Jim.

32

"Poor Jimmy Junior! Does he miss his ladylove? You dumb shit, Junior! Playing romance with these whores makes me sick. Haven't you figured out that I put her up to it?"

"What do you mean?"

"He don't mean nothin'," said Tex. "Don't pay no attention to him."

"I mean I told her to make a man out of you."

"He didn't, neither," said Tex. "He's just teasing you, Jimmy."

"Butt out, Tex!" said Big Jim.

"She liked me," said Jimmy. "She gave me these gloves."

"Let me see those," said Stoney. "Look!" He held the gloves out for Big Jim's inspection. "These are *my* gloves, Junior. I lost them in Bayonne a year ago. Now you turn up with them. I must have left them at her place."

"They're brand-new," Jimmy protested.

"They were brand-new when I lost them."

"Put them on," said Tex. "If they fit, then we know."

"I told you to butt out, hillbilly," said Big Jim.

Stoney threw the gloves on the bar. "I don't have to prove anything to a punk like you, Junior. Keep the damned things." He gave Jimmy's shoulder a scornful pat. Then he smiled. "*C'mon!* She's just a whore. Hell, Junior, they're all *whores*."

Lou Schenk, their boss, got up from a booth and came over, tough and bulky. "Push off, Stoney," he said. "You're drunk. Go home and sleep it off."

Stoney looked at Jimmy and laughed ridicule, shrugged indifference, threw an arm over Big Jim's shoulder, and allowed himself to be walked to the door. Jimmy picked up the gloves and pulled them on, tenderly.

Suddenly he convulsed, his eyes making a small shower of tears. Standing, he gripped the bar-rim hard in his gloved hands and hung his head between his arms. He looked down at a brass rail and a tin spittoon filled with floating butts.

"She was a *pig*, Junior," Stoney called back from the door.

From deep in Jimmy's throat came a sound like the growl of a wolf, and he ran out into the black-and-white lacework street after Stoney. "You bastards!" he screamed after the snow-curtained figures who walked ahead. "You liar, Stoney! She *liked* me, you rotten son-of-a-bitch!"

Lou Schenk and Tex had followed Jimmy into the street, grabbing after him. In his hurry the heavy concession-aire slipped on the iced-over sidewalk. Jimmy was only vaguely aware of Lou's curses and Tex's nervous laughter.

Ahead, Stoney detached himself from Big Jim and turned back. "Apologize, Junior, or I'll come back there and teach you some Marine Corps manners. I warn you: *Apologize!*"

From somewhere Marge had appeared. "Stop it, Stoney!" she called. "Stop it!"

"Shut up, bitch!" Stoney yelled. He stalked forward, eyes glittering drunken anger, intent on Jimmy.

Jimmy hesitated. Then Tex hissed: *"Go to, Junior! Git 'im!"* Jimmy took a step forward.

"No, no!" cried Marge. "Stop them, somebody. You'll all end up in jail!" She held a cigarette and her gesticulations tracked up and down in the gloom.

Then Stoney slipped on the ice, and Jimmy pounced on him, pummeling him with his gloved hands, hitting his face, his shoulders, his flailing arms, sometimes just hitting packed ice. It was his life he pounded. Then he felt hot flashes on his face: Marge was burning him with her cigarette, sticking it in his cheek, his temple.

"You bitch!" he heard Tex shout, and felt Marge being pulled from him. He heard her scream in short, shocking spurts. But he was in a dream, a nightmare. He pounded his life until he felt himself being pulled from Stoney's inert form by Lou Schenk, heard the concessionaire's deep soft calming voice commanding him gently to stop, to be still. Then he was being manhandled by a pair of burly blue policemen.

* * *

"I have the shakes, snakes, and the dancing bears, but I'll be all right in a few days," Jimmy's father said.

"I know you will, Dad."

"Now, what's this you want me to do?"

"I want you to sign me up so I can go in the Marines."

"You can't go in the Marines," said his mother. "You're not old enough."

"Always the nay-sayer," said his father.

"I'll be of age on my next birthday. That's old enough, if I have your permission. If you'll sign for me."

His father looked at his mother. "He can do what he wants to do if he has the courage to do it." He smiled blearily at Jimmy. "I'll sign you up."

"And be rid of you," his mother said. "That's all he wants. He'd like to sign me up, too, but I keep the rooming-house going."

"I'd like to sign up your voice," said his father, resignedly.

* * *

Stoney, Big Jim, Tex, and Lou Schenk were in the concession room getting ready for the matinee.

Jimmy felt a nervous embarrassed pride at seeing that Stoney had a black eye and a blue bruise on his jutting jaw. His stomach shook as he did a stationary swagger that said: Don't tread on me.

"Here he is," cried Big Jim. He looked at Stoney. "Aincha gonna do nothin'?"

Stoney shrugged, morose, subdued, sober.

35

"No," said Lou Schenk, "he ain't gonna do nothin', an' neither are you. I don't want no trouble among my butchers. I got a business to run. If it wasn't for me all of you'd be in jail right now." He turned his attention to Jimmy. "I like you, Junior. You got a lot of guts, showing up here. I didn't think you'd have the nerve to come in today. But I got to let you go. Stoney's my number one butcher. I need him."

"That's O.K., Lou. I figured. I just came in to say good-bye, and no hard feelings to anybody. O.K. Stoney?"

Stoney nodded. He seemed genuinely regretful.

"So—well—that's it."

Tex walked Jimmy out of the concession room and up into the lobby. "What are you going to do?"

"I'm going to join the Marines, Tex. The Marines build men. Look at Stoney. If he'd been sober, why he'da beat the crap out of me. And right, too. I don't know what got into me."

"You really mean to join the Marines?"

"If they'll have me."

"Oh, they'll have you, Junior, don't worry about that." He thought for a minute, as if remembering. "Well, it ain't nothin' here," he said, indicating the darkened theater. "It's the big burlesque out there. Hell's bells, Junior, it's all a big burlesque. You do it all."

CHAPTER TWO

SWEET LEILANI

And for a little time they prized
Themselves emparadised.
> —*Howard Nemerov*

THE NEW YORK TIMES
MAY 8, 1954

DIENBIENPHU IS LOST AFTER 55 DAYS
DULLES SAYS UNITY CAN CHECK REDS

THE NEW YORK TIMES
MAY 18, 1954

HIGH COURT BANS SCHOOL
SEGREGATION

"Cock crows, wolf bays, caterwauls, eldritch sounds ringing out and echoing back from the escarpment, weird screams meant to terrify, crazily announcing attack across fogbound spiderwebs of barbed-wired terrain. Then the poop of mortars, the red spit of burps, a flare, shedding chartreuse in its lazy swaying gravity fall, beautiful tracers burning out in air, phosphorous grenades making small midnight suns—" Buck Sergeant Robert E. Lee Sharp of Macon read to his captive audience of Marine recruits his poems of Korean conflict—recruits who had, night before, waded the blind-dark swamp of the Sea Island called Parris, shitbirds and turds up to their chins in swamp gunk, whipped on and kicked by water moccasins, Mae-Wested in the dark by boa constrictors, or so they believed. But two hundred-some-odd farm boys and city slickers scared spineless in the snakes' swamp knew it was drowning to be feared most, in the slippery dark, burdened with fifty-pound packs, rifles, helmets, cartridge-belts, canteens, bayonets, and night-blind eyes, under a star-proof vegetable roof of shingling fronds and fans. Jimmy stretched his neck like a turtle above the din of clanks splashes and shouts of terror. And always above any din Sharp's mellifluous Georgian, urging, commanding a motley crew of shitbirds and turds to become Marines, who himself was Poster-Marine, whose men thought him perfect but for the fact that he was mad as the Hatter, perfect, but for his constant, barely submerged violence, which was the song behind his words now, as he read with great beauty, vivid clarity, his martial poems of nightmare mayhem on Bunker Hill and Snipers Ridge, where he won a chestful of medals, a seemingly mad hero Marine poet drill instructor, angrier than God. At what? War, the poems told, at war, at human nature, at himself, filled with his own violence; at his recruits, too, but to save them, always to make them triumph over what he had endured, cried: "Coming! Outposts in! The sand-bagged weight of the bunker collapsed under artillery—a full barrage—pf-f-f-f BOOM—and the Reds slid in on us. Got one under my arm and slit his throat. *Now tell me about Mao, I said; I'll tell you about freedom, you two-mouthed bastard!*" Sharp scanned them, in their skivvies on the squadbay floor, across the little table he brought to his recitals. "Unnerstayend," he growled, "Mr. Kennan in Washington has devised for America a policy of containment. The Reds cain't continue to eat if they don't swallow up other countries. They don't create wealth, they re-dis-tri-bute it. Get me? They are an empire. Unnerstay-end what that is? They gotta eat up their neighbors or else they collapse. Unnerstay-end? Do you dumb shitbirds unnerstay-end what it's all about, what Bunker Hill was about—either one? About FREEDOM, you dumb turds, FREEDOM! You eat enough 'gator-doo, you'al'll learn. One o' them Reds shoots your balls off—Non emasculatatum est—" Off in another reality field, Sharp whispers, "My best buddy, from Valdosta . . ." Back. "You gonna priss like girls when you march. We gonna win the base ensign. I don't care a fiddler's bitch if the red flag goes up at a hunnerd-ten degrees. You gonna priss like girls. You gonna look PRETTY. Get me? And you know what you gonna be? Do you? You gonna be God bless America Uncle Sam's most perfect killers. Now what you gonna be?" SIR, killers, SIR! "Makes my heart sing. And if the army and the navy ever get to heaven's scene . . . What, dammit?" They will find the streets are guarded by United States Marines, SIR!

THE NEW YORK TIMES
JANUARY 28, 1955

PRESIDENT SAYS HE ALONE WILL MAKE DECISION ON FORMOSA STRAIT ACTION

EFFORTS TO CURB EISENHOWER ON FORMOSA
FADE IN SENATE
WHITE HOUSE MOVES TO DISPEL TALK IT SEEKS A
PREVENTIVE WAR

REDS RESUME SHELLING OF TACHENS AS WAY IS
OPENED FOR EVACUATION

It was cold and the mist was a frayed, gray curtain, a fine wet, disheveled lace, that rose from the gray ship's pregnant sides beneath them and up into a dark, foreboding sky, but about them distances would open like hall doors, and then they could see where they had been, or might be going, which was, sometimes, low, colorless land, too distant to see clearly, and too close and enemy-entrenched for comfort. Jimmy feared that the alarm farting would start, agonized spurts of the hysterical siren they had practiced with and for. Christ, when would the ship turn toward the glimpsed mainland? Jimmy thought of his mother and father, would they miss him? There were times when he had had doubts, but not now, now he had to believe that the whole world would miss him if the enemy did not, if he became a casualty of forces beyond the control of a stripling. There was some small comfort in knowing that the hold of the ship contained landing crafts tank, which would be some protection from fire from the shore. Oh, Jesus, why had he joined? Not for this murky ocean and that misty land. He had no answer, except to doubt the bravado of his boyhood, and to be answered with confusion, nor could his petrified friend have answered, as he could see, though his helmet was low on his brow, hiding his eyes, his useless rifle aimed toward imagined enemy hordes. Later, Jimmy read in the papers of what they were doing, of how near to war he had been; the whole world was in fact near to war. But diplomacy won the day and, after two nerve-wracking weeks of hazardous duty, of criss-cross cruising, they took a sudden scudding turn in the rough straits, making a long, curving wake, followed by swooping, screaming gulls, famished for their jetsam garbage and blurring letters of farewell to their loved ones; and, with hosannas of thanksgiving, their lucky ship set course for Hawaii, O happy day!

*   *   *

An albatross crossed the sky on that Hawaiian day when Jimmy was twenty. That day he did not have to take orders but could give them, and ordered his first legal drink, a tall, frosty, rainbow called a Singapore Sling, and strawed half the strong drink down as if it were a dime-store rickey, or a soda-fountain pop. He picked up his wallet, replaced his I.D., removed a ten-year-old photo, faded and cracked, and inspected the silvered faces of his parents. They stood before his tenth birthday cake like puckered fountain cupids, helping him to blow out his candles and in his wish. His wish then was that they would never grow old, a child's wish, born of dependency, his need for them to flourish for his sake. He looked away, about, and studied the time-worn faces of those at the bar, and wondered, if, upon his return to the mainland, his parents would look the same as always, the same as in the cracked photograph, or unrecognizably altered. Then he glanced up, and saw a long, black, tail-finned limousine, highly polished, shining moons of sun, pass out of sight on the busy street where he had entered; and, startled out of his reverie, turned about to find Waikiki Beach behind him, a keepsake postcard of one of the most important days of his life, and he wondered at the power of his first legal drink to so disorient him, for, when he entered, he was looking out at it. Then he realized that he was on a turntable, imperceptibly turning counter-clockwise, but only, of course, by the machinations of human will.

*   *   *

The 3rd Shore Party Battalion of the 4th Marines, Fleet Marine Force Pacific, Kaneohe Bay, Oahu, Territory of Hawaii, got a new education officer. Lieutenant Bland was assigned directly to Jimmy's outfit, Company B, and immediately held a white-glove inspection. Bland stopped at Jimmy's footlocker and dug into his books.

"You read Faulkner?"

"Yes, Sir!"

"What's this?"

"Paradise Lost, Sir. Milton."

"You're half through it?"

"Yes, Sir."

"I read it at Stanford," said Bland, in cultivated tones. "I took engineering, but I read a lot of literature. I'm Catholic—have you read Dante?"

"Not yet, Sir. He's next—after Milton."

"I understand you box."

"My box?" Jimmy looked down at his footlocker—was something wrong? He had a nagging ear infection and doubted what he heard.

"You're a boxer."

"Oh, yes, Sir. I'm on the boxing team."

"And you're a weight lifter?"

"Yes, Sir."

"How much can you bench press?"

"About three-twenty-five, Sir."

"Not bad. I can do about three-fifty."

"That's very good, Sir."

"You know I'm the new education officer for the battalion, don't you?"

"Yes, Sir. I've been told that."

"I want you to report to my office after inspection."

"Yes, Sir."

Jimmy duly reported and was told to sit down across the desk from Lt. Bland.

"Now here's the thing," said Bland. "I've looked over your records. I see you have a unit citation for hazardous duty in the Formosa business. I've never been in any kind of action. What was it like?"

"Boring—when we weren't scared, Sir. We were put on three LSTs and sailed down from Japan and into the Formosa Straights. We sailed back and forth along the coast of China for about two weeks, then we got an order for our ship to peel off and come here to Hawaii."

"Go on."

"That's about it. We didn't know what it was all about until we got here and read it in the papers. Then we found out we were close to war. Ike threatened the Communists with atomic weapons and they backed down. And we were given the medal."

"I bet you were glad to get here."

"Yes, Sir. It was good to know I was back in America."

"Do you think Hawaii will ever be a state?"

"Oh yes, Sir! No doubt about it."

"Do you have any close buddies in this outfit?"

"You don't have friends in the service, Sir, just military acquaintances."

"You're a bit of a loner, aren't you?"

"There's not many guys to share Milton with, Sir."

Jimmy thought Bland was a very impressive fellow, friendly but sharp. He felt that here at last was a guy he could hit it off with—too bad he was an officer. He wondered what Bland was after. He suspected that there was a method in this apparently random questioning.

"What did you do before you joined up? I see you dropped out of school."

"Sir, I was a Western Union boy for a few years. Then I was a candy butcher at Minsky's Burlesque in Newark— hawked candy, orange drinks, popcorn, girly magazines, like that, Sir."

Then Lt. Bland said, "How would you like to be a Naval Air Cadet? NavCad? You could become an officer and a pilot. I want to give you a series of academic and intelligence tests—are you willing to try?" Jimmy figured he had nothing to lose and said, "Yes, Sir—sure."

Jimmy wrote home and told his parents about this. His mother wrote back, saying that his father had completely disapproved and she agreed with his father. Elliot Whistler had lost his son by a previous marriage, the pilot, shot down in 1941. He would not have another son flying. So both were against him becoming a pilot, as his mother had been against him becoming a writer—he was trying to write poetry, inspired by Sergeant Sharp, the poet of Parris Island—a boxer, a weight lifter, a Marine, or just about anything. Even his father called her "The Negative Force." But his father and mother were united against flying, so it was two-to-one, or two-to-two, if he could count on Lieutenant Bland.

Night after night, Jimmy thought about his parents, often dreamed of them. They seemed always on the run from a bad check or an overdue rooming house bill, or in search of better sales territory or an even cheaper rent. Sometimes they moved twice in a week: twice a month was not unusual. Jimmy had rarely attended school.

Now they were superintending a new rooming house in Newark. His mother had written because his father was on a three-month jag. Someday Jimmy would come home, and go to work in a factory, and help support them, she implied. Nothing must happen to him in the meantime. That was his future, as they saw it. It seemed a very bleak future to Jimmy. He planned to go to school on the Korean G.I. Bill. He intended to become a writer. Becoming a Naval Air Cadet would eliminate a good many steps in his progress. But soon a second letter came, this time from his father, who had sobered up: by no means should he follow this dangerous course. Look at what had happened to his half-brother! His father was a fairly good writer when he was sober. He had been a W.P.A. writer, and once wrote speeches for the mayor of Newark. Jimmy remembered his father walking him along the little wall that fronted the Newark City Hall, holding his hand. He must have been about five then, and so proud of his father. Later his father was a door-to-door salesman, and fancied himself an expert in making people agree with him.

His father's letter put a damper on Jimmy's enthusiasm for cadet training. But the more tests Jimmy took, the closer he and Lt. Bland became, and Jimmy felt torn between the two.

Despite the rules against fraternization, Jimmy and Bland began to meet at Waikiki. They would sit in their bathing suits in the shade of the Banyan Court at the Moana Hotel, drink Mai-Tais, and watch the waves and the surfers roll in. Bland loaned Jimmy a book on tank warfare, another on fighting the Hucks in the Philippines. "We must never get into a land war in Asia," he told Jimmy. "Read the book and see why." Bland was probably about twenty-five, but he seemed a fountain of wisdom, which was why Jimmy did not want to disappoint him.

"Think of it," said Bland, "you'll be flying the newest jet planes! Pretty exciting, eh?"

Jimmy thought of his mother and father, and Bland noticed his frown.

"Look what I've brought along," he said. "I'm going to teach you to play chess. I give us a week and you'll be beating me."

* * *

Jimmy had made many beach landings, jumping out of the landing craft in helmet-high water while loaded down with equipment. Many times he had gone under, only getting his head back above water with the greatest effort, despite his strength. Even if he could swim, he couldn't swim in such a getup. And the truth was, that, in spite of all the time he had spent in Y.M.C.A. and other gyms, he had not learned to swim. He was taught again in the Marines, but it didn't take, and, though the Marines said he could swim, and had certified him, he did not believe it. He tried at the Armed Services Y in Honolulu, but could only keep from drowning by the most strenuous effort, which, despite his strength, he could not maintain. It was as if his forever negative mother was there to say, "You can't learn to swim at your age," as she had said, on his sixteenth birthday, when asked what he wanted to be and answered that he would like to be a writer, if he could, "You can't be a writer. You have no education." She seemed to stand by the pool, scorning his efforts—and he sank, and sank again, and again.

Another beach landing was coming up. He wasn't a malingerer, but the redundancy of these landings was getting to him. He decided to goldbrick on this one, go to sickbay with his ear infection—why he had misheard Bland at that first inspection—and spend a few days on his rack, reading and smoking Lucky Strikes. He had just started *The Revolt of Mamie Stover*, when a group of M.P.s appeared at the empty squadbay doors and called his name. He called back, and discovered that he had been assigned to a military police unit called the HASP, the Hawaiian Armed Services Police. He stuffed *Mamie Stover* in his back pocket and found himself walking into her world of prostitution and violence. This is what he got for trying to get out of something. Served him right, he guessed.

HASP headquarters was on Ala Moana in Honolulu. The HASP itself was composed of a patrol section, a motor-cycle section, an AWOL apprehension section, an investigative section, an aid station, and several lockups. All services were represented. Training was on the job. There was a barracks area on the second floor where Jimmy was assigned a bunk. This was something of a come-down from the beautiful surroundings at Kaneohe Bay, across the enchanted Pali mountains. Jimmy felt as if he had returned to Kobe, or, worse, Newark. He was assigned to the patrol section, which meant that he had to walk about like a street cop with a forty-five pistol on his hip and a nightstick in his hand, and break up fights and arrest trouble-makers. Apparently, he had been chosen for this select outfit because he was big, strong, smart, and, most of all, available. If he had gone on the beach landing this would not have happened, he reasoned. But it was a lucky break in a way, too. Now he didn't have to decide be-tween Bland's and his mother's and father's versions of his future. Not for the present, at least. That very night, he found himself patrolling Hotel Street, also known as the "Combat Zone." This was where all the action was, bars, fights, kill-ings, prostitution, etc. It was the job of the HASP to keep it under control.

He had been on the job for about two months, when he saw a drag queen followed into a men's room by two sailors. Suspecting the sailors of being up to no good, he followed them in in time to stop them from completing the beating of the drag queen that had already resulted in a long-lashed eye being popped out—shades of his childhood. One of the sailors had the drag queen's money, in an initialed clip. He arrested both sailors and took them to Ala Moana, where they were charged. An ambulance had taken the drag queen away from the bar. Next day, Jimmy received a letter from the Chief of Police, honoring his work. It turned out that the drag queen was a relative of the Chief's. Jimmy found himself to be something of a hero. Several other incidents added to his reputation. A bottle across his face also added a broken nose and several minor scars. But he was beginning to like being a cop—you could do some good, he thought.

*　　*　　*

Jimmy wrote to Lt. Bland and told him he would not be going to NavCad. Bland wrote back, telling him he had passed his one year college equivalency test, and that his I.Q. score was very high indeed. He would be crazy, wrote Bland, to miss this opportunity. "It will change your whole life."

Up or down, which way would he go? Which way *should* he go? He wrote to his parents and told them he would not rise into flight, but walk the soiled if solid ground of Hotel Street. It'll be Newark next, and Minsky's Burlesque house, back where I started from. Or a by-the-hour worker at the scissors factory on Halsey Street, or the chewing gum factory in Bayonne. That's what you really want from me, he thought. But still, he harbored dreams of his own. He thought he might go to a drama school, become an actor, and later a playwright. He filled his secret notebooks with poems and plots. He would think of lines he thought to be beautiful while patrolling among the low-life on Hotel Street, in the middle of the Combat Zone. Above the street, with its tawdriness, was the sky, blue and cloud-scudding by day, and full of stars by night, and always the perfume of sandalwood and the sea beyond.

He appeared to be a tough guy, a hard-edged, hard-nosed type, but that was only an appearance. He would check into the Armed Services YMCA, when on liberty, and spend the weekend in his room, reading. He read the Pocket Bible straight through on one weekend. As a child, in hotel rooms, he had read in the Gideon Bible. It had always been the literary content of the Bible that had interested him, the poetry. Occasionally, of a morning, he would try to swim the length of the Y's olympic-sized pool, from the deep end to the shallow, just in case his strength began to fail. He could do it with the power of his arms and chest, but nothing would allow him to float. He had to use all his strength or he would sink and drown. It wasn't that he couldn't swim but that he couldn't float.

Bland seemed to have given up on him. His parents seemed to forget him again. No letters came. He had no girlfriend. There had been a whirl of military activity and travel that precluded getting to know any women, and he had no taste for prostitutes or even B-girls, both of whom he worked among. He was lonely a good deal of the time, even in the middle of the noise and activity of Hotel Street.

But wherever you looked, people caused you trouble, or betrayed you. Jimmy had been sending money home, pointlessly, as it turned out so that he might have a nest egg to start out on, and had recently written to his parents asking if his records matched theirs. They denied ever receiving a cent. They had stolen his money—probably used it on booze—and didn't even have the good grace to be honest about it. If they had asked, Jimmy would have given them the money. It was the betrayal that hurt, the lying. They were all he knew of love and they sided together against him. They cut him out. Suddenly he couldn't breathe. He was drowning in murky water, held down by an enormous weight, something on his back, a man or a woman, holding him under. His scream was a gurgle, and he sat up on his bunk, his whole body wet. What was he going to do? He got out a pad and pencil and went into the head, where there was light, and tried to write a sonnet. By dawn's early light he had come up with—

THE NIGHT SWEATS

By our intensity, with hanging head,
we spell the wolf away, who pants and croons
outside the door, who wants us to be dead
so he may have his meal. By magic runes
we rid the world of wide-winged evil loons
whose madness mixes metaphors instead
of bringing clarity, whose looney tunes
make breathless nightmares in our sweat-wet bed.
Hear them who creep toward our peace of mind,
destructive artifices of our brains,
to wreak their havoc! Run, leave them behind!
And in the dark we try to run in chains
and can't escape because the night is mined
to blow us up in spite of all our pains.

*　*　*

Then, in the usual mysterious way of the military, Jimmy was transferred out of the HASP, and assigned back at the Kaneohe Brig to be a prison chaser, one who takes prisoners from one locale to another. The HASP had to keep their limited lockups cleared, so they would send mixed batches of Army, Navy, Marine, Air Force, whatever, to any brig or stockade that could house them, then sort them out, and the chasers would take them back to their own base lockups. Jimmy took the dog-faces to Schofield, the swab-jockeys to Pearl, and the flyboys to Hickam, shotgun at the ready.

One bright morning, Jimmy had to report to the Provost Marshal's Office over an incident in the mess hall. The prisoners had a schedule, and there was some pressure of time to get them fed and back to the brig. Jimmy had ordered about fifty prisoners to the head of the line. He had the authority to do this, but usually the prisoners had to wait their turn, along with the non-prisoners, all of whom ate in the same mess hall. There was a gung-ho corporal named Dunkel who was interested in getting ahead in the military police, another chaser, like Jimmy, but with more brig experience, though he lacked Jimmy's background in the HASP, and may have been jealous of it. Dunkel made a big stink about what Jimmy had done, demanded his sidearm, baton, and his armband right there in front of everyone, and made a virtual arrest.

Now the question of who was right was going to be settled by the Provost. Jimmy didn't give a damn who won. If he won, things would go on as usual. If Dunkel won, Jimmy would probably be placed back in his old unit, which he missed. If he could get himself back under Lt. Bland's control, he might re-think the idea about NavCad. After all, he had a right to his own life, especially after his parents had stolen his money, their latest betrayal. But the question was settled in Jimmy's favor. He had been thinking of the well-being of the prisoners and the safety of the situation. It was not a good idea to keep a large group of prisoners, anxious to eat, and to get on with their day, waiting for other units to go through ahead of them. He had used good judgement. On the other hand, it was found, Dunkel's actions had been over the top, extreme, generally not very sensible. Dunkel did not hide his hatred. Outside the Provost Marshal's Office, he spit at Jimmy's feet, and Jimmy would have to work with him for God knew how long! Sometimes winning is worse than losing, he thought.

For reasons beyond Jimmy's understanding, there was a dearth of rank on the base. The Turnkey was going stateside. He was a staff-sergeant. There were no more men of that level, only corporals, like Dunkel and himself, and privates first class and buck privates. The scuttlebutt was that one of the corporals was going to become Turnkey. Jimmy did not want the job. Let the gung-ho Dunkel have it. Jimmy was content to ferry the prisoners about. But now he feared that the incident between himself and Dunkel might put him in the lead position. That was the last thing he wanted. He had a low opinion of power-seekers. Alas, he was a poet!

In an effort to get all his troubles off his mind, he took off on liberty by himself. He thought he would go down to Hotel Street, have a few drinks, then go to a Chinese restaurant he favored and have a good meal. He was wearing slacks and a lurid Hawaiian shirt. Blond, bronzed, and athletic, he passed the entrance to an upstairs dance hall. In his experience, these countless dance halls started young girls off as hostesses and quickly turned them into prostitutes. This was ordinarily none of his business. Bad things were always happening in Hell's Half Acre. But this time his attention was caught.

A youthful female voice screamed.

An angry male voice roared.

Jimmy turned back and looked up the stairway. A man with the body of a Sumo wrestler had a pretty young Hawaiian girl pinned to the wall about half-way up a wide, twenty-foot stairway.

"What's going on up there?" Jimmy called.

"Help me," cried the girl. "I want to go home!" The girl was crying, and trying to twist loose from the big ape's grasp.

"Get lost," said Sumo, "this is none of your business." He was a bouncer type, part Polynesian, part Oriental, or some such mixture. But it was hard to tell. The light was dim in the upper reaches of the stairway. "You came here," he said to the girl, "now you stay."

"Let her go," called Jimmy.

"Mind your own business." The big man stepped into the light. Jimmy felt a cold chill run up his spine. The man's face wore a full tiger head tattoo. Jimmy got a grip on himself.

"I'm military police," he barked, and waved his wallet at the man. "Now let her go."

To locals, the Military Police was the same as the Civilian Police, since they worked together. The man let go of the girl. He seemed to be waiting for orders. Jimmy directed, "Miss, you come down here." He pointed up at the man. "You stay right where you are. Got it?"

The man gave Jimmy a surly, but assenting nod, and the girl broke free and stumbled, tears streaming, down the ten or so steps to join Jimmy.

"Stay put," Jimmy warned the ape, and took the girl's arm and walked her briskly to the corner. "There," he said, turning to her. "You're free to go."

"Please, don't leave me," she begged. "I'm afraid they'll come after me, and I don't have any money." Now Jimmy saw that she was a beautiful child, perhaps sixteen, an exquisite Polynesian girl with eyes like black full moons.

"What did you do, run away from home?"

"Yes. But it was a big mistake," she said, through tears. "I want to go home."

They walked a little way and Jimmy hailed a cab. "Tell the driver where you live." He'd never heard of it.

"What's your name?"

"Leilani Kona."

"Sweet Leilani?" he asked, opening the cab door.

"Another one. Not the original. She was a white girl."

"Have you been—uh— molested?" he asked, slipping in beside her.

"No. But it would not be so, if you hadn't come along. I have only been here today. I have heard stories, but I didn't know how bad it was down here."

"Pretty bad," said Jimmy, looking out at Hotel Street.

"You mustn't think that it is all like Hotel Street. We *are* in paradise."

"I guess I've just seen too many of the wrong places."

"You'll see, when we get to my village—you'll see how beautiful it is."

"Then why did you leave it?"

"I was full of curiosity about the wild side. You're young. Aren't you full of curiosity?"

"I come from a tough town in New Jersey called Newark. I left there to go to a tough town in Japan called Kobe. I ended up here in a tough town called Honolulu. They all seem the same to me."

"You are a tough guy, aren't you?"

He looked at her. Was she kidding him?

"Not so tough, I suppose."

"No," she said, "not so tough, I suppose."

*   *   *

When the taxi finally pulled in to the bamboo village, it reminded Jimmy of the Jungle Jim movies he had seen as a boy. He half expected to see Johnny Weissmuller in his white hunter outfit emerge from one of the grass huts. He caught the definite smell of roasting pork on the air. What appeared to be the whole village of at least two hundred souls quickly gathered around them. It appeared that Jimmy's runaway girl was not just ordinary, but a celebrity of some kind.

"They are relieved and happy to see me," she explained. "Here come my father and mother." They came open-armed and seized their daughter in a loving embrace. Leilani told Jimmy that her father could be called "the Chief," so that was how Jimmy thought of him. He was the apparent head of the village, his wife the Queen Bee. Now Jimmy saw that his Leilani was a sort of Princess.

Jimmy had expected to let the girl out, and have the cabbie take him back to downtown Honolulu, but the Chief pulled Jimmy from the cab and sent it off without him. For a moment, Jimmy thought he was going to be lynched, but then he realized that everyone was smiling. Then he thought of cannibals, but he had never heard of any on the islands. Finally, Leilani told him that her parents, indeed, everybody there, considered him a hero, who had saved her from a fate worse than death, and a big luau was in the making.

So he would eat, not be eaten. He was much relieved, and told Leilani so, who at first laughed at his fear, and now laughed at his flushed embarrassment.

"But I didn't do anything," he said. Leilani turned to her father and said a few words, then back to Jimmy: "Yes you did! I told them all about it, what the tiger-faced man was trying to do to me, and how you stopped him and brought me home."

Jimmy received the first of many affectionate pats on the back from Leilani's ham-handed father, who told him that the luau was actually for Leilani's sixteenth birthday, but that now it was for him, Jimmy, her savior, as well.

"You are going to have a real feast. We've been work-ing on it for days." He put an arm over Jimmy's shoulder. "Leilani is going to be punished for running off like this, but we'll see to that later. Right now we're so happy to have her back, we don't intend to do anything to spoil her birthday, and we intend to honor you, young man, so please enjoy your-self." A busy man, he vanished into the crowd.

"How's he going to punish you?" Jimmy asked Leilani, fearing that she might be beaten or—well, he couldn't imagine.

"Oh, he'll take some privileges away, but I have so many I probably won't miss them. Have you ever been to a real luau? I don't mean one of those beach party things."

"No."

"A luau is served as one long continuous course," she said, taking his arm and guiding him around bustling cooks. "A pig is wrapped in shiny green ti-leaves. A large hole is lined with red-hot bricks—you see here—and the pig is placed inside, covered with more ti-leaves, and slowly roasted. It takes many hours. They've been preparing this luau for several days, so everything's about ready." She pointed to a trestle table full of seafood. "There's squid, tuna, mahi-mahi and paka-paka. Poi takes the place of potatoes. Poi is baked taro bulb, mashed to a pulp and strained. You eat it with the fingers of your right hand while your left holds a piece of pork or fish. Poi is usually eaten from a calabash shell, one finger for men and two fingers for women. Don't get it wrong or they'll laugh at you. Say *he ono,* which means it is delicious. Say that a lot."

"*He ono!*"

"I think you've got it. Oh, one more thing. Nod toward the host—my father—and lift your eyebrows in apprecia-tion."

"You mean like this?" said Jimmy, making a face.

She laughed. "Anybody but my father would think you were insulting him."

"What would he think?"

"That you are a very funny guy."

A band—guitar, bass and ukulele—struck up and a few people began dancing. The Chief appeared out of the crowd and handed Jimmy a cold beer. "I thought you would like a cold one, son," he said. Jimmy had no sooner finished that beer when he was handed another one. The party was in full swing. Leilani sat with Jimmy and showed him how to eat the pork and poi in the proper Hawaiian way. Through the interstices of the trees Jimmy saw the sky over the sea explode in reds and blues and trailers of white and the moon become huge and gold and close. Morning light finally showed through the jungle fronds and fans, but the luau was still in full swing—ukuleles, deep drums and grass skirt dancing—and the Chief forced another bowl of a powerful Polynesian drink on him. He shrugged and chugalugged. It and others stayed down right into the full red dawn that came to that true paradise, blue Hawaii.

*　*　*

Jimmy woke slowly, only gradually realizing that he lay on a beach, safely up from the surf. He saw Burt Lancaster and Deborah Kerr rolling around together in the surf, making passionate love. Had he got inside the movie screen, for the beach rose right up to him, where he lay? He looked behind him and saw a seaside village nosing out of the vegetation: a little grass shack, or the corner of a little grass shack, prow emerging as if to slide down and into the water. Fleecy clouds were passing the sun's brightness down to him. The blue Pacific's horizon rose to the left of him, a tilted picture. Far off an outrigger seemed to ride on its side. He sat up with a start, and things straightened out. Lancaster and Kerr became driftwood. He took a few deep breaths of the wonderful salt sea air, and his head began to clear. But where was he? Then he heard high, tinkling laughter, and almost immediately Leilani emerged from the direction of the grass shack, carrying a tray. He smelled coffee—Leilani, of course. The luau. Her father's potent brew.

"Good morning, Mister Jim. You want some coffee?"

56

"Thanks. That smells wonderful." He took a few sips of black coffee. "What am I doing here?"

"You passed out. I thought you were safe enough—besides, I sat beside you until early dawn."

Jimmy drank more of the coffee. "You know," he said, "I never knew there were villages like this—I mean, a hundred years ago, maybe, but today . . . "

"There aren't too many of the real thing left. Kona Village is my father's idea. Did you like the luau?"

"I did. And I seem to remember people saying that it was in my honor, for bringing you home safely."

"That was a last minute change. They dedicated my birthday luau to you."

"What do you mean about the village being your father's idea?"

"This is a commercial venture. This was all an old sugar mill. My father bought up a big patch of the land, including the old mill, to make a hideaway hotel and restaurant. Visitors can come and see how the sugar mill worked. They can enjoy a luau with entertainment, dancers, etc., and sleep in a modernized version of a grass hut. It's a business. It'll be open for tourists in a few months. My father owns a number of businesses. You didn't take all this seriously, did you?"

"But they *were* speaking Hawaiian. I couldn't understand a word they said."

"They were giving you the atmosphere. Everybody here speaks perfect English. We're all Methodists. Honestly, Jimmy, I didn't think you were fooled. It wasn't our intention to make a fool of you. We, I, at least, just thought you were playing along, for the fun of it."

"What a dope I am. It must have been all that kick-a-poo joyjuice."

"Do you feel better now? The best thing to do is to take a dive in the ocean. Come on, Kimo, take your clothes off."

"Who's Kimo?"

"You. Kimo is Jim in Hawaiian. Come on, Kimo, into the ocean with you."

Jimmy stripped down to his skivvies and ran into the water with her, the trill of her laughter higher than the waves, echoing back from the taut cyclorama of blue-drum sky.

*　　*　　*

I thank my mother and father for this sixteenth year birthday gift, my diary, leather bound with heavy, dated pages which I shall ignore. I'll date as I choose. I'll be like you Auntie Mele and do things my own way. You have been gone now for nearly a year and I can tell you honestly that I miss you so much my heart could break, but won't, and I am ashamed of that. But you taught me to be strong. You were almost a hundred years old when you passed on, and you had so much left to teach me that I have decided to make this diary into a one-sided talk with you—but not really one-sided because I know I'll be able to hear you answering me and commenting on what I say—and from this time on I am going to address you directly, dear Auntie Mele, and I know that in talking to you I will learn more about life than in talking to anyone else, because you knew how to live. And you were a great adventurer, who left the islands for the mainland back in the Twenties and lived for years in San Francisco and were an artist, among many many other things. And you knew all about men, so let me get started.

Dear Auntie Mele,

You know that it is my intention to be like Nellie Bly, the great journalist and adventuress, who went Around the World in Seventy-Two Days. I thank you again for giving me that book for my thirteenth birthday. It is my inspiration. I am determined to know all about everything. You know me as I know you. So the day before my sixteenth birthday I decided to go into Honolulu—of course I have been in Honolulu many times—and go and explore the forbidden city. You know what I mean. At one time you were even part of that world. And I had my first real adventure. I was almost raped. I believe I was going to be made a part of the prostitution trade. But I was saved. A young white Marine whom I can only describe as the hero-type came to my rescue just as I was being assaulted by the most ugly, horrifying person you could imagine, or maybe not. But my hero is a strange young man himself. He was completely fooled by Dad's Village, thinking the whole thing was real. But I think the reason for him being taken in is that he is a city boy. I doubt if he has been out of a big city before. And I'm sure he knows what he is doing in such a place. And he saved me from such a place, which proves it. But Auntie Mele he is not afraid of anything but he is afraid of water. He is definitely someone to be gotten to the bottom of. He is sort of tough on the outside but very inwardly gentle, like a poet, and it turns out that he is a poet. This is a poem he wrote and keeps in his wallet, and he gave me the only copy of it that he has.

THE BROKEN CROW

Along the cliffs she wandered,
A song sublimely sung,
Along the cliffs, and pondered
The sea they overhung—

"The sea is vast and deep,
The cliffs are high and wide.

Now let me plunge in sleep,
*   And in black water hide*

My body that is dying
*   Away from loving friends,*
Away from any crying
*   And have the best of ends."*

It was a swan who dove
*   Into the sea below:*
Next day at Fisher's Cove
*   They found a broken crow.*

Her friends were there and crying.
*   It was the worst of ends.*
Oh, she who had been dying
*   Could never make amends.*

Isn't that sad and beautiful, Auntie? Kimo—that's his name: Jimmy—says that Edgar Allan Poe wrote that the death of a beautiful woman is the most poetic subject there is. How romantic! This young man is truly haunting me. Do you think that I could be in love? If you do, make the page flicker in the breeze. You do then. I love you and miss you, Auntie Mele.

Your Leilani

*   *   *

Jimmy was ordered to report to the Provost Marshal's Office to receive orientation. He was to be the new Turnkey at the brig. He had just finished reading *From Here to Eternity*, and ugly visions of Fatso, the Turnkey at Scofield, who had brutalized Maggio in the novel, came to mind. How could he, Jimmy Whistler, have gotten himself into such a situation? He bet Lt. Bland was behind this unwanted advancement. Bland knew by now that Jimmy was not going to take him up on his offer to send him to NavCad training. This was either his way of advancing Jimmy, or perhaps his way of punishing him. As he had always proclaimed, people either betray you or get you in trouble even when they don't mean to. Shun friendship, stick to military acquaintanceship. Keep people at a distance! Jimmy went to the base Chaplain.

"Isn't there some way you can get me out of this, Sir?" he asked.

"Why should you want out?"

"I don't want to be a turnkey, Sir. I'm not right for it."

"The Marine Corps thinks you're right for it."

"They're wrong."

"I doubt it. Now, if you have any other problems . . . ?"

"Don't you see, Sir, this is a mistaken attempt to help me along in my career. Lt. Bland is doing this because he thinks I ought to be in charge of something."

"I doubt if Lt. Bland has anything to do with this. This is probably the result of the incident that brought you to the attention of the Provost Mashal's Office in the first place."

Jimmy returned two more times to state his case and received the same answer: "The Marine Corps thinks you're right for it. You can't outguess the Marine Corps, son. Now just go and do your duty."

There was nothing to be done. Jimmy was Turnkey of the Kaneohe Brig, and he would have to like it or lump it. He promised himself he would be the most humane Turnkey in history. He would not allow the chasers to pull any rough stuff, especially Dunkel, who was always eager to use force. Dunkel was the kind who, if given free rein, would end up as a war criminal. But Dunkel was not going to get his way in any brig run by Jimmy.

"I'm not going to let him push those guys around," he told Leilani on one of his visits to Kona Village. They held hands and walked through the jungle to the beach. Leilani was trying to teach him to swim, as others before her had.

"There is so much tension in your body. You must relax. It is because you are so tight inside that you can't float. Try to forget about Dunkel and your mother and father and even your friend Lt. Bland. Now breathe in slowly and ease back on my arms."

"You can't hold me up," he told her, but found himself floating on her brown arms, and looking up at her great dark eyes that reflected the sunset over the horizon. "How beautiful you are," he said.   She took her hands from beneath his back and pushed him under.

"You will learn someday," she said, when he had shaken the water out of his ears.

"Learn what?" he said, laughing.

"You are like a rock, but you will learn to float. You will learn to be a floating rock. That's a rare thing."

"Impossible," he said.

"No, the islands have lava that will float."

"I don't believe it."

"You don't believe anything. That's why you can't float. Look," and she leaned back into the water and swam into the sunset, so that his eyes couldn't find her, and then she rose up beside him, a mermaid, sleek, lithe and laughing.

*　*　*

Months went by, and under Jimmy's supervision the Brig ran smoothly. But it *was* a responsibility of nightmarish proportions. Sometimes it got the better of him and he would spend the night in a Hotel Street bar, drinking into forgetfulness. One night a couple of HASP patrolmen made a routine stop in a dive and, recognizing him, started a conversation.

"Hear you're the Turnkey at Kaneohe now," one said. "Look, do you need a ride back to base? We'll get you one." They seemed concerned about him. Jimmy looked too drunk to maneuver. One of them said, "We better get him back to his brig."

62

"No, no," Jimmy protested,   then everything went blank. Next thing he knew, he was being brought to the brig barracks. It was late, after lights-out, and he found himself deserted. He stumbled his way through the bay's faint, indirect light, moonlight and watchtower light, thinking sleep, and more sleep, but there was a surprise awaiting him.

Dunkel was sitting on Jimmy's bunk, holding a glittering bayonet in each hand. Dunkel said, "I've been waiting to cut you up, you son of a bitch." Jimmy couldn't be sure, in his condition, but he thought Dunkel was drunk too. Ah yes, beside Jimmy's bunk glittered a half-empty bottle of booze. Jimmy tried to summon whatever alertness remained to him. He sized the situation up this way. If he turned and ran, Dunkel would surely pig-stick him with one of those bayonets. But Jimmy was a boxer. He knew that if you can get in close to a long-armed opponent, that opponent's arm-length, otherwise an advantage, becomes a handicap. Dunkel would find it impossible to turn those bayonets around on him. Jimmy dove at Dunkel, between his arms, and hugged the flailing chaser up and back into a metal wall locker. One of the bayonets went through a metal door and stuck, the other bounced from Dunkel's hand. They struggled there, and suddenly the wall lockers, the whole row of them, went over. Somebody turned on the lights, and Jimmy and Dunkel got a first clear look at each other. Both were bleeding. Jimmy swung, connecting with Dunkel's chin, and Dunkel sprawled on the floor, out for the count.

"He tried to kill you," someone said.

"He's drunk," Jimmy said. "A couple of you guys put him on his bunk. And don't mention this to anyone. Nobody says a word, hear me?"

*   *   *

The emerald islands of paradise were disappearing from view. Jimmy was going home, bound for the Golden Gate.

He stood on the bow of the troop transport, smoking a cigarette. There was a lot that he would never forget.

Leilani had finally taught him to float, but he doubted if he could do it without her. He hoped that he would come back and see her someday, in the not too distant future. He would come back and she would be married to some local boy and have a couple of cute little brats. He had never laid a lustful hand on her. He loved her; she would always be his sweet Leilani, his sweet dream forever, his sweet little sister, his *kaikuahine*.

He looked up and saw a queue of young men that seemed to vanish in perspective. The first in line stepped up to him.

"We don't want to bother you, Sir, but we want to thank you for the way you treated us when we were in the brig. You could have made it very tough on us, but you didn't. Thank you, Sir." Brig orders had required that the Turnkey be called "Sir." Jimmy said, "Don't call me, Sir. I always hated it."

That one stepped away with a nod and a smile, and another stepped up, saying much the same thing. And they just kept coming. Jimmy was overwhelmed. "Thank you, thank you, thank you." Then before him stood Dunkel.

"I owe you," he said. "You could have had me court-martialed and sent to Leavenworth. You knew I wanted a career in the Corps, and you gave me the chance to have it, even though I hated your guts. Semper fi, buddy."

"Semper fi, Dunkel!"

*   *   *

Dear Auntie Mele,

I feel as if I have a pound of poi in my chest. Kimo has left for the mainland and I am frightened that I'll never see him again. I couldn't go to see him off as no one knew exactly when his ship would sail. He sat aboard it for several days, but now it is gone. The leis float up to the dock but who knows which is his, or if his floated out to sea—which means that he will never come back? Auntie, I have never known anyone like him before. He has such a tough manner, sometimes, learned, I suppose, in the streets of Newark or the other cities where he was dragged, according to him, by his mother and father. But underneath that manner, which sometimes drops away completely, there is the poet. He is used to ugliness and at the same time hates it as though it were alien to him, strange and unlikely. Although he watches his language around me, I've heard him speak roughly, use rough words, and use them as naturally as I use kind ones. Violence. Betrayal. Association with monsters. And then there is his strange attachment to his parents, who, by his own account, have treated him badly. He loves them as if they were his last refuge in the world, not good, but known. Safe because known. For all this, there is a fineness about him, in him, something finer that is natural to him. He says he wears a suit of armor to protect his softness. I don't like the armor but I believe I love him. Auntie, he is so sweet to me, and calls me his little sister. He never touches me but with respect. But then, he doesn't seem to think of me as a member of the opposite sex, only as a little sister, his Sweet Leilani. But I am a real girl, and I am powerfully attracted to him. Should I follow him to the mainland? No, you would say, I must go to University and get my education; then there will be time enough to find him, if I still feel the same way. No, I must not make the mistake you say you made in following your sailor to San Francisco only to discover that he was not the man you thought him to be. I am listening to you, Auntie. But some day I am going to the mainland to go to journalism school in New York, and that is the area of the mainland where he is from. But oh, the terrible pain I feel right now! And you did become an artist in San Francisco and lived there for many years before returning, and you often told me that you loved your life there, though "the hills of San Francisco are not as high as the hills of Oahu."

Auntie dear, father and mother have taken a great liking to Kimo. Before he left, he had begun to do some work for them. He's handy with tools, and could be an excellent carpenter. And they trust him with me. After all, they look upon him as my savior. They hear him call me Little Sister. They see the way he treats me. If only they could see into my heart, as I'm sure you can, they would be afraid for me. Passion pulses through me, but I try never to show it. The Marines have done a bad job on him when it comes to swimming. I have been trying to teach him to float. I have held him under his muscled back and looked down into his green eyes and sometimes my heart skips a beat. Auntie, I don't want any other boy, ever!

CHAPTER THREE

THE SANDAL SHOP

> *. . . angelheaded hipsters burning for the*
> *ancient heavenly connection to the*
> *Starry dynamo in the machinery of night.*
> —*Allen Ginsberg*

THE NEW YORK TIMES
AUGUST 22, 1959

TOP VIETNAM RED, ACCUSED BY LAOS, IN PEIPING PARLEY

COMMUNISTS WARN U.N.

SAY 'SERIOUS CONSEQUENCES' MAY FOLLOW IF OBSERVERS GO TO TROUBLED AREA

THE NEW YORK TIMES
AUGUST 22, 1959

HAWAII BECOMES 50TH STATE

The New York office of Magazine Subscriptions Unlimited was a bustling place, filled with telephones, none of which had time to ring for being dialed. Men and women of all races, creeds, ages, and costumes kept the phones leaping to their ears and slamming back for an instant's cradling before another leap and dialing. Jimmy estimated that at least fifty people crowded the place: workers, that is; aside from those, like himself, who waited to be interviewed for a job. Smoke hung heavy like an ectoplasm in the air.

There was a man seated across the table from Jimmy, a man with great broad shoulders, made to appear broader because of the heavy overcoat he was wearing. It was February, and bitter weather: a fine time to come to New York from Hollywood; but nothing Vera and he did made any sense! The man was big, but not fat. On the contrary, one could see—for he sat pushed back from the table in a sprawling, easy posture—that, where his coat fell open, his waist was neat and narrow. But what greatly interested Jimmy about him was that he wore a beard—a rarity in the clean-shaven Fifties and a harbinger of the hirsute and swinging Sixties— every strand of which was thick as wire and glittery, coppery red. It was nearly a foot in length, and all of a piece, so that it moved with his jaw. It rayed from his chin like a Blakian sun. All this blinding hair began directly under a sensual, long lower lip, flexible and pink as the innertube of a bicycle tire. His kinky hair puffed over his ears and down to his frayed collar. On top he was nearly bald; though Jimmy was to learn that this, his first beatnik, was only twenty-eight. The big fellow seemed ill-at-ease, perhaps because Jimmy had been studying him so intently—and rudely, too, for that matter—or perhaps because he was waiting, in a place he did not wish to be to do something he had no wish to do.

In any case, after completing his application form, he behaved restively, crossing and uncrossing his legs, smoking cigarette after cigarette, thumbing through magazines, and throwing them back in the pile with a look of irritation on his benignly satanic face. Finally, he started fishing with very long, delicate fingers in an empty cigarette pack. He crumpled the pack in his fist, and startled Jimmy out of his contemplation of him by leaning across the table and, with a show of white teeth and a whisk-broom movement of beard, nearly sweeping away several magazines, asking if he could have a cigarette from him. Jimmy said, "Sure," and gave him one.

He told Jimmy he had just come back from Germany, where he had left his German wife and his two children, a boy and a girl. He had been a language teacher there, for Berlitz: had taught English to the Germans. He was in the process of breaking up with his wife, by his description a stuffily middle-class Hausfrau. He was staying with an aunt and uncle, a staid old couple, out on Long Island. They had ordered him to look for a job; and so, to appease them, he was making this half-hearted effort. But he had other things in mind, for the long run.

He told Jimmy that he had picked up a young woman on his first day in town, while wandering about in Greenwich Village, a big, strapping Fraulein, with an enormous bust and a Madonna-like face. Not the least of her virtues was that she had a sister and a brother-in-law who were "really hip, swinging." They ran a sandal shop in Brooklyn Heights, had a baby who never cried, never wore a diaper, and who was allowed free use of the floor for urinary and defecatory purposes. The brother-in-law plunked the bass fiddle, studied Zen, kept a Mulligan stew going for a month at a time, made sandals, and did odd jobs in his neighborhood. The sister was a mysterious beauty who smoked pot and sang lullabies. And in many other ways, apparently, this couple led an idyllic and primitive existence of which Rousseau would have voiced his approval. "Call me Marsayas," he said.

Marsayas told Jimmy that he was going to work his way in down there (which wouldn't prove difficult, as Rolly, the brother-in-law, had already accepted him as his guru), and stay with them for a while, at least until he could get Joan (his girlfriend) to get him a studio of his own. He was a painter, you see, and a poet, too. "Any old how," he said, "I've got to get out of my uncle's house. The old folks are driving me up the walls. Too much, too *much!* *When are you going to get a job? What are you going to do about your wife and those dear little kiddies of yours? Life is real, life is earnest. You must look to the future.* Would you believe it? They want me to be in the house by midnight!"

Jimmy agreed that that was a bit much to ask of a grown and married man, and especially one with two kids. Marsayas said that his whole family was that way, "Impossible!" His whole family were "convention-racked lunatics," or "business fiends" or "materialist maniacs."

Not Marsayas. "I'm a Zoroastrian. I believe in the power of light to conquer the forces of darkness. I believe in universal love." Jimmy was impressed, even impressed with the holes in the heels of the argyles of this gleeful gargoyle as he walked to his interview as one walks to the gallows.

Both were hired, and started the next evening at six.

Jimmy worked as fast as he could, thinking of Vera, of their latest peace pact, and worried that he might not be able to find a good, full-time job before the next rent fell due. But Marsayas, though Jimmy had heard him try a few times at first, had already given up the outlined pitch, and was engaging in long, relaxed conversations with, as the boss called them, "the Zombies."

Jimmy discovered that, though he had a certain talent for making people say yes, probably inherited from his father, by the next evening, when the supervisor called them back to verify the sales, his customers had often changed their minds. They'd claim that they had not agreed to buy a subscription at all. They'd claim that they had only accepted his offer to send them a free dictionary.

Well, either he hadn't heard right, and had pressured the "Zombies" too hard in his financial desperation, and they had changed their minds as soon as his apparently persuasive voice had clicked from their receivers; or his supervisor was a swindler, as some claimed, and was simply stealing his sales by canceling them in Jimmy's name and putting them in his own. This Jimmy suspected, but had no way of confirming, as the sales were checked by others and the order forms were out of his hands.

Rightly or wrongly, his sales were being canceled faster than he was making them. And this was the sort of thing that just could not be explained to Vera. He confided his plight to Marsayas, whose own sales hadn't added up to enough to get a cancellation from, and to his amazement Marsayas was surprised that Jimmy should be worried.

"For Chrissakes, Jim, I thought you were just working here for beer money, like me. Why don't you get that Frau of yours off her ass and out into the labor market? She an invalid?"

After work they stopped in a midtown bar for a few beers. It was one of those dives that have a food bar, and smell of corned beef and cabbage, boiled potatoes, cheap wine, draft beer, and sour people. As they made their way past the steam table and toward an empty booth, Jimmy said over the din, "I made up a poem for this place." He was somewhat exhilarated by the boisterous freedom of the quitting-time crowd and in a wild Irish brogue declaimed:

> "Ah, Dionysus, ya grapey divil deity,
> ya'd lak to have me back in Hellas
> ta guzzle in the juice of yer depravity!
> Ya know yer dirty bottled blood'll
> keep me at yer bidden.
> Ah puke it up and force it down lak cud,
> but I'll tell ya straight, ya satyr goat,
> tomorrow, ah swear, ah'm quitten!
> Ya make me drink this soupy slop,
> ah know ya do, ah know it!

Ya tease me on ta gulp the rot,
and sure'n hell ah show it.
But ya'll not beat me, goaty beast,
cuz ah tell ya straight, ya satyr goat,
tomorrow, ah swear, ah'm quitten!"

By the time he finished, several guys at a nearby table had turned to listen and raised their beer mugs in happy salute.

"I call that one 'Blarney Stoned'," said Jimmy.

Marsayas shouted in reiteration: "TOMORROW, AH SWEAR, AH'M QUITTEN!" He slammed his fist on the table. "I love it!"

"I told you I was in that Eugene O'Neill sea play, didn't I? At drama school? I couldn't lose the brogue. It just stuck. And everytime I was in a place like this—which was pretty often—a new line would come to me."

As they had agreed, they brought their poems to work with them, and now they sat and read each other's work. "GuraaaAH!" Marsayas sounded, and sipped his beer, leaving a broken ring of foam in the bristling red wires around his mouth. He held the book out and loudly recited "Late Sleeper" so that an embarrassed Jimmy thought the whole bar could hear. After all, it was not exactly a bar song.

"She never woke without the smile
That shaped that rose, her pretty mouth.
She'd lift the telephone and dial
For breakfast; then she'd have her bath,
Cheerfully free from righteous wrath.

There was no need to wait a while
To travel, study, learn a style:
Her money made her polymath.
                    She never woke.

After her bath she'd ride a mile
Around the park, in single file,
With other girls of luck and wealth,
For poise, and skill, and better health,
And wonder what one *could* revile.
                    She never woke."

He slammed Jimmy's little stapled booklet on the table, chug-a-lugged his remaining beer, and vanished. Then he was back through the crowd like an ecstatic Bacchus with four huge mugs of slopping broth, two in each big mitt. He shouted: "You, you poor fool, are among the elect, the elite, the only *true* elite on Earth. You are a *poet*!"

"Do you like them?"

"*Like* them? They're real *poems*, good as anybody going!"

Jimmy was thrilled. No one but Marsayas had ever encouraged him in his yearning to be a poet, everyone else thought he was foolish—especially Vera.

Marsayas grew serious, professorial. "Now it's time for a little applied psychology," he said. "What was that—a rondeau, a rondelet? You always write in forms, in formal verse. Nothing wrong with that. You write very well indeed. But have you read Whitman, Robinson Jeffers, any of the free versers? Your mind runs toward discipline rather than freedom. What would happen if you just exploded? Let it all hang out, let it all hang loose? Do you know about the Beats? Do you know about the new work by Robert Lowell? He drops all his old formalism in his new work. Why don't you try something like that? Break loose! What are you afraid of?"

"I'll try," said Jimmy.

It was quite a let-down, after such stimulation, to have to take himself home to Vera and her cranky, middle-class

Bohemianism, but Midnight was looming, Marsayas's curfew hour.

"Well, it won't always be like this," said Marsayas. "I'll be out of that bourgeois scene before the week-end. I'm moving into the sandal shop. Then we'll be able to drink and talk all night."

"I wish Vera would've helped me with tuition for school," Jimmy said, dreamily. "She's o.k. with drama school, though. I got that on scholarship. But I'd like to be a writer, and a writer needs more education."

"There's all kinds of writers, boyo—and all kinds of education. If you want to write, first read, read, read, then write, write, write! But if you want to go to college, well, that's a different story. Hell, I've got a masters, but I can't write poetry like your stuff." He drained a mug. "Chrissakes, Jim, who the hell is the boss in your house? Look at the lion. The king of the beasts! The lioness goes out and kills the quarry, then steps back and guards the old man while he eats."

"That's lions—not people."

"Well, people then. Do you know that the Indian brave never worked. He sent his old lady out to do it. *He* stayed at home and talked, talked *WAR* and *PEACE*," he shouted, and the whole bar, which seemed to be filled with middle-aged, unshaven men, turned to look at him, interest in their eyes, even hope.

"That's what women are meant to do," he roared on, after a bow. "Let them make the nest pretty and wait like the votary bird to be impregnated. Then you take over until the egg is laid. *Only* until then. And then you go back and keep the nest warm with wine and good conversation while they go and forage for worms. Worms of milk for the baby and worms of wine for you. I tell you that is their biological role. *They* know it, so why don't you? Don't they all want to go to work nowadays? Don't they? Well, for God's sake, let them!

"This guy Rolly I've told you about, he makes sandals—because that's art, but Jean, his wife, chews the leather. That's right. She *chews* the leather—makes it soft so Rolly can work with it. Rolly only makes one pair of sandals a week, he tells me; but Jean, with those beautiful sharp little white teeth of hers, chews enough leather for him to make twenty! He keeps her at it all day—chewing, chewing—except when she's nursing the baby, or turning on. Now that's a *wife* for you! They're in the battle for survival together—it isn't all thrown on *his* back. That's *life*—and listen, that's *love*! I tell you, Jim, once I get to Brooklyn, I'll never work another day in my life. That's my oath. I intend to dedicate myself completely to the muses."

*   *   *

Jimmy got an idea. Next Friday night, pay night, he would have next-to-nothing coming, so over the weekend he would need all the moral support he could get. He thought that the hard edge of the weekend might be softened if Vera could hear Marsayas present his version of things before he presented his own. So they made a date for Marsayas to come to Jimmy's place on Saturday and help him out.

Marsayas didn't mind telling Jimmy that he thought he was quite a coward for being so afraid of a woman, and over such a little thing as not having any money. He had never heard of a wife who wasn't at least willing to help her husband, if asked. But Marsayas had no idea what Vera was like, or of what she was capable, if angered. And Jimmy had to admit that it was more than a modest proposal that had induced him to ask Marsayas over. He was also interested in finding out what would happen when these two forces of nature came into contact. Perhaps they would vanish in a clap of thunder, and leave only a little mushroom cloud behind.

Marsayas showed up at noon on Saturday, toting a case of beer and a gallon jug of purple wine. Jimmy saw him through the window, striding down Horatio Street. He had told Vera a little about Marsayas, and that he was coming, but he did not, could not, do him justice. He went over and stood by the expensive new coffee table (which Vera had bought the day before with the last of their savings, and upon which she had laid out all the tea-time and cocktail-hour delicacies a Happy Homemaker could conceive), and waited to enjoy the immediate impact his wild man find would have upon her.

The knock came, and Vera, who was near the door, opened it; then stood, as if transfixed, gripping the knob until her little fist turned white. Jimmy thought for an instant that she was going to slam the door in his friend's face, and start screaming. But she collected herself, asking:

"*Marsayas?*"

"Vera, I presume?"

"Ha—yes!" said Vera, looking up into the aimed ends of his red rays, and finally stepping back. "Please come in—come in, please—*please!*"

Marsayas gargoyle-grinned, and slippity-slapped into the apartment on shower shoes. His naked feet were dirty, and red-and-raw-looking with the cold. Jimmy saw Vera eyeing them distastefully as the guru set his burdens down in the midst of the hors d'oeuvres. Jimmy had hoped that it would take Vera longer to get her wind back. He had hoped that, from first sight this imposing giant, Marsayas would keep her off balance. But, plain to see, she was coming back, resilient as ever.

He indicated a chair for Marsayas, and Marsayas seated himself, moving Vera's tidbits aside and putting his feet up on the table, between a bowl of cheese dip and a platter of cold cuts. Vera looked at him wide-eyed; at Jimmy, narrow-eyed; then pulled a tight meager smile back to her downy ears, and sat. Jimmy had received the first dirty look of the day. And he knew something about Vera. One dirty look meant more to follow, and maybe even along their trajectory one might find, in an hour or so, a vase, or a bottle, flying.

The thought flashed that he had better move quickly to prevent Marsayas from saying what he knew Marsayas intended to say. But then he was distracted. Marsayas said, from his recumbent position, "I hope you kids don't mind, but I took the liberty of inviting some friends of mine down—my girlfriend's sister and her husband. I thought it might do you good to meet them."

Vera stared at Marsayas, as one might stare at an oddity, trying to figure out what to make of him.

"Do us good?" she said.

"Yes. They do everyone good."

"How do you mean?"

"They're an example, an inspiration."

Marsayas removed his feet from the table long enough to fill two glasses with wine and stick them before Vera and Jimmy. He waved aside Jimmy's apology for not having done the honors, placed his horny heels back in the cold cuts, jug neatly draped on an elbow which he raised in salute, and yelled "PROSIT" loud enough to make Vera blink. They picked up their glasses and yelled "Prost!" back at him. It seemed like the right thing to do.

Then Marsayas made his gleeful gargoyle face, which put on display for Vera his big, beautiful white teeth, and said, "Why didn't you tell me you had such a pretty wife?"

Vera perked up. "Why, thank you," she said.

"Yes—yes—I must paint you some time. But first you're going to have to become more natural. These are new, hip times, Vera. Hang loose! You're the very personification of the uptight Fifties, bouffant and all. You seem . . . *constrained*—yes. Even your hair—is it dyed? A Lana Turner helmet. You'll have to get that stuff out of your hair and let it down—let it be natural—yes—" He moved the thumb of his free hand in a painterly gesture of measurement.

"And you must stop Jimmy from being a wage-slave

and help to develop him as a poet. He's the real thing." The wine bottle remained cradled in his other arm, like a baby.

Fortunately, for Jimmy could see Vera revving up for a reply, a knock came at the door. It was the Reuters. Marsayas called out introductions.

Jimmy took their coats and hats.

Rolly Reuter was a little fellow with big, lugubrious brown eyes, long black hair, and a long, silky black beard. Jean, his wife, was a striking young woman, with chatoyant greenish eyes, and beautiful long ebony hair that swam, like a dark, glittery stream, down neck and chest and out, over a more than ample, T-shirted bosom, to twin falls, stippled by nipples.

Marsayas picked up the thread of what he had been saying. But the atmosphere was irrevocably altered.

Vera was discontent. She no longer listened to Marsayas, but interjected odd, pointless questions, as if only to attract attention; and the conversation became forced and jittery. Even so, Jimmy was able to attend to the Reuters enough to see what Marsayas had meant about them. It was simple. They were in love.

He looked at Vera, popping off about something or other, that hard, mean look about the mouth, those hurt, jealous eyes, and he knew what was going on in her mind; knew that she wanted this pleasant vision of love out of her sight. It was too much for her, too uncomplicated. *Love is a simple thing . . .* his mind sang.

Jimmy envied Rolly his beautiful Jean—and he saw that Marsayas envied him, too—but tried not to show it. If Jimmy let on to the slightest admiration, Vera would make him pay—make them all pay, possibly.

The Reuters stayed for two hours and then went on their way. But Marsayas sat on, like a great blood-bubbling fixture. He finished off the last of the wine and started whittling down the case of beer he'd brought; then he dragged Vera up and danced her about to the phonograph, playing "So Rare," last of the Big Band tunes. Vera's mood brightened after Rolly took his beautiful Jean away. When Marsayas went to the bathroom, she kept on dancing by herself, whirling about the living room like the ballerina she had been trained to be. Once, she stopped, and tried to pull Jimmy to his feet to dance with her. But he refused. There was even something in her gaiety that made him nervous. He knew all too well how quickly it could change into angry hysteria. Yet she seemed happy, now; and if it hadn't been for all the misery she had caused him he'd have been glad to see her so. He'd have got up and danced with her, but for that.

*   *   *

Marsayas slept, head hanging forward, in an antiquated easy chair near the lumpy couch on which Jimmy woke. A young woman sat on the floor at Marsayas's feet, propped up against his legs, asleep, with her head in his lap. She wore a quilted kimono, and one breast bulged into view where the kimono fell open. She was a bigger, heavier version of Jean.

Jimmy looked around, through puffed, uncertain eyes. There were sandals, belts, pocketbooks, all manner of leather goods, hanging in festoons from walls and ceiling. He must have moaned; because, then, from somewhere up near the ceiling, in a dark corner, in the rear of the shop, a soft, purring voice drifted down, asking,

"Got a headache?"

It was Jean. He could see her now, or see her eyes, like a cat's, high up, glimmering in shadows.

"Are you levitating?"

"I'm on a platform. This is where Rol and I sleep. How's your wife?"

Jimmy looked around, and there behind him, under a heap of coats, was Vera. She looked a mess. Her lipstick was smeared, there were Mascara tear-stains down her cheeks,

79

and her hair looked like a burning bush.

Well, was it paradise? Was this absurd little sandal shop a heaven on earth, a sanctuary? No, he guessed not; it was just that he had come from a small, unimportant hell. And why have anything to do with any hell if you can stay in a little, bright heaven? It was just too bad that there wasn't one more of these plump, lovely creatures around, another sister with her long hair down for him.

He had been drinking beer with Marsayas for two hours before Vera grunted and woke up. She had a hangover, was angry, had slept badly (so she claimed—been mashed by him), and wanted to get out of this (whispers, harsh, in his ear) "filthy beatnik pad." She would not have Jimmy drinking again today. It was Sunday. "What *are* you, an alcoholic, like your so-called friend, Marsayas? He's a filthy beast and this sandal shop is a stinking zoo." She stomped outside "to get some clean, fresh air."

"She walked out on you last night—do you know that?" Marsayas seemed much amused by Jimmy's pickle. "You fell asleep in the car—I dumped you there, on the couch, and she got into a temper tantrum trying to wake you up. Feel your leg."

Jimmy felt around, looked at the place on his calf that hurt, and there was a large purple bruise. "It'll soon be time to go back to California," he said. "D.D. is catching up with us."

"Who's D.D.?"

"The Divorce Demon. He's been pursuing us since we got married."

"She gave you quite a pummeling before I could stop her." Marsayas laughed. "You were inert—wouldn't, or couldn't, move for love nor money."

Jimmy was beginning not to like the way Marsayas looked, the beast. He seemed to think that Jimmy's problems were a joke. But then, who could blame him? It was the truth, after all. Vera and he were a joke. They had been making public fools of themselves for three years. Why shouldn't people laugh? The thought occurred to Jimmy that maybe he had finally come face to face with the Divorce Demon. Then Marsayas broke the news:

"Your phonograph and your TV were stolen last night. Some of your clothes, too."

Rolly came in from the back and sat down, looking lugubrious. Now he reminded Jimmy a little of Chico Marx, except for the hair.

"That's the trouble with having possessions," he said; "it's not that they get stolen, but that it should hurt when they are. *Things*!" He sighed. "It's no good basing a life on *things*!" He wore such a sad face. It struck Jimmy funny that he should seem to be suffering more over Jimmy's loss than Jimmy was.

"Oh, but it's true," Rolly said, as Jimmy laughed. Then he looked at Jimmy's feet. He had given him a pair of sandals to wear. Jimmy had them on over his socks. Quite a bumbling novitiate beatnik he was. "Do they fit?" he asked. Jimmy said that they did, quite comfortably.

Marsayas went on to tell Jimmy that, after he had pulled Vera off him, she had run out into the street and stopped a car by standing with outstretched arms, like a crucifee. The car had gone off with her. Marsayas said that he had been too drunk to follow, but that after taking a nap he had driven up to Manhattan to see if he could get her to come back. He said that he had found the apartment door wide open and Vera hysterical. She told him that the man who had driven her home had threatened her, and that she had given him everything he asked for and was afraid to call the police. Trouble! *Trouble*! Four hundred, maybe five hundred, dollars worth of his hard labor stolen! His most prized possession—his typewriter. More disorder! More chaos! Well, Rolly was right. He was a fool to work for *things*.

He wasn't angry; he was just disgusted, with himself and with Vera. What a dreadful pain in the ass they must always seem to people! Ah! He thought to himself that he would go right ahead and get just as drunk as he damned well pleased; and he would start right now to demand, through an iron-clad indifference to anybody's harangue, his *rights*! But just then Vera appeared at the door, eyes shooting hot tears like sunstruck diamonds.

"I want to speak to you," she said, choking in temper.

Marsayas bent down and buried Joan's neck in the red excelsior of his beard.

"Do you hear?" Vera shouted. "I said I want to speak to you!"

Her smeared lips were pursed, her grim, envious green eyes on Marsayas.

Rolly peeked in through the curtain, from the back, but withdrew his scared, comic-Christ face when he saw Vera.

"Step outside, please," said Vera, and Jimmy felt as if he were being called out by a barroom bully. Her breath was hot, and he thought he saw a flame leap from her mouth.

He got up and walked outside, onto Henry Street, a pretty, quiet, Sunday view, reminiscent of Utrillo. He could hear tugboats tooting in the harbor, beyond the esplanade. Vera had her coat on. He was in shirtsleeves, a little chilly. He shivered. He thought that he must look like hell, unshaven, disheveled. So did Vera.

"I want you to come home with me," she said. "I've been waiting in that church over there for nearly an hour. I was not going to step one foot back in that filthy zoo of a sandal shop, with that smell of dead skin, but I did, for *you.* Now you come along with me, do you *hear*?"

"I'm staying here for a while," Jimmy said, affirming his rights. "You go ahead. I'll be along."

He was a bit tipsy—not much, but a bit; enough to think he was going to get away with facing her down—enough to think he was going to win, this time.

"No!" she said. "You come now!"

"No!" he said. "Later! I am a lion."

"You are not the king of the beasts. You're a pussycat. I suppose you'll want to grow a beard now."

"You just listen to me roar," he said.

"If you don't come now, I'll kill myself!" she shouted. The sentence rang down the hollow, empty Sunday street like a ricochetting bullet.

"No," he said; but he was weakening.

"You'll see," she yelled at him, turning, and running around the corner. "You'll see," she yelled again, farther down, out of sight.

He stood still for what seemed a long time, determined not to give in, determined to hold his ground. But then he heard her yell, "*You'll see*," from far down, toward the docks, and he thought of the harbor and the water. It came to him. She means to throw herself in. But then it occurred to him that she had won medals for swimming. How could she drown herself? And what could he do if she did take it into her idiot head to jump into the drink? He couldn't really swim at all! Had never learned, despite the Marines, despite Leilani's efforts. But he had lost already. Even to think about it was to lose.

He started running down the block, around the corner, to the river. He slowed down, occasionally, wondering what he would do when he got there. He couldn't save her! And she couldn't drown, was an expert!

He stopped running once, and began to laugh. The absurdity of what was happening struck him. He had a stitch in his side. What kind of damned crazy show was this? And what part was he intended to play? The clown who gets fished out of the drink by his wife? But, then, in an instant, he was frightened again. What was she going to do? She was capable of anything.

He started running again, and he got to the dock just in time to see Vera take off her coat, and, looking back to make sure he was watching—he felt she would have waited for him to catch up had he taken longer—jump in.

He walked the next hundred or so feet. He wondered what sort of expression he wore? Whatever it was, that miraculous crowd that gathers out of nowhere at public events such as the one taking place under the esplanade in Brooklyn Heights did not like it at all. He did not move a wee bit faster, however. In fact, he sauntered. Meantime, until three or four burly firemen, who were stationed on a fireboat docked nearby, swam in three or four strokes to rescue her, Vera swam gracefully about, doing a lovely backstroke of the sort that had won her the medals. Then she allowed herself to be saved by the florid knights of the fireboat. Unfortunately, thought Jimmy, it wasn't even necessary to knock her out; they swam back to the boat in a beautiful formation, like well-trained frogmen, Vera on point, and the knights of the fireboat took her aboard.

As for Jimmy, he just stood where he was. He may have been laughing, or he may have been crying, but whatever he was doing, it roused no sympathy for him in the heart of the crowd. It was thumbs down for him. Then one of the big, fire-colored knights stepped up to him.

"You that young lady's husband?" It sounded as much like an accusation as it did a question.

"Yes," Jimmy admitted, "I am."

"Well, whatsa matter widja? Why dinja jump in after huh?"

"I can't swim."

"Call that a 'scuse?" the fireman demanded.

Jimmy thought that he had best be careful now. He might be lynched.

"No," he said meekly.

"Well, now . . ." the fireman said, thinking. It must have

been quite a search that went on in that big head, but he came out of it empty-handed. All he could say in his state of indignation was "Get aboard!"

There was a cop on the boat. "Are you prepared to take your wife home?" he asked, adding, "Otherwise I'll have to take you both to the station." Jimmy wanted to ask what he had done, but thought better of it. He said he was. He looked at Vera, who was sitting wrapped in blankets, three or four firemen asking her questions, consoling her, and no doubt condemning him. Vera saw him, then, and stood up, stretching her arms out to him through the blankets.

"Oh, Jimmy," she cried, "take me home."

Sure he would. What did it matter now? Something had happened, something had snapped. Vera thought she had won again, but she hadn't. This time he had won. And so had protean D.D., the Divorce Demon, in the form of Marsayas, poet, painter, prophet, and king of beasts.

CHAPTER FOUR

UN ALLER ET RETOUR

> *It's the too-huge world vaulting us, and it's*
> *good-bye. But we lean forward to the next*
> *crazy venture beneath the skies.*
>   —*Jack Kerouac*

THE NEW YORK TIMES
OCTOBER 4, 1957

SOVIET UNION LAUNCHES SPUTNIK SATELLITE

THE NEW YORK TIMES
OCTOBER 4, 1957

EISENHOWER CALLS COURTS' SANCTITY LITTLE ROCK ISSUE

CLARIFIES TROOP ROLE

Jimmy had met Vera at the famous 46th Street rehearsal studio. He was there because an acquaintance of his was playing piano for a dance troupe, of which Vera was a member. She sat down next to him on a bench and dried herself with a towel. Next thing he knew they were making love at her apartment on the upper West Side. When he thought of it later, he could not remember having said or done a thing to get himself there. Nevertheless, he was complimented by her attentions. He asked himself who wouldn't be? He was a lucky dog. Everybody who met them together said that he was a lucky dog. And a dog he felt, for he suspected an invisible leash had been snapped on his fifteen and a half inch neck. He discovered very quickly too that her strong dancer's body was a very fit instrument of aggression, even violence, and he began to pull back from her emotionally only to discover that such withdrawal led to even greater aggression. She was more of a hot potato than a hot tamale, as he'd first thought, but he *was* an ex-Marine and he wasn't going to be intimidated. What he couldn't quite face was that he was being intimidated all around.

When he'd got his mustering-out pay at Camp Lejeune, he had enough to let him live a life of leisure for several months, plus the Korean G.I. Bill. The day he got out he called his Commencement Day. He would put all his earlier struggles behind him—his childhood of compelled travel and truancy, the Marine Corps, to which he owed so much, especially for restoring him to the educational level that was appropriate to his age, but about which he also had mixed emotions—the violence, the regimentation—though he would always remember the angel Leilani—and his feckless, drunken parents in their eternal basement—like Shaw, he would be the upstart son of a downstart father.

He auditioned and was immediately accepted at a well-regarded dramatic school in the heart of the theater district. He thought he would learn to act so he could learn to write plays. Later, he would attend several other dramatic schools and eventually matriculate at New York University, majoring in journalism with a minor in theater. Sometimes he seemed to know where he was going and what he wanted, but at other times he seemed confused, and sometimes lost in depression or over-excitement.

These mood swings had been diagnosed in the service as the early manifestations of manic-depression, or bi-polar syndrome, but not taken very seriously by the psychiatric department of the Tripler Medical Center in Hawaii where he had been sent for examination. One reason they might not have been taken very seriously was that Jimmy was trying to use them as a means of escaping his role as a military policeman, a role that, though he had done well enough at it, was not to his liking. But his mood swings came to play a more important part in his future life. Self-medication with alcohol was becoming a habit. He had watched his father and mother do it all his life and had sworn to himself that he would never be like them, but now—and this was one reason for his increasing tolerance of their weakness—it was beginning to seem like a genetic curse. Perhaps his father couldn't help himself, for Jimmy was having more and more trouble doing so. And didn't failure breed failure? And was it even fair of him to succeed where they had failed? His ambition made him feel a traitor to their failure. He had a secret fear of success, which he couldn't and wouldn't fully admit to himself. And with fear came equivocation.

His theater mentor, Dr. Zolauf, had turned him into somebody called Ed Fleury, just as when in their presence his parents transformed him into a six-year-old child knicknamed "Skeets," and Vera, who shared Dr. Zolauf's ambitions for Jimmy, and even spent hours on the phone discussing the so-called Ed Fleury with the good Doctor (Prague Doctorate, specializing in theater arts, successor to Erwin Piscator) and whom Jimmy was becoming convinced was more interested in the career of "Ed Fleury"—the possibility of money, wealth, and power of a star—than she was in the actual Jimmy Whistler, placed him dead center in a clanging triangle of intimidation.

Jimmy had read Sartre and could see no exit, only being and nothingness. Still, on the one hand, he was proud of this prize, Vera, this beautiful energetic dancer, whom he both desired to, and felt compelled to, introduce to his parents, and she was demanding such an introduction—"You're not ashamed of me, are you?" she would ask in the true spirit of her own paranoia. Ashamed of her! Quite the opposite. He was worried about how his pixilated parents might behave. Nevertheless, he arranged for them all to meet at P.J. Clarke's tavern, a New York landmark which was frequented by show people, average Joes and Janes, writers, and international tycoons. Clarke's had first gained fame as being the bar in which some of "The Lost Weekend" was filmed, later as a famous hold-out when much of the block on which it sat was razed and a skyscraper was built around it. He thought it a place where both Vera and his parents could feel comfortable.

Jimmy and Vera arrived first.

The place looked like a natural setting for her—a showbiz type, theatrically-lashed, with her henna'd hair piled high in a French twist.

She was a little nervous about meeting his parents, so had indulged herself with several Scotch Rockers and was casting away the false timidity that she had entered with. Jimmy looked up to see his Mother and Father make their entrance, fashionably late, he mused. He could tell by the way they leaned on each other that they had started the festivities elsewhere. Jimmy had indulged his heart-pounding, stomach-vibrating nervousness with a few Scotches as well.

Suddenly they were all sitting together. The old man was at his fourth Martini level, and was beginning to sound, as he always did at this stage, like W.C. Fields in "The Bank Dick," "My-boying" Jimmy and ogling all the women he could still see, and especially Vera who was up close.

"They're drunk," Vera hissed. "Why is he talking like W.C. Fields, and why is your mother staring at me with her eyebrow arched like that?"

"He always does that," Jimmy whispered in her reddening little ear, "and she always arches her eyebrow when she is about to attack."

"Well neither one of them better try anything with me," Vera returned with no attempt to hide what she was saying.

Fay parried with: "Who the hell do you think you're talking to, you over-painted little trollop?"

There was no doubt. Fay and Elliot had had many a few on the way here.

Elliot Whistler, now in his mid-sixties, was growing deaf. "It wasn't the trolley," he put in, out of nowhere, grinning idiotically with Martini well-being, "it was the Third Avenue El. When I was a young man—a customers' man on Wall Street—I often used to take the El right along here. I believe I have been in this bar before, in the old days, before the Crash." He turned in his seat and looked over his shoulder at the crowd at the bar. Then Jimmy felt it again, as he had many times before, the feeling that his father felt hunted, pursued. His father turned back, and there it was again—his eyes shifted from side to side and a flicker of fear danced in them, though he still wore the same foolish smile.

Fay, ignoring Vera, speaking to Jimmy, said, "They used to say your father looked just like Ray Milland."

"What," said Vera, "then this must be the sequel to 'The Lost Weekend.'" She angrily gathered her coat, pushed her way through the crowd, and out the door.

"Skeets, you can't possibly be thinking of marrying that over-painted little trollop," said Fay.

Things never improved.

They married at City Hall, with no relatives in attendance, only telekinetic scowls sent from afar.

*   *   *

By this time Jimmy had won a minor reputation as Ed Fleury, the actor, and was being groomed for some serious

90

upward moves. This put Vera in a very good mood. Think of all that shopping on Rodeo Drive! California was next. The Golden Land. Connections were being made for a part in an adventure series to be set in, of all places, Hawaii. Jimmy, or Ed Fleury, would be the star's sidekick.

"Well, you've just got to do it," Vera cried impatiently, hearing that Jimmy was not too keen on it. He was still at New York University, and was thinking about an academic career—and poetry. Vera laughed with all the scorn she could muster.

"We'll be poor as dirt. I can make more money with the June Taylor dancers in one week than you'll be making in a year at some stupid college!" Then she softened, became kittenish. "I want you to quit that damn college boy stuff and become somebody really important. You said you would—for me. . ." And, led by Dr. Zolauf, some important people in the theater had gone to the trouble of setting things up.

Jimmy:

felt:

trapped.

Besides, they had a two-year lease on their apartment, with a year to go. With that in mind, Jimmy thought maybe he could entice Vera into staying. That way he could continue the acting classes and carry on at NYU, too.

Yogi Berra, the great ball player, it was, who said when you come to a fork in the road, take it. Jimmy had discovered that he was multi-talented and was trying to walk down multiple roads at once, a metaphysical feat which was proving to be quite beyond his earthly abilities. Had he been older— perhaps. Or more emotionally balanced—maybe. But he couldn't walk a tightrope and juggle at the same time. He didn't have the wisdom of experience. And did he really want to be an actor? Having a talent for something doesn't make you desire to do it. John Barrymore was a talented actor but really desired all his life to be a painter. Perhaps his frustration at not becoming a painter led to his alcoholic downfall and death.

Jimmy had spent the last six months of his service time at Camp Lejeune in North Carolina. There he had been employed as a rifle instructor, but he had employed himself as a trainee for a new life as an actor by going on a rigid diet and losing weight, leaving his six feet at a hundred and fifty pounds. He had been weight lifting since he was thirteen, had kept it up, and was told by all that he looked in fine shape. His secret of secrets however was still that he wrote poetry. He couldn't remember when he had started writing it, only that it seemed to have always been a part of him.

Back in Hawaii, he had started reading of the New Critics in John Crowe Ransom's classic *The New Criticism*, and attributed his poetic education to them—I. A. Richards, T.S. Eliot, Yvor Winters; and also to others like R.P. Blackmur, Allen Tate, Cleanth Brooks, and to books like *The Meaning of Meaning* by Stuart Chase, and *Seven Types of Ambiguity* by William Empson. Acting required *Building a Character* by Stanislavski, which was excellent for writing fiction.

Did he want to be an actor or did he want to be a poet? Both of these professions seemed to him Quixotic avocations, the former extremely difficult of attainment, and too public for his taste, and the latter almost silly. His parents would have laughed at both, especially the Negative Force, his mother. The only encouragement in writing he had received so far was from Lieutenant Bland in Hawaii who had read one of his efforts and had pronounced it not too shabby. Until Marsayas, that was it. A big boost from Marsayas! But then, he showed his poems rarely and only to what he hoped would be a highly receptive audience, without exception an audience of one.

Dr. Zolauf insisted that Jimmy would have the easiest time any actor ever had in achieving his goals; Dr. Zolauf, who knew everyone in showbusiness, east and west, guaranteed it.

Jimmy could understand Vera's attitude—almost assured theatrical success as opposed to the uncertainty of a writing career. For teaching poetry he would need credentials. It was for these that he persisted at NYU. But he had to make a decision. As it turned out, he did not have to make a decision after all; it was made for him.

*   *   *

West Seventy-first Street in Manhattan was a shabby, low-rent neighborhood in Nineteen Fifty-eight and they lived in the worst building on the block, a big, ancient brownstone warren. Vera had complained for months that the apartment was dark and dingy and Jimmy calculated that a coat of paint might just cozy the place up enough to make her feel more at home—to subliminally contribute to cooling her on the idea of striking out for Hollywood.

Vera liked pink, so they went out and bought several gallons of pink paint. And one day when they were standing with rollers in their hands and the door open for air, the new young lady from upstairs, whom they had passed once or twice in the hall, stopped at their door, introducing herself as Lola Sherrill. She was eighteen, from Missouri, a singer, and was looking for work. Vera invited her down for supper. Lola said that she wouldn't dream of eating supper with them unless she could help them with the painting. Later Jimmy took a break and went into the kitchenette, a curtained, wall-debouched hall with a small bathroom to one side, to get a can of beer. He discovered that Vera was whipping up a big gourmet spread, to impress their new neighbor. "Paella," she said. "It's Spanish."

Jimmy drank his beer, listened to some jazz, thumbed through *War and Peace*, and after a while a knock came at the door. He opened the door, and there was Lola, in a skin-

93

tight, see-through leotard and tights. "I've come to help you paint."

Vera called from the kitchenette: "Ask Lola to come in."

Jimmy said, "Well, come on in, Lola." He felt like an endangered species. He knew that, somehow, Vera would blame him for Lola's state of undress. He said, "I'll just break out more paint."

Vera popped out. She was hot and bedraggled from cooking, paint-smeared: had been hitting the bottle. And there was Lola, dipping her cello-bottom this way and that as she painted, her see-through tights displaying with perfect clarity the flexures of each ample adorable cheek. Vera stopped short in the doorway of the kitchenette, the curtain tangled over one shoulder, took Lola in with a deep inspiration, and looked at Jimmy as if he had pulled off Lola's knickers.

Jimmy stirred paint so fast that it spattered on his shirt-less torso, turning his taut tummy pink.

Lola said, "I'm helping your husband."

Jimmy thought: "Either this is the dumbest dame I've ever met, or she has more chutzpa than a vacuum cleaner salesman in a marble hall."

Vera said, "Well, Lola, I think we should call it a day on the painting, now."

Jimmy thought it was about time for him to put his two-cents in. He said, "Maybe we can get this wall done before we quit. Why don't you just go ahead and concentrate on supper. It smells good." He meant it. They could use the help, and he didn't care what it wore, or didn't wear.

"Yes," piped Lola, "I'll help Jimmy get the painting done. I'm a good painter."

Vera went back to cooking. Pots and pans could be heard whizbanging in the kitchenette. Jimmy was having a good afternoon, even though Vera kept popping in and out;

and every time she caught him looking at Lola, which he couldn't help doing, gave him one of her You'll-pay-for-this looks.

Vera came out, Merlot in hand, finally, to survey the job. She stood with Lola and admired the wall. Jimmy heard Lola say, "I'm glad I could be of help." Vera had the table set and told them to wash and come and eat.

At last, Lola's behind was out of sight, on a chair, and her legs were under the table.

"Oh, this Paella looks delicious," she said, and Jimmy felt her pink-nailed toes walking up his leg. No shoes, either, of course. He moved his leg away to see if the walk wasn't an accident.

"Yummy!" cried Lola. "You are a *wonderful* cook, Vera," and back came the tootsies.

"She sure is," said Jimmy in a disturbed voice. No doubt about anything now. Lola was pure brass.

It seemed to Jimmy that Lola certainly knew how Vera felt, maybe could tell that Vera wasn't too stable, and was actually trying to make her crack. He did not know how else to explain Lola, a stranger, sitting there wearing next to nothing, running her chubby little toes up and down his leg while his wife looked on! Vera didn't show it, but Jimmy thought that she must know what was going on under the table.

"Why doesn't she blow up?" he asked himself, and kept moving his legs away from Lola's groping toes; but he couldn't well dodge Lola and not be obvious about it. The table was too small. Then, through his alcoholic fog, he could see that Vera was on to Lola. He could also see that Lola knew that Vera knew but didn't care what Vera thought.

They were all getting drunk. Vera slammed down her fork. "Whatever you're doing, Jimmy, I want you to stop it."

"Really, Vera, your Jimmy hasn't done anything to deserve the way you're treating him."

Jimmy got up and went to the bathroom. He took a long freedom-loving pee. "Hell, no!" he said to himself, stepping out and zipping up. "What have I done?" He was crocked, and not at all sure of what had taken place during the course of the evening.

"But if you feel that way," Jimmy heard Lola say, "I'll go up to my own place."

"Go ahead, you ungrateful little bitch!" said Vera, tears squirting from her eyes.

Lola said:

"But not till we clear the air."

"You *want* him!" cried Vera. "You *desire* him!"

"I don't want your stupid husband," Lola shouted, then looked at Jimmy apologetically. "You're just crazy, that's all! Everybody in the building knows it. You're crazy. We *all* hear you!"

Jimmy went back to the kitchenette to fix himself a drink. Now Vera was crying, Lola consoling.

"Vera's about to be violent," he thought, remembering how she cried, like a bird of prey, before she swooped; and just then she flew by him, like a great mad bird, and locked herself in the bathroom. Lola pursued; pulled at the door knob.

"She's going to kill herself!" Lola cried. Jimmy told her not to worry. "She loves every ounce of herself. She's a performer."

Vera heard him—"I heard that!"—and flew out wielding her little pink Princess safety razor. She went straight for him. He fended her off, and she kept on going into the front room. Then swaths of pink paint came back, like watery cotton candy. *Swash! Swash!*

Lola had got more than she'd bargained for. She cowered behind the freshly pinked refrigerator. *Crash!* they heard the front window break. Vera had thrown an open can of paint through it.

Sirens soon sounded through the shattered glass.

Vera heard them. She was scared now. She had done something fairly serious this time and it panicked her. She charged back into the kitchenette and locked herself in the bathroom again. "This time I really *am* going to kill myself," she shouted through the door.

Jimmy noticed that she still had the razor with her. Maybe she *was* going to do it this time. She had had enough to drink, meaning too much even for the survival instinct.

Lola put her arms around Jimmy's neck.

"What should we do?" she said, rolling big brown eyes.

He put a hand on the behind he had wanted to touch all evening, and said: "I don't know." He didn't.

Lola said, "Shall we break the door down?"

He told her that he couldn't; he had had occasion to try.

Vera screamed. It was the worst fit of many. Jimmy was more than a little scared himself. He put his drink down and put another hand on another cheek. What a behind!

The hall door was being pounded. "Open up, police!" He went to the door and opened it.

"What's going on here?"

He tried to explain the situation.

The building super, who was gay, stood behind the police. He liked Jimmy, disliked Vera. Jimmy could see that the super had been talking to the cops. They gave Lola the twice-over, but there was too much confusion. "Come on out of there," one of them called to Vera.

"I'm going to kill myself."

"Do you think she'd do it?" one of the cops asked.

"No," Jimmy said.

"Yes," said the super. "She crazy bitch. Oh, I sorry, mister, but I hear."

"I think she would," said Lola. Jimmy wondered if she wasn't hoping so.

"I will!" cried Vera.

"In that case," said a cop, "I'm calling Bellevue."

"No," Jimmy said. "Don't do that." He was weakening, as he often did, beginning to feel sorry for Vera. This was how he always lost his wars with Vera—pity.

"This is out of your hands now," said the cop. "Have you got a phone?"

"It's in here," said Lola.

The bathroom door flew open and there stood the wild woman herself. She had pink paint all over her, and looked pitiful.

"Don't let them take me to Bellevue," she cried. "Please don't let them."

"It's out of his hands," said a cop, grabbing her. "You're nuts, lady."

"They'll help you there, Vera," said Lola, nursily.

"You little. . ." fumed Vera, speech failing her, and *wham,* she threw her Princess safety razor at Lola. *Zing!* It missed. Both cops seized her arms.

Then the men in the white suits showed up. "We'll help you," they said.

Jimmy fixed himself a drink. He looked away while Vera was carried out in a straight jacket, screaming and kicking. He was not allowed to go with her. He went to the radio and turned it on. Music! Lola had assumed the role of hostess. She saw the whole menagerie out. Suddenly it was very quiet in the apartment.

Jimmy went to the window. Vera had cleared the glass out of it, but for a few jagged pieces. He leaned out and saw that there was a lovely long swath of pink paint down the front of the old brownstone. Below, there was a fracas. A small crowd watched as Vera was dragged, kicking and screaming, to the nut wagon. Lola came up behind him and put her arms around his waist.

"You poor man," she crooned.

A bitter little laugh caught in his throat. "She certainly brightened the old place up," he said. "Did they say when I can see her?"

"They said you could visit her tomorrow morning. Now you come over here and sit down. I'll fix you a fresh drink. Then, later, I'll sing you to sleep. I'm really a very good singer, you know. I'll be a star in no time."

The next morning Lola left him to find herself a singing job. She kissed him goodbye and promised more delights upon her return. Vera, however, was released to him at ten that morning. So there wasn't much chance for Lola to get at them again and Vera made it no chance at all. Jimmy was to accept that TV offer immediately. After a few phonecalls, she insisted that they leave for the west coast that very afternoon.

After all, what could be better than La La Land?

*　　*　　*

Chaos followed them to Utah. In Hollywood Jimmy wrote a poem about it. He called it:

URANIUM BLUES

Driveshaft

    distributing eighty, ninety, a hundred

  CLANG clank clank clank
outside Moab Utah
        falling dusk
long white snake line
        blacktop
shimmering off

       shimmer dimming out
mountains far

                   low ahead
smoke a cigarette   wait   smoke

wait   sky bleeding up
down behind mountains   wait

sun's hiss   sidewinder's sandshuffle rattle
first long low leap of hare

car walls away last hot sticks of sun
cigarette's smoke-signal saves you
palm it & let it go   toot
toot
                a hum   something
down the road   crosseyed lights

stand up   wave   cowboy
like the cavalry   out & under
driveshaft down   pickup's got a tow
haul you in   patch you up   come daylight
get drunk tonight

                 heigho Silver
gaining on   shadowed   etched
mountains   hauling ass   through pyramids
huge wide-based sinister cones   hundreds

through falling night   under stars
uranium
             inside mega-tons of pyramids
house up high there's Mister Big Bucks
made him a hill built him a house
them from Washington   big wigs
& queen bees

                        down here's enlisted workers'
mobiles   hauled in   you ever
seen such a one?   long as a railway car
star-glitter's ore   hot stuff's in there
just awaitin' ta burn down hell   hot damn
we going to blow up the whole
freaking world
                        break out the Coors
we got us an actor here   going to Gollywood
play you a tune   strum strum strum
sing along   sing a song of uranium
uranium blues   glitter glitter
stars all over   up & down
same whole hotdamn universe
blowin' itself up   bee–you-tiffle
all night outside on the nailedtogether
radio active porch   strumming, swigging beer
on a tilting planet   singing the Big One
BIG ONE   everything doing a slow
burn   slow burn
                        Heraclitean
rise up   up   Mister Sun
sleeping   until dark again   lit up

drive off singing   the atomic world
in the dark starbright early morning night
headlights glaring
                        singing Uranium Blues

Gratefully, Vera slept through most of it. At Bellevue
she had been prescribed something that kept her in the Sea of
Tranquility.

California was not terra incognita to Jimmy. After boot
camp at Parris Island in South Carolina, he had been flown
out to the Golden State, pack on back, on a long bench in a

prop plane that bounced him and his helmeted fellow sufferers like living bombs into the overhead at every shift of wind current and air pressure. It felt more like riding a crowded elevator at zero gravity than making a Westward-Ho advance. He was stationed at Camp Pendleton, where he underwent combat training, including a stint in the Sierra Nevada Mountains for cold weather training—snow-shoeing, skiing, living off the land, etc.—and after that he was whistled aboard a gigantic rusty tub known as a troop transport, which set out from La Jolla for Japan.

On liberty breaks, he and his buddies made trips to Tijuana, Mexico, right across the border at San Diego, or wandered up into the Hollywood Hills, where they were occasionally rousted by the police, especially the Beverly Hills private cops who watched over the homes of the stars. And returning to the mainland from Hawaii, he stopped over at Treasure Island in San Francisco Bay and partied in Frisco and Oakland—so he knew a bit about California, southern and northern. As far as Jimmy could tell, Vera had never been farther west than Las Vegas, where she had worked several times as a dancer; but Hollywood suited her perfectly, possessing a more subdued but more certain odor of money than Vegas, especially up in the hills. To some, the HOLLYWOOD sign said gold in them there hills.

THE NEW YORK TIMES
JULY 10, 1959

TWO U.S. SOLDIERS SLAIN IN VIETNAM

RED TERRORISTS KILL MAJOR AND SERGEANT—
CAPTAIN HIT IN ATTACK DURING MOVIE

Vera's first order of business was to tighten the strings between the tin cans east and west. Machinery was put into gear. It was not too late for Jimmy to become part of the Hawaiian adventure show. He must go to the studio and make a good impression on the producer, Martin Mandible, otherwise the deal was sewn up, the producer already having discussed the deal at length with Dr. Zolauf in New York. No west coast agent would be necessary. Vera could and would do most of what had to be done. Money was no deterrent. Jimmy would spend most of his days reading for a major star who was at present filming a movie but was at the same time preparing a show for Broadway from the works of a major humorist. Jimmy would read with him from a thick book until the actor had the author's words fully digested and properly interpreted, for which Jimmy would be paid a handsome weekly salary.

Vera found them an apartment on La Brea Avenue not far from Grauman's Chinese Theater, a great location at the center of things. Vera shopped for both of them. She got Jimmy properly clad in a peach shirt, grey slacks, and blue blazer, and off he went to the Beverly Hills Hotel to meet the actor, whom he found waiting to meet him at the bar.

Jack Noelle was about forty-five, Irish, with a turned-up nose, and a good-humored, rascally look about him. "You've got to be Ed Fleury," he said, as Jimmy stood tentatively near. Jack stuck out a hand for Jimmy to shake and pulled him up to a barstool with it.

"How do you like California?"

"Better this time than when I was here in the service. I got picked up by the police the last time I walked in Beverly Hills. Of course, I took a cab up here this time."

"They can tell the difference. This time you're an actor. Only a few years ago, they'd've thrown me out of here on my ear, and I was an actor then, but now, you see, a string of big roles and I'm somebody else. Did you ask for me at the desk?"

"They told me the bar."

"Completely different attitude after you asked, I bet."

"Completely."

"Well, let's go up to my suite and get to work—or would you rather have a drink first?

"Let's go to work."

In the elevator, Jack said, "Nothing but good reports about you. I was told flat out that you were going to be a star."

"It's a little overwhelming."

"It must be. It took me twenty years in the swamps before I got my first break."

"How were you able to stick it out?"

"When you love something, it's not a matter of sticking it out. They tell me that you're an ex-Marine. That'll serve you well in a lot of ways. Menace. All good actors have menace. I was in the Navy during War Two. In the Pacific."

They entered Jack's suite, ordered coffee, and got to work. When Jimmy got home to Vera that night, he was full of the excitement of working with an actor of the caliber of Jack Noelle. "I tell you, he can get an odd twist I never would have thought of. He's just hilarious. And—he said he thought I was pretty funny too."

Maybe it was being away from his essentially humorless parents, maybe it was being out of the service, away from heavy responsibility, but Jimmy was developing a greater sense of humor than he had previously understood himself to possess. Maybe it was a matter of growing up, growing older. Or maybe it was living with Vera, who took nothing lightly. Maybe it was defensive. In any case, Jimmy felt that his risibility scale was ringing at higher reaches than ever before. Vera took their present situation seriously, deadly earnest. Jimmy could not help but see it as comical, and when Vera saw this attitude manifesting itself in Jimmy, she grew as outraged as a Drill Instructor confronting a smirking recruit. Worst of all, was when Jimmy occasionally said, "What the hell am I doing here in Gollywood? The whole thing seems ridiculous."

"Don't you want to be a star?"

"Star shmar! Some of them may have talent, but they're just a bunch of assholes like everyone else." Jimmy might take a drink and add: "I want to be a poet." That could cause a whole spaghetti dinner to fly out of the kitchen. Then a phone call to New York and a lecture from Dr. Zolauf. "Tu est fou!"

But there was fear involved too. Jimmy had no one, it seemed to him, who was interested in how he felt. Even his parents were in the enemy camp, for once in full agreement with Vera. The hope of big money lay behind this unified front, it seemed to Jimmy, and he felt that he had no one to turn to. Moral support for any other way was completely lacking. With so much being staked on him, he doubted he could live up to it.

After several weeks, the big meeting with the producer was set and Jimmy duly entered the lot at Culver City, carrying everyone's hopes and dreams with him. He wandered about the studio until it was time to report to Martin Mandible's office. As he entered, he ran into the star of the series, who introduced himself, saying that he had heard many good things about Jimmy and was looking forward to working with him. New York had handed him all this on the proverbial silver platter. He thought of all the poor starving actors who would have done anything to be where he was and doing what he was doing. He felt like a naughty little boy who hadn't finished his food and was being reprimanded for the poor starving children of the world.

This was a very famous television producer of sit-coms and crime shows. This was Mister M., himself. He greeted

Jimmy like a friend, invited him to take a chair in front of his desk, and sat down behind it.

"All this is somewhat unusual, you understand, but you have come from New York with the highest recommendations. I studied your photographs, and what little of you that I could get on film. I know about your stage work. We have made a decision. You are exactly right for the part—fresh, young, handsome in a boyish sort of way, beautifully built—an ex-Marine, right? You've lifted weights as well, I can see."

Behind him, on a long table fronting the wide window through which Jimmy could see people passing in costume, and a small cottage with a sign in front—"Clifford Odets," one of Jimmy's writing heroes—were photographs of a woman and two children. Mister M. caught Jimmy looking at them.

"My wife and children." Mister M. rose and came around the desk to Jimmy and stood behind him. He named his wife and two children. Then he put his hands down the front of Jimmy's shirt and gripped his pectorals as if he had caught hold of Marilyn Monroe's front. Jimmy jumped to his feet.

"I'm sorry," said Mister M. "Did I startle you? I just wanted to see if that chest was the real thing. Please, relax. We have a contract to sign. Would you like some coffee, or perhaps a drink?"

Jimmy made a leap for the door, ran out of the studio, off the lot, and as far out of Culver City as he could get, with no taxi in sight, and stopped at the first bar he could find. Inside, he ordered a beer, lit a cigarette, and sat and thought. He tried to understand why he had done it. It had just swooped over him, like the flapping wings of a vulture. He had been in and around the theater dating back to when he was a candy butcher at Minsky's; he was used to being around gay people, he neither feared nor disliked them. Hell, he'd won a commendation in Hawaii for saving a drag queen! What had struck him? Was he just seeking an excuse to escape his situation? He needed counsel. He went to the phone and called Jack Noelle. He left the payphone number with the desk clerk. "Tell him to call me as soon as he comes in, please." He had barely got to his barstool and ordered another beer when the phone rang. It was Jack. "They called me from the hotel," he said. "What's happened?"

"I don't exactly know. Could you—would it be possible—I realize—"

"You want me to pick you up? Where are you? What's the name of the joint? I can be there in five minutes."

Fifteen or so minutes later, Jack pulled to the curb in front of Jimmy in his snazzy little rented convertible. He drove them out on the Pacific Coast Highway. "I called Mister M. He thinks you had a panic attack. Says he wants to see you as soon as possible, soon as you get yourself together. I called New York after I talked to him. Zoulauf's very upset. But mainly, I'd say, worried about you. Have you talked to Vera? Somebody probably has by now. Are you feeling better? Can you tell me now?"

"I don't think I want any of it, Jack."

"What is it—afraid?"

"Some of that, I guess. But I'm afraid it'll take me away from what I really want."

"Which is?"

"I want to write."

"Vera tells me you want to be a poet."

"Yes—well, I'd like to write other things, too. Perhaps a play. But I really love poetry."

"Ah," sighed Jack, "another Frances Farmer."

"Who's that?"

"A poet who didn't want to be a movie star. They said she was crazy. I just think she knew what she wanted but nobody would go along with her because there was no money in it. But why can't you do both? Why can't you do this first, then later on pursue the other?"

"Because I'll never go back. I have to give whatever I do everything I've got."

Jack grew thoughtful, his eyes on the traffic ahead, the beach, the blue sea. He waited a long time before he spoke. "Look," he said, finally, "I told you once that it took me twenty years to make it. Well, it was actually more like twenty-five. I'm older than I let on. I also told you that I love what I do. It's clear to me, that, even though you have reams of talent for acting, it isn't what you really love. You want me to tell you to quit. I can see that. I knew an actor once, who wanted to be a playwright. He wrote a God-awful play about ancient Rome and showed it to me. I told him it showed talent but that he ought to write a play about something he knew—the theater, for instance—and damned if he didn't write a play about me, about my long, long struggle to get somewhere, and he included a line in it that I had often said to him. The line goes: *When they come to bury me, I don't want them to say, He never did what he wanted to do.* He included that. The play was a hit. Now if you feel the way you do about this writing bug of yours, go where you'll be comfortable doing it and do it, and don't listen to anyone but your own inner voice. Follow your bliss. Come on, I'll drive you home now."

Jack let Jimmy out by Grauman's Chinese Theater to walk on the stars a little before going in to face Vera. When Jack was out of sight, Jimmy dove into a cocktail lounge and had several bourbons, which turned into a three-day Ben-Hur bender.

When he finally got home, Vera was spitting fire.

"Where have you been?"

He didn't know, but he looked like a soldier who had come in from a mine field.

Vera ordered him to strip and take a shower. When he

came out, she said, "Now listen, you stupid son-of-a-bitch, New York says everything can be fixed. They've talked to Mister M. They told him you were the most sensitive actor they had seen since Brando. They want you to call as soon as you get in. Oh my God," she said, looking more closely at him, "you're still drunk, aren't you? Well, you're an actor. Act sober, you can do it. Now for God's—"

"We're leaving tonight," said Jimmy. "Just like we left New York, we're leaving."

"Are you crazy? You can't just run out on everything. What about Jack Noelle?"

"It was Jack's idea."

"I sincerely doubt that it was Jack's idea that you should just up and leave. He's preparing that Broadway show and he's depending on you. In show business people depend on each other."

"He'll find somebody else. I have to follow my bliss."

"If you do this, you'll never get another job in show business."

"Good! I hate it!"

"You *are*! You're just crazy! Dr. Zolauf said you were *fou*! You're crazy like that damned father and mother of yours. You're all crazy! Crazy, crazy, crazy!" She threw a lamp at the wall. It bounced off, its shade crumpled, but still lit.

"With you or without you," Jimmy said. "And talk about crazy; *I* was never in Bellevue!"

"Here, this came for you," she said, and gave him a manila-envelope-in-her-fist to the solar plexus. It hurt.

"Some letter from these Huxley-Blavatsky jerks."

His stomach was tempted to propulsion, but calmed as he caught his breath. What was this? He read with pink blurred eyes: *The Association for the Study of Lucid Dreams invites you to the Hotel Paradiso in Puerto Vallarta to participate in a study in which you are to sleep and be awakened while you are dreaming and to maintain your dream and then to convert it into whatever dream you wish it to become.*

Lucid dreams, he read, *are more vivid than common dreams. Inscape is energized, so that the world of the dream is like that of Hopkins or Van Gogh, pulsating, dynamic, vital. Such imagery is sometimes said to be the manifestation of cosmic holograms, and if one is able (which we teach) to convert them, one might convert one's life, turn it into what one wanted it to be, or wished it were or had become at an earlier stage, bring time back with what and whom one loved, but in a better version, even an improved infancy; set a new course for one's self, and embark upon the friendly waters of a new life.*

He looked at her. "Somebody wants me," he said, grinning. "Somebody bought me a spa. And here's a plane ticket to Puerto Vallarta."

"Who's sending you there? Some girl?"

"I don't know. The movie people? Dr. Zolauf? Somebody. It's anonymous."

"Are you going?

"Yes. Whoever sent this to me knows I need help. This takes big money. *Some*one cares, even if you don't!"

"What am *I* supposed to do while you're loafing in a spa in Mexico?"

"Get a job in Vegas. They always need strippers. I'll be back in a week or less. I'm shot. I'm going."

"Go to hell for all I care! I'll find somebody. See if I don't!"

"I bet you will."

*   *   *

Upon arrival, Jimmy saw white gulls arise from the emerald maze in the huge garden surrounding the Hotel

Paradiso. White gulls. Don't they always arrive with a ship, following for her flotsam and jetsam? In the lobby there were a lot of dirty-smocked people crying like the gulls in Spanish and English and snippets of other tongues. His heart sank. The place reminded him of Bellevue. Before he knew what was happening, someone had given him a shot in the arm and a pill stuffed in his mouth, saying, "L.S.Dreams, Senor." Then he was in bed. Some ghostly white smock sat beside the bed with a notebook and a pen. "Go on, go on," it was saying in accented English. And he dreamed he saw an instant, which was a dewdrop in his dream . . .

Yes, a dewdrop and a stellar instant, like that of the wild gulls, pulling the air with their wide wings, an image, a vision of heavenly flight—an ascent, a transcendence—a nano-second and a shimmering drop, or, shape-shifting, a shim-mering shield, hovering in space, and what looked like a moonbeam crossed the dark—"the silver dark"—of a swirl-ing dust mote, a hazed, illumined, impossible dark, fingered, like a laser, touched the instant, the marijuana-happy high looking down at the nasty Lilliputian planet, with the most tender touch imaginable, angling this way and that, so that with each angle an entire eternal history was displayed, with all of the mass and multiplicity of life.

There was no death, but a cottage-coziness everywhere, and of us and of the mountains and the waters, seemed that all these are projections of personality, (what I see I see be-cause I am I) spiritual manifestations of the ghostly immate-rial, tilts at the dewdrop, incarnations and aspects of the All-in-all, the anomalon itself, yes, and even that sheen, that spark, on the oriflamme of time; seemed that we are the one hologram of life, and that the family portrait is the portrait of all who ever lived, with mountains and waters and creatures wild and domesticated; seemed that the holographic plate is angled for this simulacrum, this three-dimensional portrait of a universe-apparent, which portrait is not a memento mori but a glory in a turning in time, a journey around a star.

Next morning Jimmy discovered there were others there: The dying Greek Egyptologist, his fellow guest and subject of study, who spoke in his hypnotized sleep. The group, gathered in the garden, bat-eared, heard his inner voice, its *cri de coeur*. They were there to understand. They were there to change their fate. The Greek had a terminal virus of some kind, a growing vegetation of the brain. He coughed. A virus has more organized life than a star, though a star has an order of appearance, star in the sky and star on stage. There was also a famous film star with them—*è bell' attrice*—addicted, suicidal, luciously feminine, but barren. Parmenides mentored Zeno to believe in the unchanging universe behind the changing one. In Rome, the film star could only find a scrolling phantom life, too unsubstantial for her beautiful solid flesh. She sought *la dolce vita* in drugs and now, three times removed from her dream of life, she tries again though she has lost her beautiful way. Much about her reminded Jimmy of himself; he, too, was escaping promised fame and fortune.

On what seemed to be the second night, Jimmy heard the calls again, and through the next long night, material manifestations of the ghostly immaterial; or, if one is not of a fanciful turn of mind, if one prefers the psychological explanation for every sort of phenomenon, it must have been the wind he heard, and the giant hotel settling (an ancient building creaks), the water pipes gurgling, the radiators knocking, the cats in the garden, skulking; or, if one is of a physiological turn of mind, he was suffering alcohol withdrawal, plain and simple; and transformed these in his mind into the calls he thought he heard that sounded to him like the crying out of the earth's multitudinous dead. And what he felt they told him of his life's unmeaning, his time's misuse, his soul's fear, out of the vastness, the great underdarkness, caused him to writhe in his wet white sheets and sweat, glistening, like a great, limbed worm.

He awakened, startled, and, finally, he slept again, a victim of broken circadian rhythm, and dreamed of the drab furnished rooms of his infancy, the dismal corners occasionally shot with sunlight, the fascinating dust motes that were his first view of the universe.

But now, awake again, he sat in an ancient porcelain tub that smelled of chlorine and soap, pouring from a bribed-in fifth of bourbon, hearing Symphony Five—*da-da-da-dum da-da-da-dum*—frowning, smiling, frowning, smiling, for Beethoven's twittering bird-song, or Death knocking—in a tiled room full of steam, with no childhood left, a man with no toys but a cheap, green cigar.

There was no way to sleep off the memory of what is forgotten. Only the lemon morning, bringing eggs and coffee, can rewind the clock. Only the pink, shaved face. Only the white suit, the Panama. But memory's gulls were gone. That great wild rising! His old Marine 1447642 seabag was waiting. Something should have been done. Once upon a time, something that was not done still waited in disappointment.

*   *   *

"What was it like?" Vera asked, when he got home. "Were there a lot of beautiful girls there?"

"One wreck of an Italian movie star. People running around in towels. It was a drug den. Whoever sent me there thought they were doing me a favor, but as you can plainly see, I'm still drunk."

"It didn't do you any good? It didn't dry you out?"

"It hosed me down. I'm as clean as a whistle."

Ahead of them, they had a three thousand mile long argument. The Nixon-Kennedy Debates, which they caught on the car radio, were nothing compared with the Vera-Jimmy debates.

113

They parted in New York. Jimmy gave Vera the car. She was kind enough to leave him off at Rolly's sandal shop in Brooklyn Heights where he hoped to crash. She told him that she was probably going to stay at the Evangeline, a womens' residence in Manhattan, while she looked for a job and an apartment. They did not blow kisses as she drove away.

En route, Jimmy had telephoned an old military acquaintance of his, the former colonel of his base at Kaneohe, Hawaii, who was now managing the big Barnes & Noble book store in Chelsea and asked him for a job. The Colonel remembered him because of all the many complimentary things Lt. Bland had told him about this young man. He got top score in the battalion on the one-year college equivalency. Bland had also suggested to the Colonel that Jimmy be put up for Naval Air Cadet. The Colonel told Jimmy that he was very proud of him, especially more so because at that same time he had had to have his own nephew drummed out of the Corps for robbery and other crimes. The Colonel asked if Jimmy remembered.

"Yes sir," said Jimmy, "I was turnkey at the brig then."

The Colonel's nephew had brought him great shame, but at the same time Jimmy had boosted unit pride. Of course he remembered Jimmy and what could he do for him?

"I've been to university now," said Jimmy, "thanks to the G.I. Bill. Also a couple of top drama schools. I want to work with books."

"Jolly good," said the Colonel, his puffing voice sounding like Colonel Blimp. "I have just the spot available for you in the Rare Books Department."

Now this was just the thing. After the Crash Jimmy's father got a job with the Publishers Guild—sold books door-to-door. By the time he was twelve, Jimmy was selling encyclopedias, The Harvard Classics, the Wonder Book of Knowledge, etc. O, Joy! The Rare Books Department!

Goodbye movie-land. He felt himself becoming a free person. The last mistake of his youth, Vera, was next.

But soon, Vera called him at the sandal shop. A well-appointed apartment on Spring Street in the Village awaited him. She had contacted Dr. Zolauf at the Dramatic Workshop's new location at Carnegie Hall. Dr. Zolauf was of course deeply upset, but was willing to talk to Jimmy about his career as an actor, and Vera emphasized that Dr. Zolauf also wanted Jimmy and Vera to get back together. To Jimmy, this sounded more like Vera than Dr. Zolauf. If he didn't weaken because of her beautiful dancer's body, he was free. He was free, free, free. His joy at this thought was immense.

Several nights he left the snoring sandal shop and climbed up to the Esplanade and sat smoking, looking at the dancing lights of Manhattan across the dark and diamonded East River until dawn. One morning before Rolly and Jean woke, or stopped their heavy breathing, he wrote this paean to his nearly new-won freedom, which he called of course, "From the Esplanade."

> When, in the morning remnant of the moon,
> the restless city stirs beneath the stars,
> its buildings hunching in a black tableau
> that forms Prometheus from common themes
> of steel and glass and brick, I walk abroad—
> for an hour now—while night lays claim on time
> for the first time for me tonight (and now
> already it surrenders to the sun!)—
> I walk abroad requiring only love;
> that it may be a morning gift unwrapt
> from this dark shapeless parcel and received
> in utter nakedness; that it be light!
> But more than having light, I want to be
> one for whom light adventures into change,
> allowing for my lustings after it

and gives me place to say in certain praise:
O Light, allow me several such days!

*　　*　　*

After a few weeks, Jimmy could see that Rolly and Jean wanted him to leave the sandal shop, though they didn't say so. He had become an intruder in their hippie paradise, especially now that Marsayas and Joan had split for Frisco. Vera's spider-web apartment awaited him. He needed a base for his new job at the book store. Once again, life was crowding him. His best bet for the moment was to rejoin his unbearable weakness, Vera. So he temporarily caved to the ballerina's body with the tilted mind.

But it only took a few weeks for his hopes of reason to be exploded. One evening, when Jimmy, his humor temporarily lost to melancholy and his anger rising with remembrances of things past—like the long swathe of pink paint down the front of their old brownstone, like the flying Princess razor, like Vera's embarrassing crazy swim in the river and the trouble that had preceded it—just upped and grabbed his old Marine seabag and left Vera for good, walked out on all that old life to begin a new one. Good-Bye to All That, as the poet Robert Graves put it.

Was he being pushed forward by certain influences, or was he being drawn forward, by the love of poetry, crazy as that might sound? He just couldn't tell. Some of all of it, he guessed. Did he just want to be a bum, sitting under a tree with a jug of wine, writing verses, or was he a serious-minded person who was choosing Robert Frost's road less travelled by? He didn't know. Despite a difficult beginning, there remained something innocent in him, of which he was aware at reflective moments, and he often rediscovered it when he was writing poetry. He had come to think of poetry as the only good thing in his life, then as absolutely necessary to his existence. It had become his true religion.

116

The great W.H. Auden had said that young poets should concentrate on meter and rhyme, the formalist elements of poetry, because, being young, they had little experience of life and so, little to say about it. Marsayas had introduced Jimmy to Beat poetry, and at first, Jimmy wasn't sure how to take it—his father had recited Poe, Kipling, Tennyson, and he had loved them. The Beat poets seemed angry, but he, who had so much to be angry about, still preferred to escape his anger in Blake's "Songs of Innocence." Perhaps someday he should howl, for he had in him all the howls of a snared wolf—trapped, trapped, and trapped again. And he remembered: Once upon a time there were two battered suitcases, one filled with a thousand or more of his childhood drawings, his comic book, Kid Danger, many of which he made in bars while waiting for his drunken parents to go home, wherever that might be; the other suitcase filled with a thousand or more incontrovertibly dead legal documents from his father's family's wars over property, when they had had a million dollars of such, at the turn of the Century, and to relieve his father's burdens it was the ten-year-old's artistic life's work that was jettisoned. He cried then, but he did not *howl* as perhaps he should have done.

It became his habit to go down to the main aisles of the big bookstore during his lunch hour to sit and read modern poetry; and that was how he became familiar with Denise Mitchell, who clerked the Poetry aisle; or, more accurately, Jimmy became familiar with Denise's feet; or, *precisely*, with her little-toes; for his first vague awareness of her existence was the slight notice some watchman of his abstracted mind took of the large, padding sneakers and the plump little-toes, like peeping piglets, that emerged and withdrew from the holes in their sides, as Denise stepped around and over him in the service of her customers.

One day he wondered what was above those wornout sneakers, looked up from his squatting position, up and up, and saw the shadowed undersides of big, bra-less breasts, above which tilted toward him a Gertrude-Steinean head and large, plumbeous eyes dropped to the bottom of hornrims, like two black olives in Martini glasses.

"You have the most amazing concentration," she said. "How can you read in the aisles with people stepping all over you like that?"

"I learned to concentrate in a Marine squadbay."

"I notice you always read poetry."

"I'm a poet."

"I'm getting my masters at Columbia. My thesis is on John Donne. You know—'No man is an island . . .'"

"That's from a sermon."

"Hey, man, you really know Donne, don't you? I've been working on my paper for over a year. I feel like I know him inside out."

And they became friends.

Sometimes Jimmy would forego the poetry and they would take their lunch break together and sit on a bench in Union Square. Denise told Jimmy that she was an orphan. Denise's parents had left her a trust fund administered by two aunts on the West Coast, but it wasn't an awful lot. She still needed the Barnes & Noble job. Jimmy told her that he'd just left his wife and was staying at the Y. He asked Denise if she knew where he could get a cheap room and she found him a little hall room in the rooming house where she lived.

The house, owned and operated by an eagle-beaked Miss Byrdsong, and containing about twenty pigeon-coop rooms, was in the heart of Greenwich Village. In the late Fifties the low rent Village was, to Jimmy's innocent-romantic side, an American Paris. Scènes de la Vie de Bohème de Paris!

Miss Byrdsong's rent coincided with Jimmy's frugal budget. His days of lunch and drinks at the Beverly Hills Hotel were over. His room was all that Jimmy, the ex-

Marine, needed—a cot, a window, room for a table-desk—a place to write. He could read all night or write to the morning light if he felt like it. He was on the second floor. Outside his window there was a pretty shop-lined street, a spreading tree, and a fire escape he could escape to in hot weather. Right below was a little newstand-cum-cigar store. Jolly!

His new life recalled his happiest days in the service, when he would go into town and check in to a hotel with a book and spend the night or nights reading. Often he was offered a prostitute by some agent of the hotel. "I have my book," he would say, much to the surprise of the agent. He pretty much worked his way through the Western canon while he lived at Miss Byrdsong's.

Denise was a Buddhist, a Communist, and a proud lesbian. She was right three times, she told him. She began to instruct Jimmy in the Hindu Vedas, which led him to an interest in the Eastern canon—he read the *Analects* of Confucius and the *Tao*. He read *The Upanishads,* and he came to see the same life-questions and mysteries in Eastern thought that he saw in Western. Questions, questions, but not many answers.

One Friday evening as they were leaving the bookstore, Denise said: "All you do is read, write, and work. Aren't you ever lonely?"

"I've never had a chance like this before—to be quiet and alone. But sure; I get lonesome sometimes."

She told Jimmy about a friend of hers, named Phyllis, who'd recently broken off with her boyfriend, Reginald, "a real cool black cat, so she's lonely," and asked if Jimmy'd like to meet her. He said he would; and they walked over to the ominous Lower East Side one hot summer night.

Houston Street; big ugly old apartment building; Phyllis at the apartment door in a slip: a thin pale little wraith, with pale little curves of breasts and hips, and pale little legs just missing being curveless, womanly shapes so subtle that a change of light could have caused them to vanish. She had long fine hair, pale and no-colored, but with a soft sheen, a luster that, when it was noticed at all, was more an emotional response than a fact.

They talked, Jimmy feeling rather formal and incongruous in the starched dress shirt and pressed summer slacks he'd worn to work, sitting on the edge of a floored mattress, a pad, in a room lit only by stub-ends of drooling candles stuck any-whichway on the low night-cum-coffee table before him, observing the walls, painted scarlet and bright green and deep purple, and the mobiles made of coat-hangers, and the jet-black cat with golden eyes that kept leaping up from its dreams to squirt short shots of piss like a squeezed wine-bag in any direction it found itself aiming, then smugly curling up again to nap; him watching the cat, and watching Phyllis and Denise, too, and listening to them drawing—*ss-eh, ssss-eh*— on the little corn-cob pipe they passed back and forth, a pipe with a strip of tin-foil on top held by an elastic band and punctured for pot; Jimmy watching and listening and drinking the green Ballantine ale he'd brought along; and thinking, while eyeing those thin little legs like a girl-child's, how tenderly he would hold a girl like Phyllis in his arms. Gently, gently, or she might break.

But then it was time to go and he took the frail little hand proffered him and gently squeezed it; and he looked back from the door that Denise in her ambling way was closing and saw the small pale wraith in a slip fade, descend into the rear darkness of the apartment with trembling, unsteady steps, the dart-dart of retreat, like a pale butterfly into dark and ancient woods.

*   *   *

Jimmy liked Denise, and he liked Phyllis. They supplied all the female companionship he felt he could handle. They were both of a studious bent and were a welcomed and

120

refreshing change from the beauty-queen dancer, Vera. Their discussions of art and music and poetry lent a lively diversion to Jimmy's rather monastic life of work, study and writing. Sometimes the three of them would get together for a movie or a Chinese dinner. Jimmy began to look forward to their meetings and to feel a certain affection for Phyllis. Though he had sworn off women, Phyllis was a definite balm to his nerves. She was an opposite number from Vera, all right. Phyllis had had a childhood of illnesses and confinements which had molded her into a person of imagination and observation. She was thoughtful and somewhat timid. Vera, on the other hand, had been a veritable physical force. She'd had plans for her life, and Jimmy's too. She was going somewhere in the world. She was a beautiful professional dancer. She was going to point her pretty toes and kick life the way she wanted it to go, like a soccer ball. She was going to kick the poetry right out of Jimmy, but she hadn't been successful, thanks to Jack Noelle and later to Marsayas, men who knew something about bliss.

*   *   *

The season had come to stalk the wild poet.

One day as Jimmy left work at Barnes & Noble, toting an armful of books, including Gertrude Stein's *Tender Buttons*, which he particularly looked forward to perusing— indeed, looking forward enthusiastically to an evening of edification and intellectual entertainment—he was accosted by Vera.

He must come home with her immediately; he must stop all this poetry nonsense—fine enough in its place, which apparently was not in the real world—come home and try to put his acting career back together, if possible. She followed him down the street, so he changed directions, afraid to lead her to his sanctuary at Miss Byrdsong's, alternately

121

screaming and crying, all the while making her case for the superior life, the life of fame and fortune.

People stared at them, he guessed trying to figure out if he was being abusive; but he kept a steady pace, onward and upward, and finally she dropped off behind him, shouting obscenities that faded in the distance. How she had found him, he had no idea. Someone must have tipped her off. Was this the last hurrah? Hell, no! She was back the next day, and the next, and finally he decided that he had to quit Barnes & Noble to escape her, quit his access to all those wonderful old rare books and the pleasures of a regular routine, a regular life, and so he did, left without notice and no forwarding address. He told Denise not to tell anyone about Miss Byrdsong's, and he knew she wouldn't. He had to pull a second vanishing act.

"Wild bitch!" said Denise.

"You can only imagine," he said.

"You sure you want to give her up, Jimmy? She's a knockout." Denise had seen some of it.

"She's a knockout, all right. She nearly smashed in the back of my head one day with a full bottle of Scotch."

"You have all the luck, kid," said Denise, laughing.

At first, Jimmy was deeply upset and more than a little angry about these stalking incidents, but then he began to see things in another way. What Vera had succeeded in doing was to get him finally, once and for all, out of the regular life. He could take part-time jobs, anything at all, and so have more time to study and to write. His room at Miss Byrdsong's was dirt cheap, he could easily make enough as a dish-washer, car-washer, or at some other menial labor, to pay for it and to keep himself in enough food to write on. Wasn't Marsayas always saying that artists should be artists and nothing else that might take up their time or thought or energy?

Time was very much on Jimmy's mind. He was doing well enough, provided he were given world enough and time.

But a vague foreboding had begun to grip him, making the nerves under his skin twang like catgut when it came upon him—the thought that his father, who was now in his middle sixties and was, in addition, not living a very healthy or sensible life, might just drop dead on him, leaving him once again to care for his mother, a woman whom he found almost unbearable to live with. Duty would demand that he look after her, for he saw her as incapable of taking care of herself, being either mildly demented or emotionally unable to handle any of life's more serious problems.

Suppose his father died and he was compelled to look after her? Sometimes lately he felt as if he were in a race to get as much done as possible with his studies and his writing before this doom befell him. But for now, for about the first time in his young life, he felt free, a wild-oats man, a belly-up-to-the-bar boy, a poet. He had to take advantage of this opportunity, he had to adventure while he could, before the sky came crashing down on him, as it did on Henny Penny, for he knew that such a beautiful moment of freedom couldn't last. And he had just received word that one of his poems had won a 300-pound prize in an international poetry contest based in London.

Jimmy Whistler, a real poet, a prize-winning poet!

CHAPTER FIVE

CITY LIGHTS

THE NEW YORK TIMES
MAY 10, 1960

U.S. APPROVES PILL FOR BIRTH CONTROL

THE NEW YORK TIMES
AUGUST 4, 1960

DUCKLINGS FREED TO SAVE SPECIES

---

48 OF VANISHING REDHEADS
INSTALLED FOR BREEDING IN JAMAICA BAY REFUGE

THE NEW YORK TIMES
NOVEMBER 10, 1960

KENNEDY'S VICTORY WON BY CLOSE MARGIN

Vesuvio's, Frisco's dark palace of the mind, La Boheme of bars, a rich inner life and a poor exterior, postered with jazz and poetry readings, air dancing with hops, hip hips on stools, shades in the dark, Marsayas among others, his hip hips, his hops, his shades and shingle beard, draining a cold mug. Enough! Up and tall and out the door. Across the alley. Long fingers dragged along the window of the City Lights Bookshop, compelled, then in, scanning the shelves. *Howl*, and other products of the San Francisco Beat Poetry Renaissance. Then—an anomaly. An English anthology of international scope, and an international prize, Jimmy Whistler on the back cover, a winner. Thumbed through, scanned. A gleeful gargoyle, then down, down, down. "No, no, no, Jimmy," he thought, "this Danny Abse, Kingsley Amis, Philip Larkin stuff is over, all a reaction to Dylan Thomas, Alex Comfort, and George Barker, to the Apocalyptic school. But they've made their point—Apocalyptic verse can't get at the quotidian—but, Jimmy, we've gone way beyond that; we've got Ginsberg, Kerouac and Snyder. Even Robert Lowell has changed his style. Come on, boyo, get with it!" He took a second look at the Howard Sergeant anthology of international prize poems. Jimmy's poem "The Poor Boy" had won second prize over fifteen hundred entries. He read it again.

> Not having had inheritance or luck,
> undemocratically good blood or breeding,
> nor any gold come out of family stock
> that sets a young man up, preceding
> maturity and forming for it pride
> in action and aristocratic strength,
> solace in having purpose in each stride,
> and discipline that carries to its length,
> I've found myself romantically inclined,
> a muzzy mongrel with a barking mind.
>
> How I admire those men and women who
> were reared in order, dignity and pride!

You see it in their eyes, a voiceless vow,
a knowledge Levelling denied.
Here now is social change preeminent,
the mass man rises to his rightful place;
but his ascension leaves a remanent
of unredeemable darkness of disgrace
in that all art must kowtow to a taste,
now at his rising, weaned on gutter waste.

I know, for I have foraged in the lots
of blackened cities looking for a prize
of red discarded unbroken flowerpots
to place my plants, to brighten eyes.
I've shined a thousand shoes along the streets
of coughing cities all across this land.
A child, I'd enter taverns and retreats
the like of which to others would be banned.
Oh, I know poverty, unhappiness;
such things I know, I have no need to guess.

And yet a sturdy strength comes out of it,
that's undeniable; but at what cost!
The strength of street-bred children is their wit
and nerve; nobility is lost
in the hungry race of mongrels for a bone,
and Honor hangs his head before the scene.
The heart of the street urchin is a stone
ground more with each engagement, until mean.
We learn to fight and hate, but not to love,
no matter who says so. We learn to shove.

Marsayas put the book back on the shelf. He couldn't
afford it. They were living on what Joan made as a temp-sec
with Kelly Girls. He'd have to bring Joan and Kosinski and
Lani over here to see Jimmy's work. He bet Jimmy had gone

through the three hundred pound prize money by now. Too bad, he could have helped him drink it up. He stepped out of City Lights and into the hilly open air, feeling pleased in the knowledge that he had helped to create a poet. Jimmy only needed to get hip and he'd soon be writing stuff to rival the best of the Beats. He crossed over to the Hotel Alpine, just cattycorner from City Lights, his shower shoes happily flapping, snapping out a tune of poetic destiny. At the turn of the century, the question for poetry was whether to follow Swinburne or to follow Browning and Pound had pointed. Follow Browning! Marsayas felt like Pound. This is the way, Jimmy Whistler! Go west! A leader and a prophet, was Marsayas. He would write to Jimmy and explain what must be done. But—Oh, for Christ's sake!—there in front of the Alpine stood Kosinski, wearing his American flag monk's robe, complete with hood, some haute couture the artist had cut from a huge American flag he had bought at a thrift store. He had worn it in his room and occasionally around the halls of the hotel but never outside before. Marsayas lifted his head and spread his nostrils wide, smelling trouble in the wind.

*　　*　　*

A few blocks away, Leilani Kona sat on a bench in Washington Square park, transferring to a spiral notebook her experiences of the past six months. Occasionally, she would glance up from her notes and look down toward Fisherman's Wharf, which was too far to see but which played on her mind as the source of fresh sea food. It was approaching noon and she was getting hungry. She considered the long walk down to the Wharf, the short walk to the cable car, then decided on a hotdog vender who was not more than thirty feet away and was spreading pungency on the air. Miraculously, Joan appeared, handing her a hotdog.

"I was just thinking of getting one," Lani said.

127

"I got my lunch break a little early. I thought I might find you here."

"Isn't it a perfect day today?"

"Hmmn," said Joan, sitting down and biting into her hotdog. "But how can you think this is perfect when you're from Hawaii?"

"Well, it's different. You'd be surprised how dull perfect weather can get. I kind of like the changing of the seasons. Of course, I've seen all the movies, but it's different to really experience it."

"What are you writing?"

"Oh, it's just a sort of a journal. I've kept it off and on since I was sixteen. I try to explain things to myself. I pretend I'm talking to my Aunt Mele. She lived here for years."

"Here in Frisco?"

"Right here."

Joan and Marsayas had only been in Frisco for a month or so, enough time for Marsayas to have "discovered" Kosinski. The two men had immediately become great pals, and so Joan and Kosinski's girl, Lani, had been thrown together.

"I could never do that," Joan said.

"Do what?"

"Keep a journal. I've started them, but I always just give them up. I have to work."

"Don't you mind working for Marsayas . . ."

"Not really. What else would I do?"

"When I first got together with Stan he was working as a salesman. He wore a nice suit every day and a tie and he'd go off selling and come home with a reasonable amount of money and then he'd paint in the evenings and everything seemed . . . seemed. . ."

"I know. He's taken a real turn, smoking pot from a pipe all day and . . ."

"He's not like the same person. He's started wearing

that American flag all the time. He's had other mental problems. He's been put away a few times. And I can't get a straight sentence out of him anymore. Mickey Mouse! Mickey Mouse! That's all he says."

"Marsayas is worried about him too."

"Well, I don't want to desert him, but I'm beginning to think about going on to New York. That was my original intention, you know."

"I know. Frankly, I don't know what we're doing out here, either. I guess Marsayas just wanted to catch the scene. But I am a New Yorker, and I miss it. I'd just as soon head back myself. We have so many friends there."

"I think I may have a friend there, too."

"Really?

"Well, I don't know for sure. He could be anywhere. He's a Marine I met in Hawaii. In fact—you'll laugh—he was a military policeman, a member of the HASP, Hawaiian Armed Services Police? Sounds unlikely, doesn't it?"

"For *you*—yes, pretty unlikely."

"But he wasn't like what you might think. He was a very sensitive boy. I think he'd had a difficult life up to that point. He was a poet. Listen to this:

> Along the cliffs she wandered,
>   A song sublimely sung,
> Along the cliffs, and pondered
>   The sea they overhung."

"Very pretty."

"No, beautiful in its mood. Of course, there's more to it. He gave me the poem just before he left Oahu. He promised to write to me."

"Did he?"

"He sent a few cards with little notes on them. After a couple of years he sent me one to say that he had got married. Later, he sent me one saying that his wife didn't like him writing to me and that he wouldn't be sending anything more."

"Rotten gink!"

"Oh no, we weren't lovers, you see. I don't know exactly what we were. He always called me his little sister. I was only sixteen at the time, and he was eighteen, nineteen, twenty, I'm not sure. But he felt he was too old for me. We were like dear friends."

Joan looked doubtful. "Did you feel that way?"

"I don't know. When he wrote to me that he was married, I climbed up on a high cliff—just like in the poem— and jumped into the sea."

"You tried to kill yourself?"

"No. Not really. It was more of a dramatic gesture, just to satisfy myself, my anger at fate. I was never in any real danger. You know," she said, laughing, "the funny thing was, he couldn't swim. I tried to teach him but he just kept sinking. I never saw anything like it. Well, actually, I finally got him floating. Sort of. But I thought he must have swallowed a boulder to lack any buoyance at all."

"You love him, don't you?"

"Well, I guess I love the memory of him. The sweet memory."

*　*　*

Lighter fluid! That was what Marsayas smelled. Kosinski had soaked his American flag robe in lighter fluid and now he struck his pipe lighter and tried to light the pot-brimming pipe. He went up like a torch. Marsayas broke into a full gallop, across the traffic, losing one of his shower shoes behind him, and reached into the flaming red, white, and blue mass, grabbing the point of the hood. He tried to pull it off Kosinski but it was impossible. He pulled back his burnt hand and watched with the gathering, gaping crowd as a black heap formed on the sidewalk.

This event was not recorded as a suicide, nor as an immolation in protest of anything, but as an accident caused by mental confusion brought on by the excessive use of marijuana. Any moral to be drawn was drawn by the current mentality of the media, who warned against the use of drugs.

*　　*　　*

Dear Auntie Mele,

You wouldn't believe where I am. But in order to tell you where I am I have to tell you how I got here, and in order to tell you how I got here—well, It's been a while since we talked. About a month ago, in San Francisco, I started to tell you what I was doing, to bring you up to date, but I was interrupted by my girlfriend Joan and I never got back to you because something terrible happened. Oh, there's so much to tell!

First, I guess, you will be glad to know that I graduated from University of Hawaii in three years. I am now the proud possessor of a degree in English. I have also been accepted by the Columbia School of Journalism in New York. And I am on my way to New York now. Those are the bare facts. Now here are some details, Auntie Mele, some things I can only tell you.

I am no longer a virgin. I think I told you about my boyfriend at the university, but I don't think I told you that we went all the way. I can see you looking at me now with your curious smile. You were no prude. He was very handsome, Auntie Mele, and I'm not ashamed of anything. But—you can laugh now—he was as dumb as a piece of poi—only really any good for one thing. And that's about the only thing I remember about him. Well, when I graduated, I followed in your footsteps and came to San Francisco, and you are right, "The hills of Oahu are higher than the hills of San Francisco." But it is a beautiful city. I was told by people who had been there that the place to go to meet students and people in the know was a bar called Vesuvio's, and I went there and met a very nice young man named Stan Kosinski, a crazy abstract painter, and he told me about a hotel nearby that catered to beatniks—those are young people without much money, Auntie—and where a girl would be safe, so I went there with him and got a room of my own. It's in an area where everything's pretty cheap. There are all kinds of little shops, selling beads and jewelry, clothes, and all sorts of delightful stuff.

I began going out with Stan, and pretty soon we were lovers. Then along came this couple from New York—I am with them now, driving east, but stuck for the moment, as you shall soon see—and we all became friends, Joan and Marsayas and Stan and I. We attended "Ban the Bomb" rallies and stuck flowers in the barrels of rifles of marching soldiers. It is a sort of political movement. I had seen some of it back home, but here, or in Frisco at least, the peace movement is big and growing. We are looking for peace on earth, and we hope we can bring it by example. "Love not War" is our motto.

I was just sort of going along with this movement, but Stan was very very serious about it. He was also using all kinds of drugs. He was becoming fanatical. He stopped painting and destroyed all his canvasses. He began wearing an American flag costume around the hotel and then finally on the streets. People took him for a nut. Even I began to think there was something seriously wrong with him, and pretty soon I was sure of it and had almost decided to break off with him. Then something terrible happened. I don't know whether it was an accident due to his being stoned on drugs or whether it was some crazy kind of deliberate protest, but he set himself on fire, Auntie, right outside our hotel, and he died. It was in the papers and every-thing, and I was named as his wife, Lani Kosinski, and my picture was in the paper, and Joan's picture and Marsayas's picture, and the police started rousting us about drugs and anti-Americanism and everything they could think of, and Marsayas decided we should all head East. Well, that was o.k. with me, because I was on my way to New York anyway.

I'm sure you wonder how I feel about this young man, Stan Kosinski, did I love him or what? Well, I've never known anyone who was so close and who was killed in such a horrible and senseless manner. I slept with him. I made love to him. But I don't think I loved him. I think I have only really loved one boy in my life and that was Kimo. You remember me telling you about him, don't you? That was when I was sixteen. But he married somebody and that was the end of that. Sometimes I think I still love him, but what can I do?

Now here's a very strange thing, Auntie. I have discovered that Marsayas is a friend of Kimo's, of Jimmy Whistler's, and I am likely to meet him again in New York. I read a line by the poet Lawrence Ferlinghetti that goes, "Fortune has its cookies to give out . . ." and you were right, Auntie, life is very strange, and stranger still, Auntie Mele, because I'm pregnant with Stan Kosinski's child. Marsayas tells me that he knows a doctor that will get me out of trouble and that he and Joan will take care of me until it is over.

Now, about where I am—

We got out on the Mojave dessert and Marsayas's old Chevy kinda blew up. One of those tow trucks that patrol highways looking for business came along and brought us to the nearest town, which turned out to be a town used by movie people to make westerns. Half of the town isn't even real. It's all false fronts. There is, however, a real hotel—not much of one—and a real mechanic's garage. These things, from what I gather, are needed by the movie people. There's a restaurant, too. But the town is empty, and it is very eerie to be out here in what Marsayas calls "Nowheresville." We are waiting for the local mechanic to bring us a new motor for the car. The block is split on ours, whatever that means. And it'll take just about all our money to get the car fixed. So, you see what I mean when I say you wouldn't believe where I am. I am in a ghost town, and have been here for several days, each morning expecting to see a ghostly posse come riding in with the dawn. More later . . .

*   *   *

One Friday evening, Jimmy took the Hudson Tubes, boarded a rickety old Newark bus for a half hour ride, and walked up Baldwin Avenue toward the house he thought of simply as "Baldwin," a big, gray, peeling, Victorian house, full of turrets and gables, with a large, sittable porch, and a short, overstuffed lawn, buttressed with a foot high wall of stone; a rooming house where the fallen came to rise and the risen came to fall; where nothing and everything mattered; where the incurably but, it was presumed, safely, mad were "mainlined" from gloomy institutions like Vineland for the hopelessly sad and sometimes mad and even bad, to build a little life the state was duty-bound to finance; where some committed suicide and others made incessant wars on phantasmal enemies; where the dipso- and the tulipomaniac smiled different visions from the porch; where all was well and well was ill; where life was crazily life, and death death.

For some, it may have been the dawning of the Age of Aquarius, but for the Whistlers there was nothing really new about the onset of the Sixties. They had been practicing a dressed-up, permanent-waved and clean-shaved version of

134

hippiedom since Jimmy could remember. Their knockabout life-style had been initiated with the Crash of Twenty-nine and developed to a fine art during the Depression and the War, the best years of their lives. They had taken the job of superintending Baldwin while Jimmy was in the service. Fay collected the rents, kept the books, and did the cleaning, as usual, while Elliot sat at the kitchen table, amid the debris, wearing one of his ancient, handsome, tailored suits, smoking a kingsized Chesterfield, and guzzling cheap sherry.

But something new had been added. For the past few years Elliot had been taking amphetamines in the morning and shouting at the neighbors on their way to work, "*GOOD MORNING*!" and taking Miltowns at night and whispering "*sweet dreams!*" On and off he went, like a rhythmic lamp. Now in his late sixties, his hair salty; his big brown eyes rheumy; his sandalwood cheeks jowly, he looked like the collar-ad man of the Thirties thirty years later. He was an enigma, a mystery. Jimmy could not understand him, could not understand why a man who had been so successful a stock broker as to be in *Who's Who in America* in 1919 should be content to marry an uneducated former mill-girl and housemaid and sell for a living anything from Bibles to pots and pans on a door-to-door basis. Nor could he understand why Elliot had pulled him out of school after school as a child, and moved them about the country so often that no place was home. He felt that Elliot had treated him unfairly and irresponsibly, that he had destabilized his childhood and ruined his early education. No, Jimmy did not understand Elliot, but he loved him, anyway, someway, somehow, sort of.

After Elliot sank into a comatose dementia that evening, Jimmy took Fay out for a drink in a bar on Clinton Avenue, the main drag of Newark's black ghetto, a few blocks down from Baldwin, and a photographer, with a Polaroid, took a picture of them. There they sat, in a big corner booth, Jimmy in a seersucker suit and sport shirt, with his poodle-cut

Blondy curls shimmering all over his head, very self-consciously producing his best actor's profile, and Fay facing another way entirely, one eyebrow arched in her favorite look of intelligent and witty observation, as though she were about to turn to Jimmy and comment on a fandango dancer's behind; one pretty-well-manicured hand fingering her best costume necklace, the other in a frozen pose of raising a cork-tipped cigarette that, immediately upon the flashbulb's death, would be returned to the ashtray from which it had come, untouched (it was Jimmy's).

"Do you miss Vera?" she asked.

"It's peaceful. I can write."

"I never liked her—you know that."

"I know. But let's stay off her."

"She calls sometimes, asking about you, but I don't tell her anything."

"Well, don't. She used to lay in wait for me outside the bookstore. That's why I quit. It's got to be a clean break. If I went back to her, it would just be the same old thing. She was always nagging at me about being an actor. But I don't want to be an actor, I want to be a poet. I've just won a prize. I'm beginning to get somewhere."

"But, Jimmy, poets don't make any money, do they?"

Jimmy changed the subject. How could he tell her he was going to be a bum?

Bum. Beatnik. Hippie. Whoever didn't work in a factory or an office for a lifetime, and then retire, and be old, and be dead. Elliot was downwardly mobile. Fay was upwardly hopeful, but feckless. They had been hippies since the Twenties but they didn't know it, and would not have found it possible to have seen themselves that way. Fay would have said, "We always dress well," but they had been running away from bad checks for as long as Jimmy could remember. And yet Fay looked askance at Jimmy for being a poet, as had Vera. How can you love someone who doesn't love what you love? Who despises you for loving it, and despises *it* as a rival?

Jimmy being a poet was the one thing that those two, Vera and Fay, could agree on—both against it, against the only thing that really meant anything to him. Around him the world was coming apart at its seams; the Cold War seemed to be building to some terrible climacteric; but he didn't care. He knew others might disagree with him, but he felt that it was a rotten time to be young—a time when a few fools with bombs could subsume into politics every other noble human endeavor. At times he didn't care if the world blew up, although he doubted that the fools with the bombs had even the courage for a full-scale exchange. But he could take no chances. He had to write one lightening-struck poem before what may or may not come.

For Jimmy, it seemed a time of double doom. Beyond that amorphous-end-of-the-world threat that seemed to permeate the air they breathed, there was a more definite, immediate, and frightening one. It was obvious to even the casual observer that Elliot was killing himself; and, if he died, Jimmy's sense of duty would demand that he take care of Fay, an ignorant, and, as Elliot would have said, *negative* force. This prospect represented doom to Jimmy's dream of being a poet; this was the secret fear that led him to live as if nothing mattered and every day was his last. He needed time to come to grips with his work, and Elliot's self-indulgent life threatened Jimmy with Fay's negative proximity. Elliot stood between them like a guard at a gate, whether Elliot realized it or not, protecting Jimmy from Fay's destructive capacities. Fay did not simply dislike, but *hated* everything she didn't understand, and she did not understand poets or poetry. Jimmy feared Elliot's death and Fay's proximity more than he feared an atomic Armageddon. Elliot's death would be doomsday.

The next morning, sitting around the kitchen table, Fay showed Elliot the photo she and Jimmy had had taken the night before. After a few pickmeups, Elliot and Jimmy decided to buy a used Polaroid themselves at a pawn shop and take pictures of customers in the bars and night spots around Greenwich Village. After all, Jimmy reasoned, it was the weekend and he was entitled to a little recreation. He did love his father, in spite of everything, and it would give them some time together, an adventure.

Elliot was always ready to go into some kind of scheme, the crazier the better. Recently he had been talking about opening a phrenology parlor in Greenwich Village. To supplement his social security, he had been managing an Angel's Own thrift shop, where he came upon a porcelain head, the kind with the skull mapped off in sections, the sections conforming to mental and character qualities such as Conjugality, Inhabitiveness, Alimentiveness, etc. He had read up on the subject, bringing home books by or about Gall, Spurzheim, Combe, the Fowler brothers, and others among the famous bump-readers of the world. By now, he fancied himself an expert. No one knew how seriously he took it.

The photography scheme, or Jimmy's inebriated view of it that Saturday morning, was that Elliot would put up the capital for the camera and Jimmy would run around like Weegee, the famous candid photographer, taking pictures galore all over Greenwich Village, making a fortune, of course, which he'd split with Elliot, and at the same time making himself a famous Village character, like Maxwell Bodenheim or Little Joe Gould. Everybody would know him; and when he flew, busy and vigorous, in the door of a Village dive, they'd say, "Hey, there's Jimmy Whistler, the famous candid photographer, and he's packing his Polaroid!" Fay was to stay behind, and, as Elliot advised, "Keep the home fires burning" (which suited her fine, for she had, that morning, "an awful hangover"), while Elliot (who phoned downtown and got himself a leave of absence from the Angels' Own stores on the grounds of receiving medical treatment) and Jimmy went to the Village to make their fortune. As soon as they could afford to move into a Park Avenue apartment, they would send for Fay. Then she could pack up all her cleaning paraphernalia, pay back whatever money she had embezzled from Baldwin's books to its owner, Howard Burns, and give up superintending forever. She could be like the Society Ladies she was forever reading about in the columns of Dorothy Kilgallen and Cholly Knickerbocker in the newspapers.

On the train Elliot got up and swung and swayed his way to the end of the car; and, in full view of his fellow passengers, who believed he was about to pee, perhaps disappointed them by removing, with what he seemed to think was great stealth, a half-pint bottle of Haig & Haig from his hip pocket, and slugging—judging from the number of times his head bobbed—three good! stiff! drinks! He put the bottle back in his pocket, patted it; and, returning down the aisle of the racing, rocking, underground-going train, smiling and nodding in a most gentlemanly manner at the frowning or grinning faces he passed, proceeded to sit down on the wrong side of Jimmy, placing himself slowly and carefully on a young woman's lap; even having time, in his *sang froid*, to pull up the sharp creases of his shiny trousers, and to cross his legs, before the dumbstruck victim could figure out whether to scream or not. Fortunately, she was a good-natured young woman, and only tapped him on the shoulder from behind with her dainty rose-tipped fingers, saying, "Sir—oh, sir— you're sitting on my lap, sir—" Elliot finally got the message, removed himself from her lap; and, with many a courtly flourish of apology, tried to undo his wrong. Jimmy shrank in embarrassment, especially now that Elliot strap-hung over the poor, sweet kid, grinning at her, his handsome, debauched old face not an inch from hers, and his breath smelling like a tub of hooch. They pulled into the station that way, like a sideshow.

They began their career in photography, as they had planned, by making the rounds of the Village bars. In five hours of steady drinking (they *had* to have a drink in these places; it wouldn't look good to just walk in and out—as Elliot put it, "You have to spend money to make money."), they ran across one prospective customer, a tattooed sailor in a bar over near the docks who had a couple of bimbos with him and wanted them to go to a hotel and take porno pictures. He wanted to show his shipmates what a good time he had had on shore.

Elliot and Jimmy held a conference and decided not to do this because the sailor was drunk and rowdy and they didn't want to get into trouble with the law. Too bad they didn't take the gig, however, because they never got another offer of work. Their drunken dreams of fame and fortune in the art of photography were shattered that evening, as was the lens of their camera (the disappointed sailor had knocked it from Jimmy's hands). But they were resilient; they'd find another way to make a fortune. Elliot was keener than ever on the phrenology parlor and he decided to stay with Jimmy while he solidified his plans.

During the next few weeks, big Denise would come downstairs to Jimmy's breadbox of a room and create a crowd of three. They would hold long philosophical discussions, Denise touting Locke or John Dewey and whatever liberals she had in her bag, Elliot being legalistic with Coke and Blackstone and Roscoe Pound, and Jimmy spouting Bergson and the *elan vital.*

Denise and Elliot turned on and off like a couple of blinker-lights. "Here," Denise would say, "try some of these, Mr. Whistler. They'll bring you down a little."

"I've never seen any little red ones like these before," Elliot would say, like a connoisseur, studying the bottle by holding it up to the light while pulling his broken, adhesive-taped, five-and-ten-cent store glasses down to the tip of his rubicund nose. "What are they?"

"They're a barbiturate of some sort; I'm not sure."

"I don't like barbiturates, Denise. They always leave me with a headache."

"Oh, these don't, Mr. Whistler. Go ahead and try one. It's just a gentle trip down. Nice and smooth."

"Well, I'll try one—I'd like to come down just a little;" and he'd flip it in. "By the way, Denise, I was reading DeRopp on hashish. Do you suppose you could get some?"

"Oh, I don't know, Mr. Whistler, it's kind of tight right now. But I'll try." And they'd sit there, a handsome, un-shaven, grizzled old man in his stained underwear, and a big, unkempt young woman, not much more than a kid—he on the cot, and she, cross-legged, in the lotus position, on the floor at his big pink feet—exchanging pills and popping them, until neither of them was talking to the other anymore, but just talk-ing—talking to the hooded mystery guest, to the shrouded stranger.

One night, Jimmy felt a little left out of the drug induced communion his "guests" were enjoying and decided to take his last quart of ale over and see Phyllis. He tapped on her door and she invited him in to that dim psychedelic haven, her apartment. They sat side by side on the mattress and split the ale, talking and gazing into the flames of a couple of giant oozing candles stuck on the stained coffee table. Jimmy slipped his hand under Phyllis's bony bottom and pulled her closer. She did not resist. She did not resist anything for about the next half hour. Indeed, he was surprised by her boldness. She stood up and stripped in the candlelight as he lay back waiting to see. His interest was not merely sexual, and certainly not sensual. He was curious. What were her clothes hiding? She appeared in them so frail, bodiless, whispy. She had told him that she had broken up with her boyfriend, that his overtures were welcome. But the boy-friend's picture sat on a table near the mattress, overseeing the scene, a good-looking black fellow—named Reginald— of about Jimmy's size and build. What had he seen in her, this whispy girl-woman, this pale, Dachau-thin girl? She was naked in the candle-lit room, all dark out of the candles' range, and small and white as a Roswell alien, as the body of a flying-saucer creature taken from a crashed spacecraft. She stepped forward, so that he could see her face again. She had removed her glasses and her eyes looked large and dark and upward slanted, but he knew them to be pale, the palest blue, and her let-down hair was just a glow of soft light, waving about her narrow, bony shoulders, that had no meat on them, no muscle-mass at all, and tugged at his shoes, clump, clump, and his socks, and his blue jeans, and his jockey shorts, tug, tug, tug, off, off, off, and she eased herself down astraddle on him, and he held her back and rolled them over and found that he could feel himself through her paper-thin back, could al-most grip his own organ, as he thrusted in his gentlest slow-motion. But he found that there was no sensual response in her at all; she seemed merely to want to please him but did not have the strength nor the passion to be anymore respon-sive than to wait for his orgasm and in the most off-key way whisper, "That was good."

It was all a terrible letdown, an anticlimax, so to speak, and, as he withdrew, he began to laugh, a low and sorrowful laugh it was, more pain than pleasure in it, and she asked him what he was thinking.

"Thinking," he said, "I believe that's what you've been doing." But she flung herself against him and clutched at him.

"Oh I love you," she cried. But he, used to the physical passion of Vera, the athlete, the dancer, and others as physical and passionate, tried to grasp what she had got from the encounter. Her tears were genuine. He could feel them welling up in her thin breastless breastbone, throbbing in her throat, a vibration in the vein in her neck. He held her back and looked at her and everything he saw looked genuine.

"I never come," she said. "I can't come. I guess I just don't have the hormones in me. That was one of the problems Reginald and I had. He was very hurt that he couldn't make me come. He said that he just knocked himself out trying. He gave up on me. Please don't give up on me, Jimmy."

And later, when Jimmy stood and put his crumpled trousers back on, he extended his hand to Phyllis, pulled her up, and hugged her. He patted her soft, no-color hair and remembered ruefully his vow to remain unentangled with women, their demands, their needs, and sometimes, their due. He walked back to his room through the hot, humid New York night filled with city lights, vaguely trying to discern if he was sinking or swimming, or merely floating.

*　　*　　*

A week or so later, at some vague, pilled-up point, Elliot, feeling grandiose, told Denise that he had written a history of Rome. He was honest enough to say, "I didn't quite finish it, but what I did of it exceeded Gibbon, if I say so myself."

"I didn't know you were a writer, too, Mr. Whistler. Oh wow!"

"I'm a professional, Denise. The W.P.A.—you know what that is, or was?"

"Of course. My folks were New Dealers. The Works Project Administration."

"Exactly! You are a very wise young woman. You not only know ancient history, you know modern history. If it weren't for the fact that you were a woman, I should call you a gentleman and a scholar."

"Women are scholars today, Mr. Whistler."

"And Denise is very much a gentleman," said Jimmy.

She gave him a pilled-up look and he smiled back, nodding approval. Then she nodded back in a sort of salute.

Elliot said, "I wrote many a speech for Mayor Parnell of Newark. I wrote the great anti-reefer speech."

"But you didn't believe it—?"

"We writers sometimes have to say things for the public consumption. You're sophisticated enough to understand that, I dare say."

"Certainly! Oh, Mr. Whistler, you could help me so much! "

"How could I do that, my dear?"

"It's my thesis for Columbia. I've tried and I've tried and I just can't seem to write it."

"Try cutting back on the pills, Denise," said Jimmy.

"Nonsense! I find them a tremendous help—don't you, Mr. Whistler?"

"In getting the mind operating with full cargo and at full speed, indubitably, yes. Now, how can I help you?"

"I'm supposed to write a thesis on John Donne."

"I'm not sure I'm—"

"John Donne, Dad, the poet," said Jimmy.

"Of course, John Donne. The poet!"

"I'll supply you with all my notes, over two year's worth."

"And I shall have to read them. I mean—"

"I'll pay you five hundred dollars."

"Five hundred dollars?"

"I'll give you fifty to start you off."

"Yeees, I see. Now when would this thesis have to be completed?"

"As soon as possible—a month?"

"And you say you've been trying to do it for two years?"

"Yes, but I just can't get started."

"We have an agreement. Jimmy, you stand witness. I shall write this thesis before a month is out. Now, about the fifty dollars—"

Denise pulled fifty dollars from her wallet and slapped it into his big hand. "We're on our way," she said.

"We're on our way," Elliot repeated, grinning darkly. His grinning, approving teeth floated in a glass at his elbow.

*   *   *

Jimmy and Elliot were having a bit of trouble, what with Jimmy trying to work and Elliot walking up and down his back all night. In fact, they were a little sour on each other. Jimmy slept on the floor and Elliot slept on the sagging single bed, really only a cot; and they hardly had room to turn around in. Jimmy's peaceful existence was fading a little more with each day that Elliot stayed, as were his joys of a single life, because with each sleepwalking night he was almost run out of his room to the apartment on Houston Street and Phyllis. It was maddening to Jimmy. In the middle of the night Elliot would wake up from his rumbling sleep, throw his huge pink feet over the side of the bed and right onto Jimmy's back, and wobble down Jimmy's spine like a tightrope walker. Then, Hey, Presto, the lights would come on, with a *"FIAT LUX!"*

"Dad," Jimmy'd say, "for Christ's sake, do you have to walk down my back?"

"What?" Elliot would say, oblivious. "Oh, I'm sorry, my boy. I just wanted to take another Miltown and have a couple of spoonfuls of peanut butter."

"Miltown! You're like a zombie already!"

But Elliot wouldn't pay any attention to that, or perhaps couldn't.

"Have you seen that bottle of sherry I bought yesterday?"

145

Jimmy'd have to get up and look for the bottle, which was usually on the table, right under Elliot's nose, among the dirty litter of pill bottles, sticky glasses, left-over, skin-topped clam chowder cups, and the always delightful-looking sets of false teeth. Then back to sleep for an hour or two, if there weren't other trips up and down his spine, and off to work Jimmy'd go, at some temp job of the moment, feeling like Quasimodo. He wasn't doing any writing at all.

When Elliot got the chance to pick up the fifty from Denise, he already had it in his noodle to blow, and the night after she gave him the money, he vanished, leaving Jimmy to convince Denise, who had been a good friend, that he knew nothing about what his Dad was up to. The double-dealing old con-artist! Jimmy was sore. Elliot had been living on him for weeks, and Jimmy was behind in the rent, and Miss Byrdsong, was swooping down like a vulture on him for it.

Jimmy had a good idea that Elliot wouldn't show up back there; but he wasn't sure yet. So, when she asked him, he told Denise he thought his Dad had just gone to Newark for a few days to check in with his Mom; for her, Denise, not to worry; that Elliot would probably get started on her thesis while he was over there and bring it back with him when he came. That kept Denise happy for a day or two, then she started getting worried again. Jimmy called Fay. Elliot hadn't showed up. Fay was a little worried, but not too. After all, she knew Elliot. He was probably parked in some hotel room, either in New York or Newark, having a maid run his errands for him. After about a week Jimmy called Fay again and Elliot was there all right, sobering up. He had been hiding out in a Philadelphia hotel.

"What about Denise's paper?" Jimmy asked him. "Or her money?"

"Tell her I'll give her her money back as soon as I get my social security check," he said. He sounded sick, so Jimmy didn't push it too far. Only thing was, Denise was after Jimmy now. So he said: "Denise wants to know where you live. Should I tell her?"

"For God's sake, no! I'll send her the money when I get it. You can't get blood from a turnip, can you?"

Elliot sounded beat; so Jimmy said, "O.K., O.K.," and let it go at that. He knew that Elliot was going to dry out for a couple of weeks, eat, and take vitamins, and sleep, until he was his old ruddy, rosy sixty-eight year old self again. He figured Elliot would pay Denise off, now that he was getting sobered up. What he had forgotten was that Fay had been living on Howard Burns's house-money all this time, juggling the roomers' rents in the books like a champion embezzler. Elliot would have to replace that money, so he might not be able to pay Denise back. A few more days passed, and Jimmy couldn't hold Denise off any more, and he didn't have enough money to pay her himself, having to fork over every extra cent he earned to Miss Byrdsong, who had become a double-barreled bitch since Elliot had taken off, Elliot having apparently given her reason to believe that there might be something between them (the old goat); so Jimmy gave Denise the address in Newark, and his blessings into the bargain—let the principals fight it out; Jimmy was only an agent, an unwilling broker. Denise took off for Newark, angry, now, and hurt, and determined, and formidable, too.

Elliot's pomaded, neatly-combed hair stood right up on end when he saw her come in the door. She said:

"Mr. Whistler, I'm surprised at you. I thought you were a gentleman, and I discover instead that you can't be trusted. I should have remembered what Jimmy told me once about how you stole his money when he was in the Marines."

Fay smelled Elliot's blood and wanted some of it. She chimed in: "I know; it's *terrible*. Elliot, you've got to pay this girl what you owe her." Fay was only on Denise's side because she was angry at Elliot for leaving her to steal from the landlord.

Elliot had been caught off guard. His social security check was sitting on the table, right under Denise's nose. She saw it through her hornrims and said to him: "I'm going to stay right here until you pay me;" whereupon she sat down, opened *The Brothers Karamazov*, and began to read with great concentration. Elliot considered running her out, but she was too big. Fay offered her something to eat and began to prepare a little spread. Denise began cutting slices from a leg of lamb that was on the table, and that decided it. Elliot figured if he didn't get a move on to cash that check Denise would devour the whole larder. He hurried up to the supermarket on the corner, cashed his check, and hurried back, forked over the five tens to Denise, and sat down, fuming.

"Thank you, Mr. Whistler," Denise said. "I cannot say that I have enjoyed our dealings. Good day."

"Goodbye," called Fay, from the front porch, waving her to the bus stop on the corner. "Come back and see us— any friend of Jimmy's is always welcome."

A month passed and Jimmy regained his solitude at Miss Byrdsong's. Though he was working at physically demanding jobs during the day his mind seemed strangely alert and ambitious at five o'clock. Even the rejection slips that he'd taped to the wall seemed to inspire him, now that he'd won a prize.

CHAPTER SIX

THE HALF-WAY HOUSE

> *I ask you where you want to go*
> *you say nowhere*
> *but your eyes make a wish . . .*
> —*Leonard Cohen*

THE NEW YORK TIMES
APRIL 7, 1961

U.S. AND BRITAIN TO WEIGH ACTION IN VIETNAM CRISIS

THE NEW YORK TIMES
APRIL 17, 1961

ANTI-CASTRO UNITS LAND IN CUBA; REPORT FIGHTING AT BEACHHEAD; RUSK SAYS U.S. WON'T INTERVENE

Marsayas was back, his Frisco adventure having been short-circuited by the police after Stan Kosinski's death. He tried to reach Jimmy at the bookstore, and, after much cajoling, one of the clerks gave out the communal phone number for Miss Byrdsong's, which was supposed to be top secret. Denise! But Marsayas said it wasn't.

Marsayas told Jimmy that he and Joan had been looking for and had found an apartment, and invited Jimmy over to

Brooklyn for a combined homecoming and house-warming party. He had a flat on the second floor of a house in a patch of houses off the Manhattan Bridge, a house that contained, on its first floor, a small funeral parlor. When Marsayas had asked the landlady if he could use the backyard for his party, she had given permission. He had bought a keg of beer and bottles of various wines and whiskies, and it was going to be a veritable Bacchanalia, it was, yes sir! It was good to hear Marsayas's pleasant baritone.

"Where'd you get the bread?" Jimmy asked.

"Ah," said Marsayas, "Joan is prego, so I've had to go back on my vow about never working again. But it's only temporary. I'm editing How-To books. An old buddy of mine, named Butterworth, whom you'll meet—an ex-Marine like you—put me on to it. I've got my kitchen rigged up like the city room of the *New York Times*! Saturday, now—bring anybody you can get. We've brought a swinging chick back from Frisco. And—get this—she knows you. But, dig you later. Oh, I almost forgot—congrats on your poetry prize!" Bang!

*　　*　　*

Dear Auntie Mele,

Sad and weak, but relieved. Sad but hopeful too. Isn't it strange? I carried the baby, poor Stan Kosinski's baby, almost all the way across this vast land, but now it is gone, gone as if it never had been. What a shame for him! It? Stan? But I am liberated. Mother would have condemned me for doing this, I suppose, but I know that you won't. But I think, Mother is with Auntie Mele now, how long? Three years. Please, Auntie, explain to her why I had to do it. Explain it to her. She was such a good Christian girl and no one ever accused you of being that. You were practical, even as you were an adventuress. Pragmatic. You might not know what

150

that word means but it is what you were. Your booming laughter was pragmatic. Oh, I wish I were a child and in your arms again! Remember oh so many nights we slept together when I was little? Now there is no one left. Daddy is enjoying business success and, as I'm sure you know, has a new woman. He sends me money if I ask but never questions me about its use. He sent me the money for this abortion without asking what it was for, so why should I confide in him? I'm not close to anyone anymore, only you. Tonight I am so very lonely.

I drove the whole length of this huge, empty country with Marsayas and Joan and they dropped me off here, Bucks County, Pennsylvania, with his friend, Doctor Brazil, a retired doctor, who is also an artist, a painter, and who owns this farm, and who will occasionally perform an abortion for someone who needs a friend. Still, I had to pay him. But it was much less than it might have been if he hadn't been a friend of Marsayas's. He prefers, too, to keep a person like me here for rest for a few days. He says I need fresh air and good food and he supplies the latter. He's a wonderful man, and I like his paintings too.

Don't worry too much about my state of mind. I didn't love Stan Kosinski, which would have made this situation truly terrible for me, and it is only a case of the blues from which I suffer, nothing dreadful or permanent. And I mentioned being hopeful and you are probably wondering what that is about. Well, I am ninety percent certain that I am going to meet Kimo again. Marsayas told me about his friend, the poet— Jim the Poet, Marsayas calls him—Jim, Jim, Jimmy Whistler! Oh, I know he's married and all that, but at least I can see him again. Oh, Lord, how much I loved him once—or maybe still do. I have his picture in my mind. I see him then so clearly and I wonder how he will look now. Marasayas is going to come and get me and take me back to the city and I am going to stay with him and Joan 'til I get settled somewhere and Marsayas says he'll find Kimo and bring him to meet me. It's my dream come true, Auntie. Sometimes I thought that it would never, ever happen, but now here it is. I have a room on the second floor of this old farmhouse and I can see out the window from where I am, and I see the moon and think that he might be looking at it too. He is somewhere only a few hundred miles from me now. I am crying and must stop.

*   *   *

Saturday was one of those resplendent days when the sun seems to be coming from everywhere—out of the jet-streamed blue and burnished-gold of the sky, up from the city pavements, and from, as John Donne once put it, "the round earth's imagined corners." Denise and Jimmy trekked from the Village to the dark and dangerous Lower East Side along Houston Street, where the boccie-players were out in numbers and arguing in Italian across the shimmering heat waves. They picked up little Phyllis and took the subway to Brooklyn.

When they arrived, the front, parlor-floor door was propped wide open—stairs up, presumably to the party in Marsayas's flat, hall straight ahead to the open back door, yard and more party beyond. Jimmy heard Marsayas's voice booming out back, and pushed Denise and Phyllis toward it. An old Medusa with wormy hair, the landlady, presumably, popped out into the hall.

"You'll wake the dead, you beatniks!" she screamed. "You'll wake the dead!" and vanished behind a slammed door. Phyllis said: "Oh, bad vibes!"

Jimmy said, "Marsayas should have invited her."

152

"Don't be paranoid!" said Denise, smelling the food with lustfully flared nostrils. In the middle of the weedy, balloon-bobbing backyard, host and hostess had set up card tables and loaded them with cold cuts, barbequed chickens and ribs, and all the red, white, and green trimmings—plus booze and beer. Hops and fried onions in the air! A dozen or so people cavorted in grass that needed a trim.

Jimmy spotted Marsayas, raised his arm in salute, and cried: "Hail to thee, blithe spirit!"

"Jimmy!" Giant Marsayas lifted Jimmy's quarterback body and swung it in a circle as if it were a ballerina's.

Jimmy introduced his friends, one glazed with appetite and one with paranoia.

"Dig!"

"Dig!"

"Dig!"

"Dig!"

Denise dragged Phyllis to the food.

"I want to introduce you to my other buddy, Butter—ah, Butterworth."

Marsayas led Jimmy up to a blond, crew-cutted, icy-eyed chap, the only person in view who looked straighter than Jimmy. He wore a tan tropical suit.

"I've always wanted you two crazy guys to meet," said Marsayas. "Imagine—an ex-Marine poet, and an ex-Marine Platonist."

"When were you in?" asked Butterworth. "*Active*, I mean. There's no such thing as an *ex*-Marine."

"I'm very ex."

"You only think so."

"I joined at the drooping tail-end of the Korean police lunacy," Jimmy said. "I was working as a candy-butcher in Minsky's Burlesque in Newark, and I got fired over a fight. I was just seventeen and wanted to put some order in my life."

"Qualify for the Korean Bill?"

"Just."

"Use it?"

"Some of it. I dropped out. NYU and a couple of drama schools."

"Butter," said Marsayas, "was an education officer."

"I was a corporal, an M.P. I had a good friend who was an education officer, as a matter of fact."

"You, Jimmy!" cried Marsayas. "How could you?"

"What?"

"Be a cop?"

"I was young."

"You must have been," said Butterworth. "You still look young. I served in Korea. Pork Chop Hill. Heard of it?"

"Yup. Is that an officer's tropical uniform you're wearing?"

"Yeah. After Korea, I joined the active reserves. Just been on training. Didn't have anything to wear—can't go home; fallen out with the little woman. I took off my captain's bars and insignia. Tried to turn it into mufti."

"Plato was a fascist," said Marsayas. "Butter teaches philosophy," he informed Jimmy. "Plato wouldn't have any poets in his Republic."

"Poets!" said Butterworth with contempt. "It's my job to defend that flag."

Marsayas ignored Butterworth. "He's nuts. Once we're settled, I'm going to make him an Orgone Box."

"Vera needed an Orgone Box," said Jimmy.

"Wise man on that score—to get out, I mean," said Marsayas. "She'd've driven you bonkers. Lunacy's contagious, you know." He aimed the red rays of his beard over Jimmy's head and marched off. In a few minutes he was sitting on a tree stump, the central ton of a group, and reading aloud from a piece he had written on communal living among the American Indians, entitled *Sex in Longhouses*.

Jimmy went upstairs to the flat, beer in hand, to relieve himself. He found the bathroom and was about to enter it when a lovely creature flew by him, lifting her skirt and displaying soft and delightful cheeks contained in pale panties. Bam! The bathroom door was shut. Jimmy waited, looking around. He could see that Marsayas was again painting seriously—well, prolifically. The flat, what Jimmy could see of it, was filled with canvasses, wildly bespattered, a la Jackson Pollock (Marsayas was an expressionist). The kitchen overlooked the back yard; the bathroom was off the kitchen.

The bathroom was still occupado—no, it had been occupied again; because the lovely who had beaten him to it sat at the kitchen table drinking a beer with Joan. There was an empty chair near the table. Jimmy grabbed it, put it at the table, sat down, and crossed his legs tightly.

"Whoever's in the bathroom," yelled Joan, "Jimmy-the-Poet's got to pee."

"Thank you, my dear," said Jimmy. "I'm floating in it."

"I have been given to understand that you can't float."

Somebody emerged from the bathroom, but somebody got in before Jimmy could make his move. He turned back to Joan. "Wait a minute," he said. "What did you mean about me floating—not floating—whatever?"

Joan told him about Lani Kosinski.

"So that's what Marsayas meant about somebody who knows me. But . . . Kosinski? Is she married?"

"No. That's just what we call her, because when we met her she was living with a guy named Kosinski." Joan went on to tell Jimmy the sad tale of Stan Kosinski. "That's why we're back here."

"But where is she? Is she here?"

"We dropped her off with some old relatives in Pennsylvania, but Marsayas is going up to get her, I think, next week. She told me all about your Hawaiian idyl."

"God, I never thought I'd see her again."

"That's just about what she said. Were you two in love?"

"No," said Jimmy. He lit a cigarette and appeared to go off into another reality field. "Well, maybe it was puppy love, you know. It's so amazing to think of seeing her again. She was . . . like a . . . like a dream. Like Annabelle Lee—

> She was a child and I was a child
> In a kingdom by the sea. . ."

"I think you were in love," said Joan with motherly superiority.

"Leilani Kona," said Jimmy dreamily. "Sweet Leilani." His eyes came back to Joan's as if from a faraway place. "Lani Kosinski," he said, nodding affirmatively, as if to get it right.

"And no little girl, either. Wait till you see her."

Jimmy's mind began to drift back to Hawaii, when his shoulder was seized by a large hand. "Hi, dere, fluffy," came a loud, deep, heavily-accented voice.

It was Oskar, a young German painter Marsayas had befriended. Jimmy had met him before, and it was to Jimmy he spoke. He had picked up the word "fluffy" somewhere and applied it to everyone and anyone as a sort of ambiguous term of ridicule and affection. He was a handsome kid, in a black-maned, hard-featured German way: about eighteen, six-foot-five, a hundred-and-fifty pounds; wore hornrimmed glasses, like Denise, and looked intellectual. Beside him was his girlfriend, Niki Walkup, a lispy hoyden about six feet tall, an artists' model. Jimmy liked big, stringbean Oskar, who always seemed to be laughing.

Seeing the bathroom door standing ajar, Jimmy shot to his feet; "Excuse me," he said, and made for it. The bathroom was whitewashed and puzzled with light from a Venetian blind with broken, crazy slats. His bladder was flatter before he realized that somebody was sitting in the old claw-footed tub: a little woman, fully dressed. Phyllis! She was filling the room with marijuana fumes. Hmmm!

"Gee, I'm sorry," he said. "I didn't see you there."

"It's O.K., Jim" she said. "I couldn't have got up any-how."

"What's the matter?"

"I got sick. Denise made me eat cold meat, that necro-philic stuff that comes in plastic at supermarkets."

"Baloney?"

"Food from the bullshit world!" She sighed. "I puked my guts out. But it may have been that old lady—the one in the hall when we came in? She gave off bad vibes, and I'm sensitive to people, you know."

"How do *I* seem?"

"You're O.K., Jim. You're always O.K. Let's talk. Lock the door, or the madding crowd'll be in here pissing and puking and God knows what! I only opened it to see if Denise was around. Let them piss in the garden. It's a garden party, isn't it?"

Jimmy hooked the door's eye.

"I'm stoned already. I'm looking for an ontological def-inition of reality," she said.

"Me too," said Jimmy. He was getting a contact high. "Why are *you* looking?"

"Because I'm me, and I don't have big boobs."

"Yeah," said Jimmy. "It's about the same with me."

"You're very sensitive, Jimmy. "I've been reading the poetry you left at my place."

"Do you like it?"

"Yes. Did Denise tell you that we went to the Univer-sity of Washington together? We both studied poetry with Theodore Roethke."

"Did you? I like Roethke. What was he like?"

"Big! Big body, big eyes, big belly, big voice. He used to come in the classroom and jump up on his desk and recite.

He'd shout that he was the greatest love poet of all. Sometimes he'd go outside and run around the flagpole until the men in white suits came and took him away. He was scared, ontologically speaking, like me. He lived in the far field—Eternity."

"There's not much use in being scared."

"No? Let me tell you—"

She told him how she had suffered in her childhood from the most amazing series of maladies. There had been strep throats, culminating in a definite rheumatic heart; then pneumonia almost claimed her; measles and whooping cough and scarlet fever followed in close succession, leaving her little time to regain her strength from one before the next was upon her; then there had been mysterious fevers, rashes, and other symptoms that at one point had led a doctor to diagnose her as leukemic; but these had passed as strangely as they had come; and just when her poor parents, an airline pilot and a former stewardess, believed her to be on the road to recovery, she was hit by mononucleosis, and confined to her bed for nearly a year. "Is it any wonder that I'm paranoid?" she summed up. "I don't even have regular periods."

"Yes, but you survived it all. So in a way, you're a winner."

"You're nice, Jimmy. Do you think we'll all be blown off the planet?"

"No."

"You're brave."

"No, I just have an abiding faith in greed and cowardice."

"Do you think we'll put a man on the moon someday?"

"Yes; and a woman. And then, ad astra!"

"Do you think life is tragic?"

"No, mostly comic. We're all apes. Our leaders are self-important, idiot silverbacks. Madness is congenital to the human race."

She sighed. "We're young."

"And vulnerable?"

"As rocks," she said, and they both laughed.

*   *   *

Jimmy and Oskar teamed up, getting jobs at agencies with names like Strong Arm Labor, Inc., or Profit Power. Sometimes these agencies sent them out with a bunch of derelicts and winos to "knob 'em," to place samples of soap or fabric-softener on doorknobs in fancy neighborhoods. They loaded trucks, and washed cars. It was strenuous but it left time for both of them; for Oskar to paint and Jimmy to write. Then one day they found a home: a Long Island catering house where they were employed to wash dishes, change the sets in several banquet halls, etc. They worked weekends at Tony's Halfway House.

One Friday afternoon, Oskar arrived first. "Hi, dere, Fluffy!" he called from the kitchen door. "Looking for a job? We got lots of verk for you here. Know anything about shit?" He had a little cup of coffee in one big hand and a little pipe in the other. He stuck the pipe in his mouth and made spitty sounds. "Gotdammit! It's gone out again." He knocked the tobacco out of the pipe and stuck it in his pocket. "Gimme a cigarette, Fluffy."

Jimmy lit the cigarette he had given Oskar, his lighter with the Marine insignia of globe and anchor and fierce, spreading eagle glinting in the evening sun under Oskar's neatly trimmed and slightly silly black mustache. Behind Jimmy and all around the sprawling, T-shaped stucco building that housed Tony's Half-Way House was a tarmac parking lot, and expensive-looking cars were already parked here and there, glimmering in monied repose. Beyond the parking lot lay the greenery of a Long Island country town, and beyond that the town itself, and the railway station by which

159

Jimmy had come and would go, fifty dollars richer, on Sunday night.

"Oh, here you are." It was Covetti, Tony's maitre d'. Jimmy didn't like working with Covetti. They didn't click.

"Let's get busy here—Jim, Oskar—I want you to make the salad for the first party; it starts at eight—we haven't got any time for breaks. Come on, let's go!"

"Vhat da hell," cried Oskar, waving his long arms and grinning, "der's plenty of time. Ver just having a shmoke."

"Oskar—I said, let's go!"

"Gotdammit!" grumbled Oskar. But they went on into the kosher kitchen.

Tony's had two huge fully-equipped kitchens, one for kosher and one for non-kosher parties. There was actually no difference between the two kitchens except that a few rabbinical incantations had been said over the one, and all its equipment, from spoons to tureens, and was jealously guarded by Dr. Bloom, the attending rabbi. It would strike the goyem as comical, how when the kosher kitchen ran short of dishes or silverwear, all that was necessary was for one of the pearl divers to get what was needed from the non-kosher kitchen and run it through the dish-washing machines in the kosher kitchen. Having been run through one of these machines, the equipment apparently came out, not merely Jewish, but kosher. The goy boys would say, as they were waging steaming, soap-bubbling war on time and kosher appetites, "O.K., hurry up! Let's run these through. They need spoons in the Bar Mitzva. Let's make 'em kosher! Hurry up! Hurry up! Let's make 'em kosher!" Then they'd all begin to shout—the five or six, or maybe eight of them, who were working the machines—"Let's make 'em kosher! Hurry up! Let's make 'em kosher!" And they'd heave racks filled with spoons onto the conveyors where they'd rattle and splash through the washing machines and the drying machines and then they'd heave them off again—heavy, weighing twenty-five to fifty pounds, and lifted from above waist height—shouting, in drenched clothes, through steam like hot fog, "Let's make 'em kosher, boys! Hurry up! Let's make 'em kosher!"

It was as though they'd gone insane with the mechanical processes of the work and the incredible labor demanded—as if they'd forgotten themselves and were trying to remember again, by shouting, that they were there. And the roar and clatter of machines and dishes and silver was so overwhelming they had to scream to be heard above it. "Hurry up, boys," they'd hector themselves, "let's make 'em kosher!" and they'd laugh like lunatics. But that hadn't begun yet. That came at the end of each party, when the dishes and silver were beginning to run short. But before each party there was another rush, the preparative one. The pace was frantic, maddening, exhausting, and somewhere before the end came in sight, and brought with it the stimulation of hope, defeating.

Oskar and Jimmy were hosing out a garbage can in which to make salad—others were frantically chopping iceberg lettuce and celery and green bell peppers, mixing salad oil and vinegar—in would go the lot, and one of them stirring it with a broom handle.

From one of the five ballrooms they could hear music—a band warming up. There was the chapel to be prepared: a wedding, and therefore flowers to be arranged. A florist supervised this process, but they did the actual work, climbing ladders, spreading chains of roses from wall to wall. A Bar Mitzva required that great aluminum fountains be set up on tables in that ballroom, in order to spray sticky, bright-colored soft drinks into the cavities of semi-corrupted kids. Huge, round tables, like faceless targets, had to be carried from room to room, along with chairs by the hundreds; and hundreds upon hundreds of dishes had to be washed before they were used and washed as they came back in order that they could be used again, immediately, for the next course, for another party. Fruit salads had to be prepared, of canned grapefruit and orange segments and maraschino cherries, each in its individual bowl with cracked ice at the bottom, and before they were finished making these by the hundreds, the sticky, dirty bowls were coming back, waiters wheeling them in on twenty-tiered wheelers, the bowls on trays and filled with the dainties of fun—smashed green cigars, lip-sticked cigs. "Hurry up, boys! Let's make 'em kosher!" That was the call-to-arms. They might not even be in the kosher kitchen, now—they might not even be doing dishes—but they'd still scream it at one another. "Come on, boys! Hurry up! Let's make 'em kosher!"

First the fruit cocktail bowls came back, and they had metal top-pieces that had to be washed separately. Then came the big greasy soup-tureens; then almost immediately the soup bowls and under dishes. Meantime they had prepared the plates for the main dish, and now they'd be coming back, laden with leftover slop. If the boys were hungry they'd slobber down slices of beef or pieces of chicken as they worked. Then would come the truly horrible, the grotesque, dessert dishes. The standard dessert was a gooey cake, of the wedding or birthday type, topped with ice cream and over-poured with cherries jubilee. The icing was like some form of pink cement, almost impossible to scrape from the plates. Two or three of the boys became "scrapers," standing at the end of the conveyor, where there was a hole in the aluminum top, beneath which, temporarily out of sight, stood a garbage can, and, with heavy brushes, scraped this abominable stuff from the plates, while the others kept up the incredible traffic of the machines.

At this stage all of them were covered from head to foot in parti-colored muck. The cement floor itself was an inch-thicker with bright slime. Little pieces of meat, fat, and bone came floating toward them. Tobacco, broken from cigarettes and cigars, ran in among clots of pink icing and chips of cherries; their clothes became slimy rags, their shoes squeaked, and they could not see one another for the steam. And now, just when they needed it most, the first round of booze glasses would be coming in. First, the inevitable pink champagne, cheap stuff that was part of the packaged party deal. Unless the boys were too impatient or too thirsty to wait, they would scorn this. But then would come the good stuff, the Scotch and bourbon and Irish whiskey, glasses full and nearly full, any drink in the house.

"Hurry up, boys! Make 'em kosher!"

Shrieks of rowdy laughter!

Come four o'clock in the morning they'd stumble up to the attic dorm where they slept, taking some beer along with them. Soon the maloderousness of the room would become unbearable, and so they'd have to sleep.

"How's things going with Niki?" Jimmy asked.

"Not so good. Not so good," said Oskar, his long, thin form sprawled on a cot next to Jimmy's. "I tink she's sneaking out wit dat prick, Butterworth." There was moonlight from the window—stars, crickets—sleep. . . . Then they were scurrying about, getting themselves quick cups of coffee. It was two hours later, and there were tables to be moved.

"Why don't we get the hell out of this, Oskar?"

"You Gotdammed right!"

"I mean, what the hell are we living this way for?"

"Frog me?"

"Well, why don't you go back to window dressing?"

"No time. I got to paint!"

"Hurry up, boys, let's go!" It was that bustling bastard Covetti. "Come on, Jim, get that mirror polished! We've got a room to get ready."

Oskar and Jimmy vacuumed the rugs in the chapel. Oskar looked beat, his shoulders getting rounded, his chest hollow. "Listen," he said, pushing the huge vacuum as Jimmy held the cord out of the way, "let's go down to the basement tonight and get some shtuff to take home wid us—

some meat and shtuff; we put it in a box and hide it in the parking lot, ja?"

"Das is nicht eine gut idee." Oskar had taught Jimmy some German.

"How come?"

"If these mob bastards caught us stealing they'd kick the shit out of us—"

"Bah! Dey don't catch us. Vhat you think, fluffy, I'm shtupid or somepin? Ve don't get caught if ve do it my vay. It'll give us somepin to do. Now, look; here's my plan. . ."

"Ha-ha-ha-ha-ha!"

"What's so funny in here, boys?" Covetti. "Come on, let's get this vacuuming done." He left.

"Ha-ha-ha-ha-ha!"

"Fluffy Sh-vine-hoont!" said Oskar, laughing. "He makes my ass shmile. Look," he said, suddenly, a serious expression appearing on his face, his big hands to his mouth, "one of my damn front teeth is loose."

That night Jimmy and Oskar crept down to the basement and took two big pieces of roasting beef from the refrigerator. Jimmy took a scrawny, uncooked chicken too. They hid their pelf in a cardboard box, outside the garbage room. It was a clear night and the sky was sprinkled with a mess of stars, so they sat and talked and smoked and never got any sleep at all. At six they went into the kitchen and made coffee. The others came down, and they started work. Then, with dreamlike suddenness, the parties were going full tilt.

Jimmy stood behind a partition and peeked out at the revelers. He didn't know if this was a Mafia wedding or a Protestant birthday party or a Bar Mitzva or what. All the parties had run into one in his mind.

The ballroom was roaring with people; the men were wearing black-trimmed maroon tuxedos; the women were wearing lavish, frilly evening gowns. There were a few with especially silly gowns. Bridesmaids, maybe. The music was blaring and many couples were Twisting. Jimmy saw something out of the corner of his eye and looked off to his left. Down the way from him, on his side of the partition, a bald blimp of a man was rubbing his bulk over a drunken blonde. He had a green cigar in his mouth. She was holding a glass of pink champagne in one hand and a lipsticked cig in the other. The big man had her pinned to the wall. But she wasn't fighting him; on the contrary. The big man kept grinding away at her, his chubby, hairy, beringed hands on the wall behind her, above her shoulders, his body shaking like jostled jelly. The man was beginning to get frantic, now; he was perspiring and shifting his cigar around with his tongue. The woman, with some difficulty, took a sip from her champagne glass. There was a tremendous roar of music and applause from the floor. The man, heaving, panting, took one meaty mitt from the wall, reached down and, catching the blonde's dress by the hem, tore it straight up the thigh. He jiggled with himself a little, and then with her, and they both slid slowly down the wall and onto the floor. She dropped her glass and her cigarette. He spit out the stub of his cigar, and jostled— one, two, three, four—then let his weight go all over her, like a syrup.

Jimmy went back into the kitchen where he ran into Covetti, who told him to go and clean out the johns. There were two men's rooms and two ladies' rooms and all four were filled with vomit. Jimmy shoveled it up and mopped it away and wiped off the mirrors. He had a hard time with one of them in one of the ladies' rooms, where some dame had written "Dick me, Richard" in lipstick. A bit of ammonia finally got it off.

When Jimmy came back to the kosher kitchen, Covetti put him on potwalloping. He walloped them in the deep sink for what seemed a kind of tiny, Tin Pan Alley eternity. Then, deep in the evening, he was pulled off that.

There was a kind of commencement party for novitiate priests being held, and they needed extra tables. Jimmy collapsed the legs on a half dozen six-foot-in-diameter, eight-seater round tables and carted them, one at a time, out through the kosher kitchen and across the parking lot and in at another door. Inside, there were a couple of hundred rosy-cheeked, black-garbed, very drunken novitiate priests. They were sprawled about over chairs or tables, eyes-drooping or bulging, snoring or shouting. Two or three of the soberer ones occasionally carried out the bodies of their comatose comrades. The tables Jimmy brought in and set up were quickly loaded with pitchers of beer by the waiters. Bottles of whiskey were placed on each table. Joy and forgetfulness were being sung at a hundred tables around the room. At one table, "Carmina Burana" broke loose in seminary Latin.

Outside, the night was whipping up a thunderstorm.

Jimmy went to bring more tables, noticing, en route, the black-shod feet of novitiates protruding from the open windows of limousines. They reminded Jimmy of Parris Island recruits out of basic training, showing off how drunk they could get. "Onward, Christian Soldiers!" he saluted them. As he made his way out another door, a huge table in his grip, the wind caught it and gave his spine a sudden one-eighty twist. It sounded like six shots rang out from his spine, *snap snap snap, snap snap, snap!* That did it. The rest of the night he could hardly walk. He went about, bluffing everything he did, as his Buddhist pal Denise might say, in an ecstasy of agony with no Nirvana in the gloaming.

The sky broke open and the rain came straight down. It was nine o'clock, of whatever night it was.

"What night is it, Oskar?"

"Sunday," shouted Oskar, lifting a rack of scraped dessert plates onto the conveyor. "Let's make 'em kosher, boys!" Oskar took off his glasses and wiped them with his slimy apron. His face was pale and his light black beard was surfacing.

Jimmy threw down his brush and dug his nails into a particularly obstinate piece of icing. But his nails were too short and broken to do much good. He threw the plate into the hole. To hell with it! In a minute it was buried in muck.

"Three hours to go, eh?" he shouted, or tried to shout. His voice was too weak to make much noise. He adjusted his stance to accommodate his back.

"What?" shouted Oskar, angry at having his numbing concentration broken.

"Three hours to go!" Jimmy shouted.

"Yeah!" shouted Oskar: then, "Let's make 'em kosher, boys!"—madly, madly—"Let's make 'em kosher!"

Covetti came in and sent Jimmy, who could hardly walk now, limping out again to see if the washrooms needed cleaning. As Jimmy approached a ladies' room, the blonde who had been behind the partition came staggering out the door. She had the green, peaked look of one who has recently up-chucked. He noticed that the tear in her skirt was bound closed with knotted bobby pins. She wore a diamond engagement ring and a diamond-studded wedding ring above it, and she was cling-clang with bracelets. Her face looked like an oil painting that had been wiped before it was dry. Inside, she left her calling card, in the form of several little heaps of pink vomit. "That damned champagne!" Jimmy grumbled. He limped back and told Covetti that the room needed cleaning but that he wasn't going to do it. He said he'd cleaned it up once and let somebody else do it this time. He told Covetti he thought that his back was broken, and that he might sue. Covetti said that if Jimmy didn't clean it up, he could consider himself fired.

"Don't come back next week," Covetti said. Jimmy said, O.K., he wouldn't.

Covetti told Oskar to do it, but Oskar bluffed his way

out of it. "Can't you see I got dishes shtacked up? I can't do dat now." His dark eyebrows were raised, as if to say there was something the matter with Covetti's brain.

"O.K.," said Covetti. "Harrigan, you do it."

"Christ, Mr. Covetti, I'm a mixologist, not a poil-diver. I don't know how ta clean good." Harrigan was an ex-bartender, permeated with alcohol, on the bum.

"Harrigan!"

"O.K., O.K.," said Harrigan.

"Now let's go, boys, make 'em kosher!" Covetti yelled, trying in his obvious way to be in, to be democratic. Soon as Covetti left the scullery, Oskar started howling with laughter.

"Dat ugly mutterfrogger—he didn't know vhat to say to me; did you see dat?"

Then, suddenly, it was midnight. They mopped up, threw off their aprons, put their jackets on, and stood about, waiting for their pay. Tony came into the kitchen with a bottle of whiskey and gave them each a drink before he paid them.

Outside, at the garbage room, Oskar and Jimmy dug out their box of contraband. They took turns carrying it under the moon. Two big beefs and a chicken were a heavy load for workers as tired as they were, and especially for Jimmy with his bad back, but they felt obligated to take the box along. It was a symbol of some kind. But it was a symbol for Tony's Halfway House, too. A city garbage truck caught up with them on the road. Two burly types explained that Mr. Covetti told them to pick them up and take them to the station.

"You boys get up there on the garbage," said one. "There ain't no room in the cab."

"Vell, vat de hell," said Oskar. "We stink like shit any-way."

"You'll have to help me up, Oskar," said Jimmy, "my back's broken."

The truck rumbled off into the night, Jimmy and Oskar bouncing amid the garbage.

"Say, ain't dis taking a long time to get to da station?"

"Yeah," said Jimmy. "Where the hell are we?"

The truck pulled between cyclone fenced gates.

"Vhat da hell is this?"

"I think it's the city dump," said Jimmy. "But it's so goddamned dark. I can't tell where we are."

The truck started backing up. It was a dump truck and it started lifting them high into the air and sliding them forward on mounds of garbage and dumped them into a mountain of garbage and began to bury them in more garbage. The truck pulled away and vanished in the night.

"Phheeew!" cried Oskar. "Dey've dumped us like garbage! I guess dis means dey don't want me back next week, either."

Jimmy's back-pocket, paperback edition of Orwell's *Down and Out in London and Paris* was spine-split and water-logged. He threw it on the steaming, mephitic heap.

"I told you, Oskar—the weed of crime bears bitter fruit!"

"Frog me," cried Oskar, flicking foul bits of gunk away.

CHAPTER SEVEN

THE DOOR OF PERCEPTION

The sunlight on the garden
Hardens and grows cold . . .
—*Louis MacNeice*

"Post partum depression," Joan said. "Some of us get it and some don't. I've had a couple abortions in my time and it never gave me any problems. I'm pregnant now. I'm happy and healthy. You're gonna be fine, Lani."

"It wasn't so bad at first. I started feeling it after I left the farm. Maybe it was the protective surroundings, but as soon as I got in the car with Marsayas and the farm house started receding and I knew that *it* was back there and that I'd never see it again—I mean, at all—I began feeling these waves of guilt. Poor Marsayas, I cried all the way here from Bucks County and I can't seem to pull myself together."

"Well, you just stay here with us for a while. Get used to the city and get yourself into school, just like you planned. Things'll all work out."

Joan was a true earth-mother. She made Lani feel protected the way Auntie Mele had made her feel when she was a child. She put her head on Joan's big, soft bosom and wept, Joan patting her head, like a true mama. Joan could not have been more than a couple of years older than Lani, but at that moment seemed to possess the wisdom of the ages. Lani wiped her eyes and looked around at her new home—well, not a home, more of a half-way house. Maybe it was a little dump over a funeral parlor and next to the roar of the Manhattan Bridge, but Joan made it feel like a sanctuary. "I can help you fix the place up," Lani said.

"It'll give you something to do," Joan said. "Something to get your mind off this."

"And I'll finally get to see Kimo," she said, hopefully.

"Why do you call him Kimo?"

"Hawaiian for Jim."

"Kimo-the-Poet," Joan tried, then laughed. "No, honey, it just doesn't work."

"When do you think he'll come by?"

"Oh, he might pop in at any moment. He's just like Marsayas, like all these guys, totally undependable."

"That isn't how he seemed in Hawaii. He seemed . . .he seemed. . . staunch. So military, so. . .together."

"That was a long time ago, honey. He's had a terrible marriage."

"What was she like?"

"A show-biz bitch, eye-lashes out to here, all kinds of paint—oh, I suppose you could say that she was pretty good looking, in a cheap sort of way."

"He was such a clean boy. He seemed to shine."

"Well, don't expect him to be the same. He is a poet, you know, and crazy as hell, like all of them; but a lot of fun when he's not too far gone. He was an actor for a while, you know, and he can read beautifully."

"Yes, I remember how he used to read poetry to me. I thought he was the most beautiful thing I'd ever seen." She laughed, shrugged her shoulders, feeling better. "I think I'll have that glass of wine, now."

"How 'bout some pot," Joan said, lighting up, and passing the joint. "It takes all the crap out of the diapers."

While Joan and Lani talked, Jimmy and Oskar rolled in from Long Island and hit the downtown subway. "I gotta have a drink," Jimmy told Oskar, and they got off the train in search of one.

"Dat frogging money is burning a hole in your pocket," said Oskar, looking around the joint they had dived into. "And I don't think ver're welcome here. You stink, Fluffy. You see the way the people get up and move away from us? We smell like a couple of skunks, and if I look as bad as you do, dey should bury me. Look at dis shit all over us! I'm going home and take a soak in the tub for a week. And I'm gonna burn dese clothes." Oskar got up and headed toward the door.

"You handle it your way, I'll handle it mine," called Jimmy. "I'm going all the way down to Brooklyn and get drunk as the skunk that I smell like."

His stop in Brooklyn was next door to an evil smelling dive. He dove in, thinking, "I can't add much to the air in here." Five boiler-makers later he trekked across the Heights toward Marsayas's and into Chic's mafia bar. Marsayas, himself not a serious bather, did not rise from his bar stool to seize Jimmy in the usual bear-hug that was their standard greeting, but sat with a wondering look on his face, then the gleeful gargoyle appeared. "What in hell's happened to you? You looked like you climbed out of the town dump—worse—pheeewwey—you smell like you climbed out of the town dump."

"That's because I did climb out of a town dump, you dumb son-of-a-bitch! Why else would I look and smell like this. The mob boys out at Tony's Halfway House dumped us in the town dump." The denizens of Chic's, the mob bar, perked up their ears and gave him the once-over. The bartender appeared to say to Marsayas, "I'm not serving him in here."

"For God's sake, I had an accident, man. Give me a boiler-maker, quick!"

Marsayas said, "Can't you see that he's had an accident? He's got cuts all over him. Look!"

"O.K.," said the bartender and drew a beer and a shot for the victim. He handed them over at the greatest distance his arms could manage. "God, you stink like—"

"Hey," said Jimmy, "I'm closer to it than you are."

The bartender shook his head. "You got an egg shell in your hair." Marsayas reached over and carefully picked it out of Jimmy's matted hair. "There seems to be a lot of other stuff in there, too," Marsayas said.

"I don't wanna know," the bartender said.

"Another one, please," Jimmy said. The bartender repeated the order. Perhaps it was sympathy, which is hard to come by in such hard rocks as these, proving how pathetic a sight Jimmy must have seemed, but the bartender continued to serve him after that. Suddenly Jimmy had to go to the bathroom desperately. He had climbed aboard the bar stool somehow, but now he couldn't get down. "It's my back. I think I broke it."

"When they dumped you?" asked Marsayas.

"No. Before that. A table got caught in the wind and twisted my spine. Lift me down, will you?"

Marsayas lifted him down, then realized that the only way Jimmy was going to make the men's room was to be carried. "If I'm going to carry you, I might as well carry you upstairs." He lifted Jimmy in a fireman's carry and out of the bar and past the funeral parlor and up the stairs and sat him down at the kitchen table, Jimmy groaning in agony all the way.

"Look what I found," he said to Joan and Lani. "Lani, this is your poet."

"Oh my God," said Joan. "What's happened to him?"

Lani had risen at the table. This was not Kimo, this bunch of stained rags with goo in his hair and a three-day growth of beard. She leaned forward across the table to study him. He seemed to be passing out and coming back and passing out again. "What's happened to him? What's the matter with him?"

"I haven't slept in three days," Jimmy said, "I've broken my back, and I've been dumped in a town dump. I had to walk miles to the station to get the train into the city. And I've had a few drinks for the pain."

"More than a few," said Joan.

"O.K., many a few." Jimmy started laughing hysterically, then screaming as his back gripped him, then laughing again.

"Do you know who this is, Jimmy?" asked Joan.

Jimmy tried to focus. "A beautiful Hawaiian girl," he said. "I knew one just like her once. She was a child and I was a child in a kingdom by the sea."

Lani started to cry, saying, "I think he remembers."

"Give me a cigarette, will you, somebody?"

Joan said, "I'm gonna give you a bath, that's what I'm going to give you." She started to lift him, but couldn't. "Marsayas, get him in the bath tub. I don't go for that crap, but we could use some air freshener around here. Lani, light some incense!"

In a half hour they had Jimmy back at the table, dressed in Marsayas's clothes, which were too big for Jimmy and made him look like a clown. Joan had shaved him while he was in the bath tub. At least he looked clean. Joan forced some hot coffee down his throat. He looked around. "Where the hell am I?"

Lani said, "Kimo, do you know who I am?"

"I think you must be my sweet Leilani all grown up. Am I right?"

"Yes, Kimo, yes! I'm your sweet Leilani all grown up. Your little sister, remember?"

"It's like a dream," he said, and his eyes rolled back in his head and nearly disappeared. He shook his head and looked vaguely at them, grinning, and with a pale face of exhausted idiocy shouted, "Make 'em kosher!"

*   *   *

. . .and I finally met Kimo, and I must say that it was a shock. I remembered a golden boy but that was not what I found. It wasn't just that he had had an accident, Auntie Mele, but something else has happened to him, and it is so hard for me to understand how somebody who has become a true poet, as I always believed him to be, could also become what he seems to be now— reckless, drunken, and lost. I believe that the person I met would not have saved me that night in Honolulu, but would have walked right past me in my plight. I think that rock in his chest that made it so difficult for him to float has sunken him deeper than ever. My friend Joan has told me about his terrible first wife, but can one person be blamed for another person's loss of self-respect? It seems that he is also involved with another girl now. The situation is hopeless! Oh, how can anyone with the

175

soul in him to write so well not have the strength in him to live better? I know, Auntie Mele, that I am still young and don't know as much as I might at some future time, don't understand as much as I wish I did, and that, perhaps, if I knew more or understood better, I might see through the surface of what I saw and be able to detect that brave, kind, good young man that I know was there once, but it is difficult. Perhaps it is all just the process of growing up, but I feel that he has broken some part of my heart, and, after my experience with Stan Kosinski, I don't know if I want to search for the old Kimo, whom I hope is not dead. I loved him so much once. I don't know what to think.

*   *   *

A few weeks later Marsayas showed up at Miss Byrdsong's to get Jimmy to come out and play, have a few drinks with him. They went over to the White Horse Tavern, on Hudson Street, a shrine to Dylan Thomas, the great Welsh poet, who had drunk himself to death in the bar with eighteen straight shots. They bellied up to the bar. Marsayas wanted to know why he hadn't been down to see him since meeting Lani. "I think she thinks you're avoiding her," he said.

"I guess I am. I mean, you have a beautiful dream in your mind and you keep it hidden and safe from the world and it stays beautiful. Then it walks in the door and you turn it ugly and embarrassing. You've ruined the dream, you've ruined the dream in your own mind, about how you'd act and maybe you've ruined it in hers, if she ever shared it. I'm just so damned ashamed I can't go near her, you know? Has she said anything to you?"

"Naw, she doesn't talk to me much. She talks to Joan. Maybe she's said something to her."

"You see, up until that night, I always had that dream. I'm not even sure I wanted to see her again, for it to become

176

real." He looked away, then back at Marsayas. "I just blew it. It was the sweetest thing I ever had in my whole damn life—and I blew it."

"You're not the first, boyo. You're not the first."

Marsayas told Jimmy that he had some peyote and was saving it for some time when they could all get together. Jimmy suggested they meet the next night at Phyllis's apartment. Jimmy had moved in with Phyllis. After Elliot's disappearance, Miss Byrdsong had become a veritable stickler for the timely collection of rents and her admiration for artists, at least in Jimmy's case, had diminished. When Elliot failed to return she took an obvious dislike to Jimmy. "Bad vibes," as Phyllis might have put it.

Phyllis, on the other hand, offered Jimmy a haven of sorts in her psychedelic cave. She gave Jimmy the use of a tiny room in her apartment. He had some wooden milk crates for the books he was accumulating and a desk for his banged-up typewriter. In the big room, he shared the mattress with Phyllis. Phillis never interrupted. He imagined the kind of nightmare it would be to try to write with his mother around. It would be impossible for her to leave him quietly alone. Phyllis had a real admiration for Jimmy's poetry and encouraged him in his efforts, although she thought he should move away from his formalism, toward freer verse.

"Like what Roethke's doing," she said; then seemed to see a new world. "Oh!" she cried. "Your hair! Does my hair look like that?"

"Like what?" Jimmy said.

"Everybody's hair is vibrating—no, *undulating*, like every hair is a living snake!" She was high, but not nauseated from ingesting the emetic, sawdust-like peyote, but Jimmy was nauseated; his stomach was more disturbed than his brain. "I think I'm going to be sick," he said. He rose from the chanting, candle-lit circle—composed of Butterworth, Oskar's girl Niki, Denise, Marsayas, and Phyllis—a missing link, and fumbled his way into Phyllis's dark kitchen, toward the bathroom. But something stopped him, caught his eye, a streak of light coming through a pin-sized hole in the kitchen door, light from the hall outside. The hole was down low, about knee-high. Jimmy couldn't take his hypnotized eyes from it. He walked over to it to see what it was that fascinated him so. He felt perfectly sane and sober, but simply compelled. He got down on his hands and knees and looked right into—or through—the hole. No, he couldn't look all the way through it—that wasn't what his vision wanted him to do. It wanted him to look *in* the hole, not *through* it; and there in that tiny hole was a world! The rough splinters of wood pulsated, undulated—the ones facing up undulated upwards and the ones facing down undulated downward and the ones facing in undulated inwards—and they were only the frame of the scene. Toward the middle of the lower portion of this undulating circle was a pulsating pyramid upon which stood two or three undulating dignitaries of this strange world in a scene in a circle in a hole in a door. They seemed to be addressing a crowd of swinging, swaying constituents who bore long elastic spears that curled and snapped at their sides like snakes.

"Hey, somebody!" Jimmy called. "Somebody, come here, quick! Marsayas, come here—Phyllis, Niki, Butter, Denise—you've got to see this—somebody, hurry up!"

Marsayas came flapping in on his shower shoes.

"What is it?"

"Look! Look here," Jimmy said, getting up from his hands and knees and pointing at the hole. "There's a whole world in there, in that little hole. Quick, look!"

Marsayas got down on his hands and knees, as Jimmy had been, and stared into the hole, and, looking at him, Jimmy could see how silly he must have looked. Voyeurs, they were, into the fourth dimension. But Jimmy had been more interested in what was going on in that hole than in how silly he may have looked. Were the "Doors of Perception" finally opening for him?

"There's no peace there, either," said Marsayas. "Just chaos—like out here."

"You see it too, then?" Jimmy asked, excited. That was what he wanted—confirmation. "What do you see?" he asked.

"Looks like a mob of natives with assagai, arguing with their leaders. The leaders are giving the mob hell, too. Looks like trouble."

"That's it all right! You see it, too?"

"I see it," said Marsayas, with a sort of resignation. Then he jumped to his feet. "I'm getting out of here," he said, in panic reaction, and yanked the door open and ran out through the hall into the street, shower shoes going flip-flop, flip-flop, fast, as he went.

At three in the morning, after the drug had worn off, after everyone had left, Phyllis curled up in Jimmy's arms and told him that she was pregnant. Naturally, the first thing to come into Jimmy's head was that the child wasn't his. This came as a sort of reflex, a horrified spasm of emotional retreat. He didn't really believe it. But Phyllis reminded him that her former boyfriend, Reginald, was black, so Jimmy would know soon enough if the child were his.

"And you've been taking peyote? Are you crazy?"

"Don't be angry, Jimmy. It won't hurt anything."

"How do you know? And haven't you heard of the pill?"

"They make me sick."

"Everything makes you sick. You make *me* sick, you irresponsible—"

It would have been easy to describe her as having no morals, but Jimmy knew that the truth was that Phyllis had absolutely no emotional understanding of sex, and could not have been considered loose, even if she had slept with an army, like General Hooker's hookers. Jimmy just could not think of her that way. She was like a child herself. She was not a woman, really; even her brain—bright and imaginative, and yet naive—was like a child's, not a woman's. But in Jimmy's first recoil at the possibility of having a child by her, and under these circumstances, he accused her of trying to trick him. "You know damned well that if you've got anything in that little womb of yours, it'll be Reginald's."

"Oh, no, Jim! Truly, it's yours, it's yours! I know! I know!"

How did she know?

"The time. My periods—"

"You don't even have periods—"

"I do so! I do!—" She threw herself across the filthy, cat-haired mattress and cried convulsively, like a little girl.

"God Almighty, what am I doing here?" Jimmy thought. "What am I doing monkeying around with this poor little sick dame? What am I going to do with her?" He called himself a son-of-a-bitch to have ever got mixed up with her. And yet all the time he was thinking this he was filled with the most extraordinary tenderness for her. And he knew the child was his, and that he would take care of Phyllis, and not desert her. That was what he really wanted more than anything—to take care of her. Why he felt this way he couldn't have said. But he had often noticed some kind of absurd nurturing instinct in himself. It was crazy. Perhaps he loved her a little. But if he did love her, he did not love her enough to marry her, enough to see himself spending his life with her. No, no, no; something like this had even possessed him with regard to Vera—a strange sympathy, empathy almost. He must not yield to this soft side of himself. It always ended in disaster.

Jimmy walked into the kitchen and got a beer from the refrigerator. It really was, as Phyllis often said, a bullshit world. From where he stood he could see her, convulsing.

She looked ghastly. But maybe it was the light. It was always too dark in this crazily painted apartment to see. It would be daylight soon. He finished his beer, lay down beside Phyllis, and fell asleep, hoping against hope that what she had told him wasn't true. It was the sort of thing she could get wrong, wasn't it?

*   *   *

Later that morning Niki, Butterworth, and Marsayas came back in Rolly Reuter's old Pontiac. They wanted Jimmy to go with them to see Oskar and convince him that Niki and Butterworth had stayed with the rest of them all night and that there was absolutely nothing for Oskar to be concerned about. This was Niki's maneuvering, Jimmy could see that. She even had Butterworth convinced that she never intended to lead him on, that she only considered him a good friend, and furthermore had even convinced him that he had never been led on, that he had behaved like the perfect officer and gentleman, and gallant Marine, he thought himself to be. Jimmy thought he was a hypocritical martinet, philosopher or not. Who knew what had really happened? It was very vague to Jimmy, contemplating his own problems, but it was also a chance to escape his thoughts, have a beer, and think about soomebody else's mess. Distraction. They piled into Rolly's jalopy—Phyllis, too—and off they went, chitty-chitty, bang-bang.

It had been shortly after Jimmy had first met Oskar, that Oskar had started going with lisping Niki, an artists' model at the Brooklyn Museum, where Oskar studied painting under the great Hans Hoffman. Since he had met her he had become increasingly aloof, paranoid; and now he sat, up in their apartment overlooking Tompkins Square, with his beautifully shaped head in his hands, like a tired old man.

"Look," said Niki, "I've brought Jim. He'll tell you where I wath—"

181

"I don't need any froggingbody tell me vhere you vas," he said through his fingers, his German accent thicker. "Vhat da hell you try to do, make a fool out of me? Eh? Everybody get out of here!"

"They are *not* going to go! You called me a lot of names and now you're going to apologize. Tell him, Jim. Where wath I last night? Wathn't I at your place?"

"She was, Oskar." She had been, until three; where she was after that, Jimmy didn't know.

"Oh, shut up," Oskar said. Then he said: "Vhere vas Butterworth?"

"I was there, too," said Butterworth, looking very condescending, like a father with a fact.

"Sure you vas, da two of you!" said Oskar.

"Listen, Oskar," said Marsayas. "You've got this whole thing wrong. It's all in that suspicious head of yours. You've got to learn to trust people, to get rid of your hangups—"

"Listen," said Oskar, looking up—Jimmy saw that he'd been crying—"don't give me any of your bullshit. Dis is none of your damned business."

"When one of my good friends has a problem," said Marsayas, believing his own bullshit, "that problem is mine, too." He walked over and set his big frame down on the couch next to Oskar and put a big, muscular arm over Oskar's thin shoulders. "Come on, Buddy," he said in a hale-fellow-well-met voice, giving Oskar a jerk-hug. "Come on, let's get this thing cleared up."

Jimmy walked into the kitchen and helped himself to a beer from the refrigerator. He went to the front and looked out the window, down on Tompkins Square. The park was crowded, a sunny summer day crowd—mothers, babies, loafers, lovers—then he heard Oskar shouting, "GET OUT— ALL OF YOU—JUST GET OUT!"

Jimmy went into the livingroom, where everybody stood staring at the bedroom door. It still seemed to be vibrating.

"Well, can you beat that?" said Butterworth.

Jimmy could hear Oskar sobbing in the bedroom.

Laughing Oskar.

*   *   *

It happened the next day, as they were driving to Oskar's and Niki's apartment for a reprise, a return match, a second shot at lover-counseling. Marsayas—forever the officious intermeddler in his quest for universal love—had picked them up. Phyllis and Jimmy were sitting in the front seat with him. Butterworth was in the back seat, commenting on Oskar's failure to understand what Niki needed; which, according to him, was to be treated with patience and consideration by a man with a more mature sense of values than Oskar displayed. Then, suddenly, the whole front seat of the car was filled with blood.

"Jesus Christ!" Jimmy cried. "What's that?"

Phyllis had not noticed that she was bleeding, until that moment. She didn't appear to be in any great pain. But she was the color of flour-paste.

"Does it hurt, honey?" Jimmy asked, nonplussed, stupid, not knowing what to make of this horror.

"No," she said. "It's just cramping a little."

Marsayas was shaken. "Should I drive to a hospital? St. Vincent's is just across town." He didn't like this sort of thing, no, not at all.

Jimmy didn't like it any better than Marsayas did. It was horrifying to see all that blood, the blush drained from a ghost.

"No," Phyllis said. "I don't want to go to a hospital. Take me home. *Please!*"

"But you'll bleed to death," Jimmy said.

183

"No, I won't. I'll be all right as soon as I lie down. Please, take me home!"

They were closer to Phyllis's apartment on Houston Street than they were to St. Vincent's Hospital, across town, and Jimmy could see a flickering look of relief dance in Marsayas's eyes at the thought of getting rid of them as soon as possible. This wasn't his scene at all. Jimmy'd have bet that the first thing Marsayas would do after dumping them would be to get numbingly drunk.

"Oh, I'm getting blood all over the car," said Phyllis, squirming around, pushing a tattered old newspaper, that Butterworth had handed her, under her little bottom.

"Oh, hell!" said Marsayas, driving like he didn't know where he was going. "Don't worry about that; just worry about getting well."

"You see what you've done?" Butterworth said. "This is your fault, Jim."

Jimmy had an arm around Phyllis; he turned to face Butterworth, who bounced about in the back seat.

"So help me, Butterworth," he shouted over the traffic noises, "as soon as I get this straightened out, I'm going to kick your shiny teeth in."

"I'll be glad to meet you—anytime," Butterworth came back coolly.

"Shut the hell up, Butter—both of you!" Marsayas shouted. "What the hell's wrong with you? Is this any time for that?" Marsayas pulled the car to the curb in front of Phyllis's apartment house and Butterworth got out and held the door for Jimmy while he climbed over Phyllis, who had been sitting on the outside, near the window, because she liked the breeze, and got out and picked her up in his arms and carried her into the building, leaving drip-drops of blood wherever he stepped. Behind him he heard the car door slam after Butterworth, and Marsayas, burning rubber, screech the car off—Marsayas, the doctor who couldn't stand the sight of blood.

Inside, he was about to put Phyllis to bed, but she ordered him to let her down. She staggered into the bathroom and shut the door. There was much flushing, a few moans and groans, then a long silence.

Jimmy knocked on the door.

"What is it?" she called weakly.

"Are you O.K.?"

"Yes. Come in and get me, please, Jimmy; I can't walk. The door's unlocked."

Jimmy opened the door and there she sat on the john, her little bottom so small she sank into the commode like a child. There were bloody towels all over the floor. Blood everywhere. He made up his mind, then.

"I'm going outside and get a cab," he told her. There was no nearby access to a phone to call an ambulance. "You stay where you are. When I get back I'll fix you up to go to the hospital."

"I don't want to go. Please, Jimmy; I don't want to go to the hospital."

"No, Phyl, you've *got* to go to the hospital, that's all there is to it. You'll die if you don't. You'll bleed to death." But she was unconscious now, stuck in the stool like a wilted little pale-green weed in a porcelain pot.

Jimmy ran outside and hailed a cab and told the driver to wait, explaining that it was a hospital case, and ran back in and lifted her out of the commode. It went crazily through his mind that she was being treated by life like something that was meant to be flushed down the toilet. Even as he picked her up the blood poured from between her spindly legs, plopping in cherry-red gouts into the already overfilling, splashing bowl. He held her with one arm, like a rag doll, and flushed the mess away. It had to be gone. He couldn't bear it. Then he stuffed a big wad of towels between her legs and wrapped a blanket around her and carried her out to the cab. He'd had the good luck to get a sympathetic cabby. In fifteen minutes she was checked in at the hospital.

Jimmy waited to find out if she was going to be all right, and was told, eventually, that she was. She was being transfused.

He left St. Vincent's and bought himself a couple of sandwiches, a container of coffee, a six pack of beer, and went back to Phyllis's apartment (somehow he couldn't bring himself to think of it as his own, although he'd paid the last rent on it; maybe because accepting her apartment as his own would mean a final acceptance of his situation). There he ate his little meal, drank his coffee, and proceeded to sip the beer until the small hours of the morning.

Serious times were here. He had hoped for an education. He had hoped for peace and quiet in which to write. He had hoped that he'd have time to live through what had happened to him with Vera. He had hoped that somehow he'd get his guts back, and be able to deal with things again; he had hoped that he'd have time to live through his hurt and his sense of failure before life came at him again, swinging its big, clouting, medicine-ball fists. And now this. More chaos.

He sat deep into the night in that ridiculously painted apartment, with its psychedelic walls, its mobiles made from coat hangers, its filthy, furry, unframed mattress, and its mad, yellow-eyed, pee-squirting cat, Phyllis's familiar, and drank his beer and tried to understand what manner of woman-child it was to whom he was obligated in grief. What was at the center of that little soul who was carrying (or had it flushed away down the toilet?) a small pulsation of his own being, some of his own cells, his own actual life, living, living? Who was Phyllis? Did she hurt? Was she in pain now? Had he caused it? What was her unhappiness like? How felt? Like his own? Worse? Dreadful? Could she bear it? Was she afraid? Was there no way he could find in his heart her pain, her anguish?

There was a big stack of notebooks, wirebound books bought in stationery stores, books children use for homework, about twenty of them, stacked on the floor, next to the mattress, at its foot. Jimmy had seen them before, but had never paid any attention to them. He pulled the top one off the stack and opened it. It was filled with pictures of dinosaurs, tyrannosaurs, brontosaurs—all that pretty, Jurassic family— clipped from "National Geographic," looked like. He flipped back to the cover, upon which was hand-printed—

> *PHYLLY'S DIPLODOCUS BOOK,*
> *awarded to her on her ninth*
> *birthday, for being such a*
> *good, brave, and patient girl while*
> *being sick, with LOVE*
> *from Mummy and Daddy*

all in different colored crayons. It triggered something in him and he began to cry, sob out loud in the empty apartment. In a few minutes he got himself under control and put the book back. Shit, it was only a crying jag. "A crying jag, that's all it is," he told himself.

Jimmy had paid the last rent; the last one that they had paid, that is; which, to date, left them two months arrears. Why they hadn't been able to scrape together the paltry sum of seventy-five dollars a month for this mad, dingy pad, he didn't know. He guessed it was drugs and booze—expensive pastimes. He hadn't been making much, either, since quitting Barnes & Noble; only working with Oskar for Strong Arm Labor or, 'til recently, at Tony's Halfway House, or as a dishwasher in Katz's deli, across Houston Street from Phyllis's building. It hadn't seemed important to him to have money.

He had only needed enough to keep on reading and writing. But now?

Phyllis had been drawing a check of a hundred a month from her daddy, the pilot. He could have sent her a hundred a week, but he apparently had the idea of forcing her to get some kind of job, do something with herself. It would have been incomprehensible to him that she could have actually lived on only that hundred. She would write to him occasionally and tell him that she was working at this or that. Jimmy doubted if she had worked since she had been in New York. She had a reasonably good education, having completed three years at the University of Washington. But she had majored in English, and had no secretarial skills—could not type or take dictation—so there was really very little she could do to earn money. He thought of himself—a poet with a high school G.E.D. from the service. A year at NYU. Dramatic schools. Bah! Beatniks, bah!

Phyllis was likely to stay in the hospital for another week and Jimmy was absolutely broke, and the Marshal was coming around to put their things on the street. Aside from a few changes of clothes, his books and typewriter, Jimmy had nothing. But Phyllis was a magpie, a nesting bird. Like those extremely introverted lunatics who are discovered dead by the police and are written up in the tabloids, Phyllis surrounded herself with all manner of junk. Her apartment was an hallucination extended into the physical world, a secret garden wherein she could shape her own particular brand of madness in safety. Conjuring up that early image of her pale form retreating into a candle-lit and madly-colored sanctum, Jimmy thought of fear. She was like one of those soft little hermit crabs that scurry about in what appears to be terror, looking for an empty mollusk shell in which to hide. Hike, hike, get the thing up on your back, little side-walker, and, teeter-totter, off you go. But now Jimmy or life or something had caused little Phyllis to be yanked out of her shell. Here she was, soft and exposed.

It would have been easy enough to let the Marshal throw the whole works out into the street. A few months earlier Jimmy might have done just that—just upped and walked out on the whole crazy situation, split. But not now. Something had happened to him. For the first time since the early days with Vera, he was experiencing glad twinges of responsibility. But it wasn't quite a phoenix that was rising from such small sparks. Nevertheless . . . . Nevertheless . . . . Jimmy had to save Phyllis's little treasures, the whole pile of junk. And what he needed was money, "long green."

That evening he went to the hospital to visit Phyllis. But before going in, he asked the doctor in attendance how she was.

"Your wife will be all right, Mr. Whistler, but I have some bad news for you." He gave Jimmy one of those steady-eyed, professional looks.

"Well, what is it?" If Phyllis was O.K., Jimmy couldn't imagine what bad news the doctor could have for him.

"You've lost the baby," the doctor said.

Well, for God's sake, of course they had! Still, it was odd to hear it put that way—"the baby." Was it really a little living thing, then? How strange it was to think of it that way! Jimmy wondered who it was, that little soul. He went in to see Phyllis. She looked very weak. She was being fed intravenously. But, somehow, she looked better. There was just the faintest tinge of pink in her cheeks. Relief, perhaps. Or maybe fever?

"Are you all right?"

"Yes. Oh, Jimmy, I saw it. I saw it when it came out. It had a little body and a definite head, like a little person."

"That's impossible," Jimmy said. The idea of its having a shape horrified him.

"Oh, no. It really did, Jimmy. It had a little body and a head."

Jimmy couldn't stand this kind of talk, although it seemed to make Phyllis happy, somehow. Her cheeks had pinked a bit more, and her eyes were shiny. She was smiling—faintly radiant, really.

He changed the subject.

"Listen, Phylly. I've got to get the stuff out of the apartment before they come and throw it out. Is it all right with you if I move it?"

"Oh, yes. Do whatever you have to."

"O.K.; now look. I'll come back tomorrow morning, if I can, but if I don't, it's because I'm getting the stuff moved. In that case I'll be here tomorrow night, O.K.?"

"O.K. But—Jimmy?"

"Yes?"

"Are we together?"

"Yes. Don't worry about anything. The doctor said you'll be out in a week. I'll have a place for you to come to, I promise."

"Do you have any money?"

"Yes."

"Oh, Jimmy."

"Don't worry, hear?"

"No. I won't."

"I've got to get going."

"Goodbye, Jimmy."

"Goodbye, Phyl. See you later."

Jimmy gave her a kiss on the cheek and went out.

He thought he knew where he could get the money he needed. Marsayas had just received one of his editing checks. If Jimmy could get Marsayas to lend him fifty of it, he'd be able to find a furnished apartment, move Phyllis's clothes and papers and paraphernalia into it (maybe Marsayas would even drive him from one apartment to the other), and then get himself some work and pay Marsayas back and put a stock of food in, whatever Phyllis would need when she was released, and have a little nest all set for her to come home to and recuperate in. With this plan in mind, Jimmy hopped a subway down to Brooklyn.

When he got there, Marsayas and Butterworth were drinking. Jimmy was so relieved that he'd been able to put together some small vision of hope that, after a drink or two, he actually found himself in high (or slightly hysterical) spirits. Soon he was laughing and chatting away like an idiot. "Yes," he was saying, "Phyllis is going to be fine. Just fine."

"The poor little girl," said Butterworth. But Jimmy didn't pay any attention to him. He had to make himself particularly charming today. After all, he was going to borrow money. Then he noticed that there were suitcases out.

"What's up?" he said, giving a look.

"Oh," said Marsayas, "my boss at How-To Books is letting us have his cabin in Bucks County for a few weeks. We're going tonight, maybe, or tomorrow morning."

"Oh, Christ, Marsayas, that's great! But I wanted to ask a favor of you, and now . . . I suppose—"

"What was it?"

Jimmy told him.

It might have been the perfect time to ask Marsayas for money—just when he most needed it himself—because, being Marsayas, he was fond of grand gestures. The idea of giving all his money away just when he would need it probably appealed to him. But, on the other hand, he really *did* need all his money, at this particular juncture. Jimmy could read his thoughts, the mixed impulses. He'd have loved to have responded immediately, for the sake of the shock value, and thrown Jimmy his wallet. But then Jimmy knew, too, that Marsayas was thinking of Butterworth, of the negative effect that would have on him. Jimmy's heart was sinking into his stomach. But, thank God, Marsayas came through. He reached back to his hip pocket, withdrew his wallet, and handed Jimmy five tens from it. Jimmy whistled with relief; he couldn't help himself.

"But how are you going to live in Bucks County?" said Butterworth.

"I'll send him the money as soon as I get it," Jimmy said, "and more, too. Thank you, Marsayas, thank you, I can't tell you how much this means to me." Jimmy was weak and shaking with relief. Up until that moment, he'd been afraid to admit to himself how much he had been counting on Marsayas, but now he could.

"Hell, that's what buddies are for," said Marsayas, grinning his broad, gargoyle grin. He poured them each a great big waterglassful of the rot-gut he usually drank, and, beaming madly, toasted, "Prost!"

Jimmy Prosted him right back with everything he had. "Prost!" he said. *"PROST!"* he cried.

Marsayas looked as though he had shocked himself into a kind of hilarious madness. Jimmy thought he was already beginning to be frightened, have doubts.

"You have a hell of a nerve," said Butterworth, "coming here and taking money Marsayas needs for his trip."

"Leave him alone!" said Marsayas sternly. "This is my house and I won't have it!" Then he jumped to his feet, in that sudden way of his. "I'm tired of drinking this stuff," he said. "Come on. Let's go down to Chic's."

"I'm sorry," said Butterworth, "I'm not drinking with Jimmy."

"Stay here, then," said Marsayas; and, to Jimmy, "Come on." Down they went.

The day had gone wonderfully well. Jimmy felt positively blessed. All he had to do now was get out early the next morning and find a furnished room. He should have gone back to the apartment and packed, but Marsayas wanted a drinking companion, and Jimmy at least owed him that—

some company. But, as it turned out, it was a bad blunder to have stayed with him. Marsayas had nothing to do until Joan got home from work, and, when he wasn't editing a book, usually drank the day away. Now, as a result of the shock of having given a chunk of his money to Jimmy, he began to get seriously drunk, fast. Jimmy was half drunk with relief himself, and a few drinks took care of the other half. In an hour, he was only vaguely aware of Marsayas's presence, what with the noise of the juke and jammed joint, and when Jimmy looked for Marsayas an hour after that, he was gone, and Butterworth was in his place, on the barstool next to Jimmy.

"Where's Marsayas?"

"Marsayas is upstairs. He sent me down to ask you for the money back. He said you can keep five."

"But I need it," Jimmy said.

"He needs it, too."

"But I gotta have it. He said I could've it. It's you, you sonofabitch, you did this to me."

"Whatever's wrong with you, you did it to yourself. Now, gimme the money."

"Oh, *God!*" Jimmy didn't care. He was beaten, beaten. "Here," he said, and slapped the bills into Butterworth's fat, pink mitt. Butterworth walked out, winner and new champion, and Jimmy sat on his barstool, swivelling a little this way, a little that, beaten, drunk, sunk. He saw Phyllis's poor little skinny body under a sheet, and all her doodads being taken away from her, having no place to go when she was released from the hospital. He had got her into this mess and he had to get her out of it. He chug-a-lugged his beer, and went back upstairs to confront Marsayas.

When he knocked on the door, Marsayas asked who it was, although he damned well knew. That was by way of telling Jimmy that maybe he should just walk away and let it be. But Jimmy couldn't. He began to feel as though he were fighting for his very life. The whole damned thing had somehow got to be of monumental importance. He *had* to get that money. He didn't care now if he had to crawl around on the floor and beg Marsayas, licking his toes and barking—he'd have done it. He was half choaking when he said that it was himself at the door.

It came out in such a thick, broken little voice—"*Me.*"

"Come in," Marsayas called.

There they sat, around the table—Joan and Lani had come home in the interim. Joan and Jimmy had always been friends, so he could see how bad things were, because even she was giving him the fish-eye. He felt that they had been talking about him—his sad case—for his sweet Leilani gave him an almost medical once-over. Oh, his shame was boundless!

"What d'ya want?" said Marsayas. He was zonked all right, even zonked Jimmy could see that Marsayas was zonked.

"Marsayas, please," Jimmy began, his knees shaking, "I've *got* to have that money. I don't know what I'll do otherwise. *Please!* I'll give it back to you in spades." His legs were practically dancing out from beneath him.

"I can't give it to you. I need it myself. Didn't Butter tell you that?"

"Yes—but—"

"Why don't you get out of here," said Butterworth, "and leave these people alone?"

"You dirty bassard!" Jimmy cried. "You're behind this."

"I'm going to run you out of here," Butterworth said.

"Sit down, Butter!" Marsayas ordered.

"Why don't you go now," Joan put in. And that really hurt; that was it; that was too much. Butterworth was standing there on the other side of the table like Smedley Butler—Big Marine! Jimmy had known so many like him, seen that stance so often. His legs were bobbing underneath him when he made the leap, just like he had been warming up for it. He went crashing across the table and grabbed Butterworth, and then the whole thing began to fall over sideways— Jimmy, the table, Butterworth, dishes, silverware, bottles— onto Marsayas, who was half risen, and took him along with it, like a big, multiplying slide of rocks, to go crashing and bouncing on the floor.

Jimmy heard Joan and Lani screaming behind him, but all his concentration was on Butterworth, whom he had by the throat. Butterworth was kicking, and hammering on Jimmy's back with his big pink mitts. Jimmy'd throttle the sonofabitch breathless before he let go. He wouldn't talk for a month. But something looped into the collar at the back of Jimmy's neck and pulled him up, turned him in a circle, so he saw three-quarters of the room go by, saw the terrible disapproving faces of Joan and Lani, and headed him toward the door. It was Marsayas.

Then Butterworth was opening the door and Jimmy was being shoved through it. Butterworth kicked his behind on the way out. The door slammed shut. Jimmy heard it being bolted. He stood in the hall for a few minutes, getting his bearings, then wiped the tears from his eyes and, like a loose-stringed puppet, staggered down the stairs, through the funeral parlor hall, and into the street. *You hippies will wake the dead,* came echoing after him.

*　*　*

Jimmy's eyes were photophobic; the glare of the sun coming in the window was an agony. He got up, moved into a dark corner, and sat like a mole in a hole and finished his coffee. In the blood-smeared bathroom, he took a beating hot shower, then a cold one, hanging on the tarnished old brass faucets for support. He shaved with a dull blade, patching himself with toilet paper. He went to the corner greasy spoon and ate fried boiled ham and wet eggs. He went to the corner

dive and ordered a flat draft beer in a stained stein and begged
change for the antiquated telephone, which he had just discovered. He called Marsayas.

"Hello?"

It was Butterworth.

"Hello. This is Jim."

"Oh, Jim. Look, I wanna tell you something. I'm sorry
about last night. I was pretty drunk."

"Christ, so was I. And I'm sorry too."

"I suppose you want to speak to Marsayas."

"Yeah. Is he there?"

"Nope. They went to Bucks County last night—after
the fracas."

"Oh."

"But look, buddy—Semper Fi—what's the problem?"

"I've got to get Phyllis's stuff out of the apartment and
put it somewhere. The Marshal's coming to evict us. Then
I've got to get some place for her to come home to."

"Hmmm. Well, I'll tell you—where are you?"

"In a bar near her place."

"Well, look, I'll get a cab and come over there—and we
can move the stuff up here, O.K.?"

"God, yes! That'd be great!"

"O.K. I'll be right over. You wait at the house."

"O.K. I'll be there."

"So long."

"So long."

That was that. They moved all Phyllis's stuff into
Marsayas's apartment that morning, making several trips in
the cab. Butterworth paid for everything. He even helped
Jimmy pack the stuff. After the last trip, they sat down and
had a beer together. They shook hands and made friends.
Butter really wasn't such a bad old egg after all. He even
loaned Jimmy twenty bucks to maneuver on.

"Did Lani go with them?"

"No, she let me sleep on the couch and went up to Columbia this morning before I got up."

"What does she think? I mean—"

"I know what you mean. Well, I told you I was drunk. She didn't say much, as I remember, but I don't think she was too happy with you. You didn't make a hit with either of those women last night."

"Nor with you, I guess."

"Aw, shit, I told you I was drunk. We Marines have to stick together, don't we? Semper Fi, Jimmy."

"Semper Fi, Butter."

* * *

The day Phyllis was released from the hospital Jimmy checked them into a fleabag hotel in Chelsea. He'd got a few days work and had some money in his kick; but not much, not enough. They couldn't afford to go on paying high daily rates very long, not that, and eat in restaurants, too. Besides, Phyllis shouldn't have to go out to restaurants to eat. Jimmy could bring food up to her—but what would she do when Jimmy was working? The doctor told her to stay in bed for a couple of weeks. It wasn't just the miscarriage—she was anemic and a dozen other things. There were prescriptions, vitamins, etc. Phyllis suggested that she might call her father and ask him for her check a little early. That was a good idea, but it still left them with problems. Then Jimmy thought of big, sprawling Newark, right across the river, where there were two giant transient apartment house-hotels he knew of, side by side, way down on Broad Street—The Margarita and The Celeste. One could walk freely in and out of these joints. They were like hotels in that respect—with the check-in desks located somewhere on the first floor, just another apartment, only with Dutch doors, the bottom half shut, the top open, a registration book at belly height. Inside—usually a frowsy dame of middle age, with few and yellowed teeth, and a

197

skinny bald man in shirtsleeves. Cans of beer. A TV set—in summer a baseball game, in winter a Charlie Chan movie. There were large marmoreal bathrooms in the halls on every floor where one might find used condoms floating in the bowls, small packets of pills tucked away under the tubs, or decks of pornographic cards. All sorts of treasures might be found in these places, pelfs of monumental interest to pubescent boys, he remembered. And then, too, these bathrooms offered a safe location in which to smoke. The neighborhood hard rocks from ten to thirteen (the ones still young enough to have some small fear of the wrath of the public, authorities, or parents) would gather in these filthy latrines, stepping friskily over the inevitable pot-holed, sour-pee-puddles, and take their places along the rim of the tub to perform the ritual of lighting up and spraying the already foul air with Lucky Strizz streamers, which quickly broke into clouds. Then, as they smoked and talked, in the locally designed gutturals of their monosyllabic jargon, they would study the walls. It was from those walls that, as a shoeshine boy, Jimmy had learned about sex.

Jimmy decided that he and Phyllis should check out and go over to Newark to one of these half-way houses and get a furnished apartment by the week—there were always vacancies there, unlike in New York—and that's what they did.

CHAPTER EIGHT

HOME FIRES BURNING

THE NEW YORK TIMES
MAY 21, 1961

400 U.S. MARSHALS SENT TO ALABAMA AS MONTGOMERY BUS RIOTS HURT 20; PRESIDENT BIDS STATE KEEP ORDER

THE NEW YORK TIMES
MAY 23, 1961

200 MORE U.S. MARSHALS BEING SENT TO ALABAMA; F.B.I. JAILS 4 IN BUS FIRE

THE NEW YORK TIMES
JUNE 8, 1961

WEST BOYCOTTS LAOS PEACE TALK AS REDS FIGHT ON

In September, Fay and Elliot gave Jimmy a birthday party, and little Phyllis got out of bed to attend. When they arrived Fay was cooking Jimmy's birthday meal, doing marvelous, prestidiginous feats on one burner, the tiny kitchen rich with the smell of roasting chicken, stuffing, asparagus au gratin, whipped potatoes, mashed buttered rutabaga, creamed onions, peas, and there were homemade pies into the bargain. There was of course also a birthday cake, bakery model, and a great big bottle of blended whiskey. Fay was in her element. It was really her day more than it was Jimmy's. Whenever there was cooking to be done, a hopeless little place to be made as attractive as possible, and very little to do it with, Fay would exercise her thaumaturgical talents, and make a miracle.

Fay's homemaking art was largely wasted on an unappreciative audience. Phyllis's tastes in homemaking were troglodytic and bizarre; Elliot's had to do with keeping costs to a minimum: about his surroundings, he did not give a tinker's damn. Jimmy was the one most likely to appreciate Fay's efforts, so he gave her a few compliments on her curtains—no doubt copped from the Angels' Own Store—on the table setting, and what all, and she stood back happily, one small and pretty hand on her hip, surveying her labor, or the fruits thereof, and smiling. Little Phyllis stood dopily by, trying to understand what it was that Jimmy appreciated. Jimmy could almost hear her thinking, "Surely he doesn't like those silly curtains! I've never seen anything so. . . so.*middle class!*" Jimmy knew too, that, if it weren't for the fact that everything that was done here was done on a tattered shoestring, it would remind Phyllis, unpleasantly, of home. Phyllis had never got over wanting to be proud of being a fallen angel. But the place, after all, was just a tiny dump.

Fay nursed feelings much akin to those that little Phyl's mother had felt, on that day of inner coldness (which occurred somewhere in Phyllis's fifteenth or sixteenth year) when it had first occurred to her that Phyllis was never going to be a prom queen. Only what Fay was feeling differed in that she had no reason to love little Phyl, while at the same time little Phyl was, to her, growing like a parasite in her son's heart. But Fay, who under other circumstances might have confronted Phyllis with her thoughts, felt herself precluded from doing so, because her opposition to Vera had been so violent and unrelenting, because it might cause her to look like the perpetually opposing mother, and because it was apparent that Phyllis was doing Jimmy some kind of good.

Elliot was drunk already, grinning with the face that came upon him when he drank, glassy-eyed, mildly idiotic. He put his big-boned, hairless arm around Phyllis's miniature waist and pulled her to him where he sat at the crowded table, and gave her one of his wet, sloppy kisses, designed to devastate but usually producing a grimace of repulsion in the receiving party. He wore a sleeveless undershirt, a pair of lavender BVDs, and an old pair of shoes with their backs broken down that he used for slippers. He looked and acted like the empty hulk of an aging movie star, now poor and mildly maniacal. Fay treated him as you might treat a child, or as you did treat a lush, if you loved him, running about, getting him his bathrobe and helping him to put it on, catering to his whims, while at the same time pummeling him about. "Here, Elliot—please, come on, put this on—here, put your arm in the sleeve—the *sleeve*, not the neck!"

"Well, young lady, you have a nice little waistline."

"Thank you, Mr. Whistler."

"Here, Elliot, please get this on. It's embarrassing, you sitting there like that with Phyllis and Jimmy here!"

"They don't mind. You don't mind if I sit comfortably, do you, Phyllis?"

"No, I don't mind a bit, Mr. Whistler. My father always used to walk around the house in his shorts."

"A man's home is his castle, isn't it?"

"Sure, it is."

"Well, I don't care," said Fay. "You put that robe on,

Elliot. Jimmy, help him get that robe on.”

“Don’t pay any attention to the Wizard of Oz. She thinks she knows everything. She’s the Wonderful Wizard of Oz, all the wonderful things she does . . .”

“Elliot, don’t you start on me. Phyllis and Jimmy are here to have a nice time, not to listen to you pick on me.”

“It’s O.K., Mom. He’s just a little tight.”

“No, it isn’t! I want some respect around here.”

“A woman’s only a woman—”

“Stop that!”

“—but a good cigar’s a smoke!” Grinning, he looked to Phyllis for approval.

“You make him stop that, Jimmy!”

“Mom, this chicken’s fantastic. What’d you put on it?”

“Oh, yes, it’s really good, Mrs. Whistler.”

“Is it? I didn’t think it came out quite right.”

“Oh, no. It’s great.”

“That’s it, my boy. Always praise the ladies. That’s what keeps them happy. You know, Judy O’Grady and the Colonel’s Lady are sisters under their skins . . . .”

Jimmy ate like a starving aardvark, snout to the plate, snuffing it in. When everything had been reduced to bones and shells and lingering smells, he drank. He munched on a piece of Dutch apple pie and drank three quick big mixed drinks; then he had a cup of black coffee with a shot in it; then he settled down to drinking.

They all sang Happy Birthday to Jimmy. He blew out the candles. What was his wish? Fortunately, he could not tell them that it was to be somewhere else, maybe to be twenty again and sitting at the revolving bar on Waikiki, looking at a silver photograph of his tenth birthday party, or maybe to be with Leilani, her strong young arms keeping him afloat.

Then Fay and little Phyl began chatting about interior decorating.

“Cholly Knickerbocker——that society columnist——

described Mrs. Claude Mathews Haze's New York townhouse as having a pink ceiling in the living room."

"That sounds beautiful."

And Elliot was saying:

"You must read Blackstone's *Commentaries* someday, Jimmy. That book alone will teach you all about life. Life as people really live it, I mean. Yes, indeed. Who was it said, 'The life of the law has not been logic, it has been experience'?"

"I don't know, Dad."

"Well, it was somebody."

"I believe you."

And Fay was saying:

"She married one of those Garrets. You know, the Cornelius Garrets. Just *nouveau riche*—is that how you pronounce that?"

"Yes. Gee, is that right?"

"Yes *sir!*"

"Gee Whiz!"

And Jimmy said:

"Dad, how come you didn't become a lawyer?"

"Didn't have time. Started working on Wall Street when I was fourteen. As a runner. I was a rube right off the farm. I had a little room downtown. I used to study every night. You know, I wrote a history of Rome once, but I never finished it."

"Did you? Can I see it someday?"

"Oh, it's in my papers somewhere. I'll dig it out sometime and show you. Do you know that I was a very successful man in my time?" Three sheets to the wind always brought back the glory days.

"I know. You've told me. But what happened, Dad? How come we've always been so damned poor?"

"My boy, there are more important things in life than money . . . ."

"I won't ask you to name any," said Fay. "Someday I'll tell you why we've always been poor, Jimmy." There was something threatening in that remark. Jimmy remembered it.

And Phyllis said:

"But I don't want anything to do with the bullshit world."

Fay blinked at the word, "bullshit," but said:

"But if you fixed yourself up a little . . . ."

And Jimmy said:

"Dad, did you ever hear what Somerset Maugham said about money—that money is like a sixth sense without which you can't fully enjoy the other five?"

"Well, there's something in that. But you don't know—I had one of the biggest brokerages in the west. Denver. Then the Crash came, and I saw men—people jumping out of windows . . . . Oh, it was Oliver Wendell Holmes—"

"Who was?"

"The person who said 'The life of the law has not been logic, it has been experience.'"

"Have you known Denise a long time?" Fay was asking Phyllis.

"We went to school together."

"Oh, then you've really known her a long time. Has Jimmy told you what happened? About Denise and his father?"

"Yes. Wasn't that funny!"

"I think he was afraid she'd eat up everything we had if he didn't pay her. Ha-ha-ha-ha!"

"Ha—she *would* too. Denise can eat more than Jimmy."

"I bet she can."

Elliot heard this.

"Denise has the bump of alimentiveness overly developed," he said. "Look, I'll show you." He staggered into the bedroom and back out, palming his porcelain phrenological head, like Hamlet with Yorick's skull.

"Alas, poor Denise!" thought Jimmy.

"You see here?" Elliot pointed with the big index finger of his left hand, hefting the tattooed head in his right. He tapped the offending spot. "*Huge* here, on Denise—over-developed!"

"Do my head, Elliot," said Fay.

"She's just asking for it," thought Jimmy.

Elliot either didn't hear her or he ignored her.

"Jimmy's is rather large, too," he said, his huge mitt covering Jimmy's actual head like a fool's cap. He was worried about what the party food had cost. "But Denise's is even larger, more prominent. I would wager that she could eat a whole leg of lamb."

"Do my head," said Fay, like a kid asking for a treat.

"Do mine, Mr. Whistler," said Phyllis.

Elliot put the phrenological head on the table, between the remaining mashed potatoes, the chicken's skeleton, and the bottle of hooch. With a show of great concentration, eyes half-masted, he felt about Phyllis's head with both big hands, like a hairdresser giving a shampoo. "High intelligence indicated here," he said. "Strong loyalties. Perception of the feelings of others well developed—strong empathy. A very good head," he concluded.

"Do my head," Fay repeated.

Elliot swayed over behind her and felt about for a minute. He shook his head sadly.

"*Insignificant!*" he pronounced.

*   *   *

Jimmy was still suffering from a post-prandial hangover a few days later when Elliot came down to visit them at the Margarita. Elliot was still drunk; but he managed to explain his new scheme. It was his big dream, this one. He told Jimmy all about it, how he was going to set up an appointment with the Bishop at Trenton and sell that old gentleman prelate on backing him in a new chain of charity stores. He asked Jimmy if he knew the proper form of addressing a Bishop. Jimmy suggested "sir," but that seemed somehow too simple to Elliot. He thought it should be something more like "Your Eminence" or "Reverend Exceptional Father" or *something*. He stayed long enough to be served some instant Lobster Newburg (Jimmy had whipped it up with canned lobster that Phyllis had copped from a local store), to have a few snorts, sitting among the teetering stacks of books, which Jimmy had recovered from Marsayas's apartment with the help of Butterworth who had rented a truck, to be peed on by, and to pet, Phyllis's surly black, golden-eyed cat, to comment amiably that he liked their little apartment, which ran with roaches, rats, and rumpled ringdings, and staggered off into his old man's mad dreams. Mere dreams, as Yeats would say, mere dreams!

*   *   *

For the best part of a year, Niki and Oskar considered their friends in Newark to be crazy exiles from the real world of New York. But in early August, their curiosity overcame their repugnance and they visited the exiles of Newark, the lost city—their curiosity had peaked. Even so, despite the heat, without taking time to take off his thrift-store violet jacket, Oskar cried, "Forget all the greeting shit, Fluffy, Marilyn Monroe is an angel. Here, look at dis," and he threw down the *Daily News*.

DAILY NEWS
AUGUST 6, 1962

MARILYN DEAD

"Accident?"

"Suicide?"

"Murder?"

"She O.D.ed," said Phyllis.

"On purpose," said Oskar.

"They murdered her," said Niki. "She knew too much."

"About what?" asked Oskar.

"About the Kennedys," said Niki.

"About the Court," said Phyllis.

"What court?" asked Jimmy.

"The Kennedy Court," said Phyllis. "She was a courtesan."

Oskar's long dark hair looked dank with sweat, his pompadour deflated. He finally took off his jacket, opened his collar, and, sprawling in a chair, lit his pipe. He was a film buff and Marilyn's death hit him hard. Jimmy poured everyone a glass of beer.

"I've got some weed hidden away," said Phyllis.

"Later," said Jimmy.

"You knew her," said Oskar, "didn't you?"

"No—I met her sortof, once. I was a friend of Jack Noelle, who worked with her. I worked with him in Hollywood. She drove him crazy. Always late."

Oskar raised his beer—"To Marilyn," he said.

"Always late!" said Jimmy.

"Blonde all over," said Phyllis.

"I'll drink to that," said Niki.

Oskar shook his head, sadly, "Let's change the subject."

"To what?"

"Vhat do you do for verk over here?" Oskar asked.

"I've been selling photo coupons door-to-door."

"How do you do dat, Fluffy?"

Jimmy showed him a coupon book. "You buy one of these coupons for fifty-cents, take it into any Vanity Fair Photography Studio—they're all over New York, New Jersey, and Pennsylvania—and they take a bunch of pictures of you, one of which you get free for the coupon. I keep the fifty-cents—my commission. The studio shows you all the pictures they've taken, and you, being the narcissistic idiot that you are, buy the rest of the pictures at ten bucks a shot."

"You tink I could do it?"

"Sure, with your accent the right crowd would take you for a great Kraut photographer. Steichen. Stieglitz. Von-Somebodyorother. I'll take you out with me sometime."

Niki thought they were crazy, living over in Newark. "Whath there to do over here, anyhow?"

"I'm reading *The Courtier*," piped animated Phyllis, "by Castiglione."

"What do you and Oskar do?" asked Jimmy.

"The thame damned *boring* things!" said Niki.

"Well, so do we. We can do the same damn boring things in Newark that you can do in New York."

Jimmy could see that Niki was still giving Oskar a hard time. He sympathized with Oskar. He thought Oskar was a good painter. Of all the budding artists—painters, writers, musicians, actors—he'd become acquainted with, Oskar seemed the most talented and the most determined to succeed. If any of us ever makes it, it'll be Oskar, he thought. Niki, though, didn't seem to share Jimmy's high opinion of Oskar's work. She was too much in competition. Somehow, Jimmy didn't think she would chew leather for Oskar, like Rolly's Jean.

Once Niki and Oskar had left, and Phyllis had re-buried herself in *The Courtier,* Jimmy, remembering an incident that was still vivid in his mind, sat down at the typewriter and wrote:

NORMA JEAN

I was a student then and waited in
the office of a famous acting coach,
and in came Marilyn Monroe. I grinned,

but she was self-involved, not to approach.
It had begun to rain, the window showed,
and she showed too, rain on her London Fog,
blue scarf, pulled tight below her chin and bowed,
rain running down her face. I was agog,
but tried my best not to disturb her, not
to make my presence felt. She looked afraid,
and pale, and wet, and small, and sad. She seemed
so regular a pretty girl that I forgot
she was a movie star and saw instead
a girl from home of whom I'd always dreamed.

*　　*　　*

In October another famous non-leather-chewer showed up in Newark to visit the exiles. Denise sat Steinian and monumental at their rickety table. Beer and pretzels vanished before Jimmy's eyes. Between Rabelaisian mouthfuls, Denise stated her case. "I can't do this damned thesis," she said.

She was stoned on pot, or a lot of something else, but she looked worried too. "I have to have it in by November. I just can't get anywhere with it. Ever since you won that poetry prize, I've been thinking that you could write it. I don't know why I asked your dad. I should have asked you in the first place. Besides, I knew how much you loved Donne. I remember you telling me so when we first met. I could bring all my books and notes over here and you could put it all together. I know you could, Jimmy."

"I don't know . . ."

"My trust fund says that I can spend all the money I need to on education. I can give you three hundred dollars for writing it, five hundred if you type it up in good shape for me. I know you're a good typist."

"Why can't you do it yourself? You've been reading Donne for years. You've been studying at Columbia—how long has it been?"

209

"You know me, Jimmy—I just stay too stoned. I can't get my head together anymore. Please do it for me. Please. It would be the biggest favor anybody's ever done me. I'll owe you more than money—eternal gratitude."

"What do you think, Phyllis?"

"I think you should do it for her, Jimmy."

"O.K.," said Jimmy. "Get me the books. God knows, we need the money. But remember you're asking me to do in about two weeks what you haven't been able to do in well over a year. Don't expect too much."

"If I don't get my Masters, I'll still give you half. If I get it, I'll give you a hundred dollar bonus. How's that?"

"Deal!" Jimmy reached out and took Denise's big mitt and shook it.

Phyllis was in the Murphy bed with several newspapers spread about her. "Do you guys know that there's big trouble in Cuba? Senator Keating says the Russians have put in atomic missiles down there. And look at this." She waved a *New York Times*. Denise got up and took the paper.

THE NEW YORK TIMES
OCTOBER 21, 1962

PRESIDENT CUTS HIS TOUR SHORT, FLIES TO CAPITAL

HAS MILD COLD—SPECULATION RISES ON POSSIBLE URGENT WHITE HOUSE BUSINESS

Phyllis looked at them with the huge anxiety of a child. "I just know the stupid bastards are going to blow us all to hell. Look at the upper left hand corner."

THE NEW YORK TIMES
OCTOBER 21, 1962

U.S. FIRES LONG-DELAYED ATOM BLAST ABOVE PACIFIC

CLOUDS REFLECT LIGHT FROM NUCLEAR EXPLOSION
OVER JOHNSTON ISLAND,
ABOUT 100 MILES NORTHWEST OF HONOLULU.

"If you want to get your Masters, you better let Jimmy get started right away, before it's too late."

"I don't think things are that dire, my little dear," said Jimmy.

"Fuck it," said Denise. "I'm stoned anyway."

But the next morning she arrived with a sea-bag full of books and notes, which she helped Jimmy organize around his typing chair. He scanned the titles. Lawrence Babb's *The Elizabethan Malady (a study of Melancholia in English Literature from 1580 to 1642),* East Lansing: Michigan State College Press, 1951; *Book of Common Prayer,* Protestant Episcopal Church in the United States of America, 1945; Douglas Bush's *English Literature in the Earlier Seventeenth Century,* Oxford, The Clarendon Press, 1945; Charles Coffin's *John Donne and the New Philosophy*, New York, The Humanities Press, 1958; Angelo De Santi's "Litany," *The Catholic Encyclopedia,* Vol. IX, New York, McGraw-Hill, 1910; John Donne's *The Complete Poetry and Selected Prose,* Edited by Charles Coffin, New York, Random House,

1952; John Donne, *The Divine Poems*, Edited with introduction and commentary by Helen Gardner, London, Oxford University Press, 1952; John Donne's *Letters to Severall Persons of Honour,* Edited with notes by Charles Merrill, New York, Sturgis & Walton Co., 1910; Edmund Gosse's *Life and Letters of John Donne*, London, 1899; Fulke Greville's *Poems and Dramas*, edited by Geoffrey Bullough, New York, 1945; Frank Kermode's *John Donne*, London, Longmans, Green & Company, Ltd., 1957; Edward La Comte's *Grace to a Witty Sinner: A Life of Donne,* New York, Walker and Company, 1956; M.M. Mahood's *Poetry and Humanism,* London, Camelot Press, Ltd., 1950; Louis Martz's *The Poetry of Meditation*, New Haven, Yale University Press, 1954; Ronald McKerrow's *The Works of Sir Thomas Nashe,* Vol. III, (reprinted from the original edition with corrections and supplementary notes by F.P. Wilson), Oxford, 1958; Marjorie Nicolson's *The Breaking of the Circle*, Evanston, Northwestern University Press, 1950; Elizabeth Nugent's *The Thought and Culture of the English Renaissance*, Cambridge, Cambridge University Press, 1956; Francis Procter's *New History of the Book of Common Prayer,* Revised and rewritten by Walter H. Frere, London, Macmillan and Company, Ltd., 1932; *Roman Missal in Latin and English*, New York, Cincinnati and Chicago, Benziger Brothers, 1910; Robert Sharp's *From Donne to Dryden,* Chapel Hill, University of North Carolina Press, 1940; Tillyard's *The Elizabethan World Picture,* New York, Random House, n.d.; Isaak Walton's *Lives of Donne, Wotton, Hooker, Etc.,* London, Oxford University Press, 1956; George Williamson's *Seventeenth Century Contexts*, London, Faber and Faber, 1960: and a whole heap more, along with pounds of indecipherable notes on legal pads and index cards.

"Jesus Christ, Denise," said Jimmy, "you don't really expect me to read all this in the next two weeks, do you?"

Phyllis was down on the floor in her nightie looking, stacking and re-stacking the books as if they were boxes of candy. All this English Renaissance stuff squared with her Castiglione Italian visions of courts and courtiers and ladies of the courts. She loved it. "What are you going to write, Jimmy?" she asked from the enthralling stacks.

"It has to be an analysis of 'A Litany,'" Denise said. "Now this is what I want," she said, taking a long draught of beer, and Jimmy cut her off right there and then.

"I can't write that way," he said. "I'll dip into these books and put what I get together and you'll just have to settle for it. That's the only way I can do it—especially with only two weeks to do it in. Now you go ahead and get out of here and let me get to work."

"You better hurry, Jimmy," said Phyllis. "The Russian ships are heading this way."

"Will you shut up about the Russian fucking ships!"

"What am I going to do in the meantime?" asked Denise. "What happens if they blow us all to hell before I get my Master's?"

"You'll just have to remain an ignoramus."

Jimmy sat down and started typing. In a minute or so, he tore the page from the typewriter and handed it to Denise. He waited, sipping a bourbon, while she read "The object of this paper is the elucidation of John Donne's poem, "A Litany," on three levels: (1) to show exactly how the poem is, and how it is not, a litany; (2) to show that the poem is a profound moral statement of a very personal order; and (3) to show that the essential theme of the poem is John Donne's personal re-creation. I should stipulate here what is meant in this context by "*re*-creation," the word and the idea offering myriad interpretations. When I speak of re-creation in this context, I am speaking of that idea in Christian thought, the most succinct statement of which is to be found in St. Paul, in the Sixth Chapter of his Epistles to the Romans, that it is possible for the Christian believer to be re-born into life before he is dead."

Denise said, "John Donne, a born-again Christian?"

Jimmy said, "Now that's what I intend to do. Satisfied?"

Phyllis said, "Wow! Sounds good!"

Denise said, "O.K., man! Hit those keys!"

Jimmy said, "Now get the hell out of here so I can work! Go and catch a falling star. Go get with child a Mandrake root! Off you go!"

Jimmy went into total concentration and was not aware of just when Denise left or when Phyllis fell asleep, but when he stopped for a cup of coffee Denise was gone and Phyllis was snoring. Denise had been thoughtful enough to bring him a bag full of Benzedrine tablets and he began popping them down with coffee. The bullshit world of the Cuban missile crisis receded as the Elizabethan world projected itself. He lived in Donne's world until a knock came at the door. Phyllis was still sleeping. But there was natural light in the room from the window. He'd been working all night. He went to the door and opened it. Elliot stood there, drunk and disheveled, a hopeful, ingratiating look on his face.

"My boy, I came downtown on some business and I thought I'd stop in to see you. I have a nice bottle of Mr. Boston with me. Would you like a drink?"

"I'll put a shot in my coffee. What's wrong, Dad? You look kind of sick."

"It's this missile crisis," said the old man, sitting down at the rickety table among the books. "Don't you think we should all go to Denver?"

"The first place they'll hit is out west," said Jimmy, sipping his spiked coffee. "That's where all the missile silos are. They have to take them out first. We're probably safer here."

"I never thought of that. I guess you learn things like that in the Marine Corps."

"It's fairly common knowledge, Dad."

The old man looked around. "What are you doing with all these books?"

"I'm writing Denise's paper for her. The one she wanted you to write."

"Oh, yes, I rather disappointed her on that one, didn't I?"

"Look, Dad, don't be worried about this missile thing. I said that they'd have to hit our silos first, but that's not quite true. They want to hit the command centers first. That means that the stupid sons-of-bitches have each other in their sights—I mean Kennedy and Khrushchev—and they're not going to pull the trigger. If they could kill a few million of us without killing each other, they would, but they can't, so you might as well not worry about it. Remember what Voltaire said—"

"You've read Voltaire?" The old man looked at Jimmy with new-found respect. "Of course I've read Voltaire. Remember what Candide says, about how he's going to deal with life? He said that if he heard that the world was going to end tomorrow, he would just go on tending his little garden. Remember that?"

"I do, indeed! Just go on tending his little garden." The old man looked as if he had been handed the key to happiness.

"This has been a very edifying little talk. Let me have just one more drink and I'll be on my way. I have business to do. Important business. Oh, I almost forgot. I have a letter for you delivered in care of us at Baldwin." He handed Jimmy the letter. It was from Vera. The usual—a demand to see him about a divorce. She'd enclosed another letter in the envelope. It was from Dr. Zolauf. It bore no greeting. When Elliot left, Jimmy read it.

Fleury, you have not even bothered to contact me. It appears that you have dropped off the face of the earth. I've had to talk to Vera, and she doesn't know where you are most of the time. I wonder if you recognize your own ingratitude. Apparently you have no idea of the trouble and expense I went to to make you a success as an actor. I did what I did for you because in the right circumstances you could have rivaled Brando or James Dean, and you have thrown all that away, along with much good will. Vera thinks that you are unbalanced. I would use the word reckless, crazy even. Vera may still have some hope for you, but I do not. Dr. Reuben Zolauf.

"O.K.," said Jimmy, staring at the letter. "That's just fine with me. All of it."

As for Vera, Jimmy didn't want a divorce. Not yet. He was afraid his domestic nature might invite him into a marriage with Phyllis. Marriage, especially one that was all over, was good protection. In certain regards, he didn't have a great deal of respect for his own judgment. They were trying to make him feel quixotic, but he had convinced himself that he was being ruthless in his quest for an apprenticeship in poetry. Quixotic! Was Vera right? Was Dr. Zolauf right? Was he unbalanced, crazy? No, there was a method in his madness. He was going to be a poet—if only his father lived long enough to protect him from his mother, and he could stay married long enough to Vera to protect him from Phyllis.

He had made up his mind. He was going to follow his bliss, and when the time came to bury him, no one was going to say that he hadn't. Jack Noelle had taught him this lesson. Carpe diem! Jimmy crumpled the letters and tossed them into an overflowing wastepaper basket.

Phyllis was up, eating something.

The room was dark. Jimmy hit the light switch.

Phyllis was asleep.

The room was bright.

He went on working.

As though heav'n suffred earth-quakes, peace or war,
When new Townes rise, and olde demolish'd are.
They have empayld within a Zodiake
The free-borne Sunne, and keeps twelve signes awake
To watch his steps; the Goat and Crabbe controule,
And fright him backe, who els to eyther Pole,
(Did not these Tropiques fetter him) might runne:
For his course is not round; nor can the Sunne
Perfit a Circle, or maintaine his way
One inche direct . . .

"Oh, Jimmy, I hate these bastards! Why don't they do their stupid shit by themselves and leave the rest of us out of it?"

"No man is an island, Phyl. Let me work."

Jimmy wrote: *What could be more natural at this juncture, at this time in his life, and at this point in the age in which he lived, than that Donne should choose the litany as the form in which to address his God? But, while Donne is perhaps thinking of himself as a symbol for the confusions of his age* (Jimmy thought: Chaos), *his main concern—perhaps*

217

THE NEW YORK TIMES
OCTOBER 24, 1962

SOVIET CHALLENGES U.S. BLOCKADE;
INTERCEPTION OF 25 RUSSIAN SHIPS
ORDERED;
CUBA QUARANTINE BACKED BY O.A.S.

MOSCOW REPLIES

WARNS WASHINGTON RISKS NUCLEAR CONFLICT

"Jimmy, when are you going to sleep?"

"I'm just about half-way through. I'll keep going until I . . ."

He put his head down on the typewriter.

"Jimmy? Jimmy!"

THE NEW YORK TIMES
OCTOBER 25, 1962

SOME SOVIET SHIPS VEER FROM CUBA;
KHRUSHCHEV SUGGESTS SUMMIT
MEETING

"I told you once that we wouldn't blow each other up," he said to Phyllis. "Too cowardly. Remember?" But Phyllis had been scared into near catalepsy. She had stopped going

218

out altogether: sat in bed day and night, a valetudinarian, her pale hair veiled by the smoke of the pot that Niki had brought her from New York, and devoured her books on the medieval Royal Courts of Europe. She hated the present bullshit world, but adored the bullshit of the past.

Jimmy lay snoring, exhausted.

"Oh, Denise, I've never seen anything like it. He was absolutely manic, like he was on a coke-amphetamine cocktail. First he got that typewriter stand out into the middle of the room, then he stacked all your books around him like a wall, then he'd dive into one, growling the title of this book or that, then another, back and forth, up and down through the stacks. I don't know if he knew what he was looking for or what. He'd highlight, underline, dog-ear, tear out, bits from this book and that, and I don't know how he knew if he was making sense or not, but he seemed to because your thesis kept getting bigger, or then he'd cut and it would get smaller again and then bigger again, like an accordion, up and down, up and down. He'd swear, drink endless cups of coffee, take shots of whiskey, curse again, leap up and almost run around the room, and this went on for two weeks, I swear to you, without a break. He didn't sleep, he'd doze at the typewriter, then be pounding on it again. I've never seen anything like it."

"You've read it through?"

"Twice. It's beautifully organized. It's just what you want, you'll see. When he was done writing, he re-typed the whole thing as neat as a pin. He's a very fast typist. Very fast and very neat. But look at him now. He's knocked out. I've seen him do this before. He works like a madman, in a fit, then collapses."

"Let me read it. If he's done it, it's amazing. I couldn't do the damn thing for two years and he does it in two weeks, without taking any classes."

"Yes, but he knows all about Donne, so it wasn't strange material to him."

"I know. He reads Donne for fun. That's why I thought he could do it." Denise buried her face in the thesis and Phyllis went back to Castiglione.

Jimmy slept for two days and woke with one dream. He lay between his mother and his father in a small metal bed in a roominghouse in an unidentifiable city, but probably either Philadelphia or Newark. It was a very hot night. His father wore a white strapped undershirt and white BVDs, his mother, a pale pink slip. Moonlight cast in a nearby window and illuminated the area of the bed, so that he could see the hand come up from between the mattress and the wood-painted metal of the headboard. The hand was not a hand, exactly, or it was more like the hand of a monkey, but not a monkey's paw either. It was the longnailed, dirty hand-claw of a little devil, and it was trying to find him by feeling the mattress. He shrunk down out of its reach in the bed between his mother and father, but its arm was long and reached farther down, feeling here and there, looking for him. Then several other claws appeared, reaching for him as the first one was doing, and he got down to the middle of the bed, too terrified to scream, only to realize that other such claws were reaching up from the foot of the bed. He must have screamed then, for he woke his mother and father.

What's the matter? What's going on? His father got up and turned on the light. What is it? What's wrong? His mother looked about, dazed with sleep. They had never been in this house, this room, before. Although he was terrified, Jimmy forced himself to look under the bed. Nothing but dust, nothing but darkness and dust, spider webs and dust bunnies.

"What do you think it means?" asked Phyllis.

"That I'm still a child," said Jimmy. "Three years old."

"That you're pursued by devils."

"And dust bunnies," said Jimmy. Nevertheless, those two solid days and nights of sleep had revived him. He was hungry.

"How are things in Cuba?" he asked Phyllis as he fried himself a couple of eggs.

"Thank God, Jimmy, it's all settling down. The Russian ships have turned around and are heading back. Looks like we're not going to kill ourselves this time."

"I only worried about somebody making a stupid mistake," said Jimmy, eating his eggs. "This brinksmanship is idiotic. Two power-mad apes challenging each other. So Denise liked the paper, did she?"

"She loved it. She's sure she's going to get her degree."

"And we'll get our five hundred bucks, right? And a hundred bucks bonus!"

"She'll keep her word, Jimmy."

"About as much as anybody, I guess."

For the next few weeks Jimmy just rested and read, then one morning Elliot appeared at the door, hand out, as usual.

"It's near the end of the month," he said, "and I'm running a little low. You couldn't lend me a couple of dollars, could you, Jimmy?" Gad, but he had the look of a revenant, eyes like lead, nose like a rose. The old fear for his father rose up in Jimmy, then the tenderness.

"Come on in, Dad, let's have a drink."

"Good thinking, my boy! And how is the wasp-waisted little lady of kindness today?"

"I'm fine, now, Mr. Whistler, but they sure as hell had the shit scared out of me for the last couple of weeks."

"They who?"

"The bullshit world! Cuba and all that, that's who!"

"Of course. I myself even considered a tactical retreat. He who fights and runs away lives to fight another day, you know. I think that was the Scarlet Pimpernel. Douglas

Fairbanks, Senior. The real Douglas Fairbanks, not that skinny son of his."

"But you decided against the tactical retreat, eh, Dad?"

"As unbecoming an officer and a gentleman. Cannon to the left of them, cannon to the right of them, and into the breach rode the six hundred. Tennyson. I'll just sit down right here on the bed, if you don't mind." He leaned backwards wearing an expression of faith and fell across Phyllis's skinny legs. Jimmy took his free hand—the one not holding the king-sized Chesterfield—and pulled him into a sitting position.

"Now where's that drink? Ho, someone's gently rapping, tapping at your chamber door."

Jimmy went to the door and opened it. "Oh, how a gala begins!" he said. Denise stepped in wearing a smile as wide as the moon and carrying innumerable packages.

"Hail to thee, Jimmy Whistler!" she cried. "You're looking at a newly minted Master of Arts! And all hail to thee, Jimmy Whistler!" She saw Elliot. "And no thanks to you, Mr. WPA writer!"

"May I have my drink, please?" said Elliot. "Garçon! Garçon! A drink over here, and high time. Let's have a little cheerio-chin-chin!"

"Mr. Whistler," said Denise, unloading her bundles and wriggling out of her coat, "I've got something better than a drink for you. And you too, Philly. You're gonna love this."

"What is it?" cried Phyllis.

"Hashish! Number One Tangier hash! Hashish—food of the assassins!

"Voici le temps des assassins!" piped up Jimmy.

"Rimbaud—right on—now is the time of the assassins," Denise translated. Remember, Mr. Whistler, you wanted me to get you some? I had no idea you'd be here. I brought it for Philly. I know Jimmy doesn't care. But Mr. Whistler, you're gonna love it. And I've got a check here for you, Jimmy. Five hundred dollars."

Jimmy shook his head for her to be quiet, but alas, too late. Elliot smelled money.

"It appears that my visit is serendipitous," he said, raising his eyebrows.

"Do you have any cash, Denise?" asked Jimmy.

"Some."

"Have you got fifty to give me? Or that bonus you promised?"

"Yes," said Denise, looking through her big leather bag. She handed Jimmy a hundred dollars. Jimmy handed half of it to Elliot.

"Well, Mister Whistler, damned if you didn't get that fifty anyway," cried Denise, laughing. "You know you're never going to see that again, don't you, Jimmy? But what the hell! The missile crisis is over, I've got my Master's degree, and we've got booze and hash galore. C'mon, it's party time!"

"We should have a masked ball," piped Phyllis.

CHAPTER NINE

CROSSING THE BAR

Jimmy climbed hundreds of steps every night, selling the photography coupons, the muscles of his lower back cramping like nervous snakes. His back had not been right since that night at Tony's Half-Way House when the wind had whipped that huge table around on him and he had heard something crack, crack, crack. Every time he spilled himself over too much to one side or the other, he'd burst into giggle fits of false hilarity; so that, not only was he in pain, he was made to feel like a fool, giggling for no apparent reason, emitting a mouthful of bubbled laughter into some potential customer's face, while at the same time doing a kind of St. Vitus dance, attempting to relocate that spot, that exquisite point of balance, where existed dignified and painless gravity.

It was Niki who got them out of their rut. She and Oskar came over to the Margarita one day and proposed that they come to New York and stay at the loft she had rented a few months earlier. She explained that she and Oskar had taken separate apartments so that Oskar could paint and she could practice on her piano, apparently the latest of the arts and crafts she had taken up in her jealous competition with him. She could stay with Oskar at his place, she told them, until they could find a place of their own. Next day Jimmy went up to Baldwin and told Fay and Elliot that he was going back to New York.

"But it's almost Christmas," Fay objected.

"I'll come over for Christmas."

"I'm going to miss you, my boy," said semi-conscious Elliot, giving Jimmy one of his wet, sloppy kisses.

*　　*　　*

The loft was in the Lower East Side. Jimmy liked it. It was clean and neat and cheerful, a good place for him to stretch his weary bones and let his damaged back heal. He sailed supinely through a slew of Eric Ambler, Graham Greene, Dashiell Hammett, and Raymond Chandler. Jimmy loved puzzles—perhaps because he felt that his whole life was a puzzle, and one that became more complex as he lived it—and he loved to try to find the solution to these mystery stories before he was half-way through the books, then read on to see if he had been right.

Why had his own life followed the twisting, chaotic course that it had thus far? Had there been an alternative to what he had lived? Had he missed an important clue? Jimmy had begun to believe that there was an answer for everything, if only some important piece of information had not been left out. Bad mystery writers deliberately left things out, good ones gave you all the relevant information you needed to solve the case. But then, God must be a bad mystery writer. Life seemed an unsolvable riddle.

This in mind, Jimmy had begun work on a philosophical essay entitled, "AND/OR." AND included everything, everything that ever was and ever would be, all the paperclips in the world and all the universes in time. OR was each paperclip set apart from all the others, each universe set apart, each singularity. Each person was an OR and lived in the OR-world. A soldier killed others in the OR-world and was justified in the act by his reckoning of good and evil, but the AND-world was transcendent and in it was brought together all OR-worldian acts—beings, entities, paperclips—in resolution and moral solution. In the AND-world, finally, all his questions and doubts would be resolved, as at the end of a good mystery story. He wrote a poem about it, "Peace in Our Time"—

> *O yet we trust that somehow good*
> *Will be the final goal of ill . . .*
> —*Tennyson*

The poet, ignorant philosopher,
Alpha & Omega beggar, posits
AND, in an academic naming, the
world that takes all others in:

"AND," he says, "includes the All.
OR is us & even war.
AND will keep including more.
OR is reductive, what we recall

—particulars, parts, & particles
—how many ways can it be said?—

all things unborn, & all things dead,
commas, grapes, seeds, articles

of various sorts, & written ones,
all things that are not All,
all memories we can recall,
all less than All, all suns,

all galaxies, germs, & viruses,
all parts of atoms & their parts,
all stops, reverses, starts,
all flowers, roses, irises—"

She frowned. "And so you say," she said,
"that you can live with ugly war
because it's what you call an OR.
ORs also are the many dead!"

"Yes. When struck by this, I wondered
what horrid meaning it must have.
The morality of love
was made to seem almost a blunder.

And yet, I thought, morality
must include the act of war.
For Fascists must be fought, are OR,
are fragments of eternity

gone wrong in AND, the All; are Fear.
A kinder & a gentler love
has got to be beyond, above,
& other than, this OR-world, where

it must be that, if we could see
the whole of things, we'd understand
how piece by piece (& hand in hand)
things add to form in synergy

a greater than is each alone,
as also are twinned Space & Time,
or life in clay & death in lime.
Thus, in the AND, all Ors atone."

But Jimmy was a poet, not a philosopher, and here in the OR-world the essay stalled in contradictions—it fell off the paper he tried to pin it to, but it floated in his mind like the gasses of the universe, coagulating, exploding, vanishing, reappearing. Rising above his life, transcending, seeing life *sub specie eternitatis*, the practice of doing so was forming a different Jimmy, perhaps better for poetry, perhaps not so good for life, too transcendent.

Phyllis looked for work, but found nothing. Jimmy suspected she hadn't looked very hard. Her father's check hadn't come at the regular time, and Jimmy had counted on it, so he asked her if she knew what was up. She confessed that, while they'd been living in Newark, she had written her parents and told them to write her under the name Whistler.

"Yes, Mummy and Daddy," she had written, "be proud of your little girl, for she has finally met someone whom she loves and has married him." So, naturally, her father, not wanting to offend his new son-in-law, had stopped sending that much-needed stipend, that treasured check, of one hundred a month.

Since Oskar needed money too, Jimmy suggested that they go over to Bedford-Stuyvesant in Brooklyn and sell photograph coupons.

"Vhy Bed-Sty?"

"You don't think they're going to buy fifty-cent memories on Park Avenue, do you? I've got a load of coupon books and an extra sample." So off they went for a night of climbing tenement stairs and selling dreams.

The streets of Bedford-Stuyvesant were squish-squash with snow. A few unsullied flakes drifted out of the black, star-spangled sky overhead. Jimmy hurried alongside his stilt-walking companion, who had, with the help of Phyllis and Niki, stood him on his unsteady feet. He entered a tenement and painfully climbed five flights. It was torture. But he found it best to start at the top and work down, that way he'd pause for a minute and get his breath so he could talk fast, and wouldn't lose it as he descended.

The hall was musty, like rotting wood, and with a smell of sour things he couldn't identify—life and age—and the stink of kerosene fumes. Oskar was working his way toward him from the other end of the block. They would meet somewhere in the middle, in one of these crowded, collapsing houses.

He got his first sale from a sexy young lady with bejangles on her ears big as anchor chains, and sparkling thingamajigs in her soft, sly hair. Her boyfriend, a big dark guy, dressed to kill, ready for a night on the town, bought the coupons for her. He wanted a couple of pictures of her. Jimmy couldn't blame him.

He got the next three sales in one apartment from three young studs who were drinking and had fallen in love with themselves.

"You think I take a good picher, man?" one of them asked, sitting sprawled at a kitchen table, making the question sound like a challenge.

"Sure you will," Jimmy said.

"You ain't just shittin' me, is you?"

"Do I look like I'd kid you, man?"

"Sho *do*!" with which they all started to laugh.

"Hey, man," one of the other two said, producing a jug of wine, "you wanna drink?"

"Well," said Jimmy, "I only drink at Christmas."

"Well, dis is Christmath," said the third.

"So it is! Well, in that case—" Jimmy gave himself a good chug-a-lug.

"Wheeee!" said the first. "Dat man know *how* ta drink!"

Jimmy left the Three Musketeers a little happier, he hoped. Or maybe they were the three wise men and Jimmy was the babe in the woods.

He got his last two sales just before he met Oskar. This time it was from three young women—but actually only two; one of them wouldn't buy and called the other two a couple of suckers for doing so. Jimmy was afraid he'd miss Oskar in the hallway, so he hurried out. In the hall he heard Oskar yelling his head off downstairs:

"Hey, *Jim!* Wo bist du, Sh-vine! Vhere are you, you fluffy sh-vine-hoont? Hey, Sh-vine, are you up dere?"

"What'd you get, Oskar?" Jimmy called, coming down.

"Shit! Christ! A couple of bucks! Vhat'd you get?"

Jimmy told him.

"Frog me!" said Oskar, surprised at Jimmy's success.

They went to a soul-food joint and Jimmy put lots of redhot sauce on his fish sandwich and gulped himself three cups of good black hot-as-hell coffee. On the streets the nervous neons winked, the moving pageant filed, and a skinny black Santa rang his bell.

*   *   *

Niki and Oskar and Phyllis and Jimmy spent Christmas in the loft. Niki and Oskar brought up a Christmas tree and Oskar took over the decorating. They sat for hours and made chains out of colored paper and Oskar strung them back and forth across the ceiling. He got a big piece of cardboard and painted a Nativity scene on it in the broad-stroked, religious style of Roualt.

Niki brought down from her parents' house a little turkey she had roasted in their oven. She had it all stuffed, too, with raisins and grapes and nuts and all sorts of delights, and the stuffing was highly seasoned—snappy as snuff. She had the fowl all wrapped in tin foil and carried it down in a cardboard box, insulated with towels. She'd come by cab, so the unfortunate little gobbler was still warm as toast.

After dinner Jimmy gave a reading of "A Visit from St. Nick." Then Niki played the piano and they sang Christmas carols and pop Christmas songs.

There were gifts, too. Niki gave Jimmy a copy of Shakespeare's sonnets, illustrated with tableaux of the Dark Lady and the sonneteer smooching in several ways under several moons. Jimmy gave Oskar a batch of good French water-color paper. Phyllis gave Niki a little painting she had done. It was filled with those grotesque and nightmarish creatures that Jimmy suspected were for Phyllis a sort of subconscious mirror of self. There was a skinny, horrible little crab-like woman with a hump on her back, moving on all fours to her own left, indicated by the way the left arm was reaching out and also by the direction in which her glasses were looking. Actually, there were no eyes, just a pair of pink tinted glasses shaped like Phyllis's own spectacles. The body was chalk white with green spots scattered over it. In the left corner there was a sort of shrub growing out of the ground, only it was yellow and was made of separate wavery strands, like hair (peyote flashback?). From a dark area underneath the hair two beady purple eyes peeked out. Jimmy took the shrub to be himself, but Phyllis disclaimed any relationship to persons living or dead. In the right background there was a daddy-long-legs with a little blank white face, a mustache, and a black pipe extending from its mouth. To Jimmy's eye the creature looked very like Oskar.

"It *isn't* Oskar, I tell you," insisted Phyllis, vehemently. "It's a symbol!"

"Well, then," said Jimmy, "it's a symbol for Oskar."

"It is not!"

Between the yellow shrub and the crablike thing, and in the background, was a tall, graceful, beautiful brown tree with large, diamond-shaped green leaves. Its branches extended over the whole picture, and especially over the yellow shrub. The symbolism of the tree was plain enough. In fact, the whole picture was a little too clear for Jimmy's comfort. Wasn't Phyllis jealously commenting on Niki's increasing influence on Jimmy? Come on!

Two days after Christmas Niki came up with Oskar and announced that she'd had a quarrel with her parents and that they were not going to give her any more money for the loft; that Phyllis and Jimmy would have to move on the first of January; but that they shouldn't be upset because she had already found them an apartment right next door to Oskar's, and had paid a month's rent on it; that her plan was for them to move their things over there gradually during the remainder of the month—she'd dispose of her things in the loft during the same period—and that they would all then live very happily, right next door to one another. It struck Jimmy as ironic that Niki was happy enough to share Oskar's place with him, yet refused to help him with his rent; yet here she was, setting Phyllis and himself up.

The apartment was on Pitt Street, a gloomy Lower East Side slum street. It was filthy, its layers of paint and plaster dropping from its ceilings, its walls buckling and dripping brown syrup, its floor-boards warped, pot-holed. Jimmy could hear the various rodentia scurrying away underfoot. He nailed cardboard over the holes in the floor and topped that with some old, ragged pieces of linoleum that were heaped in a corner. He tried to seal the windows with cardboard too. They were all broken. What a filthy den! The rent was dirt cheap, but the dump should have been given away—or condemned, so they wouldn't have been tempted to live in it. Dirt for dirt.

Niki had handled things nicely. It crossed Jimmy's mind that it was the only place she could find near to Oskar's. She'd've put them in the Snake Pit, thought Jimmy, were it necessary, to have her own way. He had a feeling that Niki had planned this, way back in Newark, had got them arranged into an intimate little foursome, and had bound their fate together, without Oskar, Phyllis, or himself quite realizing it. But, after all, she hadn't taken on the responsibility of caring for Phyllis and Jimmy for the rest of their lives. All she had promised to do was to get them there and help them set up, which is what she had done. Inwardly, Jimmy vowed, "and that's all she's going to do, too." Oskar had become his best friend.

*   *   *

Once Jimmy and Phyllis were ensconced in their new digs, Jimmy felt he owed his folks a visit.

"Why didn't you come over for Christmas?" Fay asked, before he could get through the door.

"You promised you would. I cooked a turkey and everything, and just sat and waited and waited. I was so disappointed."

"Things happened, Mom. I just couldn't. Where's Dad?"

"Your father's moved out."

"Moved out! Where's he gone?"

"He's taken your old apartment down on Broad Street, at the Margarita, the one you and Phyllis had. He moved down there right after you left."

"But why?"

"I don't know. I don't know what's the matter with him. I think it's all those pills he takes. Or maybe he's getting senile. He's nearly ten years older than I am. He'll be seventy, you know."

"He's not senile. Far from it. If he's anything, he's hopped up. Is he drinking? Popping pills?"

"He hasn't stopped since your birthday."

Fay gave Jimmy a cup of coffee. He was glad to be there, in that tiny place. Everything looked very clean and pleasant after Pitt Street.

"He's been working on this new scheme of his," Fay went on, "about getting the Bishop to back him in a chain of charity stores."

"Yeah, he told me about that."

"What do you think of it?"

"It's crackers."

"Well, anyway, he says he has to be alone, so he can think. He says I'm a nay-sayer. But it isn't that, Jimmy; it's just that I don't see how he can do anything when he's taking all those pills and drinking all the time. How can he go to see a Bishop when he's drunk?"

"He *would*."

"Oh, I know he would. That's what I'm afraid of. Besides, that isn't the only reason he left. It's because he wants to be alone so he can drink. And do you know how much those pills of his cost him last month? Nearly a hundred dollars. I saw the bill, and I saw him take the money out of his cash box. He's not working at all, now. And there's only a few hundred dollars left. He had it up to nine hundred dollars when he was managing the Angels' Own Store. He was robbing them blind. That was the most money we've ever had at one time, and now he's spending it all. I don't know what we're going to do. He's too old to get another job. And I've got all I can do to run this house. It's a good thing we get free rent and his social security."

"Does Burns know that Dad's moved out?"

"No. I promised your father I wouldn't tell him. He'd be furious. He thinks it's terrible that your father doesn't do anything around here."

"Well—but he likes Dad."

"That's right, but he wouldn't like this. He'd be sore. Here, look at this—"

It was a note, scrawled in Elliot's very large, aggressive hand.

"*My Angel*," it said. "*I am leaving without saying good-bye because I don't want to wake you so early. But I'll be back tomorrow evening. Love and kisses from Casanova.*"

"Casanova! Gee, that doesn't sound like Dad. Was he drunk, do you suppose?"

"I suppose so. But still, it was a nice note to get. It really cheered me up. He left it yesterday morning. He spent the night here. He came up to get his heavy overcoat out of the cleaners, and it was snowing so hard I talked him into staying. He doesn't look well, either, Jimmy; he's getting gray in the face from drinking. And did you notice his eyes the last time you saw him?"

"No."

"His eyes are all mixed bloodshot and yellow. And do you know what it's from? I found out. I caught him taking some new pills, things I never saw before, and when I asked him what they were, he looked so guilty. Finally I got it out of him. The last time he went to the drug store to fill his pre-scriptions—he's got about twenty, you know, and they're all expired or faked—he asked the clerk if there was something he could take to . . . you know, to be able to make love. The clerk told him this bottle of pills would work. All they are is iron tablets—I read the label—but he's been taking them by the handful. They're turning the whites of his eyes yellow. That's what I think."

Jimmy couldn't help laughing, and Fay began to laugh too.

"I think that's why he's gone down to that house to live," Fay said, turning serious. "I think he hopes he'll find some woman in that place who'll stimulate him." Then she laughed again. "But I don't think he will."

"Oh, Mom, I think he'll come home when he gets tired of it. This is just another binge."

"I don't know," Fay said, "he's got this bug in him about going some place. He's been talking a lot about Denver, and about the old days when he had money. He's been saying that he wants to go back out to Denver before he dies."

"He always says that when he's drunk."

"But I think he means it this time. I think he'd like to take the money and go out there. It's only that he doesn't want to leave you here in the East. He'd never go anywhere unless you went. He loves you so much, Jimmy."

"I know, Mom. I love him, too, but Jesus, he has a strange way of showing it."

"But what would we do out there? I don't know what he could ever do, at his age. It's just a dream of his. Another of his crazy dreams."

Jimmy left Fay and took the bus downtown to see Elliot. He arrived just in time to be put to work. Elliot was moving.

"I've been hoping you'd call so I could get you to come over and help me carry my bags. Otherwise I'd have to pay somebody. Do you want a drink?"

Jimmy said he did. He always loved having a drink with his dad. "What's that you're wearing?" Jimmy asked, pulling his dad's jacket lapel.

"What?"

"That. . . *tie*. It's got a hula dancer on it!"

"Oh, you mean Sweet Leilani. I got it at the Angels' Own. It's really something, eh?"

"But, Dad—my God! It's a piece of *trash*. I never saw you wear a thing like that."

"Well, how about this?" said Elliot, his eyes gleaming as he flashed a huge fake diamond ring under Jimmy's nose.

"Oh, Dad! What's the matter with you?"

"The matter! Why, my boy, I've never been better! Bright-eyed, bushy tailed, and free as a bird!"

"Your eyes are like two boiled eggs!"

"I don't believe that the ladies would agree with your

assessment. Not by a long-shot," he said, winking.

He went into the closet and reached up on a shelf where a short time ago Phyllis and Jimmy had kept their box of records and pulled down a little pint bottle of whiskey. From where Jimmy was sitting, on a cardboard box packed with some of Elliot's things, he could see a whole row, at least ten little soldiers, lined up and ready in a phalanx. Elliot poured Jimmy a hooker of booze and Jimmy swallowed it. It was damned good to be out of the cold and the snow.

"Well, Dad, where are you moving to?" he asked, sitting down on the open Murphy bed.

Elliot told Jimmy that he had found a room around the corner, on Kitchen Street, in a house where they had lived twice before, once, when Jimmy was a baby, during the Depression, and once later when he was about five.

It was the house they had been living in when Jimmy had started kindergarten. He remembered that on his first day Fay had forgotten about him and he had had to find his way home by himself. He was terrified, and, in his terror, had forgotten the address of the house, which Elliot had drilled him in. He could only remember the name of the street, Kitchen, and the fact that the house in which he lived was the only one on the street that had shiny, curvy brass handrails siding its front steps. With that information a nice lady was able to bring him home to his befuddled mother.

"But why are you leaving here, Dad?"

"It's too expensive, keeping an apartment," he said. "I can get a room over there and if I want to boil water for coffee I'll use an electric plate. I'll eat in restaurants, or up at Baldwin. You can fix this electric plate, can't you?" Elliot handed the contraption to Jimmy, who looked it over.

"Yeah. It'll only take a minute," Jimmy said, seeing there was a wire loose. "Dad," he said, "why don't you go home to Mom? She's lonely up there all by herself." He took out a pen knife and started fiddling with the gadget. He wanted Elliott to remain the guard at the gate.

"No, my boy," said Elliot. Jimmy could always tell that Elliot was drunk when he started my-boying him. "No, my boy; like Garbo, I want to be alone. My head is steaming with plans and I don't want any interference. Your mother is a nay-sayer. *I* am a *yea*-sayer."

"Dad, you know, she loves you so much. She's awfully lonely." If Elliott stepped aside, would Jimmy have to take his place? The prospect sent a thrill of fear up his miserable spine.

"I love her too; but I can't live with her. You should understand that. How many times have we offered you a free room at Baldwin, and how many times have you refused it?"

"I knew she wouldn't let me concentrate—let me do my work, study, write. She'd always be calling me to *eat*—interrupting me. She doesn't understand what I'm trying to do. She doesn't understand extended concentration."

"I read some of your poetry when we were sharing your room at Miss Byrdsong's, you know. I don't understand modern poetry. I like Poe and Kipling and Tennyson—'Crossing the Bar'—but it seemed to me you knew what you were doing. I liked some of it."

"The thought of living with her scares me to death—it would kill my chance to work—she's always interrupting; she won't stick to any agreement—but it's different with you, Dad."

"No, it isn't. That's just what I've been trying to tell you. I have my dreams, too. Do you remember Tennyson's 'Ulysses'? 'There's still some noble work toward the end'—or something like that?"

"Yes. But you'll go back when you've got all your plans made, won't you?"

"We'll see. Do you want another drink?"

"Sure do."

"All right. But don't get drunk. I want you to help move me."

"Don't worry, Dad; I won't." But he did. They both did.

*   *   *

Fortunately, Kitchen Street wasn't far to go, just up the block and around the corner. When Jimmy saw the house he was disappointed, because those beautiful, shining brass handrails he remembered so gratefully were green and tarnished now. The place had become a fleabag for derelicts, drunks, and prostitutes. One of the places from which Jimmy had started out in life. The small apartments of the Depression and war years had been redivided with plaster-board into tiny compartments. It was just a flop house how, not that it had ever been anything so special, really, he supposed. But he could still remember Mrs. LaSalle, the fat lady with the pince-nez who used to own the joint. Now in her apartment—the very apartment where Elliot had written the letter to the President of the United States that resulted in having Mrs. LaSalle's son released from a prison camp—there was a horrible old virago, gin-soaked and toothless, with a nasty-snouted barking bitch of a terrier in her arms. Elliot asked her to show Jimmy the room in the basement.

"What do you think of it?" Elliot asked.

It was the only basement room; the rest of the basement was used for storage.

"This looks better to me than being way up on top. Suppose there's a fire? Down here you'd be more safe. It's all cement."

"But I like it better up there, even if it does cost a little more."

Jimmy saw what was on Elliot's mind. There wouldn't be any company down here. Upstairs, everybody kept the doors open and wandered through the halls. Jimmy thought, how ironic it was that all during his own early years Elliot always wanted a basement apartment and now he had to be up near the roof.

"O.K., it's your pick."

He hauled Elliot's bags up to the chosen compartment, on the fourth floor. But he was still sober enough to be thinking about safety, and he said to Elliot: "This place is a fire-trap, Dad. Promise me you won't stay here very long. Promise me you'll go home to Mom as soon as you get your plans made."

"We'll see," Elliot said. "We'll see, my boy; we'll see." He looked haggard and gray of face, as Fay had said, but he was still a handsome old rake.

They drank together all afternoon.

The snow stopped falling toward ten o'clock in the evening, and Jimmy decided it was time for him to get back to New York. He had obligations, responsibilities. He had Phyllis, now, to take care of.

"Why don't you stay here and spend the night with me?" Elliot said. "The snow's deep out there. Your feet'll be soaked by the time you get to New York. You can go in the morning, can't you?"

"No, Dad. I've got to go. I've got to go. Phyllis'll be wondering what happened to me." Jimmy was drunk. Could hardly walk. But he had things to do. He had things he just *had* to do. Just like Elliot. They had to do whatever it was they thought they had to do.

*　　*　　*

One evening at Pitt Street Jimmy looked into a half-filled beer bottle that had been left opened and standing out and saw six dead roaches floating atop the stale, flat beer. He was disappointed because he could have drunk the stuff. He had no aversion to warm, stale, flat beer, and had learned to put a head on it by dropping an Alka-Seltzer tablet into it. But

he wasn't about to drink any beer that had six dead roaches
floating in it, bodies like boats and legs like oars raised up, so
aimlessly. The place was filthy. He needed some order!

Phyllis went out and bought some roach spray and
Jimmy sprayed the walls, up and down, back and forth, until
there were billowing clouds of poison closing on them from
every corner. It was bitter cold out, but Jimmy knocked the
cardboard out of the windows and let the air suck the poison
out from under their noses. Then he blocked the windows
again and started in the kitchen. But before they began in the
kitchen they turned to survey the carnage. Roaches of all
sizes and shapes were swarming over the walls, dropping
with small, ticking sounds and rocking on their curled, chitinous backs, flicking, flailing, their feelers drooping.

The gas range in the kitchen was a stronghold, a fortress
of greasy grooves and baked-in crevices. Jimmy lit the oven
and watched until the top of the stove glowed red. Out they
came by the swarming hundreds, their feet burned away, their
feelers melting into kinky hairs. They ran over the stove in
desperation, panic, trying to find a place where they could put
their feet. Expectant mothers, their eggs in the chitinous cases
at their rear ends, struggled with their hindmost legs, as with
some instinct to save their offspring, to force or kick the cases
loose. Some of these had their cases dangling by only one
side when they leaped from the top of the stove. As they
landed on the floor and tried to crawl, with their burnt feet,
their dragging, kinked feelers, with their wings askew, and
their dangling, thread-hanging egg cases, Jimmy sprayed
them madly and then trampled, kicked, jumped up and down
on them, only wanting them dead.

As he was jumping up and down he saw a fat, hideous
albino roach, already like the pale ghost of its dead self, leap
from the stove. He squashed it underfoot and swore he could
hear its white shell crack and spray the pale muck of its in-
sides out: squish! But when Jimmy lifted his shoe it dragged

itself, like animated pus, into a heap of glittering brownish bodies. Hundreds of crooked legs moved sluggishly—then, here and there, with sudden convulsive speed—over the place where the ghost had gone. On the wall was a wooden plaque that held sets of false teeth, an exhibit, sold by a dental supply firm to dentists. It belonged to Oskar who was to use it for some arcane artistic purpose but who had forgetfully left it at Jimmy's. Jimmy grabbed the plaque from the wall and mashed it down atop this horrible mass of half life. Then he jumped on it, up and down, not distinguishing the sound of the breaking teeth from the sound of roaches snapping on the stove like popcorn. When he looked down there were rolling and bouncing human teeth among the slimy dead and still crawling. Shakyamuni says they will live again.

*   *   *

Fay woke the next morning and heard a radio report of a fire on Kitchen Street while she was having her coffee. The report didn't frighten her, because the number of the house given was across the street from the house in which Elliot was staying. Still, she was a bit concerned; so just to be sure she picked up the telephone and dialed the number of the superintendent of Elliot's house. The line was dead. Then she went back to the radio and dialed around the stations, looking for a further report on the fire. At ten o'clock there was a bulletin the purpose of which was to correct the address as formerly given. The announcer's voice now numbered the house where Elliot lived, and apologized for the error.

Fay was struck with fear. But only six dead; six, and Elliot had said there were at least thirty. He must be among the survivors. There was no way she could reach Jimmy immediately—he had no phone—so she called her sister Myrtle, in nearby Plainfield. Had she heard about the fire? Myrtle said that she had, on the morning news.

"That wasn't where Elliot was living, was it?" Myrtle asked cautiously. Fay told her that it was.

"Oh, my God, dear! Did you call there?"

"They don't answer!" Fay was weeping.

"Now, don't you be afraid, Fay. He probably wasn't even in the house. You just stay there and we'll be right over."

On the radio came a report naming two of the dead; but not Elliot.

"Oh, please come—yes. I can't get ahold of Jimmy. I don't know how to get him. He's over in New York somewhere with his beatnik friends and I don't even have his new address. Have you heard anything? They say six are dead. Oh, Myrtle, please come over—hurry!"

Fay dressed and went and knocked on Moe Golden's door. Moe was a taxi driver who lived in a hall room upstairs, a sickly, kindly little bachelor, who considered Elliot his friend. Fay told Moe what had happened.

"Oh, gees," said Moe, "was Elliot in there?"

"I don't know."

Moe's face, all bones and up-pointed chin, the sallow face of a man who had never been well, twisted with sudden fear, adjusted, resolved itself. "Come on," he said, "let's go down there and find out."

When they got to the house it was still smoldering, hours after the time it was estimated that the fire had started. The big old house was roofless and nearly wall-less. Fay and Moe stood on the street with the others and looked into the cubicles, where, it seemed now, only insignificant lives could have been lived—passed.

*   *   *

Jimmy had only been up for an hour, having slept late that day as a consequence of having been up so late the night before, murdering bugs. The stench of burnt roaches clung in

243

the air, an acrid, nutlike smell immixed with lingering poison fumes.

But, "Oh, blessed rage for order," he was in a room that had been swept and mopped. The stove (even its permanent stains) was glittering with the cleaning he had given it. And he was celebrating these surroundings with an early glass of cheap sherry of the type he called gasoline and a cup of black, instant coffee, when there was a rapping at the door, *rat-a-tat-tat.*

"Telegram for Whistler!" a voice called.

Jimmy went through the usual telegramaphobic reactions of persons unused to getting wired word of things. Then he read it.

JIMMY. CALL YOUR MOTHER. NIKI.

He sat down. Maybe it was the roach-murdering spree he'd been on, but he'd had an eerie feeling since getting up. He'd been doodling on a poem, and had got it completed, just before Fear with bony knuckles knocked. He'd tagged the poem "Oncoming Company," because it was about such things—eerie feelings, telegraph messengers—

> Oncoming company;
> the flooding tides, the fell
> ingrowing grave, the sea
> of place, the held in hell.
> What dark, what bleak o'clock
> swings pendulously now?
> No record on a rock
> survives the voice and vow.
>
> No record on a rock
> survives the voice and vow.
> Swings pendulously now
> that dark, that bleak o'clock
> of place, the held in hell

ingrowing grave, the sea
of flooding tides, the fell
oncoming company.

Jimmy had a fit of the creeps, gulped his gasoline, went out, made the call, and Fay told him what was up.

"Oh, now, listen, Mom; don't get excited. He probably wasn't there."

"No, Jimmy—no. He would have called me by now. He wouldn't let me worry like this."

"What have you done?" he asked. "Did you go down there? Did you check the hospitals?"

"Everywhere. Moe's been so good. He drove me everywhere. They've got a refuge set up for all the people who were burned out. Moe drove me there, but your father's not there with the rest. Then a fireman called me and said I should check at the morgue. So Moe drove me down there. He went in and looked. He said Elliot wasn't there."

"Thank God!" Jimmy said. "If he isn't there and he isn't with the others he must not have been at the house last night."

"But where is he, Jimmy?"

"I'll come right over. Stay put."

"I will. I'm waiting for Myrtle and Uncle O'Toole. They should be here any time. I don't know what's keeping them."

Fay's family consisted of two sisters, one a couple of years older than Fay, Jimmy's Aunt Myrtle, and one a couple of years younger, Jimmy's Aunt Brenda, and Aunt Myrtle's husband, whom Jimmy referred to as Uncle O'Toole. Uncle O'Toole was a retired leather worker, Aunt Myrtle a housewife who had raised five children, Jimmy's cousins on his mother's side of the family, and Aunt Brenda was the widow of a suicidal butcher, a domineering woman who was raising her three children on Social Security and as a nurse's aide.

Fay had them, and she had Jimmy, and that was about all she had.

"O.K. I'll be right over. Now don't you worry. Dad'll show up and we'll all have a drink together."

Jimmy hadn't heard any report of the fire—just what Fay had told him—so he didn't know how much to make of it. He did figure that if Elliot wasn't in a hospital, wasn't at the refuge, and wasn't in the morgue, he probably hadn't been in the fire—there seemed small chance, considering the time, of any more bodies being discovered—probably had not gone to the house at all that night, but had been off at one of his other secret places, somewhere with some crony of his, drinking, who knew? But Jimmy was sure Elliot would have called Fay, no matter what, had he known about the fire and had he had all his wits about him. He wondered if Elliot could have been dazed and gone wandering off somewhere.

Jimmy went to the Hudson Terminal to take the train through the tunnel to Newark. On the train, across the aisle from Jimmy, a man unfolded his newspaper. The headline read: *SIX DEAD IN BLAZE IN NEWARK*. That was the first he really felt scared.

*   *   *

When he got to Baldwin, Aunt Myrtle and Uncle O'Toole were there. Fay was already going into a kind of shock: she was unnaturally calm, very unlike herself. While Jimmy was on his way over, she received another call from the fireman with whom she'd spoken earlier.

The Fire Department had compiled a list of the tenants of the house and had checked them out. The count was complete: all living tenants accounted for and six dead bodies added up to a full house. Was it possible (the voice was trying to be gentle) that a mistake had been made? Did Fay have any male relatives? Was there some man who could come down to the morgue and check—just to be sure?

"I tell you, he wasn't there," said Moe. It was clear that he was reluctant to press his (and Fay's and Jimmy's) luck with a second visit.

Finally, Jimmy and Fay got him to take them back. His small, collapsed face was running with tears as he started the motor of his taxi. Aunt Myrtle sat on one side of Fay and Uncle O'Toole on the other, in the back. Jimmy sat up front with Moe. They stopped to look at the house, which was on the way to the morgue.

As Jimmy looked up at the ruin, with its blackened, still steaming timbers, and the great, jigsaw holes torn out of its walls, its roofless top, he remembered the day he had missed his mother at school and was brought home by the strange lady, and he remembered those jaunty brass banisters, which were black and crumpled now like the old horns found occasionally among the refuse heaps at the city dump, and how they had shined once, like beacons, when he was a child.

*　　*　　*

Aunt Myrtle waited with Fay and Moe while Uncle O'Toole and Jimmy went into the morgue. Jimmy could see Aunt Myrtle, round, plump, in her early sixties, sitting in the back of that idling, question-mark of a cab, hugging Fay to her, and Fay, after thirty years of marriage, just her frightened little sister again. The worst part was that Fay was not re-signed, as he was, now. Part of her was still convinced that it was all some kind of mad nightmare mistake. "I know—I just *know*—that he's alive. Suppose he were to go home while we're here?" she said.

A man in a black suit rolled them out one at a time, each time pulling the sheet aside like a magician pulling aside his cape to display a bunch of flowers, or a rabbit. After the second time Jimmy began to say "Voila!" silently, to himself.

Some of the bodies were burned terribly, literally roasted; others didn't show a mark of pink, or even a scratch,

247

despite the fact that the roof had blown off and then caved back in on them (all of the victims had been living on the top floor). These unmarked were victims of smoke inhalation. Only one of the victims was young, about thirty; all were men, white and black; the others were old, showing emaciated, debauched bodies. Elliot's was the last they saw.

When the man in the black suit pulled the sheet aside, there he lay, stark naked. He had a big pink hand up over his heart in a familiar gesture. There was a triangular, second-degree burn on his chest. His bristly hair seemed pale.

Jimmy knew that it was Elliot before the sheet had been removed. He could tell by the feet; those big pink feet, that had walked up and down on his back, were sticking out. Jimmy had seen them when he came in, but was glad when the man in the black suit led him in a different direction. Jimmy leaned down at Elliot's side and touched his hair. He wanted to kiss him, as he had done so many times before, even the last time he had seen him, when he'd moved Elliot's things up into that firetrap, but Uncle O'Toole and the man in the black suit were there.

CHAPTER TEN

GRAVITY FLOW

After the funeral, mule praises, brays . . .
—Dylan Thomas

THE DAILY NEWS
FEBRUARY 13 , 1963

SIX DEAD IN BLAZE IN NEWARK

Back at Baldwin, after a long tearful interlude during which many drinks were consumed, much to Jimmy's consternation Fay asked Uncle O'Toole, not Jimmy, what should be done. This foreshadowed the future for Jimmy, this was how it would be if he and Fay were to live together. It would always be a house divided. She would never listen to him, but he would have to listen to her. After many a few, that prospect seemed more impossible than ever. Jimmy chose to ignore all but his own inner world. He drank, smoked, and listened to the radio—"Twilight Time." His mind went passive, tuning out a conversation that seemed neither practical nor interesting. It was the best he could do in the circumstances. There was an empty room waiting to be rented in the basement of the house. He woke up several times on top of the bed in that room, rejoined the gathering, a sort of wake, really, and pleasantly rejected it once again for the quiet comfort of the bed. Each time he returned to the gathering, it seemed that there were several more people present, each time night and day seemed to have reversed themselves.

Then Niki appeared. He hadn't words to tell her how grateful he was to see her—or was he hallucinating?

"No, ith me, all right."

"It's I," he corrected. "How did you get here, how did you know?"

"When Phyllith called . . ."

"I talked to Phyllis?"

"Of courth you did. I hope you're not having black-outs."

"All I've been doing is listening to this jabberwokky and drinking. I wouldn't be surprised."

"Well," said Niki, "she refused to come over, so I decided to come over and be with you. Life support."

"Why wouldn't she come?"

"She said that funerals are the worst of the bullshit world. But I'm here, so don't worry, I'll take care of you."

Oblivion rapidly followed, but, by all reports, he was walking and talking among the others, then he drew to a consciousness of cars, and a kind of slow motion hustle and bustle, and umbrellas and complaints. The rain came down like silver nails in his father's coffin. Then he was being asked if he would say a few words and he read from his father's crumpled copy of "Crossing the Bar" by Tennyson.

> "Sunset and evening star,
>   And one clear call for me!
> And may there be no moaning of the bar,
>   When I put out to sea,
>
>   But such a tide as moving seems asleep,
>   Too full for sound and foam,
> When that which drew from out the boundless deep
>   Turns again home.
>
>   Twilight and evening bell,
>   And after that the dark!

And may there be no sadness of farewell,
   When I embark;

  For tho' from out our bourne of Time and Place
   The flood may bear me far,
I hope to see my Pilot face to face
  When I have crost the bar."

Swaying on his feet, Niki holding him as steady as possible, he stumbled over the words and got through the reading. But it didn't matter that it was a bad reading, because this was all a dream anyway, wasn't it, a nightmare, from which he would awaken, *the* nightmare, the recurring nightmare that had plagued his sleep for months, if not years? The nightmare of him trying to take care of Fay, the totally uncooperative.

Well, she now hung like a broken doll between Aunt Myrtle and Uncle O'Toole. Sometime soon now they were going to turn her over to him and that moment would represent the end of his life, the end of his poetry, the end of his dreams. He felt, suddenly, the same panic reaction that he had felt years before in the Hollywood producer's office. He began to do a little St. Vitus dance, a drunken man preparing to run for his life.

"Hold still, Jimmy," said Niki.

"I can't. My legs are running out from under me."

"I've got you," said Niki. "Hold on."

When they got back to Baldwin and the crowded little apartment, booze appeared from every side. Soon Fay had the radio blasting Chubby Checker's "Peppermint Twist." She shook like a Shaker. Really, she was hysterical. Overheard comments from the others made Jimmy think of Dylan Thomas's line, "After the funeral, mule praises, brays. . ."

"She's better off without him."

"He left her nothing."

"He was no good!"

Pale-faced Moe Golden seized Jimmy's arm. "Your father was a great tipper," he said. "A real mensch. You know what is a mensch? A human being. Someone of consequence. Someone to admire. Someone of noble character. Jimmy, your father was a real mensch, so don't listen to these gossip ghouls."

"An old reprobate," corrected somebody. "A spendthrift with nothing to spend."

"He thought he was superior!"

"Well, Jimmy will take care of her."

"Not him, he's just like his father."

"Don't lithen to them, Jimmy," said Niki, pulling him aside. "They're a bunch of old fart squares. You need some time out. Come on, I'll take you back to New York." She dragged him toward which door? But in the hall an ancient apparition croaked condolences and Jimmy invited him in. The apparition was one of Baldwin's mainliners from the madhouse. Jimmy had already grabbed his hand in a half-shake, half-supportive motion that enabled them to stagger back across the room and into chairs. Now they began to pump hands, so joyful were they to be firmly seated.

It was his old, moth-eaten and stained-stiff pajamas and robe that had caused Jimmy to take the old man for an apparition. Actually he was a handsome old duck in his eighties with tufts of white hair flopping wildly about on his head. Jimmy saw big, gnarled hands, and great, plumbeous eyes. For a moment it seemed that he had been delivered back to his father. But no, Elliot's spirit was gone from the air around them and Jimmy felt that not only he but every one on Earth remaining had lost an opportunity, a possibility, whether to know a good man or a bad didn't matter. But here was another, tenuously clinging to life's most important goal beyond survival, the manifestation of the spirit. Sobbing Jimmy of the crying jag could have taken him in his arms and danced him around the room, but his old legs would have broken and

Jimmy's would have stumbled with drink and with rising sorrow.

*   *   *

When he woke, he lay looking up at a ceiling that was like a gently lowering sky, a sky swirling with pale paradigms of cloud, shaped by shadows. His mouth was hot with cigarettes and alcohol. He popped it open to let the air cool it. He wondered about Fay, and a feeling of self-condemnation came. He wanted to cry. He hadn't cried yet. Not really— just drunken jag tears. But he wanted to cry the real thing. He *tried* to cry. It took a little while, but finally a tear came, eked, as it were, out of a small, hard eye; then came another; then a torrent, thank whatever gods may be, and he lay there and sobbed until the shaking and shuddering became mechanical; until it got too difficult to keep the tears coming; then he gave it up, quit.

Jimmy remembered the last time he saw Elliot. He felt guilty about not staying with him that night. He'd never see him again in all eternity. Oh, how he wished he'd gone back to Newark the following week as he had promised Elliot he would! He wished that he'd seen him just once more! And Phyllis. Jimmy saw his cruelty toward her, wondered what he should do. He could see it now: skinny, sickly Phyllis, Fay, himself, and the ghost of Elliot, superintending together out of a furnished, basement apartment: a valetudinarian, an unmerry, willful widow, an alcoholic poet, and a hopped-up ghost. All Jimmy had to do was to not hurt anyone and that would be the way of it. Sadly, only someone's pain could set things right.

He vaguely remembered Niki bringing him here, and was truly grateful to her. There was soft music playing on an F.M. station, mechanical lulling stuff. The radio was turned down low, so as not to wake, only to comfort his dreams; a

253

subliminal, subconscious accompaniment, and he dropped back off down to sleep.

Next morning Jimmy woke and realized he was in New York in Niki's baldaquined big bed. Niki came in from the kitchen with a rag of a kimono covering her heavy-breasted torso and long legs. She stood next to the rumpled bed and laughed at Jimmy's confusion, which was genuine.

"Did we . . . er . . ."

"No," she said, "you were too drunk. You fell athleep." She laughed again, very happily, and said: "I did my beth to theduthe you. No girl ever worked harder at it. You should have theen the trouble I had juth getting your clothes off."

"I'm sorry," he said. He felt rotten, as if he'd cheated her. "Maybe next time," he added, trying to make light of the situation. But Niki didn't seem to resent anything; unlike everyone else; on the contrary, she seemed quite contented.

"Where's Oskar?"

"Out looking for his own plathe, I hope. Would you like thomething to drink, or thome coffee?"

Jimmy reached an arm up from his supine position and pushed it under her robe and up, until his hand was on a warm round thigh. Niki watched his face, and as he moved his hand up her side, she said:

"Do you like it?"

He said he did. Then she smiled and said:

"Beer or coffee?"

He considered for a moment and said: "Beer—good and cold—crispy. Can it be done?"

"I'll have to get it from the girl nexth door. I'll be right back."

"Not from Phyllis!" he said.

"Of courth not, the other thide."

Jimmy heard her shove aside the police lock bar on the door and the door swing noisily shut behind her under the weight of the bar. He threw his legs over the side of the bed and got to his feet. He looked around for his trousers. They were in a heap on a chair. He picked them up, and it was then that he noticed that the seam was splitting in the rear. They were the last decent pair of trousers he had, and it came to him suddenly that he was getting seedy. He had his feet in the legs and the trousers halfway up to his knees, when he heard the bar on the police lock slide crankily in its groove. He had the trousers on and was about to pull the zipper up when Oskar loped into the room. Oskar stopped and looked at Jimmy and Jimmy looked back, and it was such a classic situation that Jimmy couldn't help laughing. It was absurd. Oskar said: "Oh," and Jimmy said: "I know this looks funny, Oskar, but it isn't the way you think."

"I just came to get some of my books," Oskar said, and charged about the room, grabbing things. Then Niki came in, half-dressed, disheveled, beer in hand, saw, sat down at the kitchen table, and opened a can of beer. Jimmy could see her from where he stood, in the bedroom, and she smiled at him a mischievous smile full of satisfaction. She was glad they'd been caught. He wasn't. He had just been thinking, as he was stepping into his trousers, that he was going to get out before something like this happened. He wondered if he could convince Phyllis, at least, that he had not been unfaithful to her. He doubted it. Oskar would tell her and she would believe him. But it depended, too, on what she would want to believe. If Jimmy was in some doubt as to Phyllis, however, it was very clear what Oskar wanted to believe. And he was right. Jimmy was trying to excuse himself on a technicality. He was guilty according to the spirit, if not the letter. He said:

"Listen Oskar, you've got to be—"

But Oskar said: "Oh, don't give me a lot of dat shit. Vat you tink, I'm a damned fool?"

"Leave him alone," Niki said from the kitchen. "To hell with what he thinks. Come and have your beer."

"You dirty bitch!" Oskar said, but he said it almost to himself, and he sounded tired, like he didn't care anymore.

"Oskar," Jimmy said, "won't you believe me? Nothing happened. I just got drunk after the funeral and Niki brought me here to sleep it off."

"You Gottammed liar! Vhy don't you go pull up your zipper!"

Oskar had collected a stack of paperback books that he now threw into a pillow case. He threw the little sack over his shoulder, like a hobo, and marched out through the kitchen, past Niki, with great dignity, and pulled the door open.

"You better lock the frogging door," he said, turned, and was gone.

Jimmy went into the kitchen and sat down across from Niki. She opened another can of beer and pushed it across to him.

"I wonder if Phyllis will believe us," Jimmy said.

"Aren't you going to tell her the truth?" Niki looked surprised.

"The truth is," Jimmy said, "nothing happened."

"Thath not the truth!"

Jimmy said: "She'll believe that nothing happened if you tell her it didn't."

"Why should I do that?"

"For me."

"You *are* a liar, Jimmy!"

"Look," Jimmy said, "let's not be compulsive confessors. What difference does it make as long as everybody's happy. You can get Oskar back again, too."

"But I don't want Oskar, and I don't give a damn what Phyllith thinks. I want you, you thon of a bitch."

"Then do what I ask you to do."

"I will if you'll do what I athk you to do."

"What's that?"

“Come to bed.”

“Like Butterworth and three dozen others,” he said. “Niki, you’ve been good to me and I appreciate it, but I’m not going to betray Oskar, even if he thinks I am—I have.”

“Well then, you can juth go to hell—you and Oskar and Phyllith—all of you—after what I’ve done for you—got you out of that hole in Newark! And those morons, those middle-class creeps! You can juth go to hell! I don’t want to see you anymore. Oskar either. Neither one of you.”

In a time when hurricanes were named for women, Hurricane Niki whirled about the apartment, engulfing her clothes and pulling them on like flying rags. “Don’t be here when I get back,” she yelled, and slammed the door behind her.

*　　*　　*

Jimmy had not seen Phyllis since before the funeral. He should see her. Poor little left alone dame. But instead he walked right down the dark hall, past their apartment, and out the big front door. He stood for a moment in the cold wind, looked up and down the street, then headed toward Harry’s Psychedelic Dom.

The bar was nearly empty and the quiet and gloom welcoming. A couple of stools down sat Ape, the plumber. He was a short, powerfully built man of about forty who, as a result of his proclivity for the more bizarre forms of sexual activity, preferred to frequent Bohemian bars, rather than the sort of blue-collar bar where one might expect to find him. They exchanged greetings. Then Ape told Jimmy he didn’t look so good, and Jimmy told Ape he was O.K. Ape said he had an emergency job to do, something overflowing into a flood in a tenement somewhere, and that he had hoped to get someone to help him out on it, his regular helpers being unavailable. “How ’bout you,” he said, inspired. “Would ya like ta pick up a couple five bucks say?”

257

"How long will it take?"

"Oh, nuttin'—a few hours. Do it for me, Jim. I really need somebody. I'm in a bind."

Jimmy and Ape had wrist-wrestled a number of times for a few beers. They were buddies.

"Is it going to be hard? I don't feel so hot."

"Nah, nah. Listen, movin' a few stones, dat's all."

"O.K.," Jimmy said, and Ape changed a bit. He looked Jimmy over, said:

"But, do ya feel O.K.?"

Now Jimmy wanted the money, so he wound up selling Ape on the idea of using his services, on the idea that he was fit as a fiddle. Off they went in Ape's overburdened pickup truck, down through the sloppy, winter streets of the East Village. They climbed out on East Third, and Ape yanked his huge leather bag of tools out of the back of the pickup. It had a long leather strap on it, so that he could stoop, put the strap over his shoulder, and stand up, hauling it up with him. He asked Jimmy to carry it. He had pipe, hoses, and shovels to carry. Jimmy threw the strap over his shoulder and heaved upward, but the bag did not budge. Jimmy's spine exploded with pain.

Ape shook his head. "O.K.," he said. "I'll bring it. I don't want ya should bust a gut." Up came the bag, and he walked with it and the pipe too.

The constipated building was a few doors down the block. Too bad they couldn't get the truck any closer, but there was a vandalized car in the way. The trouble was in the basement, directly below a bodega. Above the bodega there were five human-infested tall stories. The Rat and Mice Arms, East Village, Lower East Side, Manhattan, New York, New York, U.S. of A, North America, Earth, Milky Way, the Universe. A lovely place to bring up children. . . . Ape dumped his load of iron and leather on the sidewalk and pulled open the cellar doors.

Phew! Multitudes of foul-smelling molecules did a danse-macabre up their nostrils. Jimmy's stomach somersaulted in his abdomen like a little pink clown. *Now, said the Sibyl, summon up your courage, for you will need it.* Rolf Humphries' translation of *The Aeniad* ran through Jimmy's mind as if on tape.

Ape descended.

Jimmy followed.

Before the threshhold of hell they passed, and avenging Cares, pale Disease and melancholy Age, Fear and Hunger that tempt to Crime, Toil, Poverty, and Death—forms horrible to view.

"How long has this place been backed up?"

"Couple days."

"A couple of days?

"Yeah. I had so many udder jobs, I couldn't get back."

"It's a wonder the Health Department hasn't been here."

"Hey, dis is New Yawk."

The filthy ooze was a foot deep and jet black, anaerobic. "If anybody upstairs has a case of typhus, we've had it."

"Ah, I wade around in dis stuff all da time and I'm all right." Ape handed Jimmy a pair of rubber boots. "Here, put dese on."

They stood high up on a peak among peaks of the mountainous islands of rocks and gravel and mud that Ape had dug out on his previous visit. Despite the cold, hot sweat broke out on Jimmy's forehead as he pulled on the boots. His shirt and pants stuck to his skin. Outside was a cold winter day, and it was even cool here, but humid, clammy. How the hell did he get himself into these things! Ape put him to work at pulling up and stacking more of the slimy stones while he pumped some of the mephitic semi-liquid out from under them. Each time Jimmy plumped his gloved hands into the ooze to catch another slippery stone he thought of the possibilities of infection. Bacterial, protozoan, parasitic metazoan—words from books kept popping into his head. Passages! *It is inevitable that these infections, so common to the alimentary tract of man, should be found in great numbers in the feces, and even in the urine.* Talk about the alimentary tract! He was wading around in the intestinal tract of a ramshackle slum dwelling.

"What are we trying to do here anyway?"

Ape was wrapping up some hoses in the cellarway.

"Gravity flow! Dat's what we're after. Gravity flow! We gotta get dis shit runnin' out into da sewers. Dere's a block under dem stones somewheres. Dat's what's stoppin' it. We gotta find out what it is and get it out o' dere."

"What could it be?" Jimmy asked, using his curiosity as an excuse to stand up straight for a moment. His back was broken. He felt like vomiting.

"Never can tell. A few t'ings get t'rowed down da terlet and dey gadder up and make like a heap. Da pipes into da sewers is eight inches, but from what I can make out, dat drain you're clearin' is like one o' dem Roman drains—just a concave brick jobber, see, so it could happen. Den again a heavy flow might of moved a loose brick out o' place. Hard ta say. Sometimes dere's bio-foulin'. Dat's like when plankton forms up real t'ick. Hard part's findin' it. Rest is easy."

Not for another hour did Jimmy get the bright idea of tearing off the tail of his shirt and tying it over his face like a mask, stuffing the bottom down his collar. It relieved him a bit. He wished that he could pull it up over his eyes so that he couldn't see what he was digging in. He thought of Aeneus in the Infernal Regions, his only object being to see his father. He imagined how it would be if Elliot materialized. He'd be all dressed up, spick-and-span, neat as a pin, sitting at a little table on top of one of those mountains of slime, elegantly smoking a kingsized Chesterfield, watching. Fay would be there, and she and Jimmy would dig together while Elliot watched them, kindly but superior, indulging their blessed rage for order. Well, unlike Aeneas in his Infernal Regions, Jimmy wasn't going to find his father down here. *O, how willingly would they endure poverty, labor, and any other infliction, if they might but return to life!*

"Here it is!" cried Ape. "Like I t'ought, it's a brick jam."

Jimmy crawled along a ridge of a slippery mountain of detritus and got shakily to his feet beside Ape. There it was, indeed. A half dozen or so bricks had fallen apart and melted down into a red stopper. It had caught eggshells, sanitary napkins, bits of glittering glass, a thing that looked like a skinny black snake but turned out to be a coathanger, and doubtful stuff packed in layers, packed in strata. *Here is the judgment hall of Rhadamanthus, who brings to light crimes done in life, which the perpetrator vainly thought impenetrably hid.* Ape picked up a shovel and gave the red stopper a couple of tentative taps, then one clanging blow, breaking it to pieces. "Woo-ish!" it went. The sewer was hungry! What an appetite!

"I'm gonna turn on da water," Ape said. "I wanna wash dis out so's I can see how bad da damage is. Just be a minute."

"Gravity flow!" thought Jimmy. "That's what we're after. Gravity flow!" He sat down on top of the slag-heap and rested his head in his arms. He could feel his head burning through his shirtsleeves. Suddenly a little stream of water, relatively clear, trickled down the Roman canal. Jimmy remembered what he'd read in Da Vinci's Notebooks, about man being only a passageway for food. Would that he were only that, and have some peace. He would have forgiven any man his meanness—his bloody devilish power cravings—in the mood he was in. He watched the water purling away. No doubt it'd soon be carrying away nice loads of human excretion, the lost parts of bodies, dead cells, hairs, bits and parts of burnt energy, the stuff left over after the day's work, after the argument, the loving in the small bed while the kids slept fitfully nearby. Yes, there goes love. Off it goes, the domestic sewage, off to join the industrial waste, off to form the municipal sewage, to join the storm runoff, and there all to be wed and to become the combined sewage; off they go, through flush tanks and diverting weirs, through siphon spillways and sewage-treatment plants, through bar racks and fine screens and skimming tanks, through settling tanks and scum collectors, through grit chambers and sedimentation tanks, through trickling filters and activated-sludge units, through oxidation ponds and the centrifuge, through heat coagulators and into the incinerators, where, at last, all our loves go up in smoke. And the outfall works drop pure water, cleansed, unsullied by any particle of humanity, by any watery history of the human condition, into the swaying receiving waters of river and sea. Out of the water we came, onto the land, and into the sky we go, and the smoke of our loves will crowd out the light of the sun, one dark day.

Ape took the truck to get some sandwiches and a couple of bottles of beer. Jimmy fell asleep while he was gone. When Ape came back Jimmy sat up and drank beer while Ape ate a submarine sandwich and then proceeded to repair the damage. Ape could see that Jimmy was beat, so he didn't ask him to do anything more. Jimmy sat thinking and dreaming, of Anchises and Aeneus. *Have you come at last, Anchises said, long expected, and do I behold you after such perils past? O my son, how have I trembled for you as I have watched your career! O father! your image was always before me to guide and guard me. . . . Then, he endeavoured to enfold his father in his embrace, but his arms enclosed only an unsubstantial image.*

"Quite a pair, those two," thought Jimmy. "A son who thinks he's in the Infernal Regions, guided by a father who turns out to be unsubstantial. Sound familiar?"

Ape was beat too. He threw in the sponge.

"C'mon, let's go get a drink. I'll finish dis up tomorrow." Jimmy staggered along after him to the truck, and they drove up to Harry's. They jolted to a stop in front of the place and sat like two babies in a rocking carriage. Ape handed Jimmy five dollars.

They got out and went inside and there was Marsayas. He was drinking cheap cognac, half drunk. He couldn't paint or meditate, he said. Jimmy told him what he'd been up to and how he, Marsayas, had missed out on it. Marsayas made his gleeful gargoyle face and looked Jimmy up and down and said, "Yeah, I can see."

Ape laughed, plopped himself on a stool and ordered a double whiskey. Jimmy ordered cognac.

Marsayas said, "Sorry to hear about your old man. I've heard he was quite a sport."

Jimmy shrugged. "Uh-huh. I guess genetically speaking, we're all sports."

"I meant a good sport."

"I know what you meant. Thanks. Do you know what I meant?"

"I dig ya, boyo."

Jimmy left Marsayas to talk to Ape while he went into the men's room to clean up. There wasn't any soap. There weren't any towels. Jimmy pulled some toilet paper off a roll and dampened it, and wiped his face. He didn't look good. Pale as a ghost. Ghastly! His back quivered, then punched, then stabbed. Sciaticus throwing the discus for stupid Rome, he mused. He laughed hysterically.

He limped back out and drank for another hour or so; then all of a sudden the room turned upside down and Jimmy grabbed hold of the barstool, trying not to drop to the ceiling. Then he swung right side up again, very fast, as though he were on some kind of amusement park ride, and all the colors in the room became strangely vivid, unnatural.

He was terrified. Of everything. He couldn't breathe. He ran outside with only his shirt on. It was freezing.

He started to walk up the block and told himself not to be afraid, that it'd pass in a minute, but it didn't, and he started to run. His hip hurt, his legs, his back.

He turned back, dizzy, holding the fronts of buildings, and groped his way back into the bar.

Everybody looked at him—Ape, Marsayas, the bartender, others—and Marsayas said, "What's wrong?"

Jimmy didn't know what to say. He didn't know what was wrong. Then the room turned upside down again, and he saw Ape coming toward him, squat, burly, upside down.

Next thing Jimmy knew, Marsayas was carrying him along the street. When Jimmy asked him, Marsayas said that he'd fainted.

Jimmy didn't believe it. He'd never fainted in his life.

Marsayas said, "Nonetheless, boyo, you just did."

Marsayas threw Jimmy's arm over his shoulder and walked him the few blocks to the crosstown bus, pushed and pulled him aboard, and pulled him back off the bus on the West Side, then got him to St. Vincent's emergency ward. Jimmy was obstinate, did not want to be treated, but Marsayas and a doctor bullied him into it. Marsayas told the doctor that he was dealing with a nearly well-known poet, a young Dylan Thomas.

"Dylan Thomas died here," the doctor said. "That was before I was here but everybody knows about it. Acute alcoholic insult to the brain. Seventeen straight shots at the White Horse Tavern, all in a matter of minutes." He looked at Jimmy. "Is that what you're trying to pull, another Thomas?"

"I'm not trying to kill myself, if that's what you mean."

After looking Jimmy over—blood pressure, tongue depresser, temperature, stethoscope—the doctor said, "There doesn't seem to be anything wrong with him physically—that is, beside being drunk. But he's exhausted. I think we'll keep him overnight, just to be sure. I'm going to ask a psychiatrist to go up and talk with him."

Marsayas was relieved to hear the prognosis and glad to leave. He hated hospitals. Jimmy knew that, for Marsayas, it was an act of heroic proportions for his friend to have brought him here, and he thanked him. Then he was in a hospital bed, being asked questions.

"Why do you drink?"

"To feel better."

"Do you feel badly all the time? Are you unhappy?"

"My father just died."

"Oh, I see. I'm sorry. But at other times—normally?"

"Up and down."

"I've been told you are a poet."

"I'm a writer . . . a poet."

"You're depressed . . . then you feel high, full of energy. Am I right?"

"You're getting at manic depression, aren't you?"

"Have you ever been diagnosed as manic-depressive?"

"In the service. They said I had a tendency."

"And this drinking . . . this is self-medication, isn't it?"

"I suppose it is. You try to feel better."

"Have you ever heard of lithium? It's a natural substance, formed in the body. It can even out your moods. A lot of creative people are manic-depressive. I can write you a prescription."

"I'll lose it. I'm afraid to lose my passion."

"No, no, you won't lose anything. It'll just even you out—not so much down, not so much up."

Finally, Jimmy agreed to try lithium. He was released the next morning after a good, sedated night's sleep and a vitamin shot of some kind. But he didn't have any money to get the prescription for lithium filled. He did, however, find enough change in his pants pocket for a few beers.

CHAPTER ELEVEN

OBITUARY

*Poetry is of graver import
than history.*

—*Aristotle*

THE NEW YORK TIMES
FEBRUARY 27, 1963

SOVIET INDICATES 10,000 WILL
STAY ON DUTY IN CUBA;

REPORTED TO HAVE TOLD U.S. IT MUST
RETAIN 'RESIDUAL' FORCE THERE

Lights were on. Actually, only one, a deeply shaded, oddly-shaped lamp. Phyllis had already begun her dreamscape redecorating at Pitt Street and what appeared to be huge undulating petals of vivid color waved out of the woodwork onto the black walls. Seeing the place, Jimmy couldn't believe it had only been a few days since he'd gone to Newark. Everything was different, now—everything.

Now he remembered clearly that Phyllis had called him in Newark and he had asked her if she'd like to come over for the funeral and how glad he was when she had said no, because it was a relief not to have to think about, watch out for, take care of, another person. Yet the thought of Phyllis had haunted him over the whole week-end, through the Sunday burial, into the abrupt Monday escape. It was his conscience that haunted him. Phyllis came out of the bathroom and put her frail little arm over his shoulder.

"Oh, Jimmy, are you all right?"

"Of course I'm all right."

"You look terrible. Have you had anything to eat? Do you want anything to eat?"

"No. I want a drink. I come from a long line of alcoholics. You should have seen the gathering of them over there. It was like a whole division of Alcoholics Anonymous had fallen off the wagon at once. But an appropriate gathering for my father, I guess."

"I called your mother," she said. "I was beginning to wonder if you were O.K. She said she wasn't sure where you were. She wants you to call her, Jimmy. Why don't you call her up tomorrow morning and talk to her. She sounded awfully sad and lonely."

"I guess the comforting gang has finally deserted her," he said.

"Where were you, Jimmy? Where were you last night?"

"I was in the hospital."

"What? Are you all right?"

"I was just zonked. I just crashed out at Harry's."

"Before that. Were you with Niki? No, I don't want to know about it, no matter what happened."

"Well, you asked."

"Well, forget it—I don't want to know." She covered her ears with her hands.

"Hear no evil?"

She just shook her head.

"Well, O.K. Where's the beer?"

"You've got a lot of mail—mostly bills and rejections. But your agent—"

"Alex?"

"Alex sent you a note and a check. He sold another one of those Inspector McCraken stories of yours—'Murder in the Commune'."

"McCraken and his assistant Willy."

"Yes."

"To Mike Shane's again?"

"Yes. Mike Shane's Mystery Magazine."

"How much?"

"Fifty dollars."

"I'll sign it over to you and you pay the bills."

"Jimmy, I wish you wouldn't write any more of those stupid mysteries. You could be a great poet, like Auden or somebody."

"I like mystery stories. You know that. You've seen me read enough of them." Jimmy chug-a-lugged his beer and poured himself another. "I wish Inspector McCracken and Willy could solve the bitter mystery of my life," he said, and, with insouciance, blew a smoke ring.

*   *   *

It took Jimmy two weeks to work up the nerve to call Fay.

"Hello, Mom," he said. "Are you all right?"

"Yes, Jimmy, I'm fine. I'm so glad you called me. Jimmy—I wonder—wouldn't you like to come over and spend a few days with me? I haven't been alone with you since—"

"I know. I'm sorry I walked out like that, but—"

"I understand. I was so mixed up. I told your Aunt Myrtle and Uncle O'Toole that they didn't have any right to talk about you leaving so soon like that, either. I told them you had to get back to work. Are you well? Are you and Phyllis working?"

"We're just fine, Mom—fine."

"Won't you come over today?"

"No—not today, Mom—I can't."

"Jimmy—I'm very lonesome over here. Couldn't you just come over and spend the afternoon?"

"I can't today, Mom."

"Why?"

"I just can't."

"Oh. You're not drinking too much, are you?"

"*Naw*—for God's sake! Where would I get the money?"

"Do you need any money? Your father left a few hundred dollars here, and I feel that part of it belongs to you."

"No—no—I don't need any."

"Have you been working at all?"

"No—no—I haven't, but Phyllis is." It was true. Phyllis had just become gainfully, thankfully, employed that very day.

"All right."

Jimmy said goodbye into the phone but Fay had already hung up. She never waited for anybody to finish anything.

*   *   *

Fay wrote, letter after letter.

Dear Jimmy, one went, *I can't understand why it is that you won't contact me. Have I done something to you, or what is it? I told you before that I was sorry about letting Uncle O'Toole take over that way. But on the other hand, Jimmy, who have I got to rely on? I have nobody in the world but you. Don't you love me enough to come over and see me? It's been three months. Please call me.*

Then one day he was sitting alone in the apartment, thinking about a new long poem about his father to be called "Obituary," thinking about Dylan Thomas's aborted poem about *his* father, and how he would make "Obituary" different, how he would tell the story of the man, including the history that surrounded and shaped his life, and not employ a lot of cosmic thunder, as Dylan did, when a knock came at the door, and his thoughts exploded in fragments and shards, like smashed crystal. He heard Fay's insistent voice on the other side of the door. That's it, he thought, that's what I have to look forward to. She would never stop breaking up his thoughts, never stop distracting him. Hated distraction at the door, now! "Jimmy," she called, "are you there?"

He couldn't face her. He couldn't stop thinking. The poem had him.

"Jimmy? It's Mom. Are you there? Jimmy, Jimmy, Jimmy, Jimmy, Jimmy," echoing through eternity!

He sat, frozen, fear thrilling through him.

There was silence for a few minutes, then a note was slipped under the door. He could hear his mother's high heels clicking down the stairs. He stayed with his thoughts of the poem as long as he could, but finally had to go and read the note:

Jimmy, I have been here. I took the Hudson Tubes over from Newark, the way your father showed me. That's some awful ride, isn't it? I had breakfast in a little restaurant down the street from here. It was nice. Jimmy, please call me. Mom.

Oh God, God, *God,* he wanted to run out of the house and down the street and grab her in his arms! Yet she had never defended him against his father for his fair share in life, had allowed Elliot to move them all over the country and rob him of his due, his education from grade school level up, robbed him, in fact, of the savings he'd sent home all during the years he'd been in service so he'd have a little stake when he got out, and even at Elliot's death had pushed him aside in favor of Uncle O'Toole.

How could he live with her? She had not respected him in his needs and dreams, nor had seemed to care, and would never allow him to be unimpeded in his compulsion to write. She understood nothing about him or what mattered to him and would not have respected his values. And what did he

owe her? This was *his* time, *his* youth. He had a right to it.
A few days later, in a manic marathon, he wrote—

OBITUARY

Elliot Whistler (1893-1963)

Success is counted sweetest
By those who ne'er succeed.
            —Emily Dickenson

Without the mummeries of death, by fire,
but not by burning but by breath of smoke,
you died like some high god upon his pyre:
O quick, barbaric, merciful good luck!

I had so many fears for you, my father;
your ribald binges must have racked your body;
I feared some lingering illness, and I'd rather
have anything attacking one so bawdy

than an unthrilling, invalided life
spent somehow to its end in spite and temper;
though there was one thing sterner than its strife:
no death, no anything could make you whimper!

Your life was preparation for its pain:
you trained for ill and not for good, as Housman
advised his blear-eyed Shropshire lad to train
when, "moping melancholy mad," that yeoman

had rhymed the cow to death. A country boy
yourself, of Dutch and Anglo-Saxon stock,
New Jersey born and bred, hobbledehoy
and shining-faced, at fourteen, to New York

271

you went, in Nineteen-Hundred-Seven, to be
a runner on the New York Stock Exchange:
no more a rube!—No more a nonentity!—
but now (or then) a Wall Street runner, plung-

ing through the frantic, money-making crowds
America's romantic myth had brought
to conquer fortunes (time, events, becloud
so far-bygone an era, the magic sort

of moment that it was, the innocence
of fledgling fortune-hunters like yourself,
whose world of thought was Yankee common sense
and industry, who dreamed a sweet success

sometimes into existence in a trice:
opposing Mogul, Robber-baron, Tycoon,
all those first-comers who had set the price
of your success so high, O youngest son!)

Your struggle was a long one: studying
beside a late oil-lamp, O handsome youth
with raven hair!—your eyes only seeing
great dreams—reading of Rome, in law—in faith

that "Education makes the man;" with knowledge,
as Bacon'd put it, being power. Your roommate,
a brilliant graduate of Harvard College,
who one day would become a diplomat,

and later on Ambassador-at-large
in a long dead administration, instructed
you in "polish," as if you were his charge:
"Marry a rich woman," he told you once, said,

"That's my advice to you. I mean to do it
myself." Indeed, that's what he did. Not you,
though. Women meant too much. They knew you knew it,
too, handsome twenty-one, bonds salesman now,

and "Coming," as they called it then; they knew,
and loved you for it; helped you to establish
your reputation on The Street, and strew
themselves like flowers at your feet, flashing

their smiles like diamonds, their gems like teeth,
attracting and repelling, always rich
and husbanded by ghosts—a jewelled wreath
of Marley'd widows, beauties, and rich bitches,

young and old, fell about your frail young shoulders
—the day was almost won for Trumpery!
But meanwhile now the world was hurling boulders
of War, had been since Ferdinand, Humpty-Dumpty

of Peace, had fallen from the caving wall
at Sarajevo, four trenched and bloody years
before—time now for you to heed the call!
You went with other would-be "Officers

and Gentlemen" to be inducted, and
trained in the arts of martial leadership;
but suddenly, amazingly, they hand-
ed you your discharge.—We had won, had whipped

King Billy and the Ottoman Empire
(For better or for worse the deed was done!)
—and you, handsome young Elliot Whistler, Esq.,
were free to enter stormy Prohibition,

that time of Ought-not, But, and All-be-damned,
when "bathtub was synonymous with gin;"
an Eighty-nine-day-wonder, you had lammed
back into mufti—lost the veteran's pension

for my dear mother's Merry Widowhood;
but not your fault—a bureaucratic trick
that politicians played on Motherhood
is what we'll call it, for a sad laugh's sake.

Your first wife was a dopefiend. She's long dead.
The next an upright nurse—good family;
tubercular, although Bermuda bred;
and oh, British to the bone; unamatory,

or so you said, although you got a son
by her;—but not in Colorado, where
you went to help her lungs, and met someone
more amatory—Governor's daughter

she was: young, bright, and burning in her britches:
Black-Bottoming and Charlestoning and being
filled with a Flapper's ripe and bitching itches
—until you ran away from both of them.

By now you'd made the magic book—WHO'S WHO.
Success had come. You worked out of New York
and lived "Uptown"—and then the Market threw
its curve: Black Tuesday, Twenty-nine. What work

of evil genius had occurred? O fell
green hand of money! Lost hey-days! Your wife
was gone! Your son was gone, taken. What Hell
had happened and had happened here? What grief?

When, still young, you rode the Elevated,
the rumble of the wheels ground down your heart:
that iron-roar made you think quick death was fated,
thuswise against ambition raised your guard.

From then on you'd inveigh against that world
of Business, Finance, Property, Possessions
that you were trained in. Overboard you hurled
it, calling afterwards impedimenta

whatever slightest trinket stuck to you
as to summer-melting wax, which washed away
itself,—before the pierce-eyed public view!—
whatever'd stuck. The haberdashery

was all you kept: the custom-tailored suit;
silk tie; the Homburg hat; the shining shoes:
as you had worn them through the Prohibition Toot
you wore them through the sad Depression Days;

the Fylfot-War; the Eisenhower Fifties . . .
when I was there to know you, aging father:—
I, growing up by then, you in your sixties,
hair briny with the years, a heavy breather,

but still a regal, leucomelanous head—
bared now ("The man who never wears a hat"
was what they called you then—you were ahead
of time, before the style, an old pace-set-

ter—Kennedy had made bare heads official
—"My reason is to save my head of hair;
hats stop the circulation," you said; "this'll
become the style, when people learn.") Never

will I forget those idiosyncratic
quirks, those oddnesses, that set you apart
from ordinary beings so dramatic-
cally! I, walking by your side in Newark,—

where we then lived, deep in a basement flat,
where roaches climbed the walls like living paper,
and damp night brought the rustle of a rat,
—would glow to see the people look, O happier

than a rich son, to be the son of one
so striking and distinguished in appearance!
"That gent I seed you wid, are you his son?"—
Yet of the poor we were among the poorest!

You'd married Mom in Nineteen-Thirty-Two,—
one year before Repeal, deep in Depression
days. Having met in a speakeasy, you
decided to continue partying—

and did throughout the years, by fits and starts!
though making money was a difficulty
that interfered with freedom, your free hearts
went on their merry way, higgledy-piggledy,

from the Honeymoon Hotel, here in New York,
where you escaped the bill by wearing all
your wardrobe out the door, until the stork
dropped in your lap a wet, if "Wonderful!"

responsibility—which you were not
quite ready to live up to, though you tried—
"To be father, now! Why, I've forgotten how to burp a child! I'm forty-five!"

Soon fifty-five! Now, door-to-door, you sold:
bandaids, thread, pots and pans, encyclopedias
(once more you carried Bacon's quote in bold
lettering on a business card, KNOWLEDGE

IS POWER!)—Oh, a library of books!
Ah, melancholy-morbid! How you read
"The Raven," with your Barrymorish looks
to help you dramatize as you recited!

And "To the Ladies!" How that angered Mom!
You made her Judy O'Grady, not the Lady,
while you remained the Colonel! Deaf and dumb
with anger, she would wait until payday

before she made things up. The years went by.
You went to work at managing hotels
for some cheap chain; then later you would try
your hand at selling real estate; but selling

was too rough now, Old Charmer, sixty-five!
And then you read De Quincey and De Ropp:
"Why, I have never even been alive!"
And that was how you found your way to dope!

To dope and death as well! For you left home,
went to a hobo rooming house downtown,
and, three weeks later—dead! O poor poor Mom!
 "I loved him. Understood him? No." She frowned.

SIX DEAD IN BLAZE IN NEWARK, the paper said:
I read the headlines on the Hudson Tube
while on my way to Newark. Could you be dead?
Yes, I identified you at the Morgue!

Without the mummeries of death, by fire,
But not by burning but by breath of smoke,
You died like some high god upon his pyre:
O quick, barbaric, merciful good luck!

"It's wonderful," said Phyllis, looking over her glasses.

Jimmy said, "I thought a lot about how to bring it off. What I had as a negative example was Dylan Thomas's attempt to write a poem about his father. His poem never worked, and I kept wondering why. Finally, it occurred to me that Thomas was trying to employ all of his old apocalyptical tricks—blind eyes drawn by the sun and all that—and I realized that those rhetorical devices were getting in the way of his real feelings. I realized that such a poem had to be about the person, clearly biographical, and actually the person set down in his times—the story of a man and his life. That's what I was after, anyway. When I was at NYU I had to do a paper on Andrew Hamilton—"

"You mean Alexander Hamilton?"

"No, Andrew Hamilton. He was a Scottish lawyer who defended Peter Zenger in America's first freedom of speech case. Zenger ran a newspaper and said a few things that angered the powers that be, who tried to shut him down and shut him up. Hamilton won the case. But the important thing is: One of the questions I had to answer in the paper was whether Hamilton was a man of his times or not. I said that he was and my professor agreed. But the more I thought about it the more I realized or became convinced that every man and woman is a man and woman of his or her time. How can they not be? So I tried to set my father down in his times. After all, the times make us. The times we are living in are at work on us right now, making us do things we wouldn't otherwise do but also giving us chances we wouldn't otherwise have. This stupid war in Viet Nam is ruining this country, and even as individuals we'll never be the same again. We've all been smudged by its evil. You can't even go into a bar and have a quiet drink without hearing about search and destroy missions, body counts, and the latest number of sorties our planes have flown. Don't tell me it isn't doing something to all of us. See what I mean?"

"Yes, I do . . . like Castiglione, in *The Courtier*. Well, you brought it off, all right. This should be the title poem for a book. Let's get all your old poems together, the ones that have been published, and make a book. And we'll call it 'Obituary and Other Poems.' What do you think?"

"You do it," he said. "I only write these poems to explain myself to myself, my stupid life to my stupid self."

THE NEW YORK TIMES
AUGUST 29, 1963

200,000 MARCH FOR CIVIL RIGHTS IN ORDERLY WASHINGTON RALLY; PRESIDENT SEES GAIN FOR NEGRO

ACTION ASKED NOW

---

10 LEADERS OF PROTEST URGE LAWS TO END RACIAL INEQUITY

Lani hula-danced toward Jimmy to the strains of Elvis singing "Blue Hawaii," and pulled him to his feet. He tried to dance on his rubber legs, but careened past Marsayas, just in time stepping unnimbly over the record player, which was on the floor, plowing poor Lani's back into the squat, white refrigerator, which teeter-tottered softly on its little flat feet, and back across the room, into the table, so that bottles and glasses wobbled and rattled and a plate slid over the edge. Lani planted her strong, golden feet and pulled Jimmy toward her, and suddenly, when he was righted and steady for a moment, put her arms around his neck, looked so much meaning into his eyes that even he, obtuse with drink, could understand, and leaped up, throwing her legs around his waist, and kissed him, hard and harder, until it hurt. He stood so, holding her, made steady by her weight, then followed the directions given by her eyes. He put one leg forward, stepped, put the other forward, stepped again, and found himself walking, pigeon-like, out of the kitchen, through Marsayas's bedroom, and into the tiny front room where Lani had her bed. Once in that room, she slipped her legs from around his waist, took her arms from his shoulders, and closed the door behind them. As soon as her weight was gone from him, Jimmy became unsteady again. He took one feeble step toward her, found himself losing his balance, and fell backward onto her bed.

Then she undid his belt buckle, unzipped his pants, and pulled them by the cuffs, yanking and tugging, until they were off. Meanwhile Jimmy had managed with fumbling fingers to unbutton his shirt. Lani drew his jockeys down to his ankles, leaving him to kick them off. His prick patted his flat stomach as she wriggled out of her clothes, a pair of blue jeans and a turtleneck. Wine seemed to pour back and forth in his head, obliterating a thought here, a bit of clarity there. Photons from the street light outside the window flooded into the little room. They seemed checkered, black and white, or then there was a dim spotty light, enough to see by but not to see clearly by. A glowing screen stood between him and his sweet Leilani, so that he could see her, sometimes, as if she were on film. She wound her long black hair with both hands and tossed it over her curvy shoulder, then approached him. Her Polynesian, somewhat Oriental features, sometimes shadowed, cast forward suddenly in clear, determined beauty, chiseled by light. O why did this have to happen when he was drunk? For he must see her as well as he could, and he wished for a room full of light by which to witness this extraordinary event, this undreamt of moment, this moment he dared not even dream of. She was no longer the child of their hideaway beach and secret waterfall, which everyone knew, but which they thought they had held the Open Sesame for, not the child with the huge flower in her hair; no, no more, but an educated, sophisticated young woman whom he could not fathom, and who, at this moment, desired him, for some reason he could not quite comprehend. And she was on him and he was in her. Oh—he arched his back in a convulsion of expulsion. Oh—she raised her arms above her head as if in search of the ceiling, or heaven, waving them and reaching as if for the angels. All this he saw and could not answer to himself if he woke or slept, partook of a reality that was a dream or a dream that was the truth of life. He dropped and lifted his hips and cried out. She pinched his arm. "Shhhh!" And she fell forward, strangling a cry, or so it seemed in this lost corner of the universe. She lay on him, breathing, breathing, softly breathing. He thought he told her that he loved her. He thought he said: "Lani, I love you. I've always loved you." Did she answer? Did he wake, or sleep?

It was the doorbell that woke him, woke him from the most amazing dream he'd ever had. It was Hawaii and he was in the blue water looking up at the blue sky, flat on his back, floating. Lani came in, carrying a tray with two cups of coffee on it, and said that Phyllis was downstairs. Marsayas wanted to know what he should say to her.

Jimmy jumped out of bed and tried to get his thoughts together, no easy task with only a buzzy, muzzy mind to use. He said, "Tell him to tell her I'm not here."

"Don't you want to see her?" Lani asked, as if there were nothing to hide.

"No," he said. *"Tell her I'm not here."*

Lani put down the tray, went out, said something to Marsayas, and Jimmy heard him clomp down the stairs. In a moment, he heard Phyllis go down the front steps, and then he could see her stalwart, small form, huddled against rain, cross the highway, near the bridge, and disappear, finally, like an important dot erased, inadvertently, from an architect's drawing. He turned away from the window, pulled on his pants, took the tray, and went into the kitchen. Marsayas sat at the table, apparently alternating cups of coffee with glasses of wine. He looked good, healthy, a little high already.

"What did she want?" Jimmy asked.

"She didn't want to come up," Marsayas said; "she just wanted you to have your keys. She's on her way to work."

"You mean she came all the way down here to give me my keys?"

"I guess so."

"Didn't she want to see me?"

"No. She said she didn't want to bother you. I told her you were sleeping. She probably guessed with whom."

Yes, Jimmy thought, he *had* made love to little Leilani. It dawned on him again. Leilani, who was once like a little sister to him, was not little, was not even Leilani, anymore, but a beautiful young woman called Lani, and they had made love, at least he thought that they had made love. He had to cut back on this boozing.

"How did she know I was here?"

"She called last night. Don't you remember?"

"No." Jimmy had been having blackouts. Since Elliott's death he had been dodging the inevitable, trying to write, and drinking himself into oblivion every time the harsh reality of how to take care of Fay intruded. It was a balancing act that he couldn't keep up. No wonder he blacked out.

"Well, you talked to her."

"I did? Jesus Christ, I'm drinking too much."

Lani said:

"Do you want some coffee?"

"No, I want some ice-cold ale, that's what I want."

Lani put her arm around his shoulder, leaned over and poured him a tall, green, foamy glass.

"Do you want something to eat?"

"No, I'm trying to maintain a very delicate chemical balance."

Marsayas said: "Jim likes to think of himself as a drunk, that's why he won't eat. Drunks aren't supposed to eat— right?"

"Wrong. You eat all the time."

"Well, you got me that time, kiddo," Marsayas said, and drained his wine glass.

Jimmy looked around the room. It looked like a junk-yard that'd been caught in a twister. Amid the rubble, Joan sat, placid as ice floating in gin, feeding the baby. Outside, the rain beat a faint tattoo on the window panes.

Lani started to straighten up the place. Everything smelled wet, smelled of booze and wash-water, of warm milk and wet diapers and rain and of the nearby sea. The rain finally dwindled and stopped, the sun came out, and light flew in the windows like white butterflies. The fluttering light was very pleasant because Jimmy was hazy now with the ale he'd drunk. He thought it had become a very beautiful day.

"Oh, brave new world," he declaimed, reversing the meaning from the ironic to the straight-forward, "that has such people in it," and the women looked at him as if he'd gone nuts. But it was his emotion and temperature rising and rising with the new day, with the smiling sun. Marsayas understood.

Later, Marsayas and Joan took the baby out for a stroll. He said they'd be back in an hour. Jimmy flopped on the couch and took a short, snorting nap and when he got up and went into the bathroom, there was Lani, naked, sitting on the edge of the old claw-foot tub, her legs in it. Her long, rich rainbow black hair fell down in a triangular fan-shape over her golden brown shoulders and breasts, and an arm drew a razor up the curve of a calf. A Gauguin. It was so beautiful a portrait it took his breath.

Later still, he caught her by the window, looking at the back yard, the sky, and put his arms around her from behind and put his head close to her hair, to her ear, and said: "Would you like to be my girl?"

She said nothing for a few moments, then, quietly, "I don't know. I don't know."

He had wanted her to shout, "Yes! Oh, *yes!*" and turn and kiss him, and when she said, "I don't know" his heart sank to his stomach like a stone. He let her go and went back to his place at the table and poured himself another glass of ale.

Marsayas came back with Joan and the baby. "Let's go to Manhattan," he said.

"Would you like to go?" Jimmy asked Lani.

"No, I think I'll stay here. I have to write a paper . . . on Lillian Ward."

"Who's she?"

"She founded the Henry Street Settlement House."

"No kidding," said Jimmy. "I live right near there—on Pitt Street."

"I know—with Phyllis."

"Next door to Oskar," Jimmy tried to obfuscate.

"You go," Lani said. Just as well, he thought. That heart-stone was heavy and he had to get away. "Let's go," he said. "Go, go, go!"

Then the car was humming high on the Manhattan Bridge, and Jimmy could see the gulls, and they seemed to be climbing into heaven when Jimmy said: "Sweet Leilani," for no reason at all, or for his heart's sake.

"Don't feel so big about your conquest," Marsayas said, just as they slid down off the bridge and on into the Bowery.

"What do you mean?" Jimmy asked, as they headed toward the East Village.

"She spent last weekend with Butter. Besides, these Polynesian girls will sleep with anybody; it's their culture," Marsayas said, as they pulled up in front of Harry's Psychedelic Dom. "What's your excuse?"

"What do you mean?"

"Oskar told me about you and Niki."

"He caught me with my pants down, but I'm as innocent as a newborn babe. I didn't lay a hand on her—well, maybe a hand. And you're wrong about Polynesian girls, too. That sounds downright racist. At least I hope you're wrong."

"Sure, sure," said Marsayas, "tell it to the Marines."

CHAPTER TWELVE

REVELATIONS

They fuck you up, your mum and dad. . .
—*Philip Larkin*

THE NEW YORK TIMES
NOVEMBER 23, 1963

KENNEDY IS KILLED BY SNIPER AS HE RIDES IN CAR IN DALLAS; JOHNSON SWORN IN ON PLANE

LEFTIST ACCUSED

FIGURE IN PRO-CASTRO GROUP IS CHARGED—POLICEMAN SLAIN

The apartment above the funeral parlor in Brooklyn was quiet. Marsayas and Joan had taken the baby to the park, though it was a gloomy afternoon. Lani was alone with her dark and troubled thoughts. She wondered when she would see Jimmy again, and she wondered if she wanted to see him again. She looked in the bathroom mirror and saw what others had told her was a beautiful young woman. But she frowned. Her frown was creaseless, more a darkening of her eyes, a lowering of her lids. Her dark hair rested on and rolled about her shapely tan shoulders. Why did she frown? She tried a smile, showing herself even white teeth that needed no dentist, no instrument to make them shine, but it wouldn't stay. The corners of her full red lips turned down. She said, "Answer me, answer me."

Then she went into her bedroom and sat down with her diary and wrote—

I am torn between two men, Auntie Mele. One is good, direct, and decent, the other passionate, talented, and confused. I've cheated on the good man with the passionate man, and I feel all the feelings associated with such a betrayal. I feel dishonorable, adulterous, and yet neither of them has any claim on me. I am a free agent. It's my body, and my right to do as I choose with it. You never allowed yourself to be hemmed in by conventions. Butterworth, my good man, has all the qualities one should admire and respect. Jimmy, on the other hand, plunges wildly ahead, catch-as-catch-can. His drinking sometimes reaches frightening proportions, he even becomes violent on occasions.

See, compare the two. But I would bet that you would choose the latter. You told me once: passion over purpose, passion is now, purpose later. I deliberately seduced Jimmy. I simply had to have him. It was an overwhelming desire. My sense went out the window. At that moment I didn't care what happened. I'd wanted him since I was sixteen years old and there was my chance. But now that moment of madness is over. Should cooler heads prevail? I'm not so sure you'd think so. Now, take Jimmy, he lives with a girl named Phyllis who has a cat that Jimmy is not even very fond of, and yet he spent the last of his money on a vet to save the cat, who is, according to him, very old and sick anyway. Butterworth would have had it put to sleep, and that would have been the good and the kind thing to do, but not enough for Jimmy; he had to save the cat, he told me, because it was one of a kind. Well, there they are, my two Marines, in some ways much the same and in some ways so very different. If my head were to lead me, I would choose Butterworth. If my heart were to lead me, I would have to go with Jimmy Whistler. But, as Dylan Thomas once wrote: head, like heart, leads helplessly. I am lost between them. Jimmy told me recently that the police in Newark believe that the house in which his father was killed was deliberately set on fire by some crazy man with a grievance who poured gasoline in the entranceway-lobby, so that his father was murdered, at least technically speaking. Now he feels that he has to take care of his mother, but he is so afraid of her effect on his life and writing that he won't even go to see her. It's been months and months since the fire and he hasn't gone over even once. But look at it from my point of view, Auntie Mele. I have a rival in Phyllis whom I might be able to defeat, although they say he's fixated on her. Personally, I think he is hiding from life. But now it's two to one, that is, his mother and Phyllis against me. He seems to be getting farther and farther away from me because he has so many other worries. It's this thing about taking care of people and he won't take of himself. He comes down to see me occasionally now and we make love and it is the most wonderful love-making of all because I can feel his love for me when he holds me in a way I can't feel with others—never with anyone else—but then he drinks and tells me his sad story and leaves me again for Phyllis and I fear one of these days, for his mother. Point me in the right direction, Auntie Mele.

*   *   *

From her letters, which dropped at his door with the inevitability and desolation of autumn leaves, Jimmy knew the

288

sort of life Fay'd been living. He never read them anymore. He let Phyllis extract flat information from them concerning Fay's health and finances, but had her studiously avoid anything of an emotional nature. Fay was his guilt. Fay was his fear. Without Fay, he could become; with her, was the death of hope.

But Phyllis worked on him, too, in her own persistent way.

"Why don't you go and see her, Jimmy?"

"No—no—I can't yet. Leave me alone about it, will you!"

"But why? She misses you something awful."

"That's why. Because she'll trap me."

"What do you mean, trap you?"

"She'll want me to live over there with her. It'd drive me crazy to be stuck over there. I just want to be left alone. I feel like I'm being pursued. You leave me alone, too, do you hear? I'm trying to concentrate." And he turned back to the poem he was working on, "A Worker at the Waterworks."

> He watched the water purling away.
> No doubt it would soon be carrying off
> loads of human excrement, with the lost
> parts of bodies, dead cells, hairs,
> bits and parts of burnt energy, the
> stuff left over after the hard day's work,
> after the argument, the loving in the
> small bed while the kids slept fitfully.
> There the tears of his beloved melted
> into the blood, sweat, and tears of a city.
>
> Off they go, he said, the domestic sewage,
> and the storm runoff, to be wed and
> to become the combined sewage; off it goes,
> through flush tanks and scum collectors, through

grit chambers and sedimentation tanks,
through trickling filters and activated-
sludge units, through oxidation ponds
and the centrifuge, through heat coagulators
and into the incinerators, where, at last,
all our loves go up in smoke.

And the outfall works drop pure water,
cleansed, unsullied by any particle of humanity,
by any pitiful history of the human condition,
into the swaying receiving waters of river and sea.

So it went. But it soon had to end. He couldn't just walk away from his mother a few days after his father's death and never see her again.

Finally, he did, early on a November afternoon, nearly nine months after his father's death. He stood shivering in nervous sweat on the leaf-strewn front porch at Baldwin and rang the bell. In a minute he saw Fay's short, familiar figure appear in the hallway beyond the window curtain. She always got confused when a bell rang. Her eyesight had been bad since childhood, spoiled by dye and subsequent infection when she was a kid in a mill, but her harlequin-shaped glasses corrected that, and she was tilting her small, pretty head, with its waves of smoky hair, trying to see who it was. Then he could see such an expression of relief and happiness come on her face that he felt heart-stabbed with guilt. She pulled open the door and fell into his arms. She was crying more tears than seemed his due.

"Glad to see me, huh?"

"Oh my God, Jimmy, they've killed the President."

"What?"

"He's been shot in Dallas."

"Are they sure he's dead?"

"Yes, it just came on. He's dead. He's dead. Didn't you hear about it?"

"You know I don't watch television or read newspapers beside the headlines. I've had my head buried in a book all the way over here. I didn't hear a thing. I didn't see any-thing."

"Come inside. It's on the news now."

Jimmy caught a replay of the shooting. "Do they have any suspects?"

"I think so. Everybody seems to be so confused, it's hard to get anything straight."

So it was that their reconciliation turned into a death watch. They saw Lee Harvey Oswald who seemed to be sporting a black eye. He seemed to have shot a cop. But that wasn't very clear either. They stayed up all night, eating, drinking endless cups of coffee. Their personal problems dropped away like the fur of a shedding cat. They felt close, intimate, and very fearful. Was this some prelude to a soviet attack? Or a coup? Lyndon Johnson was sworn in aboard Air Force One, ninety minutes after Kennedy's death. Jackie Kennedy, still in her blood-stained suit stood at his side.

Mother and son dozed off side by side on her small bed with the TV blaring at their feet. Jimmy lost track of time. Then Lee Harvey Oswald was being taken somewhere. Then a man stepped out of the shadows and shot him. What was happening? No one seemed to know. Even Lyndon Johnson, the new President, didn't seem to know.

One morning Jimmy and Fay tried to calculate how long this nightmare movie had been running. "Wasn't that the day before yesterday?"

"No, that was when Oswald was shot."

"Oswald was shot on—was it?"

And then they watched the funeral procession in Wash-ington, little John-John saluting, the backwards stirrups on the horse, the flag-draped casket, the eternal flame. It was all

a blur from beginning to end—and of course there wasn't any
end, just a slow diminuendo of interest, emotional exhaustion,
flagging power of the senses. "Death, be not proud," Jimmy
quoted John Donne, and he and Fay began to return to the
involvements of self-interest.

Fay began to shift her thoughts from one dead man to
another, from the dead President to the dead husband, her
own. "Elliot would have hated to see Kennedy assassinated.
Oh, God, Jimmy, I wish he had come home!"

"I told him he ought to come home to you," Jimmy said.

"Well, your father wasn't a man to take other people's
advice. When he fell down and broke his arm that time, the
doctor called him *the man who prescribes for himself.* He did
things his own way, Jimmy. He never wanted you to know,
but now, I suppose, since he's gone, it doesn't matter."

"What doesn't matter?"

"Well, there are things about your father you don't
know, that he made me promise never to tell you. I suppose
he didn't want you to be ashamed of him. It's crazy when
you think about it, with all the other things he did. But this
was different, I guess. This happened before the Crash, during the boom of the Twenties, when your father was successful. A little after he was in *Who's Who.* I always thought that
was wonderful! He was responsible for his partner going to
jail. I don't know anything about stocks and bonds, so I probably don't have the story exactly right, but it seems that he
and this man who worked with him—your father called him
his junior partner—had printed and floated phoney bonds
worth about Fifty Thousand dollars. That doesn't seem so
much money now, but, back then, your father told me, it was
the equivalent of about Three Hundred Thousand."

Fay paused. She seemed to be waiting for what she was
saying to sink in, for Jimmy to say something. But Jimmy
said nothing. Fay could see that he was thinking about what
she had said. In fact his mind was racing, reviewing the

portable chaos of his life from his earliest memories and up to this blunt disclosure. A sixth sense came upon him. It told him by vibrations of sense that the answer to the biggest question of his life was finally being given. He shook inside with nerves and with hidden ironic laughter to think that Fay was playing Inspector McCracken to his Willy, to his assembled suspects, each himself. He felt that he was about to learn the solution to the mystery of his poverty-stricken, ruined childhood, and to the strange, frightened behavior of his mysterious father.

"Yes, yes. Go on."

"I only know that that's why he could never go back to Wall Street. He always believed he might get caught and serve fifteen or twenty years in prison for fraud. After that, he explained to me why we had to move all the time, why we couldn't settle down anywhere. He was always afraid some-body would find out. He felt pursued. He said there was no statute of limitations on a Federal offense. That's why we never had a proper home. That's why he became the kind of salesman that he did, selling junk, and with his background. For years he dreamed of getting back into the real business world, but he just drifted, and it became a habit during the Depression, I guess, and then finally he just seemed to give up hope. I thought you ought to know, to understand."

"Well, I never could understand why we lived the way we did, with you two dragging me all over the countryside, out of one town and into another, out of one school and into another. The older I got the more crazy it seemed. Why didn't you make him face up? It was so many years ago—it was ancient history—I don't think anybody would have charged him."

"No, no, he told me there was no statute of limitations on a Federal crime. And he firmly believed that he might go to prison. His partner served seven years. Think of it—seven years. After those seven years he was always afraid his partner would come looking for him, too. He said he would have served twenty. Really, it ruined his life."

"And ours. Or at least mine. Or at least my childhood." And when Jimmy dozed off beside Fay that night, the turned-down television still showing images of assassination, he dreamed of that haunted childhood, in which he was always a stranger, always an outsider, always truant, always behind in school, that haunting past. The sins of the fathers . . .

Jimmy finally understood that he was not a victim of an eccentric fool, a W.C. Fields prototype, but of a calculating criminal who had spent his life on the lam. But if Fay knew, why did she let Jimmy pay for Elliot's malfeasance? It was simple enough, wasn't it? She loved Elliot more than she loved him. He took her shoulder and shook her awake. "Get up," he said, "I've got to ask you something."

"What is it?" she said, putting on her glasses.

"It seemed as if the two of you were always fighting, but when it came right down to things you always took his side. Why? Why, when you could see he was wrong?"

"Didn't you ever wonder how we came to be married? A man like him to a poor girl like me. All I had ever been was a mill-girl or a maid. Over thirty years he almost gave me an education, but you have to realize how different both of us were then. He was a man-about-town and I was a nobody. We met in a speakeasy. My mother had taken me out drinking. I was a half-blind sixteen year old girl. His family was well known all over the state. My God, there was a building in downtown Plainfield named for them. But he was already on the run. He couldn't see any of his old friends. His wife had left him, taking his son, Elliot, Junior. My mother was a no-good drunk. She pushed me on him. 'Oh he's one of those rich Whistlers,' she said. I'm going to tell you the whole truth now. I had a boyfriend then, a boy closer to my own age, when I met your father. We never knew for sure whether you were his child or not. But the boyfriend ran away. It took five years, but your father finally married me. I believe you are his son. There are so many signs. But neither of us were absolutely certain. I was grateful to him, and he stuck to me for thirty years and more, and I stuck to him. There's more to these things than young people realize."

"Are you saying I'm a bastard, that you made me a bastard, in addition to everything else?"

"He was your father, Jimmy, and he loved you. He could have run away, but he didn't."

"There were times when I wished he had. There were times that I wished you had. The two of you have been lying to me ever since I was born."

Fay was crying. She took off her glasses and wiped her eyes. "Well, this is the truth. I wanted to tell you before. He didn't want you to know any of this."

"Then why are you telling me now?"

"Because he's gone and you have a right to know."

"Knowledge is Power, is that it? Knowledge is happiness? Not so long ago I finished one of the best poems I've ever written and it isn't even the truth."

"The truth is all sorts of things. What's the truth anyway? We all loved each other, didn't we? That's the truth, isn't it?"

Now he must pay by feeling the fool once again, as he had once done by trying to save her when he was sixteen by taking her away from Elliot and a basement to the majestic heights above a pizza parlor. She was nearly as dishonest as Elliot; and to think, when he was young in Hawaii, he had asked God night after night to take him and to spare them. Knowledge is Power! Knowledge is Misery! He wanted to shrink down to small, stupid childhood again and feel the wonderful wind when he ran. Oh, if only he had had this knowledge when he wrote "Obituary," but they cheated him out of getting that right, too.

"It's late," said Fay, "but let's have a beer."

"Yes," said Jimmy, heaving, "I could use one."

Fay's tactic of the night before had been diplomatic, but next morning it was aggressive. Over their first cup of coffee she said:

"I think you should settle here with me. We could run the house and you could get a job. This is a nice, comfortable apartment, don't you think?"

"But Mom, what about Phyllis and my life in New York? I can't just walk off and leave her . . ."

"Well, she's nothing to you, is she? I'm your mother."

"Sure she's something to me. I've been living with her a couple of years, don't you realize that? You act as if the reality of my life doesn't exist."

"Well, what are you going to do? Hang around over there in New York with a lot of bums and tramps? Is that your idea?"

"I don't hang around with bums and tramps."

"Well, I'd like to know what you call them. That Phyllis is obviously nothing but a little tramp. Her mother and father don't seem to want her. What is she doing in New York? Why isn't she at home, if she can't take care of herself?"

"She can take care of herself. And I don't like you calling her a tramp, either. You don't know her. She's a good little thing. She'd never hurt anyone."

"What's she doing for you? You're not thinking about marrying her, are you? Didn't you have enough trouble with Vera? You act like a fool, Jimmy. Listen to me. Your father didn't like that girl. He said that he was afraid you might marry her."

"That's not true. Dad always liked Phyllis. Besides, what I do hasn't got anything to do with her. And another thing—I'm not going to marry anybody—ever again! I don't want any woman driving me nuts the way Vera did, or the way you did Dad. Always after him about something. I could hear you screaming at him in my sleep."

"I was trying to save his life."

"Why didn't you let the poor man alone? If he wanted to drink, why didn't you let him drink in peace? Then he wouldn't have moved out."

"Because I was afraid he'd kill himself. Don't you know that he was always falling down and breaking his arms or smashing his skull? Where were you when I was taking care of him? You were running around with all your tramps, that's where."

"It wasn't my job to take care of him. It was supposed to be his job to take care of me, when I was young, but he never did it. It was supposed to be your job, too, but now I'm supposed to take care of you. Look, Mom, I have a right to do what I want to do. I'm not married to you, you know. You lived your life the way you wanted to, and you pretty much let me go to hell, and now I'm going to live mine. You didn't give me any childhood, you gave me a goddamned portable chaos. And now you're trying to steal my youth away from me. Well, you're not going to run me!"

"I'm not trying to run you. I just thought you could be of some help to me."

"Yeah, sure. You want me to sit around here with you and watch TV the rest of my life. For Christ's sake, I'm a young man!"

"Well, you don't act like a man."

"What's your idea of how a man should act?"

"Your father was a man!"

"Well, I'm doing what he did, aren't I? I'm drinking. I'm not responsible for anyone else."

"Yes, trying to imitate him. But, my God, he was an old man. You're only young. Why don't you go out and get a job?"

"In a factory? And support you and watch TV at night and never write?"

"You know I don't mean that. But look at you. You look terrible!"

"I look all right."

"You look like a bum! Are you one of those beatniks?"

"You have your ideas and I have mine."

"Then, what are you going to do?"

"Nothing—absolutely nothing—naught, nullis, nicht, nada, zero—nothing!"

"And how are you going to live! What are you going to do, let women support you?"

"Yes. Can't you tell by my fancy clothes? My limousine? I'm going to become the world's greatest gigolo. A flaneur. Does that suit you?"

"I don't know what that means, but it certainly does not. Don't you realize you're wasting your life?"

"How do you know what I'm doing? I've tried to tell you that I'm a poet. I'm learning to write!"

"Poet! You have no education."

"Whose fault is that? That's what you said when I was sixteen. I'm already a publishing poet. Besides, that's what I'm doing—trying to acquire an education. Have been—for years. Don't you know that? I don't drink all the time. I study. If you'd try for a minute to understand me, maybe you'd discover that I have some brains, that I'm not as stupid as you and Dad always thought."

"We never thought you were stupid. Don't put words in my mouth. We just thought that you weren't making good use of yourself."

"Ha! That's a fat laugh, coming from you. What use did you and Dad ever make of yourselves? Him running from basement to basement and you cleaning the toilets! *You* two lived like beatniks! I'm getting out of here. I'm going back to New York, to my tramps."

"Oh, please, don't go, Jimmy. Please stay here—just for a few days . . ."

"I'm going! Auf Wiedersehen!"

Slammed doors still vibrated as Jimmy caught the bus.

*   *   *

Fay had given Jimmy an old letter from Vera, sent to Baldwin. It contained a number he was to call.

Following her directions, Jimmy met Vera in the East Village, and they went to a lawyer downtown, near Wall Street. Jimmy still didn't know whether he wanted this divorce or not. He didn't know whether he wanted to be completely rid of Vera. After all, that dead marriage had protected him. And he didn't mind being connected to someone who was going up in the world. The past few years had been, except in writing, a spiral down for him. He looked at Vera in profile as she walked beside him and remembered her picture, along with several other members of a famous dance troupe, on a recent cover of "TV Guide"—he remembered, too, years ago, taking her to the plastic surgeon who had reshaped what had been a not unattractive conk into the standard upswept, pinched-nostrilled theatrical nose she now wore.

It was obvious to Jimmy that she had been surprised and unpleasantly so by the way he looked. She had asked Jimmy what he'd been doing, meaning what kind of work. He couldn't exaggerate his recent accomplishments; as anyone could see by his clothes, Jimmy wasn't the Rich Boy. His shoes were run through and stained a wiggly white where he'd been standing in the overflow of dishwater in restaurants, the last of his white shirts was so badly frayed that the collar could be lifted off by breaking the last few threads that held it, and his overcoat, a motheaten old tweed, had cost two-fifty at a thrift shop. It occurred to Jimmy, walking with Vera, that he would like to have a new suit. But, though he knew that the publication of many of his poems in high-brow

299

literary magazines like "The Yale Review" or "The Paris Review" would not very much impress her, he could lay one offering at her pretty, toed-out dancer's feet.

An approximately ten-year long golden age had begun for script writers and teleplaywrights around the middle of the Fifties. Writers could submit unagented scripts directly to NBC, CBS, etc., and have a reasonable prayer of getting one produced. Jimmy's agent, Alex, had persuaded Jimmy to meld together a few of his previously published McCracken and Willy mysteries into an hour-long teleplay, which Alex had sold to one of the networks as "Murder in the Commune." He told Vera about the teleplay. She seemed properly impressed but wondered why he appeared so broke. Did she hope to get some money out of him? She probably made more in one week than he made in a year. He told her that the pay wasn't that great and the sale of a script was "far and few, far and few, as the lands where the Jumblies live." That one furrowed her brow, and he guessed that she had never heard of Edward Lear. But then, he guessed that she had not heard of many things, outside the wonderful world of Capezios. "I owed money all over the place," he told her. "I'm tap city."

They signed the papers, and said farewells that appeared to be final. Vera and he were history. He didn't tell a soul. It was wonderful, in a way, to think that he *could* marry again. He wanted to marry . . . someday—the right person—to settle down, and raise a family; to start fresh. Through no fault or word or deed of Jimmy's, Phyllis had believed for so long that, when his divorce from Vera came through, she and he would be married, that he couldn't muster the heartlessness it would take to tell her that this dream of hers was merely that, a dream. Nothing could have brought him to marry her. Though he felt great affection for Phyllis, perhaps even love, he had to have a woman he could make love to, a woman who satisfied his longing for beauty and his passion for sex, which was part of that longing for beauty, and there just wasn't anything there with her. It seemed that all Jimmy could ever find was one half or the other of a woman—bits and parts. Phyllis was not the part he wanted to give his life to. To marry Phyllis would have been to go on leading a life that he wanted to escape. So he said nothing to her about his divorce. The money from his script went to pay back rent.

Lani was on his mind.

Phyllis kept her new-found job, doing clerical work for some large market research firm. Though it brought her right in to "the bullshit world," the heart of darkness, it wasn't so bad because the work was done by project, and she'd work for a few weeks, then be off for a stretch to indulge herself in her fantasy world.

CHAPTER THIRTEEN

MOVING ON

The times they are a-changin'
—*Bob Dylan*

THE NEW YORK TIMES
AUGUST 9, 1964

POLICE BREAK UP ANTIWAR RALLY

MOUNTED PATROLMEN USED AS 60 GATHER IN
MIDTOWN TO PROTEST VIETNAM ACTION

Jimmy dropped into Harry's Psychedelic Dom one day and found a worried-looking Oskar.

"Hi, der, Fluffy!"

"Hi, yourself. I didn't think we were ever going to talk again."

"Oh, dat's all bullshit. Niki's been doing dat to me ever since I met her. No reason to blame it on you."

"I told you—no matter how it looked that morning, I didn't have anything to do with her. She just got me into an embarrassing situation."

"Yeah, yeah. Ja, I got bigger problems on my mind."

"Like what?"

"Da Gotdamn draft! Dat liar Johnson says don't vote for Goldwater. He'll blow us all to hell. Me, he says, I seek no wider war. Shit, dere's already talk about increasing da draft as soon as he's elected. How come you're not worried about it, Fluffy?"

"I served three years active duty—they're not likely to call me up."

"But Budderwordth's worried."

"Butter was an officer. There's a good chance they *will* recall him."

"But you're in the reserves, aren't you?"

"Four years, but I'm way down on the list. Besides, for an enlisted man I'm getting a touch too old. I'm not worried."

"Vell, I am! My ass is crying. Dey can draft Green Card me, even if I am a Kraut citizen. What should I do, Fluffy?"

"Go to Canada."

"Wvat, me live up dere with the sled dogs?"

"Go to Montreal. It's a big city, cosmopolitan. You'll like it."

"Been up dere?"

"Once. You'll love the onion soup."

"I'll tink about it. But I need a job first. I need money ta get out of here on. Got any ideas?"

"I've been thinking about working on the docks. Want to come with me to a shape-up tomorrow night?"

"Wvat's dat mean—shape up?"

"Non-union guys. We go over and stand around and hope we get picked. Come on with me tomorrow night, it'll be like old times."

The next night they took the cross-town bus over to the West Side and ran along in an icy, slant rain, over polished cobblestones, between big green girders of the elevated West Side Highway, slipping, slapping through lively puddles and flooding ponds, the florescent inner and red-and-blue neon outer lights of *LUNCH COUNTER* giving them promise.

Across the street, beyond the girders of the West Side Highway, a big yellow mouth was open. While Jimmy drank his coffee, he watched the activity inside it. Men wearing mackintoshes or lumberjackets, hooded men, were clapping work-gloved hands together. Some held cigarettes in their teeth, and puffed a combination of smoke and steam. Many had baling hooks in their belts or hanging from their pockets. It wasn't until they finished their coffee and went over to it that Jimmy realized how huge the mouth was. There were scores of tractor-trailer trucks parked inside, and thousands of crates of all sizes and descriptions.

Oskar thought lugging those crates around all night looked too damned rough. He said he didn't think that that was a job he'd want. "Anyway, I'm too worried. I'm gonna take what money I got and go to Canada tonight. Look, Fluffy—" Oskar hugged Jimmy to him. "Maybe long time no see. I'm splitting."

Jimmy said, "After the war, pal."

"After da frogging war."

Jimmy watched as Oskar loped away into the night. He doubted Oskar would really go so abruptly. That was more Marsayas's style.

"What's in the crates?" Jimmy called to a worker, approaching the entrance.

"Vegetables," the fellow said. "All kinds."

He stood among the other men and smoked while they waited. In a few minutes a whistle blew, and the hecatomb of men who waited drew into a cluster around the sound as steel shavings draw to a magnet. Jimmy edged into the inner midst of the circle—which now re-shaped itself into a crescent. There was an institutional clock high up on a beam, by which it was exactly seven. The man with the whistle in his mouth, a hard-looking gent with a long sharp nose and expensive clothing, yelled: "O.K.!" A short, dumpy man, in not-so-expensive clothing, with a slouch-hat pulled down over his eyes, raised a clipboard toward his shadowed, flaccid cheeks, and began to jab a stubby pencil at it. The taller man winked with his lips—the whistle swung round and round in a chained arc from his manicured left forefinger—and a man stepped from the crescent and began a new crescent behind the two panjandrums, facing them, the as-yet-unchosen. The tall man kept winking his thin lips, causing his neat little black mustache to arch like a lascivious eyebrow, until half the men in the original crescent had shaped another fair-sized crescent facing it. This happened very fast. Then Mr. Mustache began to slow down, and to search among the crowd, choosing more carefully.

He picked two or three others, and then the crowd around him was getting thin enough for Mr. Important to get a good look at Jimmy, who was wearing an old pair of Wellington boots he'd got in a thrift shop, an old pair of Marine fatigues that he'd had for years, a heavy black turtle neck sweater, and an ancient, scuffed, leather jacket. He had a pair of canvas gloves on his hands, thumbs stuck into a wide black leather belt. If that costume didn't get him a job on the docks, Jimmy was going to throw the whole thing in the river.

When the big finger was pointed at him, he couldn't believe it. He pointed at himself, and said: "Me?" A few more men were picked, and then the tall chap plugged his magic mouth with the whistle, and blew!

After that night Jimmy got on three or four nights a week and life fell into a reasonable pattern of intermittent dock-work. Phyllis worked during the day (when she was on) and Jimmy'd be on his way to the docks when she came home. He'd work all night, catching those never-ending crates of vegetables as they flew down the ramp from trailers and toting them to stacks on pallets to be loaded on ships. When he'd get in, he'd clean up and read some, or on a good night, get down to writing poetry. He was now writing free verse almost exclusively. Once, he recorded his first night on the docks in a poem called "New Man on the Docks." He was taking Marsayas's advice, loosening up.

The new men were issued key-chain badges
with numbers on them, then they were
divided into workgangs and marched off,
each gang to a different tractor-trailer truck,
to off-load its vegetable green-and-gold,
later to be loaded aboard the great gray ship
that walled out the harbor view like a dam.
The trucks had aluminum ladder-like rollers
placed from their side doors and resting atop
three or four stacked crates. Half the gang
lived down at the receiving end of the roller,
and the other half lived aboard the truck
and began shooting sixty-pound crates of cabbages
down at breakneck speed. He watched
the men ahead of him catch these whooshing,
wire-wrapped rectangular cannon-balls,
the bottom inside corner ramming
into their shoulders, sending them staggering
backwards, until it was his turn
and one of them was placed in position
to be fired at him. He heard a Samaritan
behind him say, "Don't catch it in the neck,
kid." He raised his shoulder and was glad
for his leather jacket when the concussion came.
He dragged the crate down from his shoulder,
then back, catching another crate, and off
and back in the line again. Soon the crates
were being fired at him with such speed
he fell into an hypnotic trance. He had no self
left, just a dream of whooshing crates,

chalk marks, and blurred, pained faces,
and didn't wake until he felt the planet
roll out of its orbit. The universe,
the quiet and beautiful music of the spheres,
was crashing. He stood waiting for the rhythmic thud,
and no thud came. He looked up. Everyone
was leaving him, shambling off without a word.
He wiped the fast-freezing sweat from his face
on the backs of his gloves. Then he shambled away,
    too,
through the dismal morning light of the waterfront,
by ancient, devastated buildings, dreaming of sleep.

Browsing in a bookstore, Jimmy came upon Eric Hoffer's *True Believer*, and was delighted to learn that Hoffer, the great amateur philosopher, had been and still was a stevedore like himself—well, not quite like himself; for Hoffer considered himself a stevedore first and a writer second. For Jimmy it was the other way around. In fact, he had begun to feel quite the professional writer with the publication of his first collection of poems, *Obituary and Other Poems* just a few months before. Phyllis had proved a diligent agent (Alex wouldn't handle poetry.) for the book and had finally found a highly regarded small press that was willing to publish it. She was fiercely proud of him, and more than once tried to explain to Fay by phone and letter what Jimmy had accomplished, only to hear Jimmy attacked as a bum, a waster, a drunkard, and a fool.

"She just doesn't get it," Phyllis said.

"No," said Jimmy, "and she never will."

But Phyllis sent Fay a copy of the book anyway, which prompted a letter.

Dear Jimmy, Fay wrote,

I am so proud of you and so ashamed of myself for not being more of a support to you in all these years. I can't believe I am actually looking at a book by you on the table next to my arm. You always said you would do it and you have. I sat with the book a long time and read all the poems in it and cried to think that you had such feelings in you, and I never seemed to see it, did I? That poem about your father—"Obituary"—I don't know how you remembered all those things we must have told you over the years. But they're all there. It was like reading our life together. So moving. And so sad. But funny, sometimes, too.

You know, Jimmy, I only went to the sixth grade. I don't understand how things like this work. It's all a mystery to me. Maybe your father understood better than I did. I asked him once if he thought your writing was any good—you remember he was a WPA writer himself—and he said he thought you really had something and I guess he was right. I guess neither one of us ever did much for you. I know you always say you raised yourself and I suppose you really did. I guess we were just a couple of drunks. Your father and I were both pretty nice looking and I think maybe we counted too much on our looks and not enough on more important things. I wish I could help you now, but I guess it's too late. I hope I won't ever become a burden to you anyway. I guess it's a good thing I went to Catholic school or I wouldn't be able to write you this letter. That book and that poem, well, it's like a bombshell to me. Wow!

Love, Mom

P.S. I'm going to vote for Johnson. What do you think?

*   *   *

What did Jimmy think? Jimmy did not think much of any politician. Jimmy thought Oskar was probably right and that the draft would be enlarged after the election, but Goldwater's stridency scared the hell out of Jimmy. Jimmy had never cast a vote for anyone.

308

"You've *got* to vote!" cried Ishmael Reed, black activist-poet. Marsayas had introduced Jimmy to Ishy, a regular at Harry's, and they'd become friendly.

"Johnson says that Goldwater'll get us into a wider war in Viet Nam. He may even use the bomb! Johnson's promised to keep us out. You can't sit there and say that you don't feel like taking a walk of a few blocks to vote when the issues are so important. Your beer'll be here when you get back."

Phyllis had got Jimmy to register with her a month before. She, too, was terrified of Goldwater. So Jimmy walked to the voting place with Ishmael and voted for Lyndon Johnson, the first vote of his life. On the way back to Harry's, Ishmael said, "Now there won't be a wider war." Jimmy felt the delusions of virtue. He had voted for Lyndon Banal Johnson and there would be no wider war in Viet Nam. Case closed!

*   *   *

Most of the crowd at the White Horse had been to Jimmy's reading at the West Side Artists Co-Op Theatre in the West Village. Advertisements for the reading had been circulated all over and had drawn quite a crowd to hear Jimmy read from his new book, his first, for Jimmy already had a reputation for being a very good reader of his own and of other poets' work. He had been reading in coffee houses, book stores—his reading at the Gotham Book Mart had even been reviewed in several alternative press papers—libraries, and several times at the Brooklyn Museum, which had its own theatre. Unlike many poets, Jimmy was a trained actor and always gave a rousing performance, rather than a dull reading, bringing whatever text he chose alive, informing it with his pent-up passion. As one reviewer had put it, his readings were "explosive, more passionate than the whole Abby Theatre." The famous Irish theatre group had recently toured the States. Now, sprawled under a painting of Dylan Thomas,

309

Jimmy even slept with apparent passion, for he was snoring explosively. Head hanging back over his chair, intermittently roaring at the ceiling, he seemed the very definition of the roaring boy in repose; but who could tell what mysterious verbs were emanating from the besotted poet for the roar of the crowd? The reading had been an unexpected triumph. It was thought by all but a few that he'd been too drunk to go onstage, let alone to summon the necessary articulateness of a reading, but somehow he had done both and more. Once his legs had given out under him and he had dropped to one knee, like a man proposing, like Al Jolson, but in the great tradition of the theatre he had drunkenly decided to "use" this defective, if romantic, position and had managed to make it work to such a degree that the audience had stood up cheering for the collapsed poet. Now he was the semi-comatose subject of an argument between Marsayas and Butterworth. Auditors and kibitzers at the same table were Phyllis, Denise, Joan, and Lani. Phyllis, Denise and Jimmy had journeyed to Brooklyn earlier that day to join Marsayas, Joan, Butterworth and Lani at Marsayas's for the ride back over to the theatre in Marsayas's clown-crowded car.

"He'll never make it," Butterworth had said.

"He's too drunk," Lani had said. It appeared that she and Butterworth were a couple. They repeatedly touched each other—sometimes held hands—and caused Jimmy to drink the more, and more.

"I agree with Lani," said Joan. "Somebody should call up and tell them that he's not going to make it."

"Jimmy can do anything," said Denise. "Just get him there."

"I agree with Denise," said Phyllis, "he'll be great."

"_____"

"I told you he'd be great," said Phyllis, but no one was listening.

"Not only did he make it," said Butterworth. "It was one of the best readings I've ever witnessed. *Without the mummeries of death, by fire . . .*"

Lani looked at Butterworth. My God, she thought, now he's falling in love with Jimmy. Am I the only one who's worried sick about him?

"The reading was great," said Marsayas. "But it would have been better if he had had more free verse in it. Imagine how he could have done Whitman. I've heard him read Whitman, and he can really put it over. He's uptight. Why doesn't he loosen up, stop with the rhyming, stop with the meter—the metronome?"

Butterworth demurred: "He reads so well because his poetry has form and order. Do you realize what we've got here? Not just another copy-cat beatnik, but an original! He writes out of the tradition, but he makes it new. He makes it personal. It belongs to him."

. . . And on it went, Auntie Mele. Just about everybody in the White Horse had an opinion about Jimmy's work, and there sat Jimmy, dead to the world. Oh Auntie Mele, what am I to do? I suffer from the worst case of approach-avoidance in history. At the core of me I am absolutely compelled to him, but he scares the very devil out of me. Oh it's so comforting to be with Butter, who is so kind and calm, who would make such a fine husband to some lucky girl—then why do I want Jimmy so much? He told me one day in anger that I reminded him of Vera, trying to control him, trying to manipulate him—"I won't be manipulated," he shouted at me. Butter is so understandable, so direct, so simple, so honest compared with the complicated crazy mess of a Jimmy Whistler. I sure don't want another crazy Kosinski on my hands, or somebody even worse, if that's possible. A famous crazy Kosinski! Is it that I lack courage? Does Phyllis have more courage than I do, or

*   *   *

MERRY CHRISTMAS! Word went forth to the East Village: there was to be a party at the Loft, and everyone was invited, either bring your own bottle or contribute a buck or two at the door. The Loft was a series of huge, more or less empty rooms with bare floorboards, and walls of exposed ruddy brick, where a number of sculptors shared the rent for work space. A few strong wooden work benches stood about. Wild-winged mobiles, made of metal, rose from the floor and swayed from the ceiling. Unguessable creatures and things emerged from half-carved chunks of wood and rock. Folding chairs and mats held their scattered, temporary places throughout the huge rooms. A restaurant-sized aluminum steam table dominated the main room. Near it, a big wooden table swayed under the weight of its smorgasbord. Loud speakers boomed:

> *It's been a hard day's night*
> *And I've been working like a d-a-a-a-w-g—*

Jimmy grabbed a paper plate for himself and one for Phyllis, who had gone to get them drinks, and piled them high. With Denise around, one didn't figure on a second chance at the food. The big, stoned, perpetually ravenous young woman had recently emerged from a long Harlem hiatus, looking older, sadder, and sicker, but not dead yet, anyway. Behind Jimmy, as he ogled and heaped, the strong boys—some of whom were sculptors—shirts off, doing muscle feats, groaned and grunted.

> *Walk right in,*

312

Sit right down,
Baby let your hair hang down!

Jimmy turned to see Lani dart in and out of the crowd, hotly pursued by some burly drunken satyr with his belt loose and his pants half down—no, it wasn't a satyr, it was Ape, the plumber. She caught Jimmy's eye. Jimmy feigned indifference. He realized now that he had loved her at first sight. Was it first sight way back in Hawaii when she was sixteen or was it first sight in Marsayas's kitchen that night? He didn't know. He didn't care. It was biological, cellular. He did not want this knowledge, but he was confronted with it. He could not pretend that he did not feel what he felt. But she had rebuffed him. She had rebuffed him after seducing him. Now she was with Butterworth. It had hurt to the quick.

By three a.m. people lay about on the floor, singly, in pairs, and in piles, some drink-drugged, some plain drugged. The room was awash with mats, rugs, and pillows of all shapes and sizes. Jimmy saw Lani, wearing a long red dress decked with golden flowers, droop slowly down among the fallen.

Where have all the flowers gone,
Long time passing. . .

The after-image of Lani, sweet Leilani, began to fade from Jimmy's eyes. Then he saw with a jolt, a sudden shock of clarity, Butterworth with Denise, arm over shoulder, covered with blood, standing in the doorway. Butter had several dent-like cuts on his forehead, dripping in gouts. Denise was having one of her bad LSD trips. She'd wanted out, to run someplace, to escape her demon visions. Butterworth had tried to help her down the long, iron-covered, loft stairway, she'd thrown a fit, and both of them went tumbling down. Lani popped up, ran to them, tried to soothe Denise. They tried to hold her still, but Denise flailed wildly. Jimmy went over and took Denise by the shoulders and tried to pin her to a wall. But in her madness she was very strong and broke loose and slapped him back and forth across the face with both hands, nearly unhinging his jaw with the first blow. He got her back in his grip, and held her there. Then she went loose and slid down the wall into a sleep or coma or God knew what oblivion.

Lani and Butterworth tried to wake her. Someone patted her face with a wet towel, and Lani fed her coffee. At last they got her on her feet. She was docile now, whimpering and pathetic. Lani grabbed a coat and led her out the door, with Butter's aid. They must have walked Denise all the way home. None of them came back. Phyllis emerged from shadow and whispered, "Poor Denise," to Jimmy.

"Where have you been hiding?" Jimmy asked her.
"You know I don't like that violent bullshit," she said.
"She's your friend."
"Not when she's like that! Bad vibes!"

*   *   *

When Jimmy woke, he had poor Denise and her bad trip on the brain. He remembered the early days, when Denise and he worked together in the book store—how she had got him the little room at Miss Byrdsong's in which Elliot had stayed with him, and how Elliot had conned Denise out of that fifty bucks, and she'd gone over to Newark to get it—all of it was alive in his mind. Perhaps it was just sentimentality, nostalgia, the season of Good Will—but he decided to find a place where he could get a couple of quarts of cold beer and take them up as an offering to good old Denise in what was probably her hour of need. He left Phyllis sleeping, probably dreaming of the Castiglione's ducal court of Milan.

Denise now lived in an ancient dump like the one in which Elliot had died, like, but different in that the denizens of Elliot's flophouse were derelicts and winos, whereas the denizens of Denise's house were mostly starving artist types. It was a musty rooming house up the block from Harry's

314

Psychedelic Dom. Jimmy climbed four flights of stairs and banged (cheerfully, he thought) on the door. Denise moaned from within, and called: "Who's there?"

"It's me. 'Tis I, Denise; Jimmy."

She let him in, and lowered herself down on the floor, on a blanket, where she slept. She had her B.A. in Oriental studies, and it was her little resultant vanity to sleep on mats. She'd slept on a bamboo mat at Miss Byrdsong's. She had used to play the recorder (the instrument, not the machine) and would play herself to sleep at night. But, though she still slept on the floor, she no longer lived as she had in the old days. Then her little oblong box of a room had been kept in fanatic order. Its books, on neat shelves, floor to ceiling, had been arranged according to size and content; the pens on its neat desk neatly placed: a place for everything and everything in its place. This room looked like a small storage room for used books, bags of garbage, and other superfluities, and one in which all the shelves had broken and everything had caved in and commingled. It was fortunate for orderly eyes that the only light fixture was broken and ended in a frayed and dangling cord. The place was shadow-lit and dreary, the room of a drinking and drug-taking recluse. Worse yet— Jimmy spotted several syringes among the debris. Apparently Denise had learned to shoot up heroin on her Harlem hiatus. She sat in the middle of this devastation like a big, pale statue of Sorrow. She wore only a shabby pink slip, most of the fluffy tops of her big breasts exposed, showing blue veins. Her hair, which was thick, black, and kinky, was in wild disarray. Her feet were dirty, and the little toes black from sticking out the holes at the sides of her sneakers. (Jimmy still thought she must have bought her sneakers with holes in the sides.) The sneakers themselves, the crumpled black skirt, and the blood-stained man's white shirt, which she wore the night before, lay on the floor near her feet. She held her knees in her arms. She looked like a woman who didn't care what happened next, sad as an old salad, just beat.

Jimmy put the beer down on the floor by her feet, and said:

"Merry Christmas, kid! Here's something for the morning blues. Want some?"

"Oh, no man," she said quietly, groaningly, "I'm so ashamed."

"Oh, come on now. What's this? Come on, let's have some beer."

"No, man . . . no . . . it was terrible last night . . . ."

"What're you talking about. You got a little high, that's all."

She shook her head, slowly, side to side.

"Oh, Jimmy . . . Jimmy . . ."

"No. Really, Denise, you didn't do anything—" then he gave her a big, stupid smile, and added—"except freak out, fall down the stairs, and knock my jaw off its hinges—" and then he made a face of mock disapproval and said—"As a matter of fact, your conduct was . . . *deplorable.*"

She couldn't help herself. It started with a faint, blossoming, impossible-to-suppress smile, then all the tension she'd been building up exploded into laughter, and every time she looked up at him, she exploded again. While the latest of these seismic fits was in diminuendo Jimmy went looking about among the rubble for a bottle opener, found one, and opened one of the beer bottles. When her laughter had subsided, he stuck the beer bottle in her face, so that, before she could think about herself too much, she was tasting and swallowing. When she finished drinking, and put the bottle down, she looked at Jimmy seriously, and said:

"You mean you aren't angry at me?"

"Of course not. Why should I be angry?"

"I hit you."

"Oh, come off it, Denise. Drink some more beer. It'll help unscramble your brains."

She took another drink, then handed him the bottle.

"Look, kid," he said, "what are you trying to do with that bloody acid? If it sends you away to the badlands, you should skip it."

"All my trips aren't bad."

"It looks to me like most of them are. Why push it? You're going to wind up in a bad way on that stuff. At least, stick to dope. You'll be having nutty flashbacks for years on acid and you don't want that."

"I don't care. I don't care about anything. I just want to see something beautiful. Sometimes I see beautiful things."

"Doesn't look like you've seen anything beautiful lately, huh?"

"No, not lately."

"Then give it a vacation, why not?"

"Yeah, yeah, man; I will."

"Denise—you know, baby, you've got to take care of yourself a little. . . ."

She didn't say anything for a time.

Then she shrugged; said:

"I live in terrible fear, Jimmy. I look like my mother, who had heavy breasts like mine, and I saw her lean over a table so that they fell free away from her body"—she got up and walked to a little end-table, upon which books were unsteadily stacked, and demonstrated, placing her hands on the table, arms stiff, leaning forward and letting her breasts drop free—"like this, in such pain as I could never bear to see again. And six months after she'd died, my father—father— was killed in an auto wreck—" She stopped abruptly, and, distorting her face, her eyes squeezed shut by a smile so tight it looked like an exaggerated comedy mask, trying to hold back the tears that were flying from them anyoldway, she went back to the blanket and threw herself down on it, face away, without a sound.

Jimmy's own drink-unhinged nerves allowed for it, and he started damping up himself. He wiped his eyes on his sleeves, and sat on, waiting, trying to feel as little as possible.

About ten minutes later, Denise turned about, solemn, red-eyed but dried up. She said:

"Pass me the beer, please."

Jimmy did, and she drank, and then she lit herself a butt, blew smoke, smiled.

"I guess I can't do anything right," she said.

"Don't feel bad, kid," Jimmy said, "I can't either. None of us can. But we have to try, don't we?"

"What for?"

"Why not? If it don't matter, it don't matter either way, do it?"

She smiled.

He added: "Otherwise it do matter, don't it?"

She laughed.

"But seriously, kiddo, one has to figure out what one's about, dig? I used to say I was a puppet. It was true. Maybe I still am, but I'm working on it. I've been afraid of my mother, because I knew she thought I wasn't my father; and, though she didn't know it, what that meant to me then was, or would have been, that I wasn't myself, either; that I had no self, in fact. See what I mean? If I'd been myself, there could hardly have been any question as to whether or not I was my father. When you have a self, you're not afraid to take advice—not even from parents."

"Well?"

"Well, this. If we don't find, or even make up, some kind of authority for ourselves, we'll wake up at death-time to discover that everything has been pointless. That's why I'm determined, now, to become my own father. In this bloody world where no one else is willing to be your father, you have to become your own father, see; then you'll always have someone to look after you in your hour of need. Let me recite you a poem I wrote. It's called 'The Orphaned'...

> When the mood comes upon him to die
> of a loneliness deeper than death,
>
> he must speak to himself like a parent
> in a lecturing voice, but with love.
>
> He must be his own father and mother,
> and at night when he looks up at heaven,
>
> where nothing of earth seems to live,
> and the range of all things is so great
>
> as to startle the love from his breast,
> he must think of his father, the Rock,
>
> and his mother, the Dead Sea, and of
> the message he brings from the sun."

"Oh, Jimmy!"

"See what I mean? Be your own daddy and momma, then you'll be all right all right. Be big Momma. Dig?"

"I dig, Jimmy; I dig."

"Good. Why don't you start right away. What would be the first thing your momma and daddy would make you do this morning."

"Stop drinking."

"Well, let's not be Good Housekeeping domestic extremists. What's the second thing?"

"Wash my face and brush my teeth."

"Good. Why don't you do that."

"Because I don't really feel like it."

"Good. Then don't. But I mean, if that's the kind of momma you are, I guess you're just going to have a dirty kid—right?"

"Right!"

"Merry Christmas, kid!"

"Merry Christmas, Jimmy!"

*   *   *

Fay looked glum, opening the big front door. "I expected you to be here with me at Christmas."

"So I'm a day late and a dollar short," said Jimmy. "If we're going to argue, I'm going to turn around and go back to New York."

"No, it's just that I got a Christmas present—a terrible Christmas present."

Baldwin was up for sale. The neighborhood was "deteriorating," according to Howard Burns, the owner. Jimmy took Burns's "deteriorating," to refer to the recent arrival on their block of a black doctor and his family. What a joke, Jimmy thought; Baldwin was a half-way house for mad people and the neighborhood stood in stress because of a black doctor.

Fay said that Burns had offered her a room in his own home; but Jimmy could see that she didn't care for that idea. Then she said she thought—well—maybe she'd go live with Aunt Brenda, the third and youngest of the sisters, Fay, Myrtle, and Brenda, and that was an idea that Jimmy didn't care for. Brenda had two pre-adolescent children and was a bossy type. He didn't like the idea of Fay being bullied by Brenda or taken advantage of as a live-in baby-sitter.

Jimmy stayed for the rest of the week and into the New Year. They discussed the problem from every angle until the decision was made—not so much by Fay and Jimmy as by necessity. She and Jimmy would superintend a house in New York, in Chelsea or Greenwich Village, wherever they could get one. Jimmy had to help take care of her, and, at the same time, the move would alter his situation with Phyllis. He wasn't being fair staying with her when he had no intention of marrying her and he just didn't have the guts to leave. The plan, as it evolved, was to move all of Fay's things to Phyllis's, so that they'd both be in New York to look for a house. They'd rent a van in Newark, and hire Moe, the taxi driver who lived at Baldwin to drive it, and to help carry. Finding a super's job shouldn't take more than a week or two, Jimmy reckoned. Then they'd move their stuff from Phyllis's to the new house, and that'd be it. He was willing to help Fay, but he had to do it in his own way. He had to stay close to his own life. That wasn't asking too much, was it?

Phyllis had agreed to this plan. Of how she felt, Jimmy wasn't sure. She seemed to approve, in general. She knew very well what the situation was. She had known Fay for several years, and liked her well enough, with qualifications. Jimmy reminded himself that one never knew exactly what Phyllis was thinking, or how much she knew. Jimmy felt like a husband who cheats on his wife, but needs her, not exactly loves her more than he does his mistress, but feels obligated in time to her. Making this move with Fay might let him off the hook, let him worm out of having to make a final decision. He could just end up spending more time with Fay than he did with Phyllis.

They were leaving Baldwin, then. That old loony-bin had been their home, of sorts, for nearly a decade—the longest permanent address they'd had as a family. They said goodbye to the many nameless life-mad men and women who had passed their way as they'd officiated over and under that unofficial, memory-filled madhouse; but mostly they thought of Elliot, that strange, self-made failure, who'd had everything once, in another world, the world before the Crash.

*   *   *

321

The cab doors of the big rented van swung shut, Fay sat between Moe and Jimmy, and the winter wind was blowing on them, blowing their hair. Jimmy wondered what Fay was thinking. He knew she was afraid. He knew she was sad. But he suspected that, now it was done, she was looking forward to the future, too. One of her endearing as well as maddening qualities was that she neither dwelt on the past nor learned from it.

By the time they were humming on the highway she was smiling, looking about, chattering, pointing out across the choppy, lordly Hudson at the Manhattan skyline, and he could see that it was still there, the spirit, the life.

CHAPTER FOURTEEN

THE MONDRIAAN

"I have no home!" Fay wailed, drunkenly. She had her hair in her little fists and was pulling it out. "You can't be trusted, you worthless, sex-mad bum, living with a little trollop, and not even married to her! You take . . . drugs too. I know you do. And . . . so does she . . . dope fiends . . . oh, oh, oh, oh, dope fiends!"

"Mom," Jimmy said, "Phyllis wants you to stay; don't you, Phyl? There, you see? Remember we have a plan. A *plan!* Don't be afraid. Please, stick to our plan!"

Hauling Fay's possessions (Elliot's "impedimenta") from Baldwin to the van and from the van up the five flights of stairs to Phyllis's apartment had exhausted him. He was beat. He couldn't take it. He walked out, went down to a local joint, and had a beer, sat and watched an old Barbara Stanwick tear-jerker on the TV, amid the smoke and din of a shuffleboard crowd. A half hour later, Phyllis came in.

"I thought you might be here."

"How is she?"

"She's all right now. She's sleeping it off."

"I'm sorry I left you alone with her. I didn't expect it to turn out like this."

"I know," she said, smiling. "She's just drunk and exhausted. She'll be all right."

"Do you think so?"

"Sure. She's just afraid."

"Was she bad after I left?"

"Pretty bad." Phyllis laughed. "She called me every kind of name she could think of. You too."

"I'm sorry."

"Oh, I don't mind. I've been called names all my life."

"You don't deserve to be called a trollop. You're not anything like that."

"No," she said, "I'm not. But if that's what they think, I don't care. It's their problem. That's for the bullshit world."

"But it's a bad start." All their ventures ended badly, Jimmy thought, because Fay would not stick to a plan. She had no long-range vision. Her little harlequin glasses couldn't fix that.

*   *   *

At night Jimmy went to the docks and hauled crates of cabbages about. When he'd get in, in the morning, he'd hit the sack for two or three hours, and up, shower, eat breakfast, and stand about smoking while Fay fastened her earrings or brushed the cat hair from her skirt. Despite the cat hair, she managed to look nice. Enthusiastic, buoyant, she was wearing pastel woolen suits. She looked almost glamorous, at least fifteen years younger than her age of sixty. How it was that she could look positively glamorous and appealing, really girlish and pretty, after all the scrubbing she had done in hotels and rooming houses over the years, was a mystery. In certain respects she'd never matured. She was ambiguous, changeable, by turns enthusiastic and easily discouraged. After only a few days of looking, she said: "Maybe I ought to go to Brenda's." And it was this that Jimmy worried about. He feared she hadn't the will to see things through.

Jimmy passed a real estate office in Greenwich Village late one Friday afternoon, on his way to the docks. He stopped in, told the rental agent what he wanted, his qualifications, and that his mother would take the house with him. Jimmy told the rental agent her qualifications for such an important post. Think of it! A mother and son who had both been in the hotel business, who had run roominghouses, both of them able to keep transcripts and ledgers, veritable bookkeepers; people unafraid of wielding mops and brooms; attractive, well-spoken, appear to be somewhat educated—then a frown: odd, very odd!

"You say you can do electrical work?"

"Yes. Just about anything like that."

"How did you come by that knowledge?"

"I studied electrical engineering," Jimmy lied. He had read one of Marsayas's How-To books.

"You went to college?"

"I quit. But since then I've steeped myself in autodidactology. Of course, there are a few holes, but nothing that can't be plugged, as the Dutch say."

"Well—huh—may I ask just why you want to take a job as a superintendent?"

"It's my kind of work. My mother and I were made for it. *Partus sequitur ventrem,* you know. I've been doing it all my life."

"Mmmm. I see." Of course he didn't. But when he met Fay the next day he took a real shine to her, though he was worried about whether she'd be able to do such hard work. Jimmy assured him that he'd do the heavy stuff.

"O.K. then, I'll take you over to the house." After all, this was Greenwich Village.

It was one of those big, sham-quality joints that had recently appeared all over the Village. They had names like the sedate "Van Dyck" and the ultramodern "Picasso." Theirs was a big refurbished brownstone building now called "The Mondriaan," located in the block-length curve of Morton Street, between Seventh Avenue and Bedford, a quiet, quaint, tree-lined street, just out of the way of the booming Seventh Avenue shopkeeping, restaurant, and night spot area, and three minutes from the Bleeker Street stalls, stands, and Italian markets. The big front doors were thick plate-glass, which meant a great deal of cleaning. The vestibule consisted of ten wide marble-veneer stairs, and they meant a great deal of mopping. Inside, it was just narrow hallways, lined with doors with imitation brass imitation knockers that were actually doorbells that rang when the knockers were lifted, red wall-paper up the walls, an elevator full of stainless steel, and that meant a lot of wiping, and narrow marble stairs spiraling upward around the elevator to the eighth floor, top of the mark, and they meant a long trip down pushing a broom or a mop.

Near the stairwell, on every floor, there was a door opening to an incinerator chute. The agent—Bradhurst—took them down to the basement to show them the incinerator. He asked Jimmy what he thought of it, and Jimmy told him that he'd seen many incinerators in his day, but that this one was unquestionably the finest. Jimmy told Bradhurst he thought he could work with this one. He looked it over carefully, patted it approvingly, and smiled at Bradhurst.

"You like it, eh?" Bradhurst queried, apparently needing reassurance.

"I think it's just great," Jimmy said, and patted it again, at which Mr. Bradhurst seemed satisfied. Then he took Jimmy and Fay into the laundry room, where both of the machines were doing a fat, bubbly, white jiggle, and making sucking noises like a fat child eating spaghetti.

"There's a kickback switch, so instead of the fuse blowing, the power just goes off, and all you have to do is switch it back on again. But I guess you know more about than I do, eh?"

"Oh, yes—yes—" Jimmy said, hurriedly, "I know all about kickbacks."

"Good. Good. Very good," said Mr. Bradhurst.

Fay said: "May we see our apartment now?"

"Oh," said Mr. Bradhurst, "there's just one more thing I'd like to show you first. But, on second thought, this is really more for your son—I want to show him the boiler room—so I'll let you into the apartment—it's just down the hall from the boiler—and you can look it over while we take a peek in at the Big Boy—ha—that's what we call him—the boiler, I mean—the Big Boy." He let Fay into the apartment, and took Jimmy on to the boiler room. It was about thirty paces down the cement floored basement hallway from their apartment door (their door had an imitation brass imitation knocker on it too, just like the doors of the big people upstairs). They came to an iron door, with a large red-and-white sign reading *DANGER!* on it, and from inside of which emanated an ominous, pulsating sound, which encouraged Jimmy to believe that the sign had not been placed on the door for nothing.

Dapper Mr. Bradhurst bravely threw open the door and gingerly climbed down a rusty iron ladder, indicating with a nod that Jimmy should follow. Jimmy didn't care much for the idea of going into a pit with a thing that made such hideous snorts, but if Bradhurst was game, he expected it would be O.K. So he followed.

The boiler was a huge, squat black thing, which, when seen from the side, as one saw it from the door, looked like a blocky, crouching sphinx, and when seen from the front (one had to walk along a narrow cement catwalk, and put oneself practically into its chops to see it from the front) truly depicted a monster out of one's worst dreams—Moloch, a red, fire-spitting mouth with jack o' lantern teeth, that were grates; crossed, angry yellow eyes, that were lights (the crossed look having been caused by one of them being bent inwards on its metal stem), and black, zig-zagging pipes sticking out of the top of its head like crazy Medusa hair. Obviously a thing of foul disposition.

"Have you a boiler license?" queried Mr. Bradhurst.

"Why, no; I haven't. Do I need one?" In his childhood, Jimmy had lived so intimately with boilers he'd never considered a license to touch one necessary.

"Oh, my! I thought you most certainly would have a boiler license, what with all your experience in other houses. Well, we'll just have to arrange to get you one. Mr. Kreigsgeld, the owner, will come to meet you and your mother next Saturday. He'll take care of that then. And that gives you a whole week to move in and get yourselves settled before assuming your duties. Now, then, shall we go and see how your mother likes the apartment?"

It could have been bigger; it consisted of one large room, one small room (Jimmy's), and a kitchenette and bath. But it was a neat, clean, cheerful, modernistic little place, done in white (and that was good, because it was a basement apartment, and needed light), and the flooring was black rubber tile throughout. Yet, it did get plenty of light from the row of high little windows that looked to the sun in the mornings. "Curtained," Fay said, "they'll be beautiful." The bathroom was of blue tile, and clean, and nothing was chipped, for a change, and the kitchenette was functional and clean, and, surprise of surprises, everything worked.

Jimmy saw that Fay was delighted. He knew her to be thrilled at the prospect of having an apartment that offered her some chance of exercising her "not inconsiderable domestic skills," as Elliot had called them. The place was partially furnished, and Bradhurst told them that they could use any of the furniture that the former tenants had left behind, now in storage; and Fay was very busy, as Jimmy could see, thinking about where she would put this, that, and the other. In short, she was sold. She hadn't realized yet how much work there was to be done in such a building, and Jimmy didn't want to discourage her before they got started. He figured they'd find another place if this one got to be too much. But he wished that she could have been more patient, given him time to find something smaller, easier to manage. This was a very big house, and that boiler was—was—a monstrous humdinger!

Outside, Fay said:

"Oh, it's a knockout, don't you think? But I didn't want to act as if I liked it too much. I was afraid they'd cut our salary if they saw how much I liked the apartment." She laughed mischievously. "Let's go and have a glass of beer and celebrate." The "salary" to which she alluded, was fifty dollars a month. Fay was now collecting Elliot's social security check, as widow's may, but that was merely a widow's mite. Jimmy figured that would be all hers, and that, plus the salary, plus fifteen a week or so, out of his paycheck, would give her a pretty sizeable grand total—and no rent. It more than doubled her present income and it improved her circumstances in general. When she wanted to, she could go over to Plainfield and visit with Brenda, or Aunt Myrtle and Uncle O'Toole, and Jimmy would stay behind and mind the house. Then, at other times, she could watch the house and let Jimmy take off for a day. Trouble was, he'd have to hit the docks steadily three nights a week and take care of the heavy work in the house, too, every day, all day. But he had two other evenings free, during the week, and the weekends, too, or at least part of them, in which to do some writing, he hoped. Jimmy didn't think it would be too bad. The Mondriaan wasn't what he'd have taken, had he more time, had Fay not rushed him. But he didn't have time. Fay had been chomping at the bit. And it was fun that first week, when nobody knew they were there; before the house came down on them.

*　　*　　*

Owner Kreigsgeld was a sly, waxen little creature, with mean, protuberant frog-eyes, and a fishy, puckered mouth. His body seemed that of an undernourished child. He sat in their living-room with his legs neatly crossed, so as not to muss his creases, his little black patent leather shoes glitter-ing, and rubbed his nose with his thumbs, now and then, as he talked. He was a pompous, condescending little business-ghoul, who asked: "Do you understand that I expect this house to be kept clean?" and, "Do you know how to make out a receipt?" He might well have asked: "Can you read?" Bradhurst, obviously embarrassed, ventured now and then, though carefully, sycophantically, to say things like, "Oh, Mr. Kreigsgeld, Mrs. Whistler and her son know all about that. They were in the hotel business. They're very able people," and "Jim, here, has been to college—right, Jim?"

"What do you take a job like this for, then?"

"I like the work."

"Like the work?"

"Yes, Mr. Kreigsgeld, Jim is very handy with tools. He studied electricity."

"Electrical engineering," Jimmy corrected.

"Yes," said Bradhurst—"You see?"

330

"I . . . don't . . . know . . ." said Kreigsgeld. Then: "But we give you a try."

Kreigsgeld gave Bradhurst fifty dollars in an envelope for Jimmy to take with him to the Fire Department Licensing Bureau, which he, in turn, was to give to a certain Fire Captain who would make himself known.

Several days later, Jimmy sat in a waiting room beyond the partition of which a huge, examination room hummed and tested, and ran over in his mind all the details—the valves and inlet pipes and so on—of a number six-oil boiler. Then a big, burly man, with iron-grey hair and a face the color of the fires he had fought, came in. He wore no coat or hat, but the rest of his garb was that of a Fire Captain in full-dress regalia. He said:

"You Whistler?"

"That's me."

"You wanna take this test for the boiler license—right?"

"Yes, sir; I do."

"Have you studied?"

"Yes, sir—all week."

"Follow me." The Captain led him out of the office and into the hall.

So Jimmy was standing now, and what he was standing next to—aside from the fire-colored Captain—was a warning at least five feet high and three feet wide, the substance of which was an indication that anyone who should entertain the idea of bribing a public official, such as the Captain, could expect to be caught, drawn-and-quartered, and have his parts sold, at a small profit to the city, to a dog food factory. So when the Captain said: "Have you got the fifty bucks?" Jimmy hesitated, having, for a moment, the eerie sensation that he was being entrapped.

When he didn't answer, the Captain said:

"You know, the examining clerk has a lot of work on his hands. He might not be able to see you today."

Jimmy looked up at the sign, read:
WARNING!!!
and handed over the hot little bribe envelope.

"Just a minute," the Captain said, and turned his back. At the count of fifty he turned back. He put his hand on Jimmy's shoulder, said, "Good luck, son," and went back into the office again. Ten minutes later Jimmy was called in for the test. He was asked one question: What number oil does a number-six boiler use? Amazingly, Jimmy passed.

*   *   *

The super across the street had been taking care of The Mondriaan temporarily. Of course, he had his hands full with his own place, "The Dali," and wasn't doing very much for The Mondriaan, so when the notice was put up on the front door that there was a super in residence, Fay and Jimmy were hit, as if by the stuff from the fan, with complaints, requests, and demands, all of which had been neglected for months on end.

As the onslaught subsided, life at The Mondriaan took on shape and regularity. A day began at nine o'clock in the morning with Jimmy going up and sweeping the halls and stairs all the way down, through the vestibule, and on out to the sidewalk, where he gathered up the trash and sweepings to bring in and burn in the incinerator. He tended the boiler, and, if it were a day for the garbage men to come, got the twenty cans out on the street and dragged them back in when they'd been emptied. Then it was a matter of fixing light switches, unclogging toilets, installing new tiles in bathrooms where the old tiles had been chipped or had fallen out, putting new washers in leaking sink spigots, and such like odd jobs; and, of course, always waiting for the next complaint.

On the third Saturday Kreigsgeld came around, just after Fay and Jimmy had finished cleaning the house from top to bottom, banged on their door, and complained that he'd found a cigarette butt in the vestibule. Somebody had dropped it there since it was swept. They told him so, and a few other things, too, and he retreated.

Fay helped Jimmy with the cleaning, and cooked them meals that they were rarely able to eat, for the constant buzzing of doorbells, ringing of phones, etc. On Saturday mornings they did a heavy-duty cleaning job on the house from top to bottom. Jimmy'd take a five gallon pail with a wringer attached and a ten pound mop up to the eighth floor and push them, clanging and plopping, all the way down through the basement, and into their own apartment, which deserved to be kept at least as clean as the rest of the house. Ideas of Order.

While mopping, Jimmy often encountered the tenants in the hallways. And most of them proved to be perfect snobs. He hated these bucket-in-hand encounters. If he were to say "Hello," he'd get a grunt and a sidelong look, and be made to feel like an Untouchable. On the other hand, if he didn't speak, and kept his head down and his mop moving, Bradhurst would tell him later that So-and-So found him to be a rude young man. But to be got up at three o'clock in the morning to hear a drunk make complaints about his lost keys was nothing in any way unusual. Jimmy discovered that a superintendent, in one of these slick city apartment buildings, is lower than the low.

All the tenants weren't like that, of course, but the majority were. Most of them could scarcely afford to pay the exorbitant rents they were paying. Kreigsgeld, a type of man most of his tenants would look down their noses at, and for the wrong reasons, was to be admired in so having arranged things that he could get blood from such turnips. The books in their bookcases showed a slavish devotion to whatever was the fad, the prints on their walls were the selections of persons who have read only the latest, trendy intellectual claptrap and pop psychology! They worked in offices and got out their berets and sandals on weekends. It was La Boheme on a full stomach. Jimmy threw one of his extra manuscripts into the Big Boy's fiery chops in their honor. "Well, this is your life, James Whistler," he said, and he thought he heard the house applauding.

*   *   *

One Saturday morning, after working on the docks, Jimmy rode up in the elevator with Mr. MacTavish of 4-B, a silver-haired gentleman who at first struck Jimmy as a martinet, for his bearing was imperious. Jimmy was made self-consciously aware of his laborer's appearance by the older man's trim elegance.

"Were you in the Marine Corps?" asked MacTavish. "I see you're wearing Marine fatigues." He pulled a cigarette holder from his breast pocket and fitted a Camel into it.

Jimmy shot his mop handle into Parade Rest.

"Yes, sir," he said.

MacTavish cracked a smile, surprising Jimmy; for MacTavish had seemed a not only fastidious, but dour Scot. He said:

"I'm a Major in the Marine Reserves. Are you in the Reserves?"

"Three active, four reserves. I'm a short timer."

"If President Johnson persists," said MacTavish, "we could both end up in Viet Nam in a year or so."

"Ugh," said Jimmy.

"Indeed!" said MacTavish.

The elevator door opened on Four. MacTavish said: "I've a leaky faucet. Will you take a look at it?"

Jimmy hauled his mop and bucket into the hall and followed MacTavish into his apartment. There were books and papers everywhere, and, most noteworthy to Jimmy, a large manuscript next to a typewriter on a desk.

"I'll need a washer, and a wrench, and a screwdriver," Jimmy said. "Are you a writer, sir?"

334

"Not exactly. Well, in a manner of speaking. I *am* writing a book."

"I'll be right back," Jimmy said. He went down to his apartment, found the required tools, and scooped up a copy of *Obituary and Other Poems*.

MacTavish's door was open.

"I wonder," said Jimmy, thrusting the book at MacTavish, "if you'd mind having a look at this. I'd value your opinion."

"What's this—poetry? I'll look it over, though I don't see how I can be of much help to you."

"Please do, Sir," said Jimmy, though he didn't see how MacTavish could be of much help to him, either. What he really wanted was for there to be somebody among the Yahoo snobs in the Mondriaan who knew that he was a poet, and could literally, literately, and with literality, read and write. Also to a lesser degree now in German, French, and Spanish.

He bid Major MacTavish adieu, and, at top speed, descended to his forever basement, and, frenetically, typed a poem he had been thinking about in his own private eternity to be called "Hope and the Bipolar Poet."

O make me at last an Immortal born for this life,
so hard when the wind like a horse that has eaten of
  loco weed
kicks in the shining green meadow of death that is
  the bright day
beyond which the galaxies turn in dark matter like
  great carousels
with mad imagery rising and falling along their
  white ways,
all celestial combustion and anger as if there were
  truth in the gods
and I had come from their birth to mine that happened
  in heat

in the bowels of the ship of the universe powered by
    diamonds,
dead glitters of light burnt in the cones of the sky. O
    Heraclitean Fire,
forgive one who has not known the one pinch of peace
held in the index and thumb of the chef who concocted
    this terrible stew,
brew that biology seeks in its crystals that fall like the
    fall of each phylum
down the great day of time, no matter all time be an
    infinite cloud,
O Fire have mercy and snuff out the wick of your
    running black wax
and spare me the waste of beginnings, evolutions,
    and ends.

STOP, stop, poor soul, for the fire at the center of self
    is the fire at all distances,
emanation and flow like the oceans of life serve
    likewise the Heraclitean Fire
though the walking world is of mercury sulphur and
    salt, sex, sun and sand,
yet the fire heats the shards till they melt, reshaping
    them in their clay and
thereby a new entity is formed bearing the heart's
    evergreen name of Hope.

CHAPTER FIFTEEN

"THE BULLSHIT WORLD"

THE NEW YORK TIMES
FEBRUARY 22, 1965

MALCOLM X SHOT TO DEATH
AT RALLY HERE

MALCOLM KNEW HE WAS A 'MARKED MAN'

Phyllis called Jimmy late in January to tell him that her parents were coming East for a visit—just a week-end—and she wanted him to go with her to show them around. In fact, she wanted Jimmy to play husband, which is what those two poor deluded people still thought him to be—their son-in-law. The father, of course, had been in and out of New York often, in the past few years, being, as he was, an airline pilot for a major airline, and having had, for a time, a regular run between New York and Seattle. About a year ago, he had been switched to a run between Seattle and Tokyo, and that had saved Jimmy and Phyllis a great many headaches. Before that, when in New York, he'd tried to meet Jimmy several times, but Jimmy had always somehow avoided the encounter. Phyllis had met her father uptown several times, but had told him that her "husband" was called away, was sick, had to work, was drafted—any lie she could think up to save Jimmy the meeting and still not make her father suspicious. But this time her parents had written: "We are coming East to see a few shows, but more especially to meet Jim. We sincerely hope that nothing will happen to make that impossible."

"You've just got to meet them, Jimmy," Phyllis said. "I don't think they believe me when I tell them about you anymore. Please, Jimmy; just this once."

Jimmy couldn't find it in his heart to refuse her. But, on the other hand, he didn't like the idea of pulling off such an imposture. He had serious things on his mind now. Serious things. He didn't want to lie to a couple of (probably) nice people, to make them think he was their son-in-law. Phyllis shouldn't have told them that they were married in the first place, but surely she should have told them that they weren't, by now. Nevertheless, that was the situation.

Well, that was the half of it. As if things weren't complicated enough, Jimmy's "in-laws" were coming to New York on the same weekend on which Fay had invited Aunt Myrtle and Uncle O'Toole to visit. It was going to be a busy weekend.

Fay worked very hard on their super's basement apartment all week. She had polished the furniture, put up new curtains, waxed and rewaxed the rubber-tiled floor till it was gleaming—in short, she had prepared it for the inspection of her fastidious big sister, Aunt Myrtle, and for the enjoyment of her equally fastidious brother-in-law, Uncle Albert O'Toole. It was Fay's intention to show her lace-curtain Irish relatives how well she was doing—and, indeed, the apartment looked very pretty, entirely satisfactory for that purpose. By Friday afternoon, she had a roast pork in the oven, three pies baked, hors d'oeuvres on a platter on the table, drinks mixed, etc., and was in the process of getting herself dressed to receive her visitors. Jimmy, too, was getting himself dressed in his best bib and tucker.

He'd accumulated a few clothes in the past year, and was now able to make himself fairly presentable in a well-cut, good-fitting suit, a chocolate shirt, cream-colored tie, and a new pair of oxblood loafers.

Fay and Jimmy had discussed the situation, and decided upon a plan of action. Since Fay had no intention of meeting Phyllis's parents and palming herself off as Phyllis's mother-in-law, Jimmy would tell Phyllis's parents that his Mother was away, visiting her sister in New Jersey, and that he had been unable to get in touch with her in time to have her back in New York to meet them. It was a frail story, but Jimmy thought he'd be able to bluff it through. Furthermore, he'd tell them that he'd volunteered to help keep the house that she superintended in good shape while she was away, and that would give him an excuse to spend some time with Fay and Aunt Myrtle and Uncle O'Toole. A lot would depend upon what Phyllis's parents wanted to do; and, of course, upon what Aunt Myrtle and Uncle O'Toole wanted to do. First, Jimmy was to wait and meet and greet Aunt Myrtle and Uncle O'Toole when they arrived at five, then he'd make some excuse or other and leave and go over to pick up Phyllis, and, from there, go uptown to the hotel where Phyllis's parents were staying, and meet them.

At ten minutes after five the doorbell rang, Jimmy pushed the buzzer, asked who was there, over the speaker, and heard Uncle O'Toole, his voice full of static, say, "Jimmy? Is that you, Jimmy? Uncle O'Toole here. How do we find you?" They were in the lobby. Jimmy went upstairs and led them back down.

Nervous laughter.

Confusion.

Hugs and kisses.

"Say, Jim, this is a pretty fancy building," said Uncle O'Toole.

"What a lovely apartment!" said Aunt Myrtle.

"Do you mean you get this apartment free?" asked Uncle O'Toole. "Do you get tips, Jimmy? Well, let *me* give you a tip. Save your money. Ha-ha!"

"What lovely curtains!" said Aunt Myrtle.

"What smells so good?" asked Uncle O'Toole.

"Fay, you look lovely!" said Aunt Myrtle.

"You're lookin' good, Jimmy," said Uncle O'Toole. "Lost a little weight?"

"Do you get a salary here, too?" asked Aunt Myrtle.

"Quite a deal you've got here," said Uncle O'Toole.

They all sat down and had a couple of drinks together; then Jimmy excused himself, saying that he had to go over to the docks to pick up his pay check, and that he'd be back as soon as possible.

He grabbed a taxi out on Seventh Avenue and scooted over to pick up Phyllis. When he got there, she was all aflutter. She was worried about how she looked, but Jimmy couldn't remember the last time he'd seen her looking so nice. She had her fine, pale hair in an upsweep, and was wearing a pretty teal suit. She wanted to know if she looked nice, and he told her that she did.

"Oh, this is such a lot of bullshit," she said nervously. "If only I didn't have to pretend with them."

Jimmy's sentiments exactly. Then she donned her lined tan raincoat and picked up her little native-American beaded pocketbook, and spoiled the whole thing.

"Haven't you got another purse to carry?"

"What's wrong with this one?"

"It looks like you picked it out of an ashcan somewhere in New Mexico," he said.

"Well, it's the only one I've got," she snapped angrily.

When they got out of the subway in the midtown area, Jimmy stepped into a store and bought a plain black pocketbook for her.

"But what'll I do with this one?"

"Put it inside the black one."

"Bullshit!" she said, as she did so.

Jimmy stopped her again, taking his handkerchief and wiping off some of the excess rouge from her face. He hadn't noticed it in the house, but out in the daylight she looked like she had a target on each cheek. Ordinarily, she never wore makeup, and, surprisingly, for a girl who could paint pictures, was considered by some to be a serious artist, she had developed no skill whatever in the use of makeup. Jimmy, on the other hand, had been taught to do theatrical makeup. He stood, dabbing at her with his handkerchief, trying to tone her down a bit, while she cursed and complained, full of impatience.

"To hell with it!" she said. "Come on; let's go!"

"Well, you don't want to look like you're ready for a war dance, do you?"

"To hell with it! It's just a lot of bullshit."

The poor little thing. She was more nervous than he was, and he wasn't exactly calm.

Her parents were staying at a good hotel in the upper-midtown area. At the desk, Phyllis called their room. They were told to come right up.

Jimmy felt embarrassed getting into the elevator. The incongruity of their situation struck him. He disliked himself for feeling it, but Phyllis embarrassed him. She hadn't stood still for his treatment, and her makeup was smeared. The black pocketbook he'd bought her in such a hurry seemed far too large and awkward for her (still, it was an improvement over the beaded Indian one that was contained in it). And Jimmy could see, now, that her pretty teal suit had black cat hairs all over it; and her stockings hung loose and twisted on her thin legs. Some of the upsweep of her hair had come tumbling down, and despite the autumnal chill, she had beads of nervous sweat on her forehead, corrugating her face powder. Little Phyllis was not beautiful, but had she had the instinct for adornment of a primitive, she could have made herself appear quite attractive. But the instinct for adornment was completely missing from her personality. Makeup was missing from her makeup. Looking at her, Jimmy wondered what her parents would think. Here he was—tall, well-built, and, by most accounts, good-looking. Would they think he was some kind of fortune hunter, taking advantage of their little Phyllis? Some kind of rogue? How could they ever understand how it was that Phyllis and he had got together? How could they understand the tenderness he felt for her, his admiration of her gutsyness and her artistry? How, perhaps, theirs was a case of friendship gone too far?

The elevator stopped: they got out and found the appropriate door and knocked.

"How do I look?" Phyllis asked.

"Fine," Jimmy said. "You look fine."

The door was opened by a round-faced, good-humored looking man of medium height, wearing a grey pilot's uniform. He had a ruddy complexion, blue eyes, and close-cropped salt-and-pepper hair. He was holding a cocktail glass in his hand.

"Daddy," Phyllis said, and threw her arms around his neck. Then she pulled away and turned to Jimmy, saying:

"Daddy, I want you to meet my husband, Jimmy. Jimmy Whistler."

The pilot, smiling, extended a hand to Jimmy. Jimmy took it and shook it.

"So you're my son-in-law, are you?" he said; and Jimmy thought for an instant that he doubted it. "Meet your mother-in-law, Jimmy." A slim, attractive woman stepped forward.

"Mummy!" Phyllis cried, and threw herself into her mother's arms as she had into her father's. When "Mummy" had disengaged herself, she came to Jimmy, put her arms around his neck, and planted a kiss on him.

"My, Phyl, but your husband is a handsome young man," she said, and then to Jimmy: "I want to welcome you into our family, Jimmy. Do you realize that you and Phyl have been married for over three years and this is the first time I've laid eyes on you. Well, I certainly like what I see."

Jimmy felt crummy. How could he have ever got himself into something like this?

"Have a drink, Jimmy?" asked the pilot.

"Yes," he said, "please."

"Canadian Club?"

"Fine."

"Soda?"

"Please."

"Ice?"

"Please."

"Well, Phyl . . ." said the mother, holding her daughter at arm's-length and looking at her, "you look just fine. Married life seems to agree with you."

"Yes," said the father, handing Jimmy a drink, "you look well, kitten. You know," he said, speaking to Jimmy, "Phyl was a sickly little girl. She had one thing after another. Not like her sister at all. Her sister was a regular little butterball. But Phyl looks like she's putting on some weight, now, too, dear," he said, addressing his wife, "doesn't she?"

"Yes, she looks wonderful."

"I bet," said the father, "that you make her eat; don't you, Jimmy?"

"Yes, I try." It was true; but Phyllis was anorexic.

"Oh, I can see it," said the mother.

"Why don't we eat now?" said the father. "Let's go down to the restaurant and we'll all have a nice dinner. How's that sound?"

They went down to the hotel dining room and ate. The mother had fried shrimp, and Phyllis and the father and Jimmy had Lobster Newburgh. Jimmy was so nervous during the meal that he choked. All he could think of was getting away from these good people before he tipped his hand. They weren't unusually inquisitive, but naturally they had a great many questions to ask of the young man whom they thought to be their son-in-law. That was what they took him for, it seemed. And they seemed to like him, too. Jimmy wondered how Phyllis was going to explain this away in years to come. She'd probably tell them that they'd got a divorce on the grounds of mental cruelty and Jimmy's stock with them would hit bottom. Even now, that future time troubled him.

Phyllis was ecstatically happy. Jimmy could see that she was very proud of having got herself married, in their eyes. Probably she never thought the day would come when a young man whom she could claim as her husband would sit at a table with herself and her parents and please them so. For her sake, Jimmy was very attentive to her, and tried to show the parents that he loved her, which, in fact, he did. But he felt that the whole thing was not only preposterous, but sad. He knew in his heart that he wouldn't be with Phyl much longer, and this seemed an awful crime to commit near the end of their time together.

They left her parents that night with the understanding that they would meet at ten the next morning and that they'd take a tour of New York together, and, later, Saturday evening, they'd all go to a play, and afterwards have a few drinks and a snack somewhere. Phyllis knew that Aunt Myrtle and Uncle O'Toole were at The Mondriaan, so she didn't object to Jimmy taking a different train and going straight there. When he kissed her goodbye on the subway platform, she thanked him for going to meet her parents, and said: "Wasn't it really nice? I mean, they're real squares, but aren't they nice? Do you like them, Jimmy?"

Jimmy said that it was and that they were and that he did.

"Oh, Jimmy, why can't we be really married?" she asked wistfully.

He felt like a criminal.

When he got to The Mondriaan, there was a party in full swing. Fay was dancing with Uncle O'Toole, and Aunt Myrtle was engaged in a monologue about her grandchildren. They were three sozzled sheets in the wind. Jimmy sat down, nervously exhausted, but relieved to be at home, and let Aunt Myrtle chatter at him while he drank a good stiff drink.

Aunt Myrtle was only about two years older than Fay; but Fay, who'd kept her figure, looked about twenty years younger. Uncle O'Toole, who referred to himself as "a tough guy from Joisey," was a lean, dapper man in his late sixties. He did not have the same settled appearance as his wife. He was a wiry, energetic man, full of fun.

"Let's go out somewhere," he said. "This is Greenwich Village, ain't it? Let's go out and get a look at some characters, whatdaya say?"

"Now, O'Toole," Aunt Myrtle put in, "we can't afford to spend—"

"What the hell, Myrt!" said Uncle O'Toole. "You only live once, right Jimmy? Whatdaya say, Fay? Shouldn't we go out and see the characters?"

Uncle O'Toole won the day, or the evening. Jimmy took them out to a place on Seventh Avenue where beer was served in pitchers and a banjo-band played Gay Nineties music. They loved it. They sang with the band and drank the beer until none of them could talk or walk normally, and then Jimmy took them home in a cab. Fay gave them her bed and she took Jimmy's and Jimmy left them all there, puffing and snoring, and went over to Phyllis's to sleep. He set the alarm, and next morning, bright and early, he was there when they came to.

Uncle O'Toole leaped out of bed as full of energy as he'd been early the day before. Aunt Myrtle seemed groggier, but came around fast after an eye-opener. Fay had a hangover, and felt sick. She spent some time in the bathroom, throwing up. Jimmy felt like he was sleep-walking.

Aunt Myrtle wanted to know if there was much of that "mess-sin-ation" around Greenwich Village.

Jimmy gathered that she meant the mixing of the races. "About as much as anywhere," he told her, never having thought much about it.

Uncle O'Toole said:

"I don't approve of that; do you, Jimmy?"

Jimmy told him that he had nothing against it. "I wouldn't go out of my way to marry a black woman," he said, treading where the ice was thin, "but if I fell in love with a black woman, and we wanted to marry each other, I'd marry her."

"You *would*!" exclaimed Uncle O'Toole, shocked. "But suppose you had a daughter," he said, explaining the problem succinctly, "you wouldn't want your daughter to marry one, would you?"

"Well," Jimmy said, "it looks like if I had already married one, and I had a daughter, I couldn't offer much of an objection to my daughter marrying one, too, could I?"

"Mmmm," said Uncle O'Toole, thoughtfully. "I see your point."

"You're not going to marry one, are you?" asked Aunt Myrtle, genuinely frightened.

"I haven't been asked."

"My God, Fay," cried Aunt Myrtle, "Jimmy isn't thinking of marrying a colored girl, is he?"

"He's only teasing you," Fay said, with a fleeting vision of Dorothy Lamour in a sarong. Jimmy had mentioned Lani to her on a few occasions.

"Oh," said Uncle O'Toole, "I get it," and laughed. Aunt Myrtle said:

"Well, for a minute there, I thought my poor sister was going to become the grandmother of a pickaninny. And me the great-aunt of one. You mustn't do that to her, Jimmy. I know you've got some weird ideas, but she's had a hard enough life as it was, with your father." The thought inspired her. "Oh, what a strange man your father was! I wouldn't have put it past *him* to marry a colored girl."

"Now let's leave him out of this," said Fay. "He's gone to his rest. Let's not talk about him when he's not here to defend himself."

"Well, I was thinking of the life he led you. My dear Albert has never treated me in such a way. He's worked hard all his life. He always supported his wife and children; didn't you, dear?"

"Yeah," said Uncle O'Toole devilishly, "but sometimes I think maybe old Elliot had the right idea."

"Oh," said Aunt Myrtle, turning red, "to say such a thing!"

Jimmy left them there to hash that out, while he went uptown with Phyllis to meet her parents. When he got back from taking a scenic cruise around Manhattan Island, from looking at the "ant-like" people from atop the Empire State Building, and from climbing into the Statue of Liberty's head, the same discussion was still underway at The Mondriaan.

"Why did that man wear his hair like that?" asked Aunt Myrtle.

"He looked like a girl," Uncle O'Toole said.

"Why do you live over here?" Aunt Myrtle wanted to know.

"Was he queer?" asked Uncle O'Toole.

"I'd like to see a lesbian," said Aunt Myrtle.

Next thing Jimmy knew, he was coming out of a theatre on Forty-sixth Street, having just slept through a Rogers & Hammerstein revival. Years before, Dr. Zolauf had introduced him to them at Carnegie Hall. "You've got to be carefully taught," came to mind.

Phyllis and he walked hand in hand, ahead of her parents. Phyllis said:

"They really love you, Jimmy."

He'd been turning on the charm. Once, in drama school, he played the Hairy Ape, and he felt suddenly swept with nostalgia for the part.

Then he was at The Mondriaan again, sitting at the table, and Aunt Myrtle, now thoroughly sloshed, was saying:

"Let's go out and see if we can find a lesbian bar."

"Let's go out, Jimmy," said Uncle O'Toole. I want to see some Bohemians."

Jimmy took them to the White Horse Tavern.

"This is where Dylan Thomas drank himself to death," he said.

But it cut no ice with Aunt Myrtle. Far as she could see, it was just a dump. And who was this Dylan Thomas and where did he get such a funny name?

"He was a famous Welsh poet," said Jimmy.

"Famous for getting drunk and not supporting his wife and children," Uncle O'Toole said, showing a dumbfounding knowledge of modern literature. "I heard all about the bum." This turned several poetic faces in the crowd. The White Horse was a shrine to the Welsh poet.

"Your Uncle O'Toole knows just about everything," said Aunt Myrtle with pride and conviction. "Go ahead, ask him about something."

Jimmy sat, dazed, smiling, his head nodding approval, his mouth in a frozen smiling rictus.

Phyllis's parents left on Sunday afternoon. "We are so glad to have you in the family, Jimmy," her mother said. And to Phyllis: "You take good care of our son-in-law, Phylly, do you hear?"

Then Aunt Myrtle and Uncle O'Toole left on Sunday evening.

"See you all of a sudden," Uncle O'Toole said waggishly.

"We've had a wonderful time," Aunt Myrtle said, "even if I didn't get to see any lesbians."

*　　*　　*

Jimmy met Butterworth in Harry's one afternoon. Every time he saw Butter he was reminded of that day in the car, with Phyllis hemorrhaging, and Butter condemning him for what he'd done to her. He did not like being reminded of that unfair assessment. But then, too, he remembered Butter being so helpful and considerate when it came to taking care of Phyllis's things. And that night at the loft party when he'd tried to help Denise.

"Hi, Jimbo," he said. "I've been looking for you, but I haven't seen you around. It's about Lani."

"Lani? I haven't seen her since the loft party. I thought you and she were an item." Jimmy sometimes wondered if he was going mad. Maybe it was the drinking, but sometimes exaggeration got the best of him. It seemed that he'd developed a history for Lani and Butterworth, a history that he half believed. Maybe he was kidding himself, letting himself off the hook a little. The crazy green-eyed monster sometimes saw what wasn't there.

"No, no. We're not an item. It's strictly Platonic."

"Are you still teaching philosophy someplace?"

"No. That went, along with my wife."

"Anyhow, how do you know how I thought it was between you and Lani?"

"I just know how you think, that's all. Now listen to me a minute—" at which Jimmy shrugged, turned to face the bar, and began to sip his beer—"In the first place," Butterworth was speaking down into the back of Jimmy's right ear, "I have never put a hand on Lani—"

Jimmy knew he was lying, but said, "That's none of my business."

"—I know it isn't! But I'm telling you anyway. I'm telling you for Lani's sake, not for yours or mine. All I ever did with her was to escort her—take her a few places. We're just friends, that's all. I don't know who else she might be seeing, but that's neither here nor there. Anyway, you know that she keeps a journal, don't you?"

Jimmy shook his head. He did not know that.

"Well, she does. And she left it out on the table last week—she'd gone shopping and left me there—and I read part of it. I really don't know what possessed me. I guess I'm nosey."

"You mean there's something about me in it?"

"Why, man, the thing's full of you! You're it! There isn't anything else. Nothing that looks like it matters, anyhow. Women are foolish creatures! Yet the fact remains— let's say you occupy most of her recorded thoughts. As Yeats once said:

> It's certain that fine women eat
> A crazy salad with their meat."

"Marsayas told me once you were gonna beat me up 'cause I was seeing her."

"I did say something rash like that one night when I was in my cups. But that was a long time ago. You were doing Phyllis wrong. Still are, probably. If not with Lani, with someone else. But there it is. I'm afraid my own affections have shifted. As I said before, I'm not saying this for your benefit. I'm saying it because there's a dame up there who won't be at peace till she has you."

"My God! I've always known you were a romantic, but this is disgusting!"

"Be that as it may, I'm doing what I think is right. Maybe butting in is right sometimes. Besides, I might not see you again. I've been called up. I'm on my way to Quantico and then, probably, Nam. Now, Lani's going to be in here at about seven to have a going-away drink with me. *You* go away, and don't get drunk, and come back then. What do you say?"

After a moment's reflection, Jimmy said, "O.K." Then, he said: "Look, Butter, here's a handshake for you, for luck in Nam. What do *you* say?" And they shook hands.

"Semper Fi, Butter."

"Semper Fi, Jimbo."

"By the way, Jimmy, I think you're one hell of a good poet."

"Thanks, Butter. Am I good enough to be cast out of the Republic?"

"Absolutely."

Jimmy followed Butterworth's suggestion, came back at seven, and there she was. Butterworth left them about eight. At eleven, Lani and Jimmy went up to her new place, which turned out to be right around the corner from Harry's. They sat across from each other at a wobbly kitchen table, sipping beer.

"I'm afraid it's a bit of a dump," Lani said, "but I'm glad to have a place of my own. I've got to keep expenses down. Tuition and everything. You know how it is." Lani nearly tipped over her beer glass with a wave of her hand. She grabbed the glass with both hands to steady it.

Jimmy faked a glance around, but was not really interested in where they were. He saw them back in Oahu in a cove of glistening water, the sun breaking apart and painting the scene with a soft violence of evening. "Do you remember those days in Hawaii—I mean, our days?"

"Of course I do," she said softly, "but you were different then. You weren't a famous poet."

"There are no famous poets—just real poets and fake ones. I don't want to be a famous, successful poet—it's a ridiculous conception—I just want to be a real poet. That's all I ever wanted to be."

"Even back then?"

"It was in me then. Some of my earliest memories are of Elliot Whistler reciting poetry to me. The magic of it never left me."

"Why do you call your father Elliot Whistler?"

"Because I'm not even sure that he was my father." He waved his hand in dismissal. "He *was* my father, of course. But my mother's even managed to throw some doubt on that."

"But you loved him, didn't you?"

"I loved him. I hated him. I love her. I hate her. She loved him. She hated him. He—what? Who knew? He loved me, I think, in his own way. But selfish people—it's not easy for them to love. When you love, you have to put someone else ahead of yourself. Neither one of them were ever able to do that. And that's a shame, because loving is better than being loved."

"I think I could do that," Lani ventured. She cast her eyes away.

"I think I could too, given a chance."

"I love you, Jim," Lani whispered. "I have since the first moment I saw you."

"Same here," he said.

Neither of them said another word for a full five minutes. Then Lani looked up from her thoughts and said, "But Phyllis, your mother . . ."

"It's an obstacle course."

"Do you think we can run it together?"

"We have to try."

The New York Times
March 7, 1965

3,500 U.S. MARINES GOING TO VIET NAM TO BOLSTER BASE

2 BATTALIONS FOR DANANG ARE FIRST LAND COMBAT TROOPS COMMITTED BY WASHINGTON

A month later, Fay answered the telephone one afternoon and it was Lani. Jimmy wasn't home so Lani left a message. She was going to Hawaii to see her father. Her plane left at noon. When Jimmy arrived Fay wanted to know more about who this "Lani" was.

Jimmy had written to Fay from Hawaii years ago telling her about Leilani, the girl he had saved from a fate worse than death, he had told her the story a number of times, he had even mentioned that he had encountered her here in New York, but Fay never listened. Sometimes he wondered what the use of talking to her was. He said, "That's Lani, the Hawaiian girl I told you about."

"You mean that girl, the one whose parents gave you the luau?"

"Yes."

"Have you been seeing her?"

"Yeah, I told you, I've seen her a few times." He didn't want to go too deeply into it. He didn't want to have to explain and explain. But oh God, why had Lani taken off like this? She'd been in flight for at least an hour now, out of his reach. His impulse to run over to her place faded with that realization. He tried to cover up his frustration, keep things casual, smiling, but he could tell that Fay sensed something in the wind. "Do you like her better than you do Phyllis?"

"I like everybody."

"But Leilani—you told me she was a native girl."

"I told you that she was a local girl—in Hawaii."

"Does that mean that she's a colored girl of some kind?"

"We're all some kind of color, aren't we? She's Polynesian, Hawaiian. She's a beautiful girl. An absolute beauty. I've told you before who she looks like, Dorothy Lamour, only thinner and taller" then, more seriously, "or maybe a little like Nancy Kwan. Do you know who that is? She's made a few movies. She was Suzie Wong—in 'The World of Suzie Wong.' Did you see that movie?"

"Oh yes. Oh. She was a beautiful girl!"

"Well Lani looks a little like her."

"But she's not white, is she?"

"Not exactly white, no, golden. What difference does that make?"

"Are you involved with her?"

"We're friends. I've known the girl since she was sixteen and I was, maybe nineteen or twenty. You don't seem to remember anything about my life, do you?"

"You don't know anything about my life, either."

"Oh, let's not fuss."

"Well, I demand to know what's going on. Oh, I almost forgot, she told me to tell you that a friend of yours named Butter-something—"

"Butterworth?"

"Yes, I think that's it. Butterworth—"

"What about him?"

"He's dead."

"Oh, no!"

"Killed in Viet Nam. Was he a friend of yours?"

"Yes. I'm going on down to the bar. See you later."

Jimmy ordered a boiler-maker and watched the endless war news on television. Butter was just a number. The beer and shot hit him like bombs. What number was Butter? "Butter, Butter, Butter," he said. In an hour his thoughts began to wander. Then he cursed the fact that Fay would not or could not make friends of her own. She counted on him for company. "Oh, do you have to go out again tonight?" ran her refrain. "Why can't you stay at home with me and watch TV? Don't leave me tonight, please, Jimmy!" It got so that he began to sneak about, getting ready to go out, feeling guilt-ridden.

And Phyllis: "When are you going to come over? What, not till Saturday?" Jimmy was dizzy with it. He didn't know whom he'd told what. He broke promises left and right because he couldn't remember having made them. But they forced him to make them, anyway, or else there'd be more trouble, which he was sick of. After consuming four more boiler-makers, Jimmy shocked the denizens of Mulroony's Irish Pub, a dockside bar, who were staring down a civil rights march on TV, by shouting, "Set my people free!" They thought the young Caucasian, who looked like a born member of their set, must have been sympathetic to a cause that they did not have much sympathy with. Little could they know whose civil rights he was thinking of. But he was sick of the racism that his emotional transcendence had been tolerating at home and on the docks, and within a week he had written what he thought of as a love song to the beautiful women of all the races of the world. He called it "Transformations."

If in place of my lady's eyes
there were other eyes as beautiful,
if this woman had other eyes;

if my lady's eyes were emerald
like the Irish Isles and this woman's eyes
were violet like the flower;

if in place of my lady's hair
there was other hair as long and
wonderful to see and touch;

if this woman had different hair;
if my lady's hair was shot with gold and silver,
but not gray, and this woman's hair

was of that Oriental black, flashing green,
or rainbowed; if in place of my lady's ears,
other ears perched upon this woman's head;

if my lady's ears were curly, tiny cakes
with pink and white icing, cherried perhaps,
and this woman's ears were brown and pendant,

with lobes like long strong loops, hung with spiral shells;
if in place of my lady's upswept nose
there was the aquiline, or bulbous, or flat and flared;

if instead of my lady's pink aureoles
there were two burnished copper coins,
and if they made complete my lady's

perky breasts and the others did the same
for the pendulous breasts of the woman
by whom my lady was being replaced;

if my lady's slender waist vanished and became another's,
girdled with lacy jeweled chains instead of Shantung Pongee
silk,
pale as Caucasian chalk or the limestone cliffs of Dover,

with belly button out instead of belly button in;
if my lady's pale round thighs, untouched by sun,
were found to be the lithe, athletic thighs

of a bronzed goddess who bathed all day in sun,

or thighs of Oriental gold or Melanotic mocha;
if my lady's ballerina's calves had been replaced

by hunger's calves in stockings made in diamond net;
if my lady's ankleted, once-bound feet, impossibly small,
should be replaced by webbed paddle-feet, ruby-toed,

and dusted with reflective sand; and if my lady's
smiling mouth, containing chicklets-in-a-row,
should be replaced by the bitter, appealing mouth

of someone else, another woman, with buff dentures
that had chewed raw meat, like a leopard's;
if, in short, my lady were replaced in her entirety,

and I beheld her there, upon that high pedestal
where I had placed her, should I approve?
If her soul could be the same, despite

the physical transformation; if she could say
the same words, the words that I had almost
come to understand, after ages of agonizing struggle,

I think that I should not know that she was a different lady,
another woman, nor would it be true, in essence,
any more than I would be a different lover

without my beret, my bouquet of dew-damp,
fresh-cut, long-stemmed roses,
and my cornucopia of poetry.

*　　*　　*

*And that's how we left it, Auntie.　That night
Jimmy behaved as he had when we'd been together
when we were kids, just a kiss goodnight and he left.
But everything's changed now.　We're going to be
together always. We both know it.　But something*

has happened now that is a great threat to this wonderful recognition. I've told you, Auntie Mele, that I don't use the birth control pill. It's too new, and I am afraid that something bad will be discovered about it in time. I use a diaphragm. And I must have made an awfully terrible mistake when I slept with Butterworth. I'm pregnant. I am terrified of telling Jimmy. Now that everything is really beginning again with us, how can I tell him? You can imagine what the consequences might be. But as if things could not be worse, as if to disprove that, they get worse. Butterworth had no one but me at the end— even his ex-wife had vanished—and so I was to be notified if something happened to him in Viet Nam, and something has happened to him in Viet Nam— he's been killed. The notification says KILLED IN ACTION. And that he was awarded a Purple Heart and a Bronze Star. He was only there less than a month. I must be a wicked girl, Auntie Mele, for I feel so little at the death of this kind young man, only a vague, generalized sadness at the fact of his death and the fact of this awful war. Why do women sleep with men they don't love? All that was on my mind or in my heart apparently was to insist on my independence of Jimmy, and it has caused me to commit the worst crime of my life—to not love a dead hero enough to feel deeply his loss, to feel free at word of his death, to abort his child. What kind of woman am I? I only have one answer, only one thing can explain it, I am so in love with another man—no, not merely in love. I love another man beyond my ability to control what should be my finer feelings with regard to others. We are all out of our own control, Auntie Mele—you knew that—and we feel what we feel and we can't do a thing about it.

CHAPTER SIXTEEN

THE BEAUTIFUL DAY

> *I have considered and found*
> *A mouth I cannot leave . . .*
> *—Theodore Roethke*

THE NEW YORK TIMES
APRIL 18, 1965

STUDENTS PICKET AT WHITE HOUSE

15,000 WHITE HOUSE PICKETS DENOUNCE
VIETNAM WAR

THE NEW YORK TIMES
JUNE 25, 1965

POPE TO REDEFINE BIRTH CURB STAND

PRESSES COMMISSION TO RUSH STUDY OF SUBJECT

Fay left on a Thursday afternoon, intending to spend the remainder of the day and Friday and part of Saturday with Aunt Myrtle and Uncle O'Toole, and from Saturday afternoon until Monday morning with Aunt Brenda. She said she'd be back from Jersey before noon on Monday. Just after she left, the Big Boy boiler had a nervous breakdown. Jimmy barely had time to get the repairman in to doctor it up before he had to leave to go to work on the docks. And when he got to the docks, more bad news was waiting for him. It seemed that, as a result of a union shake-up, they would no longer hire extras; this was to be his last night. Furthermore, due to bookkeeping complications, there would be no pay that morning.

"Wait for the mail," he was told. He walked home broke, feeling exhausted from a night of hauling crates. He turned on the TV and looked at the test-patterns, then took a shower and brushed his teeth and fixed himself a drink. Five in the morning seemed to be the only hour of the day at The Mondriaan when it was quiet, when there wasn't a bell ringing or something blowing up, and he savored Saint Chrysostum's golden silence. He threw himself on Fay's big bed, took three or four sips of his drink; and next thing he knew someone was knocking on the door, claiming him from a nodding doze.

The dim morning light that had been showing behind the curtains had turned to gold. It was eight-thirty. Well, he'd got a couple of hours sleep anyway, before the onslaught. He went to the door and pulled it open, determined to give short shrift to whoever was there; but, after a second of focusing into the dim basement, all his states—of sleep, of exhaustion, of depression, of defeat—were shaken, like the colored glass in a kaleidoscope, into a bright new pattern—of awakening, of energy, of delight, of Lani—for it was Lani standing at the door.

"Honey!" he cried. "It's you!"

"It's me," Lani said, smiling. "Aloha! Greetings from Hawaii! I just got off the plane an hour ago." She threw her arms around Jimmy's neck and they kissed; and kissed again; and again.

Jimmy said:

"Come on inside, honey, and let's lock the door, before my charges come down on us."

Inside, he said:

"I can't believe it. I didn't think you'd be back for another week or so."

"I just couldn't stay away from you anymore. I told my Dad all about you. And he certainly remembered *you*. Oh, sweet-ass, I'm so glad to see you! I love you so much, Jim! Let me kiss you again." And she threw her arms around his neck and they kissed again.

Then she said: "Look, I've brought you some coffee cake—and here—here's a present." Jimmy tore the package open. It was a copy of Theodore Roethke's poems: *Words for the Wind*.

The telephone rang, but Jimmy didn't answer. The speaker buzzed, but he spoke not. The doorbell rang, but he didn't go.

Hours later, in the late afternoon, they were awakened by someone trying to get in at the window. Lani was naked in his arms. They looked at each other, and laughed, hearing a voice from outside, saying:

"The superintendent must be down there." It was the voice of a female tenant. The man's voice was unfamiliar, as he said:

"The real estate office sent me over to see an apartment. They said there'd be somebody here." He sounded cranky.

"Well, I'm certain that he's down there," said the woman. "I've been doing my laundry all afternoon, and I haven't seen him come out. He's sleeping on the job again, that's all. Here, bang on the windows. Wake him up!"

Bang, bang, bang, came the sound of a shoe on the window.

"Hello, down there! Are you there?" the man called. "Hello! Hello, down there? You, super, come out of there! We know you're down there."

Lani giggled, and Jimmy put a finger to his lips and went *sssshhhh!*

"Well, this is a fine thing," said the man. "I've been ringing the bell for a half hour."

"We need a new superintendent," the woman said. "This one's terrible. I've heard he's a *poet*."

Lani buried her face in a pillow, and Jimmy could hear muffled laughter.

Silence. Apparently all was clear.

Lani turned her face up from the pillow and said: "Let's get dressed and go out to eat. I'm starved."

"Me too. But I don't have much money. They didn't pay us this morning."

"Why not?"

"They're laying off all the extras."

"For how long?"

"I don't know. Maybe permanently. Anyway, I'm going to have to start looking for something else to do. I'm in a real bind, what with Mom and the house, and all."

"Let's go out anyway. I've got a few dollars. It'll lift your spirits."

"O.K. We'll pool what we've got."

"We've got enough for one good day, anyway."

It was afternoon, and they were hungry. They went to an Italian restaurant on Bleeker Street, had antipasto, spaghetti, Chianti, and coffee, then toured some Village bars. By moontime, they were running out of money. They were in a fancy dive on Seventh Avenue, seated at the bar. Toward the rear, at a table, there was a party going on. A well-heeled old gentleman seemed to be at the center of the festivities. Once, in glancing around the room, Jimmy'd caught his eye. Now, as Lani passed his table on her way to the ladies' room, the old gentleman extended a polite hand to stop her, and Jimmy watched as he spoke to her for several minutes. She smiled as they talked, and the others with the old man smiled, and everything appeared to be all right, so Jimmy didn't think much of it; but he asked the bartender who the old gentleman was.

"That's Vito D'Ambrosia, the Olive Oil King," he was told. "That's his wife sitting next to him. It's his eightieth birthday." The bartender pushed his nose flat, indicating Mafia.

Lani went on into the ladies' room, and everything went back to normal at the old man's table. But as Lani was on her way back to Jimmy, the old man stopped her again. He nodded his head toward Jimmy, smiled, and put something into Lani's hand. Lani appeared to thank the old man and joined Jimmy at the bar.

"What was all that about?"

"He invited us to his table. He said that it was his birthday, and that he was rich and didn't know how to spend all his money before he died, and that we looked like young lovers, and that he would like to see us have a good time."

"What'd you say?"

"I thanked him and said I was sorry, but that we were leaving soon."

"And what was that he gave you?"

"I don't know. I didn't even look at it. He said for us to have a drink on him. I'm supposed to give it to you," at which she handed Jimmy a crumpled bill. "It's probably a five dollar bill."

"That was nice of him. But I guess we'd better go, honey. A five spot won't get us very far in a joint like this."

They got up and went to the door, where Jimmy stopped to nod at the old gentleman, who raised his glass in reply, and smiled, and Lani and Jimmy stepped out onto Seventh Avenue.

"Let's look," Lani said.

"No, let's get away from here first. I don't want anyone to see us pulling it out right away. It looks like we're broke and greedy."

"We are," Lani said.

They walked a block, then stopped under a street light. Jimmy got the bill out of his pocket and they looked at it. It was a fifty dollar bill.

"He must have made a mistake," Lani said. "Shouldn't we take it back?"

"I hate to say so, but I think we ought to."

They went back to the bar.

When they got there, the table at which the old man and his party had sat was empty.

"They just left," the bartender said.

"Do you know where I can get in touch with the old gentleman?" Jimmy asked.

"I do," the bartender said, smiling, "but I'm not supposed to tell you. He told me that, if you came back, I was to tell you that you was to keep what he give you—that it was a gift from his wife."

Suddenly they had a pocketful of money and a weekend ahead of them in which to spend it. Their good luck seemed to them a sign of cosmic approval. They went to a place where they could dance, and drank and danced and talked for hours.

Lani was in an euphoric mood, but at one point she grew serious. "Kimo," she said, "what with the big build-up in Vietnam, do you think there's any chance of you being called to active duty, like poor . . . dead . . . Butterworth?"

"Not much," Jimmy said. "Butter was an active reservist. I served three years active duty and four inactive. I'm out. I don't think they'll be calling on me."

"I've been worried about that. And I've been worried about something else, too . . ." she said, looking down into her glass of gin and tonic. "There's something else . . . I've got to tell you." Her eyes had gone from sparkling happiness to dull brown seriousness to a fearful glitter. Jimmy heaved in his chair for fear of what might come. He motioned for her to go on.

"That's why I went home," she said—"to see if I couldn't think what to do. I went out to Auntie Mele's grave and talked to her. She told me I should be brave and come back and tell you the whole truth."

"Lani, you're making me nervous. Tell me what it is."

"I'm . . . in trouble."

"You're pregnant? We haven't made love in months— not till today. Wait a minute, it's Butterworth's, isn't it?"

"Yes. Kimo, please, don't speak too quickly." She held her hand up as if to fend him off. "Please, Kimo, don't let this change it all. I love you so much. It was an accident. It shouldn't have happened. I want you to speak, but I'm afraid of what you're going to say."

"Well, I haven't said anything, have I?"

"I thought I'd go somewhere and have it taken care of."

"I don't like the sound of that—have it taken care of." Lani studied Jimmy's frowning face. She was never sure of what was going on in there. She said:

"There's doctor Brazil in Bucks County—"

"Look," Jimmy said, "I have nothing against abortion. I think women should be able to decide this. But this is different."

"How different? What do you mean?"

He threw out his hands. He looked angry. His speech came flooding: "This is Butterworth's kid, and old Butter is lying out there dead somewhere, the last of his line, as he used to say. Haven't there been enough casualties already in this God-damned war?"

"What are you saying? Are you saying I should have the baby?"

"It's no good. Butter's dead. The kid should live."

"You want me to raise it by myself?" Tears formed in her eyes.

"I'll help you raise it. It'll be our kid."

She was stunned. She tried to sort this out. It was the last thing she would ever have dreamed of. She'd been deeply depressed after the Kosinski abortion. The possibility of not having an abortion had winged in from a blue sky. As she sat looking at Jimmy, trying to read him, uncontrollably her mind was making new pictures. Wherever it came from, she couldn't say, but she said: "Would you be willing to carry it in one of those slings—you know, the kind where the baby hangs in front?"

"Like a pack—only in front? Sure."

"Kimo, do you mean it?"

"Of course I mean it."

The tears dripped down her cheeks and dropped off onto the table. Jimmy could see that she was dumbfounded, couldn't speak, just stared at him.

"Come on," he said, "let's dance."

Finally, exhausted, they went home to The Mondriaan and to bed. But next morning they were up and out with the rising sun and the early bird. They walked all the way down to Battery Park, had coffee at a sunny, breezy, outdoor table with a green umbrella over it, and took a ride on the Staten Island Ferry.

Winds were blowing up the water, choppy, but the sun was warm overhead, a bright light, below and through which the gulls flapped and fluttered, hovered and swooped. They leaned against the railing of the ferry boat, side by side, watching the water change from slate to white and back to slate again, watching as barges moved slowly along the bay waters, watching as upright little tugs pulled and pushed dumb, gray, sheep-like ships with all their might, and Lani's expression became serious and she said: "What are we going to do, Kimo? What next?"

"I'm going to tell Phyllis about us. I'm going to break off with her, that's all. There's nothing else to be done. I've been thinking about it and thinking about it, and it looks as if there isn't any way of doing it—of us getting together—without hurting her. It's a damn shame. It seems like somebody always has to get hurt."

"I know," Lani said. "I've been thinking about it, too. When I was home, I went out to our place, outside the village, where we used to play, remember?"

"Where you taught me to float—or almost taught me. Of course I remember." But did he remember it as it really was, as Lani had seen it recently? He doubted that he could, because the paradise he remembered was too beautiful for this world—O if only he could see it again and it be truly what he remembered—he could perhaps believe in the goodness of life then.

"I tried to relive our time together there. I concentrated and concentrated, and tried to bring it back, and, oh wonderful, it began to come back, as if we were there together again, or back there together then, and I saw us both like children, and I knew I loved you because I knew what was inside you and I knew you loved me even then even if you didn't know it or felt that you had to hide it. When I saw us together there, when I could see it again, when I remembered how I told you over and over that you must trust life in order to float—and that's the really important part, that you must trust life—I knew that we should be together, that I should take my own advice, the advice I gave you, and trust life, and you, you must learn to trust life, and I'm going to help you learn to do that, just as I tried to do back then."

She paused. She stepped in front of him and held his shoulders, and her intense dark eyes held him, and she said: "You know, Jim, if you want to wait—I mean, while you square things with Phyllis and your mom, if you think putting it off is a good idea—I won't push you to do it. You can take your time. Wait until you think it's the right time, I mean.

What I'm trying to say is, you don't have to worry about me. I'll wait. I'll wait until hell freezes over."

They stopped-over in Staten Island and had hotdogs at a stand, then took the next ferry back to Manhattan. From the Manhattan ferry landing they took a bus uptown through Wall Street and on into Greenwich Village. Then they went to see a movie on Eighth Street, a love story, a war story, "The Cranes are Flying," and after the movie they walked across town to Lani's new East Village apartment. When they settled down to sleep that night Jimmy dreamed of the times they had nearly lost each other and he hugged Lani closer to him and kissed her sleeping eyes. God, he loved her!

*   *   *

On Monday morning the sidewalk in front of The Mondriaan was strewn with litter, as if a garbage truck had lost its balance. If Kreigsgeld had seen it in a mess like that he'd have raised hell. Not only that, but there were finger-prints and smudges and kid's soap-mark graffiti all over the big plate-glass doors. Jimmy pushed one open and peeked into the vestibule. Cigarette butts, cigar butts, candy wrap-pers, and—the master stroke—a little heap of vomit on the third stair near the wall, a dog's regurgitation, probably.

Just as Jimmy was about to make his way into the house, by the basement entrance, he was accosted by the superinten-dent from across the street, the one who had taken care of The Mondriaan before Fay and he took over. The superintendent of The Dali had "gas heat," or so he had informed Jimmy sev-eral times, great pride ringing in his voice. To have oil heat was to be a superintendent who had to get dirty, but to have gas heat was to be a superintendent of higher standing, an aristocrat among superintendents. He who has gas heat wears frilly bright pink shirts, a cravat stuck in his collar, stands about all day and has nothing to do but to smoke colored cig-arettes in a long ivory holder. He who has gas heat is always organized, is efficient, is never in the kind of fix Jimmy always found himself in. He who has gas heat said (speaking in an unidentifiable, middle-European accent):

"Say, when if you're gonna sweep here? Dis paper blows on me. How about it?"

Jimmy told him he was going to get right at it.

"Good," he said. "You know, but son-of-a-bitch, I couldn't get my front clean."

Jimmy said, "As soon as I get it cleaned up, I'll come over and do your sidewalk, too. O.K.?"

"Sure, O.K." He smiled at Jimmy, and looked at his crotch. "Pretty busy you got, eh?" He smiled again, and motioned his head disdainfully at the Mondriaan.

"That's a tough joint to be. Goddamn, she drived me nuts. Had nay trouble wid da boiler?"

"No, not so far," Jimmy lied, not wanting to give ruffles the supremacy he was seeking.

"Ho, gees. Dat t'ing out all winter. The pipples go crazy. No hot water. No heat. My God! I scaired dey would kill me. She's no good, da Big Boy. She break, watch!" He pucker-smiled and looked down at Jimmy's crotch again. "Lottsa work, eh?"

"Looks like I've got a week's work out here alone."

"Ya," he said. "Nice day, though. If tomorrow bees like today, son-of-a-bitch, dat's what I hope!"

"Me too."

"Well, see you, buddy. O.K.?"

"O.K.," Jimmy said, and descended the steps.

Inside the basement door stood one of the long-faced horsey girls (there were two of them: Fay and Jimmy called them the horsey girls because they often wore riding dress, and in their apartment they each had an English saddle, a collection of riding crops, and the sets of dull little spurs they hooked to their boots to kick horses with: the walls of their apartment were covered with pictures of horses, and the biggest picture was a painting of a horse, executed in such a way as to make the horse indistinguishable from any other horse who ever galloped, and underneath which was written, on a brass plate attached to the frame: Seabiscuit. She had a sour look on her face, and, when she saw Jimmy, she said:

"Mr. Whistler! I have troid and troid to locate you. These washing machines have simply been a terrible nuisance. One of them isn't working at all. And the other overflows every time it's used. You simply must do something about this. And there hasn't been any hot water *all* weekend, I-ther."

"I'll get right on it. You say there hasn't been any hot water?"

"Not a drop."

"Boiler must have gone on the blink."

"I should say!" She stomped off in her boots, slapping a puff of her jodhpurs with a riding crop, and in a few seconds Jimmy heard the elevator clanging and wheezing as it lifted her, temporarily, out of his hair.

"Christ!" he said aloud. "The whole place has gone to pieces in a day and a half."

He went in to look at the incinerator, thinking that he'd just as well set fire to whatever was collected in it before he swept up the front. He opened the incinerator door and looked in. God! There wasn't room for enough air to get in there to start a fire with. He'd have to pull half of that stuff out, burn the other half, and then stuff the rest back in and burn that. He thought he'd do that as soon as he got the front of the house swept up, but he had to change his mind on that score, because he couldn't get the incinerator door shut again. So he started pulling the trash out of the incinerator. He was beginning to get frantic, thinking that old Kreigsgeld might show up.

He pulled and tugged the stuff out of the incinerator's mouth: an old girdle, a fluffy pink slipper, a milk container with a condom on it, a half empty box of doggy biscuits, an empty caviar tin, a five pound bag of rotten potatoes, a Teddy bear, a broken riding crop (ah!), an old pair of men's shoes, tied together at the laces, an empty can of crabmeat, foot plasters, an old stained jockstrap, a framed photograph of Harry Truman, an empty six-pack of beer cans, a sewing kit (Jimmy set that aside); and before long he was knee-deep in rubble. He reached into this heap, that completely surrounded him, and filled the little incinerator room, grabbed an old newspaper, set fire to it, and threw it into the incinerator's mouth. *Whoo-ooooosh!* Up went the flames!

He stood there for a couple of minutes, sweat dripping from every gaping pore, looking like the chimney sweep he was, to see that the fire was burning properly, then closed the incinerator door, leaving the grate open so that the fire could get air, and waded through the debris, on out into the basement.

He hurried into the apartment, got the keys, opened the storage room door, where were located the kickback switches, and pushed the fallen one back up. There was a gurgling sound, a roar, and then a sweet and steady jiggling noise, meaning that the washing machine that didn't work had been overloaded, causing it to throw the switch mid-cycle, and now it was, like any dumb machine, completing the job it had started by doing the second stage of a phantom laundry.

Jimmy was in a sweat for fair, now.

He grabbed a broom, a mop, and a pail, and pulled them out of the storage room, locked the door, and took the works into the apartment. Stepping in, he almost broke a leg slipping on the stack of complaints that had been shoved under the door. He dropped his equipment, grabbed the phone, and called the boiler repair service. Fortunately, he was told, there was a service truck equipped with a radio in the neighborhood. Jimmy could expect help at any time. Then he made another hurried call to the washing machine repair service. Be around that afternoon, he was told. He grabbed the pail and took it into the bathroom, to fill it at the tub. He caught a fleeting glimpse of himself in the bathroom mirror and looked away. His face was beaded all over with perspiration and smeared with soot. He needed a shave. His eyes were red. His curly, disheveled hair caused him to look more like a Medusa than a man. In fact, that glimpse he'd caught of himself very nearly stopped him in his tracks. He wondered, for an instant, if Kreigsgeld would rather find *him* looking nice and the house a shambles, or him a shambles and the house looking nice. How long would it take him to shave? He decided that he'd better stick to cleaning up the house. He hopped into the elevator and rode up to the eighth floor and began sweeping and mopping down in lightning-like strokes. By this time, he wasn't thinking too clearly. Everything had to be done and it all had to be done at once. That was all he could understand about the situation. He didn't even stop to wonder why everybody had left bags and boxes of trash outside their doors. He didn't even stop to think about it, when on the eighth floor he tried to put one of these bags in the incinerator chute and found that the chute was stuffed. Instead, he took the bag and put it in the elevator, and all the rest of the bags and boxes went into the elevator, too, as he worked his way down the stairs.

In the basement, when he rang the elevator buzzer and it dropped down to him with a squeak and a shudder and he opened the door, he found it as full, it seemed, as the incinerator had been; only, unlike the incinerator, one of the items in the elevator walked out of the door under its own locomotion. It was the horsey girl, and she had a bag of garbage in each arm, each bag filled with unburnable bottles.

"I have never seen anything like this," she complained. "Why is all this garbage in the elevator?"

"To get it down here," Jimmy said, in short temper.

"Well," she said, "if you would unclog the incinerator chute, you would be able to get the garbage to its proper place in a more convenient and expeditious manner, don't you think? I, personally, don't care to ride in elevators full of garbage, and I doubt if the rest of the tenants would appreciate it either. Is the washing machine working yet?"

"One of them is," Jimmy said, stuffing garbage in a garbage can.

"Thank heavens!" she exclaimed, and went to look.

Jimmy loaded four garbage cans with the stuff from the elevator, and left them standing there as he ran outside to sweep up the front.

He was plying the broom like a madman, sweeping everything up, including poodle and Great Dane droppings, when he heard a scream from the basement. He looked behind him and saw that there was smoke billowing out of the basement door, which he'd left propped open. "Fire! Fire!" It was the horsey girl.

Jimmy looked around him, his wits scattered. What to do? He saw the dainty super across the street bob up out of his basement and disappear again. Jimmy made a beeline for his own basement door, held his breath, and dove in. But it seemed that this was not to be his heroic day. Instead of finding the damsel in distress, he ran into her, and both of them went sprawling on the floor. It appeared that if Jimmy had just stayed out of the doorway, she'd have found her freedom. Now they floundered about, not able to see, and held onto each other in a most familiar way. Jimmy wondered if she didn't take advantage of the situation.

They finally groped their way outside.

"My Gawd!" she said, standing next to Jimmy, watching as the smoke beclouded and darkened the street. Jimmy heard a voice and looked up. A tenant that Jimmy had dubbed "The Countess" for obvious reasons, had her head stuck out of her window (he could see the two heads of her two poodles, too). She wanted to know if the house was on fire.

"Just the basement," Jimmy called up to her. He felt a bit unhinged. Then, sirens wailing, bells tolling, two fire trucks pulled to the curb. In they went, the men of whatever squad it was: hoses crisscrossing the little street. Dogs barked. People stared. Firemen cursed. Bells rang. Sirens screamed. Cars pulled up. Traffic snarled. And Jimmy wept.

Then, suddenly, it was over.

"You didn't have any fire there, sonny," he was told by a red-faced Captain (who looked very like the one Jimmy had given the bribe to). "Your incinerator backed up. Chute was clogged; pushed the smoke back down. You gotta keep that chute open."

He turned to a fireman who was standing nearby. "I told you that was it, didn't I? Hell, this place is famous." Behind the fireman to whom the Captain was speaking, lurked the super of The Dali. The Captain looked over at him. "Happened three times when you were taking care of the place. Didn't it?" he called to He-Who-Has-Gas.

"Yes, sir, Captain. Three times backs she up on me. I the one who called now."

"Good man," said the Captain. He turned back to Jimmy. "You're new, eh?"

"Yes, sir."

"Well, I'll give you a break, sonny. I gave Frilly-Front there a nice ticket. But I don't want to be called out to this damn place no more, got it? I got real fires to fight."

"Yes, sir," Jimmy said, and slunk away.

By five o'clock that afternoon things were under control. Jimmy'd got most of the mess the firemen had made cleaned up. He'd got all the trash burned (making certain first that the chute was clear), and he got the front walk and the vestibule cleaned. The washing machine repair man came a bit earlier than expected and fixed the broken machine. The boiler repair man had come and had got the Big Boy growling properly, so as to make heat and hot water, and Jimmy had got all his soot and grease cleaned up after him. Cleanliness and Order had been restored. He straightened up the apartment at odd moments, so that Fay wouldn't come home and find a mess. He shaved and showered and put on clean clothes; and, not having to go to the docks on this Monday night, he felt momentarily relieved. But he was disgusted, discouraged, exhausted, undermined; in short, feeling rotten. He'd expected Fay to be back by now. She'd probably decided to stay on an extra day. Probably having a few drinks and a good time with Aunt Myrtle and Uncle O'Toole. It was better that she hadn't come home, in the middle of all this commotion. But Jimmy wished she were here now, so he could go out without feeling that the place would cave in while he was gone. He felt like walking out on the damned place for good and ever. It'd been wrong of him to stay the whole weekend with Lani, and not come over to check on things. But any house that can't be left alone for a day and a half ought to be razed, buried, shoveled under.

In the middle of it all, Mr. MacTavish tapped Jimmy on the shoulder. "Nice bit of chaos you have here," he said. "Would you say this is the right way, the wrong way, or the Marine way?"

"I'm sorry for the mess," Jimmy said.

"No, no, I'm not here to complain." He was smiling. "I came down to return your book. These poems are very interesting. When you get a chance, drop up and let's have a talk."

Jimmy stuck the book in his back pocket. The basement door of the elevator was sliding shut before he thought to call thanks after Mr. MacTavish.

Then Fay showed up. She was tired from her trip over and wanted a tall, cool drink. That was fine. But after a *few* tall cool drinks Jimmy found himself with a tipsy Fay on his hands, and that wasn't so fine.

"I can't take this anymore . . ." she cried.

"What do you mean, Mom?"

"This place is no good for me. All I do is work around here . . . and you're always going off and leaving me all alone . . . always out with one of your hussies . . . I want to live in Plainfield, where I have friends . . . I don't like this place at all! I don't like Greenwich Village and all these peculiar people!"

"Well, I'm a grown man, Mom. You don't expect me to stay home all the time, do you?"

"You could stay home with your mother once in a while," she said. "You leave me here with this whole house on my shoulders."

"Well, you leave me here alone all the time, too; don't you? You've just got back from Plainfield, haven't you?"

"Yes, and now you'll walk out."

"Well," Jimmy fibbed, "I've been stuck in here all week-end, haven't I?"

"I'm doing you a favor," she said, "staying here. I just want to see you get on your feet, otherwise I'd live over in Plainfield."

"Well, what about me? Aren't I doing you a favor, too? I thought I was. You have more money now, don't you?"

Fay banged her glass on the kitchen table and started wailing at the top of her lungs about being unloved and mistreated and left alone. Jimmy was afraid that somebody would call the cops. There were a lot of people in the house who didn't like them, and who would leap at the chance of putting them on the spot. Then Jimmy thought that he might be able to scare Fay out of her hysterics by pretending to call Aunt Brenda and asking her to come and take Fay back to Jersey. But before he knew it, he was actually putting the call through. Fay was still wailing in the background when Brenda came on the line. Jimmy looked at Fay, and decided to go ahead with it. He told Brenda roughly what was happening, and, after considerable hemming and hawing, she agreed to drive over from Jersey and take Fay back. Jimmy figured that, if he could get Fay quiet by the time Brenda came, he'd just ask Brenda to come in for a visit. He didn't want to send Fay away, really. It didn't seem right. But he wasn't quite able to handle the situation either. And he was afraid they'd be fired out of the place before they could get themselves organized. They especially needed the house, right now, with the docks closing up.

Finally, Fay quieted down and just sat and sobbed. Jimmy tried to console her, but it wasn't much good. She had it in her head that he was the cause of all her troubles, whatever they were. He was her only resource, and he'd failed her. She believed that she was unwanted, unloved, lost and alone, and there wasn't anything Jimmy could say to shake her out of it. It was a good plain crying jag. But finally even the sobbing subsided. She went into the bathroom and washed her face, and came out all made up again, and aglow.

Jimmy asked her if she didn't want some coffee and she answered that what she wanted was for him to fix her a nice drink in a clean glass and to put some ice in it. He did that, and gave it to her, and then she asked him what he'd told Brenda.

"I told her you were sick," he said, lying.

"Is she coming over?"

"Yes."

"Do you want me to go back with her?"

"I think it'd be better if you did, Mom. And as soon as you feel better—in a day or two—I'll come over and get you."

"What about the house?"

"I'll take care of it."

They had a few more drinks together, and talked on, reasonably, until Brenda came. She didn't bother to come in— just honked her horn outside until they heard it. Jimmy took Fay out to the car.

Fay was all submissiveness now. She'd completely worn herself out. At the last minute, Jimmy wanted to make her stay, but when he saw Brenda scowling behind the wheel, he thought better of it. Brenda'd be sore as a hornet, coming all the way to New York for nothing. Fay was thinking the same thing. Jimmy had a feeling that she wanted to stay but thought it was best to go along. Leading her to the car, he felt like an Aztec priest taking a human sacrifice to the altar. But he knew too that Fay could handle herself with Brenda, whose bark was worse than her bite. Brenda'd bully and domineer, if she could, but she loved Fay, too. She was Fay's big little sister, after all.

It was clear that Fay wanted to be in closer contact with her family, to live in her home town, where things and people were familiar. She didn't like the people who lived in The Mondriaan. They were foreign to her, alien, snobs. Besides, The Mondriaan was too demanding. The little house Brenda was renting had a nice room in it for her. Brenda would let her have it cheap; she'd just have to do a bit of work around the house and keep an eye on the kids, that was all.

Well, there it was.

Jimmy couldn't keep the house going by himself; and, even if he could, as soon as the owner discovered that Fay had gone, they'd certainly ask him to go, too. The Mondriaan was a two-person post. So there was no question about it, Jimmy was going to have to leave—and pretty shortly. But where was he going? Even if the owner let him stay on alone, he'd have to be at The Mondriaan by day, and he was losing his night job on the docks, and where could he get another job that was near the house, that paid well, and that occupied him only three nights a week? He couldn't see himself working five nights a week on one job, and five, or really seven, days a week at The Mondriaan, and writing too. That was a bit much, he thought. Besides, the house was a nightmare. He wanted out of it himself.

He needed cheering up. This might be a good time to drop in on Mr. MacTavish to hear—he hoped—something encouraging on his poetry.

MacTavish was pleased to see him. He let him in, gave him a seat and a Scotch, and got down to cases.

"I'm writing a book on copywriting—so, you see, I'm not one of your regular writers. I'm in the ad business. Now you're a damned good poet, young man—and an ex-Marine into the bargain. What more could I ask?"

Jimmy did not get his drift. "Thank you, sir, but I—"

"Too good for copywriting, are you?"

"Are you offering me a job?"

"I am, indeed!"

"But I don't know anything about advertising, about copywriting—"

"In an age of beatnik verse, competent formal lyric poets are hard to find, and I know all about copywriting. I had occasion to speak to your mother. She told me you had been a salesman."

"Several times."

"What kind? Not a sales clerk in a store?"

"No. Door-to-door. Everything."

"Very good! Copywriting is just peddling in print, son. Well, are you interested?"

Hooray! It was the Salvation Army on the march! He heard drums and tootles!

CHAPTER SEVENTEEN

BLACKOUT

> *Out of the cradle endlessly rocking,*
> *Out of the mockingbird's throat. . .*
> —*Whitman*

"Do you love Lani?" Here it was, Jimmy's Moment of Truth.

"No, no, Phyl. It's just sex." He still didn't want to hurt Phyllis.

"Well, I know I'm no good that way, and, as long as you love me, that's all I care about. I don't care if you want to make love to her. If that's what you've been doing anyway, what difference does it make? As long as we have our life together . . ."

It seemed impossible to break off with her. Jimmy gave up the effort. A professorial look came upon him. He began to thumb tobacco into a pipe he'd recently acquired. In a moment he spoke from a cloud of wise and pungent smoke. He told her about his new job offer. She listened, a mocking, scornful look on her face, then said: "Sure, the great middle class has its arms wide open to you, and you, you blind-poet

380

fool, you're going to walk right in, whistling. But the bullshit world is no good for you, Jimmy. You go up to the American Rubber Climax Building and—"

"The American Metal Climax Building."

"Whatever. The world is mad with lies, Jimmy. You go up there and you'll tell lies all day."

"All I do is tell lies anyway. I *was* an actor, you know. I might as well get paid for it."

"Oh, you *tell* lies, but you don't *write* them. You write true and beautiful things. And you know that stuff is a deep fake . . ."

"It's just selling products."

"But I don't mean that it's a fake that way, I mean that it's fake poetry. Pretty soon you'll think you're writing and you won't be, and then you won't write the real stuff, because these jingles will satisfy you. It'll please you. You know, Jimmy, it always surprises me to realize how naive you are. Have you been writing any good poetry, anyway, lately?"

"I've tried. But then, you know, Phyl, the only good poet is a dead poet. You know what Faulkner said: We all start out wanting to be poets and find out that it's too hard, then we try to become short story writers and find out that that's too hard, and that's how we all end up as novelists, or in my case, a writer of television scripts."

"A dead poet is a poet who isn't writing poetry, Jimmy. Have you seen this review?"

"No. Who's it by?"

"Oh, some anonymous Kirkus reviewer, I think. He says that Whistler's 'Obituary' immediately engages the reader's attention by its detailed verisimilitude and narrative pace unclogged by sentimentality, yet flowing with fidelity for his father, who perishes *Without the mummeries of death, by fire . . .*"

"It just goes to show you how much he knows. 'Flows with fidelity for his father . . .' Always faithful, that's me. Semper fidelis. I didn't even know my old man was a crook when I wrote that poem, and maybe he wasn't even my old man, anyway."

"You were faithful to what you knew. That's my point."

"That poem makes me feel like a fool. Poetry makes me feel like a fool. It's about time I made some money."

"Your scripts make money."

"I haven't sold one in a month of Sundays. The market's gone."

"I refuse to believe that you can't write honestly and not make money."

"You know what it is, Phyl? It's the bullshit world."

*　　*　　*

Jimmy called Fay and told her about his new job as a copywriter in an ad agency, told her that he would have to leave The Mondriaan, that she would have to come over and get her things. It was just as well with Fay. She was going live with Brenda, who had an extra room, and would help her out by paying her to watch the kids. Brenda would drive Fay over to pick up her things.

Jimmy moved what little he had into Lani's apartment. He felt badly about Bradhurst, but screw Kreigsgeld! For the next month Jimmy stayed with Lani and didn't go to see Phyllis at all. It was the cowardly way to do things, he knew, but that was the way he did them. He just didn't know what else to say or do. He didn't want to be forced to tell her that he didn't love her—besides, it wasn't true. That was the whole problem. If he hadn't loved her, he could have brought himself to say: "Look here, Phyl, I love Lani, and I'm going to leave you for her;" but he did love Phyllis. Now that Lani had become his lover, Phyllis had become his little sister. Besides, he tried not to think of it like that—that he was (actually had) separated from her. He was simply playing house with Lani, the woman he loved. They'd get up in the morning, and

once Lani's morning sickness had subsided, she'd fix breakfast, and they'd go to work—she to a new television job—she
had dropped her studies at Columbia for some practical experience in journalism—he to MacTavish's Agency, where he
was finding copywriting more unendurable than superintending The Mondriaan, despite the fact that he was now on
lithium and feeling neither the ups nor downs of life—and
come home and eat supper together, go to bed and read and
make love and listen to music on the radio together, and every
day they grew closer, more attuned to each other, more alike,
more one, until there was no letting go and no turning back,
especially as, month after month, Lani ballooned in preg-
nancy and finally had to be taken to St. Vincent's to give birth
to Butterworth's boy.

It was a very hard birth. The cord was tied around the
baby's neck like a hangman's noose. The doctors finally settled for a Caesarean section. Jimmy looked at the baby for
the first time and thought, This is a child for the new age, a
golden brown Hawaiian-featured baby with what almost
looked like a blond crew-cut.

"What a dumpling you are," he said. "This world killed
your dad and tried to hang you, but here you are, faithful to
life." Then he said to the baby's exhausted beautiful mother,

"I've got a name for him if you approve. What do you
say we call him Semper Fi?"

"That's a crazy name," she said, "but you're the poet.
What will we call him for short? We can't go around saying
'Semper Fi' this and 'Semper Fi' that."

"We'll just call him 'Fi' for short—'Fi' this and 'Fi'
that."

It took strength for her to laugh and then she fell back
on the pillows, exhausted. "Are you serious, Kimo?"

"Semper Fi Butterworth. Yes, I am absolutely serious."

"Well," she said, drifting off, "we'll talk about it later."

But Jimmy was determined. He looked at the sleeping mother and said, "He's my son and he's going to be called Semper Fi, and he'll be faithful to himself and to others and to his mother and his father—both fathers—and to his wife, when he gets one."

Lani was released from the hospital a week later. But she was still weak and would have to stay in bed another week at least.

Jimmy fixed Lani breakfast and served it to her in bed before going to work. In the morning he also fixed something for her to eat for lunch, something all ready to slip in the oven and heat up. Every night he got out the cookbook and tried to make her something nourishing and tasty for supper. He bought a chess set and taught her how to play, and during her convalescence they played by the hour with Semper Fi's cradle pulled close by. Jimmy even went out and rented a television set for Lani to watch during the day when she was too tired to read. On November 9, 1965, Lani watched a report that former President Dwight D. Eisenhower had been taken to Fort Gordon Army Hospital in Georgia with a mild heart disturbance. President Johnson was recuperating at his ranch in Texas from his recent gall bladder operation. A twenty-one year old pacifist named Roger Allen La Porte, shades of Kosinski, set himself on fire in front of the United Nations Building to protest the Vietnam war. Jimmy wouldn't have watched the news, "a mere sketch of human madness," he'd've said; but television news was going to be Lani's life, so she took a professional interest in what Jimmy called "mere information." He would have asked, paraphrasing T.S. Eliot, "Where is the wisdom we have lost in knowledge, where is the knowledge we have lost in information?"

Well, Jimmy was a poet and Lani was a journalist. Even so, weak as she was, she fell asleep with little Semper Fi in her arms and the television on. Jimmy came home from the

American Metal Climax Building and found them so. He decided to let her and the baby dream on. He had work to do. He had work to do because he had big news for Lani when she woke up. He had picked up the vestibule mail box mail and found a contract and a big retainer in it, along with a long letter from a west coast and Hawaiian production company who wanted to use a script of his for the opener of a series, set in Hawaii, and had hopes that he would consider relocating to Hawaii to write more scripts in the same series and to oversee the series story-lines in general. If this turned out to be what it seemed to be, they were going to be rich. The script was called "H.A.S.P.," and was the story, much elaborated, fictionalized, and romanticized, of two Hawaiian Armed Services Policemen and their adventures on the streets of Honolulu. Of course it derived from his own experiences in Hawaii, in the pre-statehood days.

The production company had asked for some changes and he was anxious to get right to work on them, so anxious that he decided not to take his lithium that night, and he felt the old manic twinges of a man raring to go. He had just set up for work, when, at 5:27 p.m., the television and every light in the house went out.

At first, Jimmy thought a fuse had blown, but then he looked toward the kitchen window to see that it was as black as night out where New York should have been glittering with evening lights. He went to the window to see better. No lights anywhere. He wondered if the nation was under attack. Lani and Semper Fi dreamed sweetly on. He thought he'd better find out what was going on.

He went down to Harry's Psychedelic Dom to find out what he could about it. As he approached the bar he could see dozens of dancing candles through the plateglass windows. The place was buzzing with gossip. There was a Russian invasion, a Martian landing, a World War or a War of the Worlds, who knew? Finally they got the story straight.

Somebody had a transistor radio and the news came over it that there was an extensive power failure, reaching from Canada to New York. It was all very exciting, and called for a drink.

A blackout party began in Harry's, with most of the gang in attendance. Denise was there, and Jimmy took a seat at her table. From time to time a denizen of the neighborhood banged on the door and was allowed entry—Harry had bolted the door as soon as the lights went out—and one of these times it turned out to be Phyllis who was banging. Phyllis seated herself with Jimmy and Denise. Somebody at the bar started singing "Where Have All the Flowers Gone" and the crowd joined in. Soon everyone was singing.

> *Where have all the flowers gone,*
> *Long time paa-a-sing,*
> *Where have all the flowers gone,*
> *Long time ago. . .*

They had a few drinks, and speculated about the blackout. Then Phyllis said she wanted to get back downtown to her apartment, now that she knew the country wasn't being attacked or anything, and insisted that Jimmy take her home. He told her that Lani was asleep upstairs, and that he was going right back to her. There were at least a dozen people in the bar who knew Phyllis and would be willing to take her home. Denise could handle herself as well as any man. Let her walk with Phyllis. But Phyllis said that if Jimmy didn't take her, that would be it. Jimmy told her that he couldn't leave Lani alone and asleep up there that long, and sick, too, and with the baby—

"You mean Butterworth's little bastard, don't you?" she said—and flew out the door in a temper. Denise went along after her and Jimmy went back to Lani and the baby. Lani was still sleeping.

Next day he went down to Phyllis's and told her that he was leaving her. She said she'd been tight the night before and didn't mean to act the way she did. Jimmy told her that it had nothing to do with that. He tried to tell her, in the most gentle way he knew, that he had to be with Lani. But there wasn't any nice or easy way to do what he was doing. He wished that Denise had never brought him to the Lower East Side to meet Phyllis that summer day long ago; then this day that had come only to hurt Phyllis would not have come. He wished, too, that he could have taken Phyllis in his arms and kissed her, but that would have been only to hurt her more. She watched as Jimmy gathered up his remaining things and put them in boxes and carried the boxes down to the street. She even helped him, and then went to find a taxi for him while he carried the last box down.

Jimmy didn't have much left at her place, a few clothes and books, a few manuscripts, that was all. While he was at The Mondriaan he'd gradually got most of his stuff over there. Phyllis asked him for a book or two, and a picture that he'd drawn—and he gave her whatever she wanted. He knew that she only wanted the things as mementos. He'd've given her an arm in expiation, if he could.

She stood in the doorway of her tall tenement building and watched as he put his things in the back seat of a cab. Finally, he couldn't stand it anymore, and he went over to her and kissed her on the cheek. Then he climbed into the cab and looked at her for a instant, a wan little thing with no-color hair and moist, pale blue eyes, and told the cabby to get going. "Go!" he said.

CHAPTER EIGHTEEN

LOVE IT OR LEAVE IT

*The old Lie; Dulce et Decorum est
Pro patria mori.*
—Wilfred Owen

DEMOCRATS ALTER PLANS ON POVERTY

HOUSE MAJORITY MAPS CUT IN FUNDS FOR COMMUNITY ACTION

U.S. SAYS IT HAS LOST 376 PLANES IN VIETNAM WAR

Christmas, New Year's, spring, and in June the full birth and burst of summer—time marched on to the vibes of deep dark tubas and bright brass trumpets, and Jimmy tried to keep in step. One evening he came home still shuddering from the subway and found Lani waiting for him with a letter from Marsayas.

Dear Boyo,
Well, as you must have figured out by now, we decided to split the scene once and for all. It was no good anymore.

I was getting too old for it. You know, middle-age is beginning to encroach on me. If I'm going to do anything, I got to get busy and stop playing. How about you, Boyo, what are you going to do? I hope this little epistle finds you. I'm sending it to Lani with a forward on it, because, when we took off, it looked like you two might make it. I'd like to hear whether you did or not, and the rest of it too. By the way, I'm sorry for that crack I made once about Lani. Guess I was just coming down on you. Do you remember what I said? If not, good!

I'm taking a chance and enclosing a picture of me & family. (The kid's getting big, ain't he?) Some one of these days I'd like to have you come out here to the Pennsylvania woods and split a bottle of my homemade stuff with me. And, I've got some great other stuff to share. Doctor Brazil brought back some yagé from South America. Don't know if I told you, he's the doctor who took care of Lani that time. He's selling me this dump, little by little and officially, I'm caretaker of his whole spread when he's off on one of his medicinal research trips. Besides being a terrific painter, he's also an honest-to-God Shaman! No kidding!

Joan's working in town (got a sitter for the kid there). I wish you could see my new paintings. I've made a complete change of style. Total expressionism, plus Zen. I think you'd like them.

I want to tell you how sorry I am about not saying goodbye. It was just that, once I decided to get out, everything about the East Village gave me the creeps—even you. But I've got a bit of time and space on the situation now.

Well, Boyo, if you ever get this, do me a favor and answer it, will you? Old Marsayas has a big heart, and you're in it. Ooooom! Huuuumm!

The picture enclosed showed an older, fatter but healthier-looking Marsayas holding a small replica of himself on his shoulders in a piggy-back position, his gargoyle face in a big grin, and a slimmer, more mature Joan standing at his side, smiling into sunlight. The front porch of a slat-board house showed in the immediate background, with a huge bird's foot shadow of a tree striking across it.

P.S. Jimbo, I'd just about got through writing the other letter when I got a phone call from a guy who was in Nam with Butter. Jimmy, Butter is dead. The guy said he was killed by friendly fire and then he kind of laughed ruefully and said Butter was murdered by some of his own men. He was "fragged," he said, and he was there. I said, "What's fragged?" And the guy said somebody drops a fragmentation grenade behind you and bang, your dead, blown to pieces. I said who in hell would have done a thing like that to old Butter and the guy said Butter had a reputation for being a pain in the ass. A martinet. You know yourself how annoying Butter could be sometime with his straightness. It seems like this kind of thing happens to officers over there all the time. I said will there be some kind of investigation, and the guy just laughed again. Gees, Boyo, I know you and Butter didn't always get along, but I know you kind of got together before he went over and this must be bad news for you and it sure is for me. He was an okay guy, just a little stuffy, not anything really bad in him. I'm sorry to bring you such tidings from the front but I thought you'd want to know. The army covers this stuff up, you know—bravely killed in battle, etc. More bullshit! I thought Lani would want to know too. Maybe— you decide. Well, you tell anyone you think it might mean something to, okay? I'm just going to sign off and have one for Butter. I'll tell you what—at noon on Thursday next (this should surely have reached you by then) you raise one for him and so will I. The great ape Johnson has got another decent guy killed—and for what? It's not about him and the Kremlin. It's not about him and China. It's not about him and Ho! It's about us. It's about Butter and the rest of us and our lives. And when in hell will this damned madness ever end?

*   *   *

Which madness? Jimmy wondered, for it seemed that one madness led to another. Of course Marsayas had meant the war, but that was the umbrella madness underneath which the others flourished. It seemed a catalyst for every kind of lunacy and every kind of lunatic reaction to every kind of lunacy. It was always the big dark shadow overhead, the protean umbrella that threatened to turn at any second into the big mushroom, the one that would tower upwards higher than the sky and blot out the sun and surround the globe with radiant toxicity, the little big bang.

The whole of America was sick with this thing, but sometimes that was just too big to worry about, sometimes people had to deal with the little madnesses that, somehow, even if they turned out to be pure illusion, seemed to be spawned by the big one. Minor plagues swept through the Village and the Lower East Side, some with far-reaching consequences, so that those who survived would learn to suffer later. Venereal diseases were rampant, soldiers, driven insane, were beginning to return, some of whom had suffered terribly, physically, emotionally, both, and were being tormented by anti-war protesters, who called them baby-killers. Soon everybody was wearing hippie rags, some made from the remnants of uniforms. Many of these vets were black and therefore dealt a double blow to their pride, being treated once again as not only inferior because of color but also because they had gone to serve their country. But the bearded ones who called them names were being called names in their turn, and "Bearded Hippie" was usually followed by the command to "Love it or leave it." Trouble was, for those with that attitude, that many of the soldiers were becoming indistinguishable from the hippies, were in fact becoming hippies. If these could be called factions, they shared one thing in common—drugs. Overdosed bodies were being found everywhere, on roofs, in doorways, on sidewalks, wherever they fell, another lost generation.

And so it was that one day on his way home from work, Jimmy stepped into the vestibule of Lani's apartment house and found . . . a body. He stepped closer and looked down—a heap of rags in a dark corner of the hall, dark curly hair, sneakered feet sticking out from under a huge army overcoat and *oh no!* little toes sticking out from the worn-away sides of the sneakers. He dropped down on his haunches beside the still form, shaking his head slowly from side to side.

He got up, ran out of the building and found a police car, always cruising around the Lower East Side, and was driven back to the house to show the police what he had found.

"You say you know her?" said the driver, turning to him in the back seat.

"She's a friend of mine."

"She may have been a friend of yours but she nobody's sweetheart now," said the other cop.

"Are you on the stuff, too? Let me see those arms."

"Lay off," said his partner. "It's illegal." They pulled to the curb, got out, and the two patrolmen pushed through the big front doors, Jimmy lagging behind. He did not want to see again.

"It's just that it makes me so Goddamned mad. This ought to be a lesson for you, sonny." He pushed Jimmy toward the body. "Look, she was shooting up. The needle's still in her arm. She must have got hold of some of that pure smack they're dishing out up in Harlem. Too much for her."

"I don't use heroin. I don't do drugs. I drink."

"She got any relatives we can notify?"

"A couple of aunts in Seattle, but I have no address for them. I can take you to her apartment, maybe you can find something there." Jimmy felt unsteady . . . . *it tolls for thee, it tolls for thee* . . . ran repeatedly through his mind.

The other cop said, "I got her address here in her bag. Also needles and all kinds of crap. There's a bag with some beer in it over in the corner."

"She must have been coming to see me," Jimmy said, "then stopped here . . . to shoot up."

After telling the police where he could be found, if needed, Jimmy wobbled up the stairs and into the apartment. He told Lani about Denise and they both sat down and slowly drank Denise's warm beer.

"Why didn't you come up here and get me?" Lani asked after a while. "I can't believe it."

"I didn't want you to see her like that. I didn't think you'd want to see her like that, either. Was I wrong?"

"No. No. Poor Denise. This place is like hell," Lani said after a few minutes. "I'm glad we're getting out. I want to go back to Hawaii. You know that. I've had enough. I want to go home. And, thank God, we have the chance now."

"Damn, Denise!" Jimmy cried. "She just couldn't take care of herself."

"And you can take care of everybody, because your parents were a couple of drunks and you feel guilty and responsible and think that you have to take care of everybody, but you can't take care of yourself anymore than poor Denise could."

Jimmy looked at her, nonplussed. After a moment's consideration, he said, "I guess you wanted to say that for a long time. Feel better now?"

"No," said Lani. "But it did take me getting pregnant to get you away from Phyllis, didn't it?"

*　　*　　*

Lani and Jimmy planned to get married. They wanted that symbolic act, something that would bind them in the eyes of the world; so that, from then on, the two of them and little Semper Fi could stand together against any look of the world's eyes, and the world would know who and what they were to one another—for *its* information, not theirs—and know that to challenge one would be to challenge the other. And they were anxious to leave the Lower East Side, even Manhattan, even the mainland, with its Boston bus protesters and it's Southern sheriffs. Hawaii beckoned.

But before leaving the mainland Jimmy wanted to go to Bucks County and see Marsayas for what he thought might be the last time for a long time. He wanted Lani to go with him but she wouldn't. She said that, although Doctor Brazil had been good to her, his farm held a bad memory. He should go alone. She had plenty to keep her busy in New York with the baby. And besides, she'd got hold of a few copies of the Honolulu "Advertiser," was looking for a new place there, and making plans for their departure.

"Just a couple of days," he said, kissing her good-bye at the Port Authority station. He kissed the baby, and headed off to see Marsayas.

CHAPTER NINETEEN

ARGONAUTS

Back out of all this now too much for us . . .
—*Robert Frost*

THE NEW YORK TIMES
JULY 18, 1966

SOVIET ARTISTS APPEAL TO THOSE IN U.S. ON WAR

LEADING SOVIET CULTURAL FIGURES GALINA ULANOVA,
THE PRIMA BALLERINA, AND ARAM KHACHATURIAN,
THE COMPOSER, APPEALED TODAY TO
LEADERS IN THE ARTS IN THE U. S.
TO PROTEST AGAINST
"THE CRIMINAL WAR" IN VIETNAM

"Hail to thee, blithe spirit!" Jimmy shouted, spotting Marsayas in the dusty parking lot at a country station in Pennsylvania. They hugged each other and Marsayas drove them across the countryside and then through Doctor Brazil's farm and finally to his outlying cabin.

"Who is this Doctor Brazil, anyway?" asked Jimmy, as he bounced along, trying to light a cigarette.

"Why, Christ, Jimmy, where have you been? He's famous! Didn't I tell you? He was a pal of Aldous Huxley's and knows Timothy Leary. He's a medical doctor and a terrific painter. His paintings are psychedelic. He uses what he calls glow paint. When he came back from the Amazon a couple of months ago, he brought all the ingredients needed to make a wonderful spiritual potion. We'll try it later. Sorry you won't get to meet him—he's off somewhere making a documentary."

That evening Jimmy drank what felt like gallons of home-brewed beer with Marsayas and Joan, patty-caked with little Marsayas, who used his daddy's gargoyle grin to charm him, all to the strains of Ravi Shankar. After Joan and the toddler went off to bed Marsayas and Jimmy sat together drinking deep into the night. Jimmy told Marsayas about the Hawaii deal in the offing. Of course Marsayas saw writing for television as a "damned freaky sellout. You're a true damn poet, you jerk, why on earth you'd want to do that, I can't figure. Me, I've given up writing poetry completely, I haven't got the stuff. But like I said years ago, you're among the elect, you dope, a true poet. I'm sticking with my painting." Marsayas gurguggled some beer and rumbled internally.

"I wanted to tell you about Denise, too. And then Butterworth. But you had no way of knowing about the baby. We call him Semper Fi. Lani and I have little Semper Fi and we'll be married soon. Before we take off for Hawaii, any-way." Jimmy felt drunk on Marsayas's brew. Something happened to the night. It vanished. Jimmy slept peacefully that night for the first time in a long while—until the sun burst through the window like a golden glove, punching him in in-stead of out.

He still held a mug of splashing instant coffee in his mitt as Marsayas drove them all in his bouncing, shaking old parti-colored jalopy off to what he called the waterfall, explaining that it was a swimming hole whose cold water would soon wake Jimmy up and snap him out of his hangover.

"And I hope you're up to trying some of Doctor Brazil's yagé potion. It's only a mild hallucinogen, but, believe me, it'll make the whole experience miraculous. It's all about nature, Jimbo, inside and out. It's about more than getting close to it. It's about *being* nature. It has removed from me the ugliness of the residual of any ambition. You need it. You'll love it!"

They left the car creaking in the sun and stumbled down the embankment—Marsayas leading the way. Joan feared for the toddler a bit because the embankment was steep, but they dropped into the shallow from the rocks without incident. It was merely a smooth shallow pond, purling slightly, only a foot deep. On a lower level, was a kind of natural slide that had been worn into the rock by the rush and rub of the water.

One could slide down this into a deeper pool, perhaps four feet in depth. It was too small to swim in, they could get only about three overhand strokes and they were up against a smooth wall of red rock. Jimmy and Marsayas tried to deepen it by throwing up the stones at the bottom, but they could go on doing that forever and they were here for fun and not work, so their labor was short.

The toddler had to be kept up in the higher, shallower pool, Joan attending. Marsayas and Jimmy joined them and sat down on the hot stone to enjoy some cold beer from sweating cans.

There was a small concrete bridge down below the deeper pool and a pickup truck whizzed by over it, otherwise no sound but water and talk and laughter, shrill cries from the baby. Below the bridge the water dropped in a steep fall and then, after a rushing meander, into the lake. The lake was very large and dark and Marsayas claimed that a phantom chief beat an ominous tattoo upon a tom-tom out there at night.

Marsayas chanted in a low mysticism-packed voice— "*The voice of the white birds from every quarter cried out, You have lost your country, You have lost your country!* His whole tribe was wiped out by the white man and he was out for justice. Of course scientists say the night rumblings are made by natural gas, a less impressive explanation, don't ya think?"

After the beer they took a plunge in the water and then Marsayas said he'd heard that somewhere upstream was a great waterfall, one that fell for perhaps a hundred feet—not a Niagara, but a fair cataract and it was supposedly located in a canyon of considerable beauty—and would Jimmy like to hike up the stream with him to find it.

Jimmy said he would and they started off together up the shallows.

Marsayas had been roughing it in a woodland way for over a year now and moved along at a good pace over the slippery rocks, sometimes through the water, sometimes along the bank, but more often through the water, because the bank was quite steep most of the way and often it was non-existent, only a sheer wall of rock in its place.

He looked a mythological figure of a man, tall and broad and beefy of shoulder, red and bushily bearded, sharp-eyed, visored cap pulled low for the sun: he moved sure-footed as a goat—or not quite that, for he did slip occasionally, but even a mountain goat might have slipped on these watery stones.

Jimmy kept apace about twenty yards behind and it took his whole attention focused upon where he was next to step to keep him from dropping farther behind. They were no longer boys and this delicate goat-walking on watery stone was an effort, of the body but then more of the will. Jimmy wished Lani were here to see this beautiful place.

Where were they going? Where? And why? Why make the effort?

Back at the lower pools near the bridge there was rest on the hot stone with beer, kept cold by the cold purling water and the shade of the rock over it; so why this little odyssey, this minor quest? Why be Argonauts? What was the grail they were after?

When Jimmy looked up Marsayas had disappeared ahead of him and he saw a long gently rising glassy piece of water, reflecting mountains, bushes, trees, and below the crazily slanting mountains, bushes and trees all the little gems half buried in a slippery silt, as if the flow of the water had discovered a sunken treasure, brightly colored arrowheads, axes, peacepipe fixtures, as yet all un-manufactured—the raw material of a stone culture, the proud stuff of the phantom drummer of the lake and casting over it all, over the reflected, layered escarpments, over the faint tiny rock flowers, little bits of bright blue, scarlet, and gold, fool's gold, the reflected sky and the mysterious shadows of unseen birds, wind-caught leaves, swaying lazy branches and Jimmy wondered where was Marsayas: had he fallen so far behind in this amazing world, was all this sudden glare and shadow too much to be accepted, was he no longer any part of it, that could flow with it all at will, or without will, without the consultation with will, as Jimmy imagined the red shadows who were men and women that had flashed here once had been able to do? But those men and women had had to fight the chaos around them, too.

Then Jimmy saw Marsayas, as he came wading knee-deep in water around the long bend and he was standing on a rock his arms akimbo and breathing hard; Jimmy could see his back heave; he turned toward Jimmy and motioned and pointed up through the trees and Jimmy followed his gaze and saw deeply hidden a small cabin grayed by weather.

Marsayas grinned and pointed. "A poet!" he called and turned to his task of getting from one rock to another, the mountain goat.

Again they came upon a small waterfall with a sharp declivity and they had to work their way around it up the steep embankment of black mud and moss. Their feet and fingers ripped and upheaved the fine smooth moss as they scurried, a bit fearful of taking a long uncontrollable slide backwards and on to the jutting rocks and then they were able to drop down again into the cool water at the top of what Marsayas said he thought was the penultimate fall and the mud was washed from their feet and Jimmy dipped his hands in the water and rinsed the mud from his knees.

The water here was only about four inches deep but stepping into it he was alarmed by its pressure and for an instant thought it might overtopple him and send him headlong down the fall to crack his head on the rocks below, but he was learning already that to deal with nature one must relax: it is the only "safe" way, Marsayas said.

Marsayas was teaching him not to fight the stone under his bruised feet but to put down a foot with all its muscles loose and to let it find its shape on the earth: otherwise it wouldn't be accepted and rejection was the danger. How much of this damned chaotic world was he fated to endure?

Had he begun sliding down the muddy bank he should have forced himself to relax, to go limp and to accept his fate and he was already winning a faith that helped him believe that he should have merely slid over those jutty rocks like a piece of mossy mud and gone on sliding down and down and down the great fall under the bridge and meandered, making with his body some mystic hieroglyphs in the water, until he fell gently into the lake without hurt.

He might have passed Joan and the baby and called good-bye to them. He might have been ushered into that dark frothy water by low drums at twilight. Would life be so bad? Life? Life without Lani?

But now Marsayas and Jimmy came upon an exceedingly long and narrow place which, except for the fact that it was all moss and stone and gurgling, rushing water and the fact that it was so terribly deep a trench in the high mountains, reminded Jimmy of one of those canals that city workmen dig in which to lay pipe for sewers (he'd had first-hand knowledge of such labor) and he felt like a workman on break as he and Marsayas sat, panting, and smoked a cigarette and looked up the long alley at the fall there, perhaps a hundred yards ahead and Marsayas said, "Here, take a swig of this." He unbuttoned the pocket on his shorts and withdrew a little flask. "It's Doctor Brazil's spiritual potion—made with herbs right from the Amazon. Smoother'n peyote, more friendly than L.S.D." He handed the flask to Jimmy.

"Sure." Jimmy drank. They passed the flask back and forth and sat awhile, listening to the splashing waters, soaking the sun. Light seemed to bounce from the multifoliate greens surrounding them and streak back upward toward the radiant sky.

"What do you think, Jim? Should we keep on going?"

Jimmy didn't know what it was that made him sense the larger fall beyond the smaller, perhaps it was some accurate unconscious reading of the lay of the land, or something vibratory in the rocks, but it seemed something else which he was forced to say was a kind of indescribable sensation.

Jimmy sensed a great booming mystery that was also a sort of magical silence beyond and he said, "Yes, let's go on. Yes, he thought to himself, I'm going on. The word "yes" felt like a mantra and he found himself thinking or saying "yes, yes, yes!"

This was a treacherous place, for the water was deep and rushing with great, foaming force down its narrow confines and there was just moss-slippery rock edging steeply up into the thickest bramble and tangle of green life Jimmy could remember ever having seen: but somehow they found their way onto a wide open flat place and the water was gentle again, almost still but for a slight observable upper purling, a rippling and it was all open here, wide and open again and Jimmy felt as if he had been in a tunnel and was now out again in the open.

But there was yet a sense of being low. It must have been due to the sense of height ahead, because they were already quite high up. They had come nearly two miles steadily upward and that was from a high place itself.

Yes, the feeling of being low must have been because of the great height Jimmy sensed ahead. Or because of the mountains rising all around him: or because the azure and pink-streaked sky still seemed to be so high above. He had an image of men casting for trout with long, flexible poles, men with wading boots and colorful flies pinned all over their hats: pipes in their mouths. And when he looked up Marsayas was gone—gone again!

And for all Jimmy had learned his feet were badly bruised, cut even and he would have been limping had he been walking on soft grass, so he had to take ridiculous delicate little steps, like a baby's steps and he'd probably be left so far behind he'd be ashamed to be such a tenderfoot.

And Jimmy wondered, with his Zen Master, what were the punishments of them that serve the Evil One, of those who cannot make their living except through violence to Being. And he saw Marsayas, ahead, standing in the center of a great open place and the water up to his knees and he pointed up, crying over the natural sounds "Look! Look!"

And Jimmy took one last look at his poor wretched feet to see that they were well placed on the slippery-as-ice rocks and looked up to where Marsayas pointed and saw an over-awing escarpment circling round them in deep beautiful folds of rock and placed them in a kind of canyon.

And his feet slipped and up they went most idiotically into the air and down he went plunging and thrashing and laughing like a fool, but he kept his plaid slouch hat that Marsayas had given him above the water and a bit of his fore-head and he came up making an absurd joke of how the beauty of the place had knocked him over and Marsayas at first afraid Jimmy had hurt himself began to laugh and Jimmy looked in his hat and best of all his smokes were still dry, and so he scampered on in the sun drying off and caught up with

Marsayas and right around a bend in this enormous place—there was the waterfall.

They pulled themselves up on some rocks and Marsayas lit a joint and passed it to Jimmy. They looked around and Jimmy thought I must never let the details of this quest blur in memory. I must get right back to Marsayas's ramshackle old cabin and scribe the magic of it all. Oh—

The waterfall came down for a hundred feet or more, then hit an odd rock and fell out like an opening fan across itself; so it was like two falls, one down, one crossing that, like translucent lovers entwined and undulating and above them, below a deep blue twilit heaven, a great cliff hung, weighted with trees.

Jimmy knew a mystic place when he saw one; a tabernacle. He saw a cloud. "It looks like an Indian chief," he said, panting. "See, he's in full regalia."

Marsayas said, "What's that strand?"

"It's a peace pipe," said Jimmy.

* * *

Back at the old creaky car, in the shade, Joan and little Marsayas had been waiting. She'd been listening to the radio. As Jimmy and Marsayas approached, she called to them:

"I've just heard about what the fascists have done to a bunch of kids at Kent State! It's all over the radio! There was a protest. The National Guard shot them!"

Jimmy, climbing into the back seat, said, " Hell, the National Guard don't know how to shoot."

Marsayas said, "It was the morons in charge that told them to shoot." He slid into the driver's seat, turned the dashboard knob, and leaned his head toward the radio. "The bastards shot a bunch of kids—a frosh—"

"What's a frosh?" said Joan.

"A freshman—one of 'em, the stupid kid." Marsayas was red-faced with anger. "Apparently, there's no limit to

Nixon's thuggery. The goddamned bomb people want us to keep a flag up at half-staff forever!"

*   *   *

After returning to the city, Jimmy tried to work on his script, but was distracted by the Kent State massacre which filled the media. The abbreviation "frosh" that Marsayas had used for "freshman" played in his ear. As the open window next to him blew him traffic horn salutes, he caught a rhythm. He thought of the poem he had begun to write as a dirge— "Dirge for the Dead Students."

> She'd only come to look
> When bullets broke her flesh
> A frosh, she held a book
> > When bullets broke her flesh
> > With almost wistful sighs
> > Her face was round and fresh
> With almost wistful sighs
> The bullets raped her body
> With almost wistful sighs
> > They pierced her gentle body
> > And her book dropped open to
> > A page all torn and bloody
> Her book dropped open to
> A torn and bloody page
> Containing nothing new
> > A torn and bloody page
> > Each child must learn to read
> > A "History of Our Age"
> Each child must learn to read
> O study, students, study
> This "History of Greed"
> > O study, students, study
> > Learn what they want from you
> > Another age as bloody

Is what they want from you
Another age befouled
And nothing else will do
    Another age befouled
    By Great-Granddaddy's Greed
    (No wonder Ginsberg Howled!)
O Great-Granddaddy's Greed
Sucks, like a Vampire Bat,
The blood of his living seed
    Sucks, like a Vampire Bat
    The blood of our youth away
    Sucks, like a cornered rat,
The Pestilence of Our Day
And spits into our faces
The horrors of Our Day
    And spits into our faces
    Spreading disease and death
    That virus among the races
Spreading disease and death
Destruction throughout the world
With its maddening murderous breath
    Destruction throughout the world
    That Malthusian explanation
    Picture the bombs being hurled
That Malthusian explanation
And a baby crying for shelter
While the Senate is on vacation
    And a baby crying for shelter
    And her mother and father dead
    And the bombs dropping helter-skelter
And her mother and father dead
And the President making decisions
(Who will his daughter wed?)
    And the President making decisions
    Search and Destroy is the way

And the President making revisions
Destroy all their crops on the way
And the baby is blown to pieces
While the President goes to pray
  And the baby is blown to pieces
  While the President speaks to God
  And the rich collect rent on their leases
While the President speaks to God
And the students are shot for complaining
And the Haves of the world think it odd
  That the students (who Have) are complaining
  (These children have so much to learn!)
  And the government's busy explaining
For these children have so much to learn
In double-talk tripled twice over
How we keep what we get when we earn
  In double-talk tripled twice over
  How Ends do all Means justify
  In News-Speak all wrapped up in clover
How Ends do all Means justify
And death to the man who denies it
So, hush up, dear students, or die!
  For death comes to him who denies it
  As many dead children could tell
  And praise to the bastard who buys it
As many dead children could tell
And four dead students provided
A proof in the sun when they fell
  These four dead students provided
  Us all with a living example
  That day in the sun when they tried it
Gave us proof and a living example
Of what the "Great" in their greed are about
And four dead students are ample
  To show what the State is about

(Christ, any one baby who died
Should have left us no shadow of doubt!)
Now four young students have died
Shot dead in the name of the law
(But in fact for the lies they denied)
SHOT DEAD IN THE NAME OF THE LAW
FOR THE TERRIBLE TRUTH THAT THEY SAW.

Lani and Jimmy tried to live a normal domestic life, stayed away from others, whom Jimmy said always and only caused chaos—"Mice on a mudball!"—and shortly thereafter, they were married by a Justice of the Peace. And so things were when Fay telephoned to say that she had won a settlement on Elliot's case; and not a bad one, considering that he didn't have many working years ahead of him when he was killed. In fact, his working years were over, but nobody knew that for certain but Jimmy and Fay. But five other men were killed in that fire, so the insurance company was glad to settle out of court, rather than have six widows to face up to, and a jury that would be sympathetic to them.

Jimmy met Fay at the Port Authority bus station and brought her home to his and Lani's apartment, where Lani was preparing a version of sweet-and-sour Hawaiian pork, with all the trimmings, even poi, to impress her mother-in-law. Fay was wearing a whole new outfit—suit, hat, gloves, purse, shoes, the works—and looked like the Merry Widow herself.

"I've wanted to meet you for so long," she said. "Jimmy, she's exquisite. Do you know who you look like?" she said to Lani. "You look just like that movie star—you know, the one who played Suzie Wong."

"Thank you very much," said Lani. "Nancy Kwan is a beautiful girl. I'm flattered, but I think she's Eurasian. I'm Hawaiian."

"Are Hawaiians Americans? I mean, I know Hawaii is a state now, but does that mean that native Hawaiians are Americans?"

"Born and raised," said Lani, laughing.

"And you two have known each other since Jimmy was stationed in Hawaii, haven't you?"

"Since we were both a lot younger," said Jimmy.

"Well," said Fay, "I can't wait to see my first grandchild. Now what have you called him? I couldn't get it quite straight."

"Semper Fi Butterworth Whistler," said Jimmy, leading Fay into the little living room.

Fay looked blank. She shook her head. "What is Semper whatever? Is that an Hawaiian name?"

"It's Latin for always faithful. It's the Marine motto, Mom."

"Well, Jimmy, if that isn't the strangest . . . well, what is the Butter, Butter—what is that other . . . "

"We named him for an old buddy in the Marine Corps. Butterworth."

"Well that's a nice . . . clear name. Can I see him?"

They took her into the bedroom to see Semper Fi. Fay stood and stared at the baby for a long time. Then she said, "Well, he's adorable. He looks like both of you. Isn't that strange? I mean, the blond hair and the brown skin—it's, well, it's striking. What a beautiful little boy. And look at those big brown eyes! Oh, look, he's smiling. He's smiling at his grandma."

She leaned down toward the crib. "Yes, you know it's your grandma, don't you?" Semper Fi gurgled and sputtered spit. He was a happy little tot.

After eating, Fay said, "Now let me tell you my other news. Not only have I got some money, but I've met a wonderful man." It seemed that she'd met a man in a bar over in Plainfield, a charming man, and good-looking, by her lights.

He was a construction worker a bit younger than she, and drank like a fish, but he was lots of fun, she said, an Irishman. Was she thinking of getting married?

"God, no!" But she didn't intend to sit around doing nothing the rest of her life, or to join the Golden Age Club either. It seemed that this gentleman friend of hers worked in Florida in the winters, and she thought she might go down there with him on his next trip. "I always wanted to see Florida," she said. What did Aunt Myrtle and Uncle O'Toole think about all this? "Oh, they think I'm terrible. They think I'm a loose woman."

"Uncle O'Toole has a Victorian viewpoint," said Jimmy to Lani.

"I told him," Fay said, "just because I'm in my sixties doesn't mean that I have to sit around waiting to die. Everybody takes me for much younger, anyway. And as your father used to say—when he was sober, that is—life was meant to be lived." Her half-blind eyes were blurred away by tinted glasses.

AFTER

God knew because somebody had to know. You begin to think that way as middle age oozes out of your skin and knocks some of the hair off your head. Know what? Where we all went, he guessed. Fay was the last of them. He had had to fly from Hawaii to Florida to attend her funeral, now he was flying back. Well, she was pretty old. "Better off dead," his step-father had said. "She couldn't see to watch television or to read a newspaper, with the macular degeneration. But she still tried to watch your show. I had to read your name on the credits. That always gave her a kick. Written by James Whistler. She loved that. It made her a little bit of a celebrity. And when you were written up in the Orlando papers, I had to cut the pieces out and put them in a frame, even though she couldn't see them. And her hearing! We got her a new hearing aid with the money you sent, but the hearing expert said they had reached the top level and she still couldn't hear much. You'd have to shout. My throat would ache with shouting at her. And the colostomy was a terrible problem. I read the instructions to her, but she never wore it right. She'd leave the belt loose all day and night, so it would just hang there and pull at her skin as it filled up. She had to have her skin treated a number of times. But you couldn't tell her anything. She couldn't seem to learn—or wouldn't. I used to get so pissed at her, I'd have to go out to a bar to cool off. Yeah, I think she's better off now that it's all over. Want a cold one?"

"The Wizard of Oz," thought Jimmy. "All the wonderful things she does. All the wonderful things she did, I mean." He felt the plane lift off from Los Angeles. She hadn't been alone though. Aunt Myrtle and Uncle O'Toole had moved to Orlando and they had been in close proximity to one another for nearly twenty years, had grown old and enfeebled together and had all died at nearly the same time. But Aunt

Myrtle had paid her own way into the earth; Fay, on the other hand, had set nothing aside with which to take care of her last expenses. Jimmy looked out over the vast Pacific and remembered his first trip across to Japan on that troop transport so many years ago, out of La Jolla to Kobe, where he was surprised to see a huge neon Coca-Cola sign near the dock. That was only nine years after the atomic bombs had been dropped on Hiroshima and Nagasaki. When they were dropped, his grandmother had stood on her back stoop and said that she had heard that nobody would be able to live in those places for a hundred years.

He remembered looking up at her—he was about ten—and feeling terror at the thought of such a horrible thing; but only nine years later, there he was, in Kobe, standing on deck, watching a blinking Coca-Cola sign. Was life strange, or wasn't it? Anyway, the first thing that his step-father had said to him was that he needed money to pay for Fay's funeral and plot. He laughed a little to himself. She had done it to him one last time. Several thousand dollars. He wrote the check. He wrote another check for his step-father, without being asked. After all, he had plenty of money, thanks to real estate investments alone. He had followed his bliss as a writer like a rainbow to the pot of gold. The television serial, set in that green paradise, and several mystery novels had done it. "Act the way you want to be and soon you'll be the way you act." He had taken that advice from a carnival machine and it had worked.

Fay was the last of the past. He took out a notebook and pen and began to scribble. Notes for a Memoir, he wrote. What did he want to say, high in the sky? What should he say of a poet gone wrong? What should he say of a successful television writer? Now he had money enough to protect him so that he could be a poet. And now because he had the money, he wondered was he still a poet? He looked out at constantly shifting, but now dark and gloomy ocean miles below and he wondered what had ever happened. The past was so exciting. He was dull. He had sold out and then it was over. When he was young, pain or not, it was fun to be alive, to be challenging the world. He tried to remember when he was young, and poor, a shoeshine boy, the poem he wrote about Lola Albright, when he shined the movie star's shoes. He remembered being a Western Union boy and getting his family out of a basement. Should he write about that? Or maybe when he was a candy butcher at Minsky's Burlesque. Or when he was a young Marine and first met Lani, or when he met Vera, his dancing negative. Or when he met Marsayas, his greatest friend? Should he put this stuff in a book? He scribbled on. Would this stuff make something worth reading? The plane bounced. It startled him out of his reverie. And now . . . and now he paused, lit a cigarette, caught at the sleeve of a passing stewardess, and ordered another Scotch. He belonged to Alcoholics Anonymous, and he had given several of his AA friends his promise that he would not let go while on this sad trip, but, what the hell, why should he keep his word? Who ever kept his or her word to him? Nobody, not even Lani, not even his Undine of paradisal pools. The stewardess brought him his Scotch and he held it, studying its flickering iodine color. Alcoholics on both sides of the family, wasn't the stuff in his genes? Wasn't there some deep-seated weakness in him, something he had never been able to rid himself of, despite his best efforts? And yet, he had not done so badly with his life, the upstart son of a downstart father, as Shaw had called himself, he was a respected writer. But he was finally alone. He was alone up here above the clouds, the tops of which now looked like a red-gold desert with the sun beating down on them, alone up here, and alone down there in chaotic paradise, for, after nearly ten years of blissful marriage to Sweet Leilani herself, and two children, the boys, Semper Fi and the second one they called Aquarius, he had been left for another man, an Hawaiian television producer, who had more time for her because he shared in and supported her career in television. Well, Jimmy could see her tonight—on the news. He could see her every night on the news. And he could see Lani anytime, if he asked her to see him, because they were still friends—because they still had their youth in common: the days of splashing about on the beach behind her village, days of innocence.

With the years, he had come to realize something about himself, that, from the earliest days of his life, it seemed, he had been trying to hold on to innocence, and later to recapture it. And despite all the evils of life he had been witness to, he still pursued innocence, a pursuit that others of his age had long since dropped. His cynicism was only skin-deep, a protective armor. Or, to put it another way, deep inside the tough guy the poet was still struggling to get out. What was it about? It was about a dream. It was about a dream called Aquarius. It was about innocence. He sat there way above the planet and wrote a poem called "Aquarius."

We dreamed the Golden Age
we wanted you to be,
our long hair hanging loose
and blowing in the wind,
our beads, our sandals,
jingling, flapping on our
feet, our feet encrusted
with good Woodstock mud,
smoking a joint, and nodding,
wordless, for it seemed we had
no words with which to
get beyond the chaos of the
conscience back in that time
of undeclared and endless war,
and back to Batman, Robin,
and the Joker's gang, where

Good was understandable,
for not at all complex,
and Evil slunk away,
its lesson learned.

And, thinking of those days reminded him that he would like to ask his sons—Semper Fi and Aquarius—to join him on a trip to Washington to see the new Viet Nam Wall Memorial and perhaps trace Butterworth's name.

He had a cottage and a garden now and he could go out to the garden and lie down under the trees and dream and read poetry and write poetry as he had always wanted to do. And he had found that he did not mind being alone with himself. He agreed with himself, even if no one else did. And it cheered him to think that he would be there in only a few more hours—if the plane didn't crash or go into sad lonely eternal geosynchronous orbit.

LAST POEMS

of

JAMES WHISTLER

THE SHADE

I would rejoin myself, deserted long ago,
that wandering shade somewhere in its separate time.
They say that the spirit hovers above the body while we
  sleep
and if we awaken suddenly we are dazed until it returns.
I would rejoin my earliest remembrance and start anew.
Travelling warily all roads,
I would be a dangerous companion for the unwary,
a disturbance in the calm weather of thought.
But that shade, transparent as an angel fish,
luminous at night as the moon on a mote of dust,
O, the lost bodiless distant song of that shade!
What wilderness of calm does it wander
bravely seeking the way home to chaos?

DARK CANZONE

Considerate la vostra semenza . . .
—*Dante*

From when some wandering primate first discovered
that vocal cords had formed within its throat:
when thorax wind was blown, and it discovered
a modulation of its grunts, discovered
it had a tongue that could articulate
more subtly than it had presumed; discovered,
in fact, its ur-humanity; discovered
that it was different from monkeys, wiser,
and could communicate a plan; was wiser,
one than the other, in this gift; discovered,
in short, itself as special being, poet,
it sang in lamentation for the poet,
O felt itself the oddest ape, a poet,
and, with the weight of what it knew, discovered
the truest nature of itself as poet,
that it must bear the burden of the poet,
harsh bile of truth that rises in the throat
and burns the vocal cords of every poet.
For meaning murders innocence, the poet
learns, word by word; and to articulate
as in a grammar, to articulate
as words demand, and so to be a poet
is to be that most special being, stranger
than any other animal—but wiser?
It felt itself the strangest thing, much stranger
than any other animal—a poet—
for words had made it thuswise stranger.
But was it better being this much wiser?
What had this primate after all discovered?
Who really thinks it's better to be wiser?

Who doesn't know it's sadder to be wiser?
Who envies words blown through a poet's throat?
What poet hasn't wished to cut its throat?
If grammar makes for meaning, is it wiser
to be a special being, to articulate
the truth words find—or not articulate?
It may be braver to articulate,
to be an animal, yet strangely wiser,
but is it wisdom to articulate
the grunts of animals, articulate
from them the existential life of poet
among the primates, to articulate—
syntactically commanded—articulate
the place in nature that we have discovered,
the death in nature that we have discovered?
Grunt one last grunt! Enough! Articulate
no more! Oh, envy nothing from the throat
of any poet! Let it cut its throat!
Oh, let the primate poet cut its throat
before it's forced on to articulate,
by sending lamentations through its throat,
from its self-fabled heart and out its throat,
how truly sad it is to be a little wiser
than other animals that have a throat
but have no vocal cords within that throat
which they can use to make themselves a poet
who sings the lamentations of a poet,
a sadder wiser primate prophet poet,
whose ordered language has at last discovered
what happy animals have not discovered . . . .
What is it animals have not discovered,
which leaves them happier than any poet?
The ordered thought of death! It might be wiser
for nature never to articulate.

THE WAR OF THE NINE AND THE SIX

Jane Goodall tells of the Nine and the Six,
the Chimps' War,
of how a tribe of fifteen male chimps
divided, Nine and Six,
and made new camps.

The Nine, she writes, because stronger
numerically, attacked
the Six, several to one,
isolating, murdering each of them,
until there were none.

These had been sons and fathers,
friends and brothers,
but had become two nations,
sniffing at borders—
foreign relations.

NOW, THE FOX!

We suffer from reminiscences . . .
— Karl Menninger

A thousand times I've had this urban dream &
asked a doctor what it meant
 to no avail. "It was the city's grip on
an impressionable child,"
 one doctor told me. I was dropped once down a
hellish, pitch-black pit, a deep
 dumbwaiter shaft, & fell a floor before I
landed, more or less intact.
 I bear a scar above my eye. Could that be
it, dropped by a drunken man,
 a family friend, when I was still an infant?
Meaning harmlessly to play,
 he swore off drink, I'm told. In any case I
have these nightmares constantly,
 & doubt if they will ever go away. Waking,
after one, I'm shaken to
 the bone. I live now in the country, where I
hoped to find diminishment
 of terror, over time. But here's the strange part:
rabies is a major threat
 here in the country in the summer—dogs &
cats can get it from the wild-
 life teeming in the woods—& just the other
night I dreamed a foaming fox
 that chased me back into the cityscape I
hoped so much to free myself
 from, years before, by coming to the country.
Waking horror brought me new
 concern for peace of mind & where to find it.

NO

The world says No.
It has a genius for No.
Everything is No.
In the beginning was Yes
but the world says No.
By the world I mean the people.
The people No.
The people say No.
Authority says No.
Power says Yes to itself
but No to everyone else: it says No.
The police say No.
Sometimes, assuredly,
it is necessary to say No.
But I say No,
it is not always necessary to say No.
When the new child wishes
someone always says No.
When the dog barks
at his own wagging tail,
someone says No.
When the cat runs sideways,
his back up, playing,
someone says No,
you'll break the lamp.
The world says No.
When someone has a new idea,
the world says No.
The world likes to say No.
No means I know better.
No means I am stronger.

No means I am Yes and No.
The world says No.
The people say No.
Authority says No.
Power says No.
The police say No.
The teacher says No.
Love might even say No.
No is the genius of the world.

THE SOULS

Outside on a green lawn a giant water-oak conducts a
    sunset.
    Some unsteady hum has summoned us out of our houses.
My ancient lady friend, who lives nearby, is jawing now,
    and wears
    an awed-holy expression as she says they are souls, yes
        sir.
And they are everywhere, they wade the dusky clouds, they
    are
    giant black-winged fruits hanging, falling, bouncing. The
        green
is black with them. And neighbors stare; they worry for
    their

cars and pickups. If they get into the red berries, it's hell on
    paint. Shoot them. No, they are beautiful. They are a
        menace.
Look out below! They rise and wheel, kaleidoscopic, inside
    rings
    of themselves. They set themselves against the sky, black
        on blue.
They caw. They are telling themselves, or us, something.
    They caw and caw, and what is it they are saying, so
earpiercingly, holes through your eardrums, through your
    brain,

as if lasered? Then they settle again, like a black blizzard
    of huge coal flakes. The souls come back to visit us, to
        tell
us that they know everything now. Now their sharp yellow
    beaks
    pierce the lawn. They are busier than worms, in a feast
of famishment, an ecstasy of appetite. Now, she says,

the nonagenarian, I'll soon be with them, and then
it's always now for me like them. The souls have found
    their

bodies. I don't know which is which, but somewhere, there,
    is everyone who died, all the loved ones, and even the
        others,
the ones that nobody loved, they are all there now, she says.
    I stare as deep as I can see. They are every blessed
place—on roofs, looking down, in trees, on bushes, under,
    over, and around. Some seem to be waiting, some tug
at the turning-emerald lawn in the lowering light: and now

how do they know to rise suddenly, and become one wide
    black wing? How do they know to circle and circle in
        unison,
one boomerang black wing composed of so many blood-
    beating,
    sky-rowing black wings? How do they know when it's
        time
to fly along a horizon, rimmed with rising red? The souls,
    they know, they know! I think it must be out of some
        distant
folklore that the old lady speaks, eyes fixed, waving them
    goodbye.

COPPERHEADS

The New York Draft Riots

Vanish these walls, vanish this wealth, with visionary
   eyes that see
back to hot July 1863. Vanish where wealth shines
   shopping on Fifth
Avenue, five minutes from the lion-braced library,
   where I turn down
my book. Vanish these great, gray walls, to see when
   this mirage
was another, of a white-winged building housing
   motherless humanity.
Try to see out of the eyes of two hundred frightened
   black orphans

and their saviors, or, better, the eyes of one little girl
   under her bed,
who is to be beaten to sleep and burned alive. They
   come now, the first,
malignant rumble of mobs is heard. A giant, bearing a
   huge American flag,
appears. Ten thousand men and women follow. They
   shout: *NO DRAFT*;
shout: *KILL THE NIGGERS*! One mob of ten thousand,
   among many mobs,
one mad mob, is coming; Copperheads coming; but
   Mary doesn't know

what they are. Snakes, she is told; and, people like
   snakes. Snakes?
What does it mean?   But behind them the sky is red, as
   if the sun had
set in broad day, as if it had hit the earth and bounced
   back to the sky

in cones of flame, like upward teeth, serrating the
    downward, hot blue.
The fireworks for the Fourth, a week before, had shaken
    her.
Looking everywhere, she saw no arms to hold her.
    BOOM BOOM!

Now again—*BOOM BOOM!* But this is wilder, worse.
    She caps her ears,
her eyes rolling for a mother, while the giant bearing
    Old Glory juts
his lantern jaw toward the white-winged building where
    she hides terror
in tears, holding her braided, ribboned head as, between
    her ten-year-old
fingers, distorted clangor of malignant mob-voice
    penetrates with
curses and screams of coves and harpies, liquored-up
    looters, drink-mad,

blood-mouthed molls, ill-wind-shifted, now, toward
    Mary in the white-winged
Colored Orphan Asylum on Fifth Avenue, the ghost-
    building, inside tall
wealth, that I can reach in five minutes from this great,
    gray library,
close my book and walk out into the Fifth Avenue
    festival of limousines
and be inside of its smoldering, ectoplasmic doors with
    the orphan children,
who are always poorest, with Mary, who hides under
    her bed, her eyes

spraying terror, shutting her ears to the Fourth of July
    or, now,

a week later, to the flag-bearing giant leading a mob
    through the present
affluent Fifth Avenue shoppers to *BOOM BOOM KILL
    THE NIGGERS*
NO DRAFT KILL, outside the library window on Fifth
    Avenue, inside of,
behind, through, the tremendous modern traffic stalled
    at red, frustrated,
Manhattan-honking. *KILL!* Mary sees feet, fast feet.
    She doesn't

understand that the children are being herded out to
    safety, to
Blackwell's Island on the East River. Mary sees feet
scurry by her bed, sees a watery world, like one sub-
    merged, when she
looks out. Then, above her bed, something huge and
    malignant appears,
something too big. An evil thing! She will not come out
    from under, she will
not, as the white-winged building shakes like her body
    with battering

and the doors are pulled from their hinges. Mary tries
    to find her mother
inside of herself, and finds an entrance and a dark hall.
    She goes in,
finds herself upright, her legs steady under her. She
    pats the bodice
of her pink dress, straightens her pink ribbon—for she
    knows her mother
waits at the end of the dark hall—as the giant lifts her to
    the sky—
knows a door will open at the end of the dark hall—and
    dashes her ten-

year-old body down. Great doors open, her mother
    shimmers with beauty,
with long, strong, brown open arms. In fury at his loss,
    the giant howls
after the escaping orphans, and flames rise up around
    him as he moves,
touching, touching the pitiful beds of orphans, touching
    and torching,
his small mad head hissing, spitting curses upon
    Lincoln, the top-
hatted ape, and Greeley, and niggers, niggers, for his
    tongue would fork

with curses if it could, as the white-winged asylum
    crumbles
in flames inside of the facades of now with its *BEEP
    BEEP* of prosperity.
As if the great library walls had vanished, as if the
    market values of now,
with their multi-millions of construction, were trans-
    parent, there
stands the Colored Orphan Asylum, and there inside is
    Mary, hiding under
her bed. Mary and the flag-bearing giant. Mary and the
    mad mob. I lean

back in my library chair and push up my glasses. I am
    trying to see more
clearly. I think I don't understand any more than Mary
    did,
as the lion-braced library walls form around me again,
    shutting me off
from my shopping, struggling fellow Americans on
    Fifth Avenue, outside,

who cannot see the white-winged Colored Orphan
   Asylum as they pass it.
But I know that all hurts must be outlived as humanity
   presses forward.

CHRONICLE

Out of the mustard tang that filled my mouth
with the vivid day once when wind
brought itself riffling through my short golden mane
like the hand of God being the cub's mother's tongue
came that time when life was endless wonder
and listening to the wind take away laughter
as a chime with wings as little silver
stars afloat like darting butterflies
as sipping hummingbirds at one long meal
within that wind on such wide wings
as monarchs never know nor hummingbirds
but boys and girls flying their youth
wantonly was my dear time wasted
and now it is bells for a stopped watch
where I have ground my teeth out
my novel of ten thousand pages
empty as my mouth.

OLD WOMEN, PAUSING

Old women, pausing, standing midblock on a hill
or midlevel on subway steps, waiting for breath,
their shopping bags hanging from toughened hands,
their eyes back in girlhood, perhaps, or ahead,
on the next meal, the contents of the bags
cooked and served, their honor again earned,
exist away from where they are, the grade or incline
slowly flattening, reversing, as their hearts calm
and their breath comes slower, more peacefully;
and so they stand, with the stillness of statues,
black-coated, black-shod, eyes straight ahead,
wisps of pale hair riffling slightly with the breeze,
waiting for breath, ahead of or behind where they are.
—So all of us, ahead of or behind where we are
or separated from what we are, not complete,
having left part of ourselves behind,
not having done that which we hoped to do,
not having attained to that which we hoped to attain,
all like old women, standing midblock on a hill,
waiting for breath, ahead of or behind where we are.

THOSE WHO DIE IN THEIR SLEEP

When the mind is wakeful
and the eyes are shut,
ears buried in their pillows
hear the song and
then it fades behind them
as on a distant shore,
and some drown then
and can never hear again
the song of the dreaming mind
singing its own mystery,
but now the song of the non-
life of the non-mind, of
the stars wheeling to Nowhere,
of time ending, snuffing out
the stars, one by one, the song
of all that has never known
of its own existence.

WHERE ARE YOU?

>*to Leilani*

What life does to us
is strange, too strange,
I suppose, for many to
think about. But I
think about it, about
how you were here,
right here with the
rest of us, and now
are not, are gone into
the ground and maybe
are waving in the grass,
or are sitting silent
there, being the rock,
or are looming up
and reaching out,
being the tree, or are
drifting easily down
the street, being
the leaves burning
and the smoke.

Where are you?
You cannot not be anywhere.
I want you to come back;
but you can't, I know.
I can fan the air
with my hands and
do no good. I was
sitting here, right here,
with you, and you were

436

saying or doing something
and I was not attending,
I was thinking my own
thoughts, but what
are they now? I
should have listened
deeply to you. I
should have recorded
your voice in my mind,
so that I could hear you
again and again until
I myself am smoke.

OLD CHORISTERS

Singers
of our generation
are turning up
dead. A serial
killer
is injecting
them
with cancer
heart disease
and stroke.
This police
silhouette
of the killer
isn't made
of his head,
but of his
twisted mind,
made
of a brain
to answer
for his crimes
of torture
perpetrated
on so many
choristers.
With a rough
cat-tongue
he licked flesh
from bones
and made
the other
mercy-kill
to make
amends.
Look,
from
a high bridge,
as highway god,
he drops
stones on old bones!
Even the sap
of trees is worried
up the trunk
as the killer
waits
for an autumnal
weariness of
leaves.
I am
Time's agent
his tool
he brags.
Singers
of our generation
think that this
is a serial crime,
but have
no choice
but to
become ringers
and to pull
the ropes
and toll
the bell.

A HUNDRED YEARS

Although the sea won't pose,
the picture that the boardwalk takes is clear.
In each ear, the old man says, he has a baby mouse
that squeals sometimes and makes the surf high-pitched.
A hundred years of being here, he says,
seems merely like a day, a day with many nights.
Once, he kept the old lighthouse, once, a tackle shop,
and once he was a fisherman himself, also selectman
   once,
but then he laughs and says he married twice.
Most of the Earth, he says, is sea,
most of a man is water,
and mother comes from *mare* and *meer* and others,
the sea we swim before our birth.
Once, too, he was a farmer,
and calved the cows inland, but not for long.
The sea must call him back, he must have the sea,
or the sea have him.
In a hundred years you learn a thing or two,
he says, but not so much as you might think.
Mostly it's the magic of it all.
You are born with that, you have that right away,
but then there's sex, and then there's all
that business in between that's meant to keep us going,
the race I mean, and you forget the magic
in the business, the busyness, he adds,
and you work hard, and you are tired a lot, and only see
   the sea,
as with your mind and not that sense the youngest have
that's gained again in age, when time's more free,
and you can feel the flow of life right on your skin.
You feel the wind, now, I don't doubt, but do you feel
the other thing? Do you feel the secret thing?

Do you feel the thing behind the wind?
Aldebaran was so bright last night,
I 'most could take it in my hand,
not so simple as a jewel, but a spiritual thing.
When I look at the sea, or at the stars at night,
I do not fear my hundred years as you might think.
They do not wish to go or stay.
They are always here with you and everything.

FLASHBACKS

You are doing something thoroughly mundane one day,
say, peeling carrots, and you are suddenly where
you once were while your hands go on with their work
and you are staring into the sun from under a shed
roof, where you and your other are arguing over
what you have done and now you remember that part,
the part of it that was about what you had done:
then you are wondering why you did it, what
ever possessed you to do such a stupid thing,
and it occurs to you as it has in a past you've
almost forgotten that you might have been arrested
for doing such a thing and no wonder that you and
your other argued over it, how could it have been
otherwise?
                Of course it was a terrible mistake
to have made: it was a wonder that your other stayed
with you, who had done such a thing, but in the shed
in the last light of evening you finally made up and
even now you experience the sweetness of the kiss
of forgiveness as if it were warming your lips as you
peel the last of the carrots and you remember what
you are supposed to be doing though it is difficult
to draw away from that moment in the sunset shed
that seems somehow to be happening as you stand
where you are: but then you realize that you have cut
yourself and are bleeding. You must bandage your finger.
You must wash the carrots and cook them. You must not
forget this event, you think, as you have so many others.

ELEGY FOR THE LEADER BIRD

This compass-headed bird,
>   dead-reckoning South in Fall,
arcing its bloody breast
>   above the roof and cawing
some kind of bold farewell
>   to higher air and leaderless
V'd fliers off on it,
>   was shot (we saw and heard),
and staggered in the sky,
>   dripping blood and guts
down on the lobstered roofers
>   working in the sun.
It sang its downfall swan
>   song silently, now, spread
its wings, and then, as silent
>   as its eyes, it lay
resting on the roof,
>   face up, and looked at clouds,
(and some sweet heaven we
>   could almost see); but soon
pain shook it like an angry
>   nurse, so one good roofer
struck head from body with
>   a spade, merciful severance,
and catwalked off, bloody
>   spade dragging on the tiles,
a man of dirty duty,
>   unlike the murderer
of song, the wanton boy-
>   in-man, who pellet-shot
the bird (the shot we heard);
>   and this once musical,
most bright and beautiful,
>   small dust was part of all.

THE NURSING HOME

There are more women than
men in the nursing home and
more men than old doctors.

Staff doctors visit once a
month. The few old men do
very little but sleep. Two

or three of them occasionally
gather outside in clear
weather for a smoke, which

is allowed them. I suppose
those in charge feel that
it can make no difference

now, and it brings the old
men a little pleasure. I
sit and chat with them

sometimes. Perhaps "chat"
is a bit too lively a word
to describe what passes for

conversation during these
puffing sessions. A lot
of low grunting goes on.

There is one old man who
is afflicted with bone
cancer and who says, in

high good humor, that his

guarantees have run out.
He was a travelling salesman

in women's wear, and still
remembers how much he loved
women. Many of the women

have become little girls
again. They carry dolls
about with them, mostly

rag-dolls, I suppose so
they can't injure themselves
when they squeeze them.

To see these toothless,
balding old ladies, frail
as twigs, clutching these dolls,

is heartbreaking. Oh, to love
something! It's still there.
It has been in them since

they were little and had dirty
knees and bows in their hair.
Some recognize me now, and,

when I give them a wave,
they wave back. It's a
wonderful feeling to make

contact, but it is difficult
to tell how much they know.
The care-givers are kind and
efficient. They are mostly

young, and apparently try
to imbue the old with some of

their zest for life, but
of course the old know all
that already--or knew and have

forgotten it. I wonder,
can the young reverse their
situations with the old

and see themselves looking up
at such fresh faces from the
vantage of bed or wheelchair

or walker? I am too young
to join the old here in the
nursing home, this metaphor

(or is it the tenor of a
metaphor?) for the last days,
but I am too old

to feel the buoyancy of the
young; so, at least for the
context of the nursing home,

I have arrived at yet another
awkward age. After visiting
my mother, who is only partly

present, I go out and sit
with the old men and have a
smoke. We hope for clear days.

THE LOSS

When the blackbird stood on the chimney and called,
poking her beak at the clear blue ice of the sky,
I watched from inside the frame of an old wooden house
across from the once two-chimneyed house where she stood,
heard her cry crack the ice of the sky that day
from the wrongest of chimneys, the wrongest.
The bricks lay scattered next to the house.
The big nest of hay had blown away.
The ugly babies now lived in the barn,
but for one, who had drowned in the well.

MEMENTO MORI

When these blow-dried twigs
finally fall, or are deracinated,
tangled in some last, accomplished comb,
or in the glib fingers of a lover
fine-boned and sharp-nailed enough

to play tweezers, the scarred skin
will gleam nakedly in the mirror,
burnished by sun and overhead bulb
and, quick as life, we shall have been
transformed into a meditative monk,

skull-capped and burnoosed, who
belongs to the Monastery of Maturity,
and bears on his weary shoulders,
silently, to his last small cell,
his own *memento mori*.

A PILE OF LEAVES

They lose their scent,
that freshness of
beginning, but
something replaces it,
some odor on the air
out of the eternal
olla podrida of
decay, a gift,
folded in dimensions
not yet understood,
tied with the
string theory,
bowed and ribboned
with a Monarch's
living wings. They
tap the earth,
dissolve into pure
spirit—of leaves,
of cells, of atoms
—and return,
bodiless angels,
to the place from which
all is projected,
where intelligent
spirits prepare
for new flight,
the old injuries
understood,
assimilated,
forgiven.

DEATH

What do I know about death?
It is a question one must
occasionally ask oneself
Death who are you what are you
No metaphor will do
because that is merely
a likening of one thing
to another thing, which
when it comes to death
is impossible, for
death being unknown
anything we should
choose would be
arbitrarily chosen
and therefore
would be a bad
metaphor nobody
being able to say
how close or distant
the vehicle
from the tenor
the subject being
death. How then
do we approach this
unsubject this
antisubject this
but you see
even here
is a metaphor
even here
we are at a loss
that we are asking
a question for which
the only answer
is death.

AT THE GATE

Between the greater-soul and fleshed reality are particles, the final tangible reaches of our thought, seeming like something singing out beyond the rugged tabletops of testable existence; and if we had eyes to see this outlandish world, we might see a swirling of mysterious cloudy forms, a blending of ourselves and our surroundings in a mystical dancing light, in salty jewels, our cloudy arms and hands would try to reach our cloudy chairs and sink and blend into a mad phantasmagoria and we should be afraid until we learned that we were part of it, our bodies swirling clouds of atoms. But what's important is that we would be seeing at the gate just beyond which is the home of Mystery, source of Soul, which is our truest life, our centrum, and now where would we be if we stepped forward, through the gate, through the mysterious clouds of unknowing? This makeshift shadowy world is metaphor, which is our chariot of choice, our light-inducting darkproof vehicle ready to ride the road and river of space and time, to deliver us from evil, which is all that isn't in the vision of the cloud-bodied hungry soul when it goes through the gate to the mystery of unanswering love, and we see from there how all things flow outward toward wisdom and back upon themselves toward joy and that love is always answering, is the cloud formed into self, which is others and all, at once.

BALLAD OF THE BURNT-OUT BARD

Old Duracell, old Mazda-man
you've got to keep the light—
it's growing dim inside you
but that's no time to hide you—
there's just a chance you might
say something shedding light.
Old candle-wick, old burnt-out bard
old hairy ears and snout,
you gouty worn-out lout—
oh, call yourself a name, old cuss—
because you weren't the best,
and yet you know it doesn't matter,
no, not in the stinking least.
　　Old geeze, don't lose your grip,
don't fall and break your hip—
you've got to keep the light, baldspot,
you've got to keep the light,
because there's just a Chinaman's chance
if you keep the light, old souse,
if you keep the light,
there's still a chance, though mad, mad, mad,
that there's something left to add.
　　You've got to keep the light, old piles,
you've got to keep the light.
You know you've been a dog,
oh, you've behaved like a *trayf* old hog,
but somehow in your life
you've had a loving wife,
so there must be something good about you,
you lousy lucky lout you—
all I ask of you, old dripping candle,
is just to keep the blessed light,
and show a flash of pluck, old duck,

and with a bit of luck
you might come up with something
worthy of the world that you've surveyed.
    You've been around so long now
you've got to hold some light,
whether hell or heaven
is waiting with its leaven
to galvanize you new again
for better or for worse,
old man of steel, who once pumped iron,
don't listen to that deathly siren,
you've got to keep the light a while,
you've got to keep that gap-toothed smile,
you've got to keep the light alive
inside your horrible old hide,
because you still might do a thing
that's worthy of its doing,
you've got to keep the light, old pipe,
you've got to keep the light.
    You've written many a poem, old bard,
and published many too,
but I've got news for you, old bard,
I've got news for you—
you haven't any right, old cough,
not to keep the light.
You don't get off like that, old shakes
slide off the roof like that—
there's plenty time to die, old guy,
plenty time to die,
so keep on humping light, old bard,
pumping, pumping light!

SONNET: THE BOSNIAN CHERRY

> *. . . the explosion appears to have*
> *shocked the tree into blossom.*
> *—Reuters*

Friends, look with faithless unbelieving eyes
upon this miracle the bomb has wrought,
as now, in shocked conversion, I tell you
of spring against the devastated skies
of winter war, the hopelessness war brought,
and how, enveloped in explosive blue
of acrid smoke, this tree could still devise
beyond predictability. It caught
the shell's enormous heat, and grew
fluid with sap, miraculous with surprise
of spring, for all combatants to be taught
anew a faith unlearned by deathly cries,
a blossoming the human heart has sought
with every hopeful spring—a sweet-Peace Prize.

HOUDINI AND THE DYING SWAN

Where was he? Was it a tunnel?
But he had come to a wall,
a slimy, wormy wall.
He must break through.
He must break out.
He felt for a tool.

Naked, she lay back in the tub,
white as a white swan, long-necked
as a swan, thin as a silken thread,
her gloriously thick dark hair
piled loosely up, collapsing
onto her wide, sloping shoulders,
dark, water-dipped ringlets forming,
her swan's-down skin pinking,
steam misting her swan song,
her suicide with water and razor.

II

They concentrated. A glittering
company. Rich. Celebrated.
They waited for the great Houdini.
His monument was dark, unmoving.
The stars glittered, like the company.
Half a minute. They breathed
in short, shuddering breaths,
and waited. Houdini heard:
"Houdini, do not disappoint us,
for we must believe that Death
cannot take us, utterly."

Tearing at the wall, his long
yellow fingernails cracked off,
ricocheted; then he heard:
"I am dying, dying . . ." He drew back,
prepared to throw his body at the wall
—he must *break through . . .*

III

The steaming water in the marble tub
was streaked in ribbons of red.
She was going to die, that *he* would know,
her lover, what he had done.
He had killed beauty
in neglect and pursuit of money.
He would be sorry. Her long lashes locked.
It was like a dream, and she was falling,
falling over a dark sea, which now she struck.
The noise jolted her. It was like
breaking plaster, like tumbling bricks,
like an earthquake. Her eyelids rolled back
to see a mad-eyed specter
emerge from a great, gaping hole
torn through tiles. Her dizzy mind,
half-bloodless, saw the bloodless form,
and fainted. Houdini lifted her from
the marble tub and taped her wrists.
He put her in her bed and tugged
the bell pull. She was too beautiful to die.
A great grandfather clock obliterated
the last of midnight. A doorknob turned,
and he went back the way that he had come.

Houdini darkened into death.

OLD ICARUS

Grandchildren turning
their faces from
drooling kisses
to avoid
what you have
become:
teeth like graveyard
stones, sunken cheeks
pockmarked
(where once,
as a boy,
the feathers went),
wens, wild hairs.

The wax your father poured
has melted
and the feathers,
plumes he placed so carefully,
flew, fell,
and you fell
into the sea
but did not drown,
owning a future,
as you did,
long enough
to hug your grandchildren
close and have them
turn away.

TOWARD THE END

One long winter at Revere Beach in Massachusetts,
with snow banked up two feet or more at the door,
I read Karl Marx's romantic tales from Dickens.
I discovered that the essence of that big tome
was somewhere in the first fifty pages,
where Marx gives out with his theory of value,
i.e., that the labor that is put into something
invests it with value. A flattering fallacy.
I had worked as a laborer much of my young life
and knew that if two hundred men moved a pile of shit
weighing two hundred tons two feet from its original
location—it was still a pile of shit.
Shovelling shit was something I knew about,
something you don't learn much about in the
reading room of the British Museum,
so Marx was a big disappointment to me.
And was it true that if God did not exist
everything was permissible, as in *The Brothers
Karamazov*? I went through the *Great Books
of the Western World*, the *Cambridge Ancient Histories*,
etc., etc., and in the end came to the conclusion
that all learning is meant to teach only one thing:
how little one knows. Now, in the face of the Great Dark,
I know that I know nothing—well, little of importance,
a few apparent facts, a wet paper bag full of information,
so, toward the end, now, though still seeking to understand,
I only read poetry or look up at the mysterious stars.

BECAUSE

in the port-cities they have found everything out and
Aristotle-like have put everything into categories
and the unicorn is an ungulate because they say so
because the fine-print of the unreligious sun says we circle it
it is not for us but we for it because the moon hit us
and bounced off instead of was born of our first spin
because the ninth planet is an invading comet caught
and because there is no now and there never has been

because we look upon ourselves in savannas past
knuckling to water because we see the white lemming's hole
in the snow smashed down by hooves and hear its pitiful
chirp of counter-aggression because the avalanche
indifferently buries the contested world of the snow
valley because stars die because we believe in facts
and because the deluge led to the ark because because
and because we bury our dead and dig up their bones

because the unsoundness of our judgments lead to sound
judgment and because facts are facts and we must reckon
and because the sea is cruel and because time flies
because the wind blows down our houses and because
we remember the snow hare and the hawk because
because the dove is taken in air by the eagle
and because space is either empty or full of dark matter
because galaxies hold for a long time their pinwheel-shapes

because time and space are curved and we can blow
    ourselves up
and because we blow ourselves up constantly and because
it makes us wonder because doesn't it mean something
because we are riding a mud-ball through space because
we were born here and because we have categories and

because we dig up our bones and dogs dig our bones up
and because we are not even safe in pyramids because
we dig ourselves up and look upon our own bones

459

HEART FAILURE

I have made my moon landing at night
by way of the emergency ward,
on the strong black arm of a nurse.
My wife is the other woman,
and between the two women I enter,
seeing, reflected in glass, my red car
half up on a curb, and mal-angled,
the glare of the high beams showing
my terrified wife's confusion.

There is no air in that car,
there is no air in the night,
but there is air in the hose that the nurse
claps to my turning-blue face,
and strength in her arms that are used to
the harsh struggles that have plagued her existence,
strength that I finally can share in.

I lie in a gown in a room,
and the silent killer says nothing.
He signalled, I guess, with red flags.
I paid no attention. I'd developed
an elephant's hide, an armor for the arrows
of insult that poor boys endure.
From childhood, when I was raw,
and my nerves could actually bleed,
I worked on this suit of armor,
oiled it and flexed it and shined it,
but now it belonged to them,
the doctors who probed me with wonder.
"Didn't you notice a thing?
You sound like a sidewinder, rattling."
"I thought I'd caught cold in the chest."

But I had no desire to know
because I had no desire to stop.
I could see that they thought, "What a fool!"
All but the black nurse, who knew
how the poor slid the slippery slope
that poverty, stress, and high blood pressure
grade for the struggling-upward.
She pulled at my ear, and said, "Tough guy!
He don't take no crap from his heart."
She knew how the pressure builds up,
as you climb in the ignorant ghetto,
until you would break, or be broken.

"How you doing, baby doll? Better?"
"Yes, but now I'm embarrassed."
—embarrassed at being so weak,
ashamed of my heart that can fail,
ashamed to have such a heart—
no lionheart, no Coreleone, I.
But they tell me it's stress that's at fault:
the heart is okay, the tests show.
The angel nurse flattens my hair,
pulls at my ear, and says, "Go!—"

THE URN

Containing the Night Thoughts of a Sexagenarian

It is this heavenly tale, that the child in one could wish for,
that keeps me awake tonight, on the eve of my sixtieth year,
fearing death and wishing for grace, not knowing what
either is, or even if either is, though the unbreathing
stillness of bodies has me fairly convinced of the
former, and of the latter I have seen so little as to
doubt what I have seen as aberrant, some twist in the
air and light that, so full of desire for the magic of
exemption, I have deluded myself, half knowing
I lied, half believing my own white lie. But by
sixty I've come to believe that the only grace
is the goodness of the rational mind, and the
only evil the old instinctive animal brain, the
knob of the cerebellum, seeking its own satis-
factions of food and sex and selfhood, the
ultimate isolate one, that yet does not
understand that we are together in this
flowing, amazing hologram, with
or without a creator that may or
may not care; that, come alive, we
have every right to judge the nature
of existence, for, however arrived
at, our brains are analytic, not made
to hunker down in obeisance to
riddling gods, nor to any phantom
that hides in a cloud of unknowing.
For we have one another and have
courage and the hope of courage
and the practice of courage,
to help us, and, when the
wind is calm, and

the waters lean down
for the moon, we have
lonely senses to share till
at last our time has run out. Now,
as I think in the night, somewhat afraid
of the day that will see me another year older and
that much closer to death, I mark the speed of time
that has seen me, a moment ago, a child walking home from
school, or a man going off to harm's way, or this or that or
the other, and think of these things that we have, of others
and courage and love, of human intelligence used as it plainly
was meant to be used, and I think that I'll sleep and awaken
less anxious than I was considering a heavenly tale, for in the
realist reality, the closest thing to the truth, there is finally a
peace of mind that is a grace in a sweet surrender. It is the
heavenly tale that the child in one should wish for. *It* will
allow me to sleep in the night of my sixtieth year.

ANTHOLOGIES ARE SAD

Impressed by smoking-ember music,
as I have always been, drinking gin,
and reading the poets of the past—
who are in anachronistic pain
as if alive, striving, thriving
today—I think of today's.

I have a new anthology,
one including me,
with, alas, dates.
Most have only births and dashes,
a few the flying ashes,
the smoking music, of the past—
dates that say, *At last! At last!*

What then of Berryman
and those other merry men
and women who were human—
in pain and joy—alive?
In the anthologies they thrive,
possessing their due dates!

So now I turn a page,
afraid to find my final age;
and, though my last is but a dash,
I feel the flutter of ash.

THE FUTURIST

And then we must replace you, Death, for you must go
with the combustion engine down the tube of time
and all will laugh at you as they do now at blimps
and bleeding, flapping wooden wings for flight and leeches
on the back for purifying blood, for in the future, Death,
hiatus will replace you, the storage called cryonics,
the deep freeze, or some such method to define
and discipline ourselves, to give a shape to time
and render meaningful our lives as you do now,
O wisdom-wasting Death, when life is lived poetically,
in many stanzas, each building on the last, developing
its theme, so that an open-sequence poem of life
is lived and not a golden drop of honey-wisdom wasted
that cost us generation after generation,
O Future, in long darkness climbing unto you.

REVIEW

"*A Portable Chaos* is an historical novel that brings to life the transformation of the United States from the conforming Fifties to the volcanic social eruptions of the "swinging Sixties"—from the private chaos of Jimmy Whistler's childhood to the public chaos of his youth, the former shaping himself, the latter shaping all Americans."

That describes this novel and it is true. It is a great American novel and it is indeed set against that chaotic and transformative period of American history. We follow eighteen year old Jimmy Whistler, from the bottom rung of America's social ladder, to his time in the Marines in Hawaii, where he meets Leilani, a girl destined to be the love of his life. Discharged, he returns to New York, a city churning with the chaos of the Sixties. Jimmy mines the very heart of that chaotic New York as an actor and a writer, one who sees himself as a poet. He hangs out with the denizens of the theatre and the hippies who seek the extremes of the chaos.

He survives these soul and health destroying years and reunites with Leilani. Married to Leilani, two loved children, seeing his writing succeed on television, they now live in Hawaii. So you think he lives happily ever after. Get ready for disappointment. Nothing lasts forever. Leilani leaves him to pursue her own career. He is left with his two sons and his poetry, always his poetry. This is a bitter sweet story, one that charts the uncertainty of life in America today and attests to the myth portrayed in the Norman Rockwell covers.

But don't read this book for any of these reasons. Read it to be captured by characters who are brought to life better than any you've ever encountered. Read it to be enthralled by dialogue so real that you are taken inside the life of each. Read it to experience what it's like to be a

voyeur and an eavesdropper on every page. Read it to feel
the poetic resonance of the language. Read it to experience
E M Schorb, a writer who will, from now on, stand at the
top of your reading list.

Pat Mullan
Novelist, Poet, and Critic

NOTES

Grateful acknowledgement is given to the following publications in which some of the poems in this novel have appeared:

The Formalist, Gallery (UK), *The Great American Poetry Show, Vol. 3,* Hot Metal Press.com, The Hudson Review, *Keats Prize Poems,* London Literary Editions, Ltd. (UK), Measure, *The Meridian Anthology,* North Carolina Literary Review, *Peace is Our Profession: Poems and Passages of War Protest,* Poetry Salzburg Review (AU), SPRING: The Journal of the E.E. Cummings Society, Sparrow '62, Virginia Quarterly Review, and The Yale Review.

Acknowledgement is also given to the following publications in which some of James Whistler's Last Poems appeared:

Agenda (UK), The American Scholar, *Anthology of Magazine Verse & Yearbook of Modern Poetry 1976,* Atlanta Review, Blue Unicorn, The Classical Outlook, Context South, Deronda Review, Dream International Quarterly, Free Lunch, Ginosko Literary Journal, Haight Ashbury Literary Journal, The Hudson Review, *In Whatever Houses We May Visit* (Anthology), American College of Physicians, The Iowa Review, The Literary Review, Measure, New Letters, The New Welsh Review, Nimrod, North American Review, OffCourse, A Literary Journal, Outposts (UK), *The Phoenix Rising from the Ashes* (Anthology) (CA), Poetry Daily, Poetry Life & Times (UK), Princeton Arts Review, The Raleigh News and Observer, The Sewanee Review, Shenandoah, Southern Humanities Review, Southern Poetry Review, SPRING: The Journal of the E.E. Cummings Society, St. Sebastian Review, Stand (UK), The Tennessee Quarterly, Virginia Quarterly Review, War, Literature & The Arts, Wascana Review (CA), Whiskey Island Magazine, and The Yale Review.

"Dirge for the Dead Students" which was widely circulated on college campuses after the tragic incident which occurred at Kent State University in May, 1970, has been set to music by the composer Daniel Jahn, and appears as the centerpiece of his anti-war musical program, "Noon/Afternoon: American Poetry in Song," which was given inaugural performances in New York, Provincetown, and Boston. The poem was also published and distributed as a broadside by SANE: Citizens' Organization for a Sane World; and included in the well-known anthology, *Peace is Our Profession: Poems and Passages of War Protest*. It is also part of the May 4 Resource Center collection at Kent State University Library.

Grateful acknowledgement is given to the Lannan Foundation and the Provincetown Fine Arts Work Center, to the North Carolina Arts Council, and to the Ludwig Vogelstein Foundation, for the fellowships, grants, and awards which helped provide the time and freedom to write many of these chapters.

ERIC HOFFER AWARD WINNER

A Portable Chaos

Award Citation

A Portable Chaos opens with a stream-of-consciousness flashback to a childhood incident that resembles James Joyce's "Portrait of the Artist as a Young Man," which gains significance as the novel unfolds, and you come to appreciate it. The main character is a decent guy overflowing with un-tapped potential, who walks away from opportunities and the wrong sort of success and follows his bliss as a poet. After a pretty squalid time living "la vie Boheme" (vividly written, conjuring up the ghosts of 1960s' past), he emerges from the slough and finds validation, the girl, fame, fortune, content-ment, and reconciliation with all those pesky childhood demons.

This was a well-plotted, well-characterized, and solidly written story. *A Portable Chaos* has everything you want in good literature—poignant writing, drama, and redemption.

Christopher Klim, Senior Editor, *The US Review of Books*